Regency
Collection

A
Regency
Captain's
Prize

MARGARET McPHEE

MILLS &
BOON

Published in Great Britain 2016
by Mills & Boon, an imprint of Harlequin (UK) Limited,
Eton House, 18-24 Paradise Road, Richmond, Surrey, TW9 1SR

A REGENCY CAPTAIN'S PRIZE © 2016 Harlequin Books S.A.

The Captain's Forbidden Miss © 2008 Margaret McPhee
His Mask of Retribution © 2012 Margaret McPhee

ISBN: 978-0-263-91766-6

052-0216

Harlequin (UK) policy is to use papers that are natural, renewable and recyclable products and made from wood grown in sustainable forests. The logging and manufacturing processes conform to the legal environmental regulations of the country of origin.

Printed and bound
by CPI Group (UK) Ltd, Croydon, CR0 4YY

The Captain's Forbidden Miss

MARGARET McPHEE

Margaret McPhee loves to use her imagination—an essential requirement for a scientist. However, when she realised that her imagination was inspired more by the historical romances she loves to read rather than by her experiments, she decided to put the stories down on paper. She has since left her scientific life behind and enjoys cycling in the Scottish countryside, tea and cakes.

Chapter One

Central Portugal—31 October 1810

High up in the deserted village of Telemos in the mountains north of Punhete, Josephine Mallington was desperately trying to staunch the young rifleman's bleeding when the French began their charge. She stayed where she was, kneeling by the soldier on the dusty stone floor of the old monastery in which her father and his men had taken refuge. The French hail of bullets through the holes where windows had once stood continued as the French dragoon troopers began to surge forwards in a great mass, the sound of their *pas de charge* loud even above the roar of gunpowder.

'*En avant! En avant! Vive la République!*' She heard their cries.

All around was the acrid stench of gunpowder and of fresh spilt blood. Stones that had for three hundred years sheltered monks and priests and holy Mass now witnessed carnage. Most of her father's men were dead, Sarah and Mary too. The remaining men began to run.

The rifleman's hand within hers jerked and then went limp. Josie looked down and saw that life had left him, and, for all the surrounding chaos, the horror of it so shocked her that for a moment she could not shift her stare from his lifeless eyes.

'Josie! For God's sake, get over here, girl!'

Her father's voice shook her from the daze, and she heard the thudding of the French axes as they struck again and again against the thick heavy wood of the monastery's front door. She uncurled her fingers from those of the dead soldier and, slipping the shawl from her shoulders, she draped it to cover his face.

'Papa?' Her eyes roved over the bloody ruins.

Bodies lay dead and dying throughout the hall. Men that Josie had known in life lay still and grotesque in death—her father's men—the men of the Fifth Battalion of the British 60th Regiment of Foot. Josie had seen death before, more death than any young woman should see, but never death like this.

'Stay low and move quickly, Josie. And hurry—we do not have much time.'

On her hands and knees she crawled to where her father and a small group of his men crouched. Dirt and blood smeared their faces and showed as dark patches against the deep green of their jackets and the blue of their trousers.

She felt her father's arms around her, pulling her into the huddle of men.

'Are you hurt?'

'I am fine,' she said, even though *'fine'* was hardly the word to describe how she was feeling.

He nodded and set her from him. She heard her father speak again, but this time his words were not for her. 'The door will not hold them much longer. We must make for the uppermost floor. Follow me.'

She did as her father instructed, responding to the strength and authority in his voice as much as any of his men would have done, pausing only to collect the rifle, cartridges and powder horn from a dead rifleman, and taking care to keep her eyes averted from the gaping wound in his chest. Clutching the rifle and ammunition to her, she fled with the men, following her father out of the hall, past the door through which the French axes had almost hacked, and up the wide stone staircase.

They ran up two flights of stairs and into a room at the front of the building. Miraculously the key was still in the lock of the door. As it turned beneath her father's hand, she heard the resounding thud of the front door being thrown open and knew that the French were in. They heard the sound of many French feet below running into the great hall and then the booted footfalls began to climb the stairs that would lead them to the room that housed the few remaining riflemen.

There was little to mark Lieutenant Colonel Mallington from his riflemen save his bearing and the innate authority that he emanated. His jacket was of the same dark green, with black frogging, scarlet facings and silver buttons, but on his shoulder was a silver thread wing and around his waist was the red sash of rank. His riding boots were easily unnoticed and his fur-trimmed pelisse lay abandoned somewhere in the great hall below.

Within their hiding place, Josie listened while her father spoke to his men. 'We need to draw this out as long as we possibly can, to give our messengers the best chance of reaching General Lord Wellington with the news.' Lieutenant Colonel Mallington's face was strong and fearless. He looked each one of his men in the eye.

Josie saw the respect on the riflemen's faces.

Her father continued, 'The French force are marching through these hills on a secret mission. General Foy, who leads the column of French infantry and its cavalry detachment, is taking a message from General Massena to Napoleon Bonaparte himself. He will travel first to Ciudad Rodrigo in Spain and then to Paris.'

The men stood quiet and listened to what their lieutenant colonel was saying.

'Massena is requesting reinforcements.'

'And General Lord Wellington knows nothing of it,' added Sergeant Braun. 'And if Massena gets his reinforcements…'

'That is why it is imperative that Wellington is forewarned of this,' said Lieutenant Colonel Mallington. 'It is only half an hour since our men left with the message. If Foy and his army realise that we have despatched messengers, then they will go after them. We must ensure that does not happen. We must buy Captain Hartmann and Lieutenant Meyer enough time to get clear of these hills.'

The men nodded, thin-lipped, narrow-eyed, determined in their conviction.

'And that is why we will not surrender this day,' the Lieutenant Colonel said, 'but fight to the death. Our sacrifice will ensure that Wellington will not be taken unawares by a reinforced French army, thus saving the lives of many of our men. Our six lives for our messengers.' He paused and looked solemnly at his men. 'Our six lives to save many.'

Within the room was silence, and beyond rang the clatter of French boots.

'Six men to win a war,' he finished.

'Six men and one sharpshooting woman,' said Josie, meeting her father's gaze and indicating her rifle.

And then one by one the men began cheer. 'For victory!' they shouted.

'For the King and for freedom!' boomed Lieutenant Colonel Mallington.

A raucous hurrah sounded in response.

'No man shall come through that door alive,' said Sergeant Braun.

Another cheer. And one by one the men positioned themselves at either side of the door and readied their weapons.

'Josie.' Her father's voice had quietened and softened in tone.

She came to him, stood beside him, knowing that this was it, knowing that there were no more escapes to be had. For all the men's bravado, Josie was well aware what her father's order would cost them all.

A single touch of his fingers against her cheek. 'Forgive me,' he said.

She kissed his hand. 'There is nothing to forgive.'

'I never should have brought you back here.'

'I wanted to come,' she said, 'you know how I hated it in England. I've been happy here.'

'Josie, I wish—'

But Lieutenant Colonel Mallington's words were cut short. There was no more time to talk. A French voice sounded from beyond the door, demanding surrender.

Lieutenant Colonel Mallington drew Josie a grim smile. 'We will not surrender!' he bellowed in English.

Twice more the French voice asked that they yield, and twice more Lieutenant Colonel Mallington refused.

'Then you have sealed your fate,' said the highly accented voice in English.

Josie cut the paper of a cartridge with the gunflint to release the bullet, poured the gunpowder into the rifle's barrel and rammed the bullet home before priming the lock. Her father gestured her to crouch closest to the corner farthest from the door. He signed for the men to hunker down and aim their weapons.

The French unleashed their musket fire, their bullets thudding into the thick wooden door.

Wait, instructed the Lieutenant Colonel's hand signal.

For Josie that was the hardest time, crouched there in the small room, her finger poised by the trigger, her heart racing somewhere near the base of her throat, knowing that they were all going to die, and disbelieving it all the same. Never had the minutes stretched so long. Her mouth was so dry she could not swallow, and still her father would not let them fire. He wanted one last stand, one last blaze of glory that would hold the Frenchmen at bay until the very last moment. And still the bullets kept on coming, and still the six men and Josie waited, until at last the door began to weaken and great chunks of wood fell from it, exposing holes through which Josie could see the mass of men crammed into the corridor outside, their uniforms so similar in colour to that of her father and his men that she could have imagined they were British riflemen just the same.

'Now!' came the order.

And what remained of their section of the Fifth Battalion of the 60th Foot let loose their shots.

Josie could never be sure how long the mêlée lasted. It might have been seconds; it seemed like hours. Her arms and shoulders ached from firing and reloading the rifle, yet still she kept going. It was an impossible cause, and one by one the riflemen went down fighting, until there was only Sergeant Braun, Josie and her father. Then Lieutenant Colonel Mallington gave a grunt, clutched a hand to his chest, and through his fingers Josie could see the stain of spreading blood. He staggered backwards until he slumped against the wall, the blade of his sword clattering uselessly to the floor. As Lieutenant Colonel Mallington's strength failed, he slithered down the wall to land half sitting, half lying at its base.

'Papa!' In two steps she had reached him and was pressing the sword back into his hand where he lay.

His breathing was laboured and the blood was spreading across his coat.

Sergeant Braun heard her cry, and positioned himself in front of the Lieutenant Colonel and his daughter, firing shot after shot, and reloading his rifle so fast as to make Josie's paltry efforts seem laughable, and all the while roaring his defiance at the French force that had not yet crossed the threshold where the skeleton of the door still balanced. It seemed that he stood there an eternity, that one man holding back the full force of the French 8th Dragoons, until at last his body jerked with the impact of one bullet and then another and another, and he crumpled to the ground to lie in a crimson pool.

There was no more musket fire.

Josie moved to stand defensively in front of her father, aiming her rifle through the gun smoke, her breathing ragged and loud in the sudden silence.

The holed and splintered wood that had been the door fell inwards suddenly, landing with a crash upon the floor of the barren room that housed the bodies of the riflemen. There was silence as the smoke cleared to show Josie exactly what she faced.

The French had not moved. They still stood clustered outside around the doorway, in their green coats so reminiscent of the 60th's. Even the facings on their coats were of a similar red coloration; the difference lay in their white breeches and black riding boots, their brass buttons and single white crossbelts and most of all in the brass helmets with black horsehair crests that they wore upon their heads. Even across the distance she could see their faces beneath those helmets—lean and hard and ruthless—and she saw the disbelief that flitted across them when they realised whom it was that they faced.

She heard the command, *'Ne tirez pas!'* and knew that they would hold their fire. And then the man who had issued that command stepped through the doorway into the room.

He was dressed in a similar green jacket to that of his men, but with the white epaulettes upon his shoulders and a leopardskin band around his helmet that was given only to officers. He looked too young to wear the small, silver grenades in the carmine turnbacks in the tail of his jacket. He was tall and well muscled. Beneath the polish of his helmet his hair was short and dark, and down the length of his left cheek he carried a scar. In his hand was a beautifully weighted sabre, from the hilt of which hung a long, golden tassel.

When he spoke his voice was hard and flinty and highly accented. 'Lieutenant Colonel Mallington.'

Josie heard her father's gasp of shock and she raised the rifle higher, aiming it at the Frenchman.

'Dammartin?' She could hear the incredulity in her father's voice.

'You recognise me from my father, Major Jean Dammartin, perhaps. I understand that you knew him. I am Captain Pierre Dammartin and I have waited a long time to meet you, Lieutenant Colonel Mallington,' said the Frenchman.

'Good Lord!' said her father. 'You are his very image.'

The Frenchman's smile was cold and hard. He made no move, just stood there, seemingly relishing the moment.

'Josie,' her father called with urgency.

Josie kept the rifle trained on the French Captain, but she glanced down at her father. He was pale and weak with lines of pain etched around his eyes.

'Papa?'

'Let him approach. I must speak with him.'

Her gaze swung back to the Frenchman, whose eyes were dark and stony. They watched one another across the small distance.

'Josie,' her father said again. 'Do as I say.'

She was loathed to let the enemy any closer to her father, but she knew that she had little choice. Perhaps her father had a trick up his sleeve, a small pistol or a knife with which to turn the situation to their advantage. If they could but capture the French Captain and bargain for just a little more time....

Josie stepped to the side, leaving the approach to her father free, yet never taking her eyes from the Frenchman's face.

The French Captain's sabre sat easily in his hand as if it were an old friend with which he was so comfortable that he ceased to notice it. He advanced forwards to stand before the Lieutenant Colonel, taking the place that Josie had just vacated, waiting with a closed expression for what the older man would say.

And all the while Josie kept the rifle trained upon the Frenchman's heart, and the French soldiers kept their muskets trained upon her.

'Captain Dammartin.' Her father beckoned him closer.

The Frenchman did not move.

Lieutenant Colonel Mallington managed to smile at the young man's resistance. 'You are of the same mould as your father. He was a most worthy opponent.'

'Thank you, Lieutenant Colonel.' Dammartin's mouth was grim. 'A compliment indeed.'

The Lieutenant Colonel's eyes slid to Josie. 'She is my daughter, all that I have left in this world.' Then his gaze was back fixed on Dammartin. 'I do not need to ask that you treat her honourably. I already know that, as Jean Dammartin's son, you will do nothing other.' He coughed and blood flecked red and fresh upon his lips.

Dammartin's eyes glittered dangerously. 'Do you indeed, Lieutenant Colonel?' He slowly extended his sword arm until the edge of the blade was only inches from the Lieutenant Colonel's face. 'You are very certain for a man in your position.'

The French dragoons in the background smiled and sniggered. Dammartin held up a hand to silence them.

Josie took a step closer to the French Captain, the weight of the raised rifle pulling at her arms. She showed no weakness, just tightened her finger slightly against the trigger and took another step closer, keeping the rifle's muzzle aimed at Dammartin's chest. 'Lower your sword, sir,' she said, 'or I shall put a bullet through you.'

'No, Josie!' came her father's strained voice.

'Think of what my men will do if you pull the trigger,' Dammartin said.

'I think of what you will do if I do not,' she replied.

Their gazes locked, each refusing to look away, as if that would determine whether the sabre blade or the rifle trigger moved first.

'Josie!' Her father coughed again, and she heard his gasp of pain. 'Lay down your weapon.'

Her eyes darted to her father's face, unable to believe his words. 'We will not surrender,' she said in a parody of his earlier words.

'Josie.' His bloodstained fingers beckoned her down, their movement weak and fluttering with a control that was fast ebbing.

One last look at Dammartin, who let his blade fall back a little, and, keeping the rifle pointed in his direction, she crouched lower to hear what her father would say.

'Our fight is done. We can do no more this day.'

'No—' she started to protest, but he silenced her with a touch of his hand.

'I am dying.'

'No, Papa,' she whispered, but she knew from the blood that soaked his jacket and the glistening pallor of his face that what he said was true.

'Give up your weapon, Josie. Captain Dammartin is an honourable man. He will keep you safe.'

'No! How can you say such a thing? He is the enemy. I will not do it, Papa!'

'Defiance of an order is insubordination,' he said, and tried to laugh, but the smile on his face was a grimace, and the effort only brought on a fresh coughing fit.

The sight of the blood dribbling from the corner of his mouth brought a cry to Josie's lips. 'Papa!' Without so much as a glance as Dammartin, she abandoned the rifle on the floor, and clutched one hand to her father's. The other touched gently to his face.

The light was fading from his eyes. 'Trust him, Josie,' he whispered so quietly that she had to bend low to catch his words. 'Enemy or not, the Dammartins are good men.'

She stared at him, unable to comprehend why he would say such a thing of the man who looked at them with such hatred in his eyes.

'Promise me that you will yield to him.'

She felt the tremble in her lower lip and bit down hard upon it to hide the weakness.

'Promise me, Josie,' her father whispered, and she could hear the plea in his failing voice.

She said the only words that she could. 'I promise, Papa.' And she pressed a kiss to his cheek.

'That's my girl.' His words were the faintest whisper.

Josie's tears rolled, warm and wet.

'Captain Dammartin,' Lieutenant Colonel Mallington commanded, and it seemed that something of the old power was back in his voice.

Josie's heart leapt. Perhaps he would not die after all. She felt him move her fingers to his other hand, watched him reach out towards Dammartin, saw the strength of his hand as he gripped the Frenchman's fingers.

'I commend Josephine to your care. See that she is kept safe until you can return her to the British lines.'

Her father's gaze held the Frenchman's. It was the last sight Lieutenant Colonel Mallington saw. A sigh sounded within the cold stone room of the Portuguese monastery, and then there was silence, and her father's hand was limp and lifeless within Josie's.

'Papa?' she whispered.

His eyes still stared unseeing at the Frenchman.

'Papa!' The realisation of what had just happened cracked her voice. She pressed her cheek to his, wrapped her arms around his bloodstained body, and the sob that tore from her was to those that had heard a thousand cries and screams of pain and death still terrible to hear. Outside the room men that had both perpetrated and suffered injury for the past hour stood silent with respect.

When at last she let her father's body go and moved her face from his, it was Dammartin's fingers that swept a shutting of the Lieutenant Colonel's eyes, and Dammartin's hand that took hers to raise her to her feet. She barely heard the order that he snapped to his men, or noticed the parting of the sea of men to let her through. Neither did she notice Captain Dammartin's grim expression as he led her from the room.

The French camped that night in the same deserted village in which they had fought, the men sleeping within the shells of the buildings, their campfires peppering light across the darkness of the rocky landscape. The smell of cooking lingered in the air even though the meagre stew had long since been devoured.

Pierre Dammartin, Captain of the 8th Dragoons in Napoleon's Army of Portugal, had wanted the English Lieutenant Colonel taken alive. The only reason that he had tempered his assault against the riflemen hiding in the empty monastery was because he had heard that it was Mallington who commanded them. He wanted Mallington alive because he wanted the pleasure of personally dispatching the Lieutenant Colonel to his maker.

For a year and a half Dammartin had wanted to meet Mallington across a battlefield. He had dreamt of looking into Mallington's eyes while he told him who he was. He wanted to ask the Englishman the question he had been asking himself for the past eighteen months. Barely an hour ago it had seemed that his prayers had been answered and Mallington delivered into his hands in the most unlikely of places.

Mallington had not been easily beaten despite the difference in numbers, one section of a British company against one hundred and twenty mounted men backed by a whole battalion of infantry. Indeed, Mallington's men had fought to the death rather than let themselves be taken, refusing Dammartin's offers that they surrender. The fight had lasted longer than Dammartin could have anticipated. And even at its conclusion, when Dammartin had walked into that blood-splattered room in the monastery, he had not been satisfied. True, Dammartin had looked into Mallington's face and revealed his identity. But Mallington's reaction had not been what he expected, and there had been no time for questions. The moment for which the Captain had so longed had left him unexpectedly disgruntled. Especially because of Mallington's daughter.

He stood by the window in the dilapidated cottage that was situated at the foot of the road that led up to the monastery. A few men still drifted around the place. He could hear the soft murmur of their voices and see their dark shapes by the light of the fires. Soon they would be bedding down for the night, just as the thousands of men in the canonments around Santarém not so far away to the south would be doing. Above, the sky was a spread of deep, dark, inky blue studded with the brilliance of diamond stars. And he knew that the temperature was dropping and that the cold would be biting. Tomorrow General Foy would lead them across the mountains towards Ciudad Rodrigo and they would leave behind the ruined monastery at Telemos and the dead riflemen and Mallington. He heard Lamont move behind him.

'Your coffee, Pierre.'

He accepted the tin mug from his sergeant's hands. 'Thank you.' The brown liquid was bitter, but warming. 'Has Major La Roque sent for me yet?'

'No.' Lamont smiled, revealing his crooked teeth. 'He is too busy with his dinner and his drink.'

'He is making me wait until morning then,' said Dammartin, 'to haul me over the coals.'

Lamont shrugged his shoulders. He was a small, wiry man with eyes so dark as to appear black. His skin was lined and weatherbeaten, his hair a dark, grizzled grey. Lamont knew how to handle a musket better than any man in Dammartin's company. Despite the fact he had grown up the son of a fishmonger and Dammartin the son of a distinguished military major, the two had become close friends.

'The riflemen refused the option of surrender. They were like demons. Never before have I seen the British fight until there is not a man left alive. It was no easy task to overcome them. The Major must know that.'

Dammartin met his gaze, knowing that his sergeant understood very well that the fight had been unnecessarily prolonged by Dammartin's refusal to storm the monastery until the last. 'The Major will only be concerned with the delay this has cost us. General Foy will not be pleased. One day of marching and we do not even make it past Abrantes.'

Lamont sniffed and wiped his nose with the back of his hand. 'The cost was worth it. You wanted the English Lieutenant Colonel alive so that you might watch him die.'

Dammartin said nothing.

'You have waited a long time to kill him, and now he is dead.'

'But not by my hand.'

'Does it make any difference? He is dead just the same.'

'I wanted to look into his eyes while I killed him. I wanted to watch his reaction when I told him who I was, to see that he understood, to feel his fear.'

'And today that is what you did. This Mallington looked upon you with his dying breath. It is done, Captain. Your father is avenged.'

The line of Dammartin's mouth was hard. He said nothing. It was true that Dammartin had looked into Mallington's face and revealed his identity. But thereafter nothing had been as the French Captain anticipated, and he was left feeling cheated.

Lamont fetched his own battered tin mug and sat down

on his pack by the fire he had lit on the hearth. Steam rose in wisps from the steaming-hot coffee. Lamont wrapped his hands around the mug, seemingly impervious to the scald of the heat, and gazed into the flames. 'Perhaps my ears deceived me, Captain, but I thought the Englishman said the girl was his daughter.'

'He did.'

'Sacré bleu!' cursed the Sergeant. 'It shows the nature of this Lieutenant Colonel Mallington. Only a crazy Englishman would bring his daughter with him to war.' The Sergeant drilled a forefinger against the side of his head. 'Crazy.'

'So it would seem,' said Dammartin, remembering the image of the girl standing alone and seemingly unafraid before the men of the 8th Dragoons to defend her father.

'She is so young, so fragile looking. It does not seem possible that she could have survived this hell of a country.'

'So fragile that her bullets are lodged in half our men,' said Dammartin sourly.

'That is the truth,' Lamont said soberly, and took a gulp of his coffee.

Dammartin retrieved a small, silver hip flask from his pocket and loosened the cap. 'Brandy? To keep the damp from your bones tonight.'

Lamont gave a grin and nodded, holding the still-steaming tin mug up.

Dammartin poured a liberal dousing of the amber liquid into the proffered mug before doing likewise with his own. 'Why should Mallington have sacrificed his men over a deserted village in the middle of nowhere? It makes no sense. Wellington's forces are all down at the lines of Torres Vedras and Lisbon. What was Mallington even doing up here?'

The sergeant shrugged. 'A scouting party? They were riflemen after all.'

'Perhaps—' Dammartin sipped his coffee '—Mademoiselle Mallington may be able to shed some light on her father's actions.'

Lamont glanced up quickly at the young captain. 'You mean to interrogate her?'

'She is the only one still alive. Who else can tell us?' Dammartin's expression was unyielding.

'The English Lieutenant Colonel gave her into your care,' protested Lamont. 'She's only a girl.'

Dammartin glared unconvinced.

'She's the daughter of a gentleman, and today she watched her father die.'

'She is the daughter of a scoundrel, and an English scoundrel at that,' Dammartin corrected. 'She handled that rifle as good as any man and she is not to be trusted. Where is Mademoiselle Mallington now?'

'Locked in the cellar below.'

Dammartin drained his mug and set it down. 'Then it would seem that I have work to do this evening.'

Lamont stopped nursing his coffee to look at Dammartin. 'I pray, my friend and captain, that you are certain as to what you are about to do.'

'Never more so,' said Dammartin, and walked from the room.

Chapter Two

Josie sat perched on one of the dusty wooden crates, hugging her arms around her body, trying to keep out the worst of the damp chill. Wherever she looked, it seemed that she saw not the darkness of the cellar in which the French soldiers had locked her, but her father's face so pale and still in death, the blood seeping from his mouth to stain his lips and dribble down his chin. Even when she squeezed her eyes shut, she could not dislodge that image. All around in the dulled silence she heard again the crack and bang of rifles and muskets and the cries of dying men. She stoppered her hands to her ears, trying to block out the terrible sounds, but it did not make any difference, no matter how hard she pressed.

That morning she had been part of a section of twenty-five men and three women. She had collected the water from the spring behind the monastery and boiled it up to make her father's tea, taking the place of his batman for that short time as was her habit. They had laughed and drunk the brew and eaten the porridge oats that were so warming against the cold.

She remembered just those few hours ago in the afternoon when her father had told her of the column of Frenchmen marching through these hills and how he would have to go in closer to discover what they were about. Papa and a handful of men had gone, leaving Josie and the others in the old monastery, cooking up a stew of rabbit for the evening meal. But the small party's return had been panicked and hurried, retreating from the pursuit of the French, scrambling to send their captain and first lieutenant with news to General Lord Wellington. And then Josie's world had exploded. Papa would not laugh again. He was gone. They were all gone. All except Josie.

Even though she had seen their broken bodies and heard her father's last drawn breath, she could not really believe that it was so. It was like some horrific nightmare from which she would awaken. None of it seemed real. Yet Josie knew that it was, and the knowledge curdled a sourness in her stomach. And still the images flashed before her eyes, like illustrations of Dante's *Inferno*, and still the racket roared in her ears, and her throat tightened and her stomach revolted, and she stumbled through the blackness to the corner of the cellar and bent over to be as sick as a dog. Only when her stomach had been thoroughly emptied did she experience some respite from the torture.

She wiped her mouth on her handkerchief and steadied herself against the wall. Taking a deep breath, she felt her way back to the wooden box on which she had been seated.

It seemed that she sat there an eternity in the chilled darkness before the footfalls sounded: booted soles coming down the same stairs over which the French soldiers had dragged her. One set only, heading towards the cellar. Josie braced herself, stifling the fear that crept through her belly, and waited for what was to come. There was the scrape of metal as the key was turned in the lock, and the door was thrown open.

The light of the lantern dazzled her. She turned her face away, squinting her eyes. Then the lantern moved to the side; as her eyes began to adjust to the light, Josie found herself looking at the French captain whom her father had called Dammartin.

'Mademoiselle Mallington,' he said, and crossed the threshold into the cellar. His lantern illuminated the dark, dismal prison as he came to stand before her.

He seemed much bigger than she remembered. The dust and dirt had been brushed from the green of his jacket, and its red collar and cuffs stood bright and proud. The jacket's single, central line of brass buttons gleamed within the flickering light. His white breeches met knee-high, black leather boots and, unlike the last time they had met, he was not wearing the brass helmet of the dragoons. Beneath the light of the lantern his hair was shorn short and looked as dark as his mood. She could see that the stare in his eyes was stony and the line of his mouth was hard and arrogant. In that, at least, her memory served her well.

'Captain Dammartin.' She got to her feet.

'Sit down,' he commanded in English.

She felt her hackles rise. There was something in the quietness of his tone that smacked of danger. She thought she would defy him, but it seemed in that moment that she heard again her father's voice, *Trust him, Josie.* Trust him, when her every instinct screamed to do otherwise? She hesitated, torn between obeying her father and her own instinct.

He shrugged a nonchalant shoulder. 'Stand, then, if you prefer. It makes no difference to me.' There was a silence while he studied her, his eyes intense and scrutinising.

Josie's heart was thrashing madly within her chest, but

she made no show of her discomfort; she met his gaze and held it.

Each stared at the other in a contest of wills, as if to look away would be to admit weakness.

'I have some questions that I wish to ask you,' Dammartin said, still not breaking his gaze.

Josie felt her legs begin to shake and she wished that she had sat down, but she could not very well do so now. She curled her toes tight within her boots, and pressed her knees firmly together, tensing her muscles, forcing her legs to stay still. 'As I have of you, sir.'

He did not even look surprised. 'Then we shall take it in turns,' he said. '*Ladies* first.' And there was an emphasis on the word '*ladies*' that suggested she was no such thing.

'My father's body… Is he… Have you…?'

'Your father lies where he fell,' he said harshly.

'You have not given him a burial?'

'Did Lieutenant Colonel Mallington take time to bury Frenchmen? Each side buries its own.'

'In a battle situation, but this is different!'

'Is it?' he asked, and still their gazes held. 'I was under the impression, *mademoiselle*, that we were engaged in battle this day.'

She averted her gaze down to the floor, suddenly afraid that she would betray the grief and pain and shock that threatened to overwhelm her. '*Battle*' was too plain, too ordinary a word to describe what had taken place that day in the deserted village of Telemos. Twenty-seven lives had been lost, her father's among them. Only when she knew that the weakness had passed did she glance back up at him. 'But there is no one left to bury him.'

'So it would seem.'

His answer seemed to echo between them.

'I would request that you give him a decent burial.'

'No.'

She felt her breath rush in a gasp of disbelief. 'No?'

'No,' he affirmed.

She stared at him with angry, defiant eyes. 'My father told me that you were an honourable man. It appears that he was grossly mistaken in his opinion.'

He raised an eyebrow at that, but said nothing.

'You will leave him as carrion for wild animals to feed upon?'

'It is the normal course of things upon a battlefield.'

She took a single step towards him, her fingers curled to fists by her sides. 'You are despicable!'

'You are the first to tell me so,' he said.

She glared at him, seeing the dislike in his eyes, the hard determination in his mouth, this loathsome man to whom her father had entrusted her. 'Then give me a spade and I will dig his grave myself.'

'That is not possible, *mademoiselle*.'

Her mouth gaped at his refusal.

'You wish Lieutenant Colonel Mallington's body to be buried? It is a simple matter. It shall be done—'

'But you said—'

'It shall be done,' he repeated, 'as soon as you answer my questions.'

Fear prickled at the back of Josie's neck, and trickled down her spine. She shivered, suspecting all too well the nature of the French captain's questions. Carefully and deliberately, she fixed a bland expression upon her face and prayed for courage.

Pierre Dammartin watched the girl closely and knew then that he had not been wrong in his supposition. 'So tell me, Mademoiselle Mallington, what were riflemen of the Fifth Battalion of the 60th Regiment doing in Telemos?'

'I do not know.'

'Come now, *mademoiselle*. I find that hard to believe.'

'Why so? Surely you do not think my father would discuss such things with me? I assure you that it is not the done thing for British army officers to discuss their orders with their daughters.'

He smiled a small, tight smile at that. 'But is it the done thing for British army officers to take their daughters on campaign with them? To have them fight alongside their men?'

'It is not so unusual for officers to take their families, and as for fighting, I did so only at the end and out of necessity.'

He ignored her last comment. 'What of your mother, where is she?'

The girl looked at him defiantly. 'She is dead, sir.'

He said nothing. She was Mallington's daughter. What had Mallington cared for Major Dammartin's wife or family? The simple answer was nothing.

'Tell me of your father's men.'

'There is nothing to tell.' Her voice was light and fearless, almost taunting in its tone.

'From where did you march?'

'I cannot recall.'

He raised an eyebrow at that. The girl was either stupid or brave, and from what he had seen of Mademoiselle Mallington so far, he was willing to bet on the latter. 'When did you arrive in Telemos?'

She glanced away. 'A few days ago.'

'Which day precisely?'

'I cannot remember.'

'Think harder, *mademoiselle*…' he stepped closer, knowing that his proximity would intimidate her '…and I am sure that the answer will come to you.'

She took a step back. 'It might have been Monday.'

She was lying. Everything about her proclaimed it to be so: the way her gaze flitted away before coming back to meet his too boldly, too defiantly; her posture; the flutter of her hands to touch nervously against her mouth.

'Monday?'

'Yes.'

'How many men?'

'I am not sure.'

'Hazard a guess.' Another step forward.

And again she edged back. 'A hundred,' she uttered with angry defiance.

'A large number.' He raised an eyebrow, knowing from the scattering of corpses that there had been nowhere near that number of men.

'Yes.'

He watched her. 'Did you ride with your father, or walk with the men, *mademoiselle*?'

She looked up at him, and he could see the puzzlement beneath the thick suspicion. There was the shortest of pauses before she said, 'I rode a donkey, the same as the other women.'

'You are telling me that the unmarried daughter of the Lieutenant Colonel rode with the company's whores?'

'They were not whores,' she said hotly. 'They were wives to the men.'

'And your father was happy to leave you with them while he rode ahead with his officers on horseback? How very caring of him,' he ridiculed.

'Do not dare to judge him. You are not fit to speak his name!'

'Only fit to kill the bastard,' he murmured in French.

'Scoundrel!' she cursed him.

He smiled. 'Who took the horses?'

All of the anger drained from her in an instant. She

froze, caught unawares. He saw the tiny flicker of fear in her eyes and knew that he had guessed right.

'I do not know what you mean,' she said, but the words were measured and careful.

'There are only two horses stabled at the monastery. Where are the others?'

Beneath the glow of the lantern her face paled. There was a pause. 'We shot the others for food.'

'Really,' he said, 'you shot the horses and left the donkeys?'

'Yes.' One hand slid to encase the other and she stood there facing him, with her head held high, as demure as any lady, and lying through her teeth.

'I see.' He watched her grip tighten until the knuckles shone white. He looked directly into her eyes and stepped closer until only the lantern separated them.

She tried to back away, but her legs caught against the wooden crate positioned behind her and she would have fallen had he not steadied her. Quite deliberately, he left his hand where it was, curled around her upper arm.

'You would do better to tell me the truth, Mademoiselle Mallington,' he said quietly. He saw the pulse jump in her neck, could almost hear the skittering thud of her heart within the silence of the cellar. Her eyes were wide and her skin so pale as to appear that it had been carved from alabaster. She was smaller than he remembered from the shoot-out in the room in the monastery, the top of her head reaching only to his shoulder. Perhaps it was the rifle that had lent her the illusion of height. They were standing so close that he could see the long lashes that fanned her eyes and hear the shallowness of her breath.

'Do you want to start again?' The softness of his words did not hide the steel beneath them.

She shook her head, and he noticed the fair tendrils of

hair that had escaped her pins curl around her neck. 'No, sir.' Her words were as quiet as his, and Dammartin could only admire her courage.

'Very well.' He knew what he must do. The task was not pleasant, but it would give him the answers that the girl would not. Yet still he stood there, staring at her, as much as she stared at him, until he stepped abruptly away. 'We shall continue our conversation at a later time.' And he was gone, leaving her once more in the dark solitude of the cellar.

Josie still glared at the door long after it had closed behind him. Her heart was racing so fast that she thought she might faint, but still she did not move to sit down. Her eyes strained through the darkness, seeing nothing, her ears hearing the steady climb of his feet back up the stairs. Her arm throbbed where his hand had been even though his grip had been so light as to barely be a restraint.

She pressed her fingers hard to her lips as if to catch back all of the words she had spoken.

What had she revealed? Nothing that he would not already have known, yet Josie knew that was not true. The Frenchman's face had told her it was so. He knew about the horses, and if he knew about that, then it would not be so very long before he knew the rest.

Her lies had been feeble, obvious and pathetic. Dammartin did not believe her, that much was evident. And he would be back. Her stomach turned over at the thought.

It had taken an hour for twenty-seven men and women to die so that General Lord Wellington might be warned of Massena's scheme. In the space of a matter of minutes Josie had almost negated their sacrifice if Captain Hartmann and Lieutenant Meyer had not yet reached Wellington. How much time would it take the two men to weave their way back to Lisbon? The future of the British army at the lines of Torres Vedras rested on that and Josie's ability to prevent, or at least delay, Dammartin's discovery that the messengers had been sent. And that was not something in which she had the slightest degree of confidence.

Not for the first time Josie wondered if her father would have done better to let her die with him in the monastery. For all Papa's assurance of Pierre Dammartin's honour, she had a feeling that the French Captain was going to prove a most determined enemy.

It took almost half an hour for Dammartin, his lieutenant, Molyneux, and his sergeant, Lamont, to finish the gruesome activity that the girl's reticence to talk had forced them to. The night was dark, the moon a thin, defined crescent. They worked by the light of flambeaux, moving from corpse to corpse, examining the uniforms that garbed the stiffened, cold bodies that had once been a formidable fighting force for Britain, noting down what they found. And with each one Dammartin felt the futility of the loss. As prisoners of war they would have lost no honour. They had fought bravely, and the French had acknowledged that. Yet they had laid down their lives seemingly in a pointless gesture of defiance.

Three times Dammartin had given them the opportunity to surrender, and three times Mallington had rejected it. Time had been running out. Dammartin knew he had already delayed too long, that General Foy and Major La Roque would arrive to take over if Dammartin did not bring the matter to a close, and Dammartin's chance would have been lost. In the end he had been forced to storm the monastery, just as La Roque had ordered.

He pushed such thoughts from his mind and forced himself to concentrate on the task before him. It seemed a long time before they had finally been able to rinse the blood from their hands and make for the stables.

With the flambeaux held low, they scrutinised the marks and patterns of feet and hooves impressed upon the ground.

'What do you think?' Dammartin asked of his lieutenant. Molyneux had been trained in tracking, and when it came to his expertise in this field, there was no one's opinion that Dammartin trusted more.

'Two men and two horses heading off in the direction of the track over there. Prints are still fairly fresh. They probably left some time this afternoon.'

'It is as I thought,' said Dammartin. 'We have found what we were looking for.' It all made sense. Now he understood why Mallington had fought so hard for so long. Not for Telemos. The village was of little importance to the British regiment. But time was, and time was what they had bought for their messengers, and paid for with their lives. He gave a sigh and moved to instruct a pursuit team.

Josie was in the midst of a dream in which the battle of Telemos was being fought again. She shouted the warning to her father, snatching up the dead man's weapon, running up the staircase, loading and firing at the pursuing French. Her bullet travelled down the gun's rifled barrel, cutting with a deadly accuracy through the air to land within the Frenchman's chest. Smoke from the gunpowder drifted across her face, filling her nose with its stench, catching in her throat, drawing a curtain before her eyes so that she could not see. She heard the stagger of his footsteps, and then he was there, falling to his knees before her, his blood so rich and red spilling on to the hem of her dress. She looked down as the enemy soldier turned his face up to hers and the horror caught in her throat, for the face was that of Captain Pierre Dammartin.

She opened her eyes and the nightmare was gone, leaving behind only its sickening dread. Her heart was thumping in her chest, and, despite the icy temperature of the cellar, the sheen of sweat was slick upon her forehead and upper lip. She caught her breath, sat up from her awkward slump against the stack of wooden boxes, and rubbed at the ache in her back. As she did so, she heard the step of boots upon the stairs and knew that he was coming back, and her heart raced all the faster.

She struggled up to her feet, ignoring the sudden dizziness that it brought, felt herself sway in the darkness and sat rapidly back down. The last thing she wanted Dammartin to see was her faint.

And then he was there, through the door before she was even aware that the key had turned within the lock.

He looked tired and there was fresh dust upon his coat and a smear of dirt upon his cheek. The expression on his face was impassive, and she wondered what he had been doing. How much time had passed since he had questioned her? Minutes, hours? Josie did not know.

He set the lantern down upon a box at the side of the room and moved to stand before her. Josie knew that this time there was a difference in his attitude. His eyes were filled with such darkness and determination that she remembered the stories of interrogation and torture and felt the fear squirm deep in the pit of her stomach. Tales of bravery and singular distinction, men who had defied all to withhold the information that their enemy sought. And something in Josie quailed because she knew that she had not a fraction of that bravery and that just the prospect of what Dammartin could do to her made her feel nauseous. She swallowed and wetted the dryness of her lips.

If Dammartin noticed that she had forsaken her defiance of refusing to remain seated, he made no mention of it. Instead he drew up a crate and sat down before her, adjusting the long sabre that hung by his side as he did so.

She waited for what he would do.

'Do you wish to tell me of the horses, Mademoiselle Mallington?'

'I have told you what I know,' she said, feigning a calmness, and looked down to the darkness of the soil below her feet.

'No, *mademoiselle*, you have told me very little of that.'

In the silence that followed, the scrabble of rodents could be heard from the corner of the cellar.

'Your father sent two men to warn your General Wellington of our march.'

She felt the shock widen her eyes, freeze her into position upon the discomfort of the hard wooden crate. He could not know. It was not possible. Not unless… She stayed as she was, head bent, so that he would not see the fear in her eyes.

'Have you nothing to say, *mademoiselle*? Nothing to ask me?'

The breath was lodged, unmoving in her throat at the thought that Hartmann and Meyer might be captured. She forced its release and slowly raised her head until she could look into his eyes. There she saw ruthlessness and such certainty as to make her shiver.

'No,' she said. 'There is nothing.' Her voice was gritty with the strain of emotion.

His eyes were black in the lantern light as her gaze met his. They stared at each other with only the sound of their breath in the dampness of the cellar, and the tightness of tension winding around them.

'Denial is pointless. I know already the truth. Make this easier for us both, *mademoiselle*.'

She could hear the chilling determination in those few words so quietly uttered. The worst of imaginings were already crowding in her mind.

He was still looking at her and the distance between them seemed to shrink, so that the implacable resolution of the man was almost overwhelming.

It was as if there was something heavy crushing against her chest, making it hard to pull the breath into her lungs and she could feel a slight tremble throughout her body. She curled her fingers tight and pressed her knees together so that the Frenchman would not see it. She swallowed down the lump in her throat, praying that her voice would not shake as much as the rest of her.

Part of her argued that there was no point in lying anymore. Dammartin knew about the messengers already. And the other part of her, the small part that had kept her going throughout that nightmare year in England, refused to yield.

'I will not.' Her words seemed to echo in the silence and she felt her teeth begin to chatter.

'What would you say if I told you that we have captured your messengers?'

She got to her feet, ignoring the way that the cellar seemed to spin around her and the sudden lightness in her head that made her feel that she would faint. 'You are lying!'

Dammartin stood too. He smiled, and his smile was wicked and cold. 'Am I?'

They faced each other across the small space, the tension stretched between them.

'If you wish to know of the messengers, *mademoiselle*,

you will tell me what your father and his men were doing in these hills.'

From somewhere she found the strength to keep standing, to keep looking him in the eye. All of the fear was crowding in around her, pressing down on her, choking her. If the French had captured Hartmann and Meyer, all hope was gone. Her father's message would never reach Wellington. It had all been in vain. All of today. All of the sacrifice.

'I am not privy to my father's orders.' Her gaze held his, refusing to look away, angry disbelief vying with grief and misery and wretchedness.

A terrible desolation swept through her. The tremble had progressed so that her legs were shaking in earnest now, and the cold sweat of fear prickled beneath her arms. She thought again of what it would mean if the French truly had captured her father's messengers. A fresh wave of hopelessness swept over her at the thought, and as the moisture welled in her eyes she squeezed them shut to prevent the tears that threatened to fall. Yet, all of her effort was not enough. To her mortification, a single tear escaped to roll down her cheek. She snatched it away, praying that Dammartin had not noticed, and opened her eyes to stare her defiance.

'Are you crying, *mademoiselle*?' And she thought she could hear the undertone of mockery in his words. He looked at her with his dark eyes and harsh, inscrutable expression.

She glared at him. 'I will tell you nothing, nothing,' she cried. 'You may do what you will.'

'*Mademoiselle*, you have not yet begun to realise the possibilities of what I may do to you.' He leaned his face down close to hers. 'And when you do realise, then you will tell me everything that I want to know.'

Her heart ceased to beat, her lungs did not breathe as she looked up into the dark promise in his eyes.

His hand was around her arm, and he pulled her forwards and began to guide her towards the door.

'No!' She struggled against him, panicked at where he might be taking her and felt him grab her other arm, forcing her round to look at him once more.

'Mademoiselle Mallington,' he said harshly. 'The hour grows late and the ice forms in the air. If I leave you here, without warmth, without food or water, it is likely that you will be dead by morning.'

'Why would you care?' she demanded.

He paused and then spoke with slow deliberation, 'Because you have not yet answered my questions.'

Josie shivered. She did not know if he was lying about Hartmann and Meyer, but she did know that despite all of her fear and despair she had no wish to die. She ceased her struggle and let him lead her out of the cellar and up the creaking staircase into the heart of the little cottage.

The room into which he took her was small and spartan, its floor clean but littered with makeshift blanket beds and army baggage. A fire was roaring in the fireplace at which a small, grizzled man in a French sergeant's uniform was toasting bread and brewing coffee. His small, black eyes registered no surprise at her appearance.

'Capitaine,' the man uttered, and gave a nod in Dammartin's direction.

She sat down warily on the edge of the blanket that Dammartin indicated, trying to clear the fog of exhaustion from her brain, trying to remain alert for the first hint of a trap. There was nothing.

The small sergeant placed some toasted bread and raisins and a cup of coffee on the floor by her side before he and Dammartin busied themselves with their own bread.

Josie looked at the food set before her. The smell of the toasted bread coaxed a hunger in her stomach that had not been there before. Slowly, without casting a single glance in the Frenchmen's direction, she ate the bread and drank the coffee. And all the while she was aware of every move that the enemy made and the quiet words that they spoke to one another, thinking that she could not understand.

The logs on the fire cracked and gradually the room grew warm and no matter how hard she fought against it, Josie felt the exhaustion of all that had happened that day begin to claim her. She struggled, forcing her eyes open, forcing herself to stay upright, to stay aware of Captain Dammartin until, at last, she could fight it no more, and the French Captain faded as she succumbed to the black nothingness of sleep.

It was late and yet Pierre Dammartin sat by the fire, despite the fatigue that pulled upon his muscles and stung at his eyes. His gaze wandered from the flicker of the dying flames to the silhouette of the girl lying close by. The blanket rose and fell with the small, rhythmic movement of her breath. Mallington's daughter. Just the thought of who she was brought back all of the bitterness and anger that her father's death ought to have destroyed.

Sergeant Lamont sucked at his long clay pipe and nodded in the girl's direction. 'Did you get what you wanted from her?'

What had he wanted? To know why Mallington had been up here, the details of his men, of his messengers; her realisation that her defiance was useless, that she could not hide the truth from him. 'Unfortunately, my friend, Mademoiselle Mallington proved most unhelpful.'

Lamont's gaze darted in Dammartin's direction, his brow rising in surprise. 'You were gentle with her, then?'

The firelight flickered, casting shadows across Dammartin's face, highlighting his scar and emphasising the strong, harsh line of his jaw. 'Not particularly.'

'Pierre.' Lamont gave a sigh and shook his head.

'Did you really think that she would be in such a hurry to spill the answers we seek? The woman faced us alone with a rifle to defend her father.'

'She is just a girl, Pierre. She must have been afraid.'

'She was frightened, for all she tried to hide it.'

'Yet still she told you nothing?'

'The girl has courage, I will give her that.'

Lamont sucked harder on his pipe and nodded.

Dammartin thought of the girl's single teardrop and the tremble of her lips. Tears and emotion were ever a woman's weapons, he thought dismissively, but even as he thought it, he knew that was not the case with Mademoiselle Mallington. Given half a chance she would have taken a rifle and shot him through the heart, and that knowledge wrung from him a grudging respect.

'Do you mean to question her again tomorrow?'

'Yes. I suspect that she knows more than she is telling.'

Lamont frowned. 'Interrogating women goes against the grain.'

'We must make an exception for Mademoiselle Mallington.'

'Pierre…' admonished the Sergeant.

Dammartin passed Lamont his hip flask of brandy. 'What the hell am I going to do with her, Claude?'

'I do not know,' Lamont shrugged. 'That Mallington entrusted her to you makes me wonder as to the old man's mind. Why else would he give his daughter over to the son of the man that he murdered?'

'To appease his own conscience, leaving her to face the revenge from which he himself fled?' Dammartin's eyes glittered darkly as he received the flask back from Lamont and took a swig. He sat there for a while longer, mulling over all that happened that day, and when finally he slept, the sleep was troubled and dark.

Dammartin slept late, not wakening until the light of morning had dawned, and with a mood that had not improved. Disgruntlement sat upon him as a mantle even though he had reached a decision on what to do with the girl. He rolled over, feeling the chill of the morning air, and cast an eye over at Mademoiselle Mallington. Her blanket lay empty upon the floor. Josephine Mallington was gone.

'Merde!' he swore, and threw aside the thickness of his great coat that had covered him the whole night through. Then he was up and over there, touching his fingers to the blanket, feeling its coldness. Mademoiselle Mallington had not just vacated it, then.

He opened the door from the room, stepped over the two sentries who were dozing.

They blinked and scrabbled to their feet, saluting their captain.

'Where is the girl?'

The men looked sheepish. 'She needed to use the latrine, sir.'

Dammartin could not keep the incredulity from his voice. 'And you let her go unaccompanied?'

'It did not seem right to accompany your woman in such things,' one of the men offered.

'Mademoiselle Mallington is not my woman,' snapped Dammartin. 'She is my prisoner.'

'We thought—'

Dammartin's look said it all.

The sentries fell silent as Dammartin strode off to find Mallington's daughter.

Chapter Three

Josie hitched up her skirts and ran up the worn stone stairs within the monastery. She could not help but remember the last time she had made this journey. Only yesterday afternoon, and already it seemed a lifetime ago. This time she was alone with only the echo of her own footsteps for company. She reached the top of the stairs, and, hesitating there, braced herself to see once more the horror of what lay not so very far beyond. Her hand clutched upon the banister, tracing the bullet-gouged wood. Then she walked slowly and steadily towards the room in which the 60th had made its last stand.

The doorway was open; the wood remnants that had formed the once sturdy door had been tidied to a pile at the side. Blood splatters marked the walls and had dried in pools upon the floor. The smell of it still lingered in the room, despite the great portal of a window within the room and the lack of a door. Of her father and those of his men that had fought so bravely there was no sign. Josie stared, and stared some more. Their bodies were gone. Their weapons were gone. Their pouches of bullets and powder were gone. Only the stain of their blood remained.

She backed out of the room, retraced her steps down the stairs and peeped into the great hall. The rabbit stew still hung in the corner above the blackened ashes of the fire. The stone floor flags were stained with blood. Yet here, as in the room upstairs, there were no bodies. She turned, moving silently, making her way through to the back and the stables. The two horses were no longer there; nor were the donkeys. Of the supplies there was no trace.

Josie's heart began to race. Her feet led her farther out on to the land that had once been the monastery's garden. And there they were.

She stopped, her eyes moving over the mounds of freshly dug earth. At the front, one grave stood on its own, distinct from the others by virtue of its position. She moved forwards without knowing that she did so, coming to stand by that single grave. Only the wind sounded in the silent, sombre greyness of the morning light. For a long time Josie just stood there, unaware of the chill of the air or the first stirrings that had begun to sound from the Frenchmen's camp. And for the first time she wondered if perhaps her father had been right, and that Captain Dammartin was not, after all, a man completely without honour.

It was not difficult to trace Josie's path. Several of his men had seen the girl go into the monastery. No one challenged her. No one accosted her. Some knew that she was the English Lieutenant Colonel's daughter. Others thought, as had the sentries, that she was now their captain's woman. The misconception irked Dammartin, almost as much as the thought of her escape had done. Yet he knew that it was not the prospect of escape that had led her back to the monastery.

He found her kneeling by her father's grave.

Dammartin stood quietly by the stables, watching her.

Her fair hair was plaited roughly in a pigtail that hung down over her back and her skin was pale. Her head was bowed as if in prayer so that he could not see her face. She wore no shawl, and Dammartin could see that her figure was both neat and slender. He supposed she must be cold.

Her dress was dark brown and of good quality, but covered in dirt and dust and the stains of others' blood. The boots on her feet were worn and scuffed, hardly fitting for a Lieutenant Colonel's daughter, but then holding the 8th at bay with a single rifle was hardly fitting for such a woman, either. He watched her, unwilling to interrupt her grieving, knowing what it was to lose a father. So he stood and he waited, and never once did he take his eyes from Josephine Mallington.

Josie felt Captain Dammartin's presence almost as soon as he arrived, but she did not move from her kneeling. She knew that she would not pass this way again and she had come to bid her father and his men goodbye in the only way she knew how, and she was not going to let the French Captain stop her. Only when she was finished did she get to her feet. One last look at the mass expanse of graves, and then she turned and walked towards Captain Dammartin.

She stopped just short of him, looking up to see his face in the dawning daylight. His hair was a deep, dark brown that ruffled beneath the breeze. Despite the winter months, his skin still carried the faint colour of the sun. The ferocity of the weather had not left him unmarked. Dammartin's features were regular, his mouth hard and slim, his nose strong and straight. The daylight showed the scar that ran the length of his left cheek in stark clarity. It lent him a brooding, sinister look and she was glad that she was much more in control of herself this morning.

'Mademoiselle Mallington,' he said, and she could see

that his eyes were not black as she had thought last night, but the colour of clear, rich honey.

'Captain Dammartin.' She glanced away towards the graves, and then back again at him. 'Thank you.' She spoke coolly but politely enough.

A small tilt of his head served as acknowledgement.

'After what you said…I did not think…' Her words trailed off.

'I was always going to have the men buried. They fought like heroes. They deserved an honourable burial. We French respect bravery.' There was an almost mocking tone to his voice, implying that the British had no such respect. 'And as for your father…' He left what he would have said unfinished.

Beyond the monastery she could hear the sound of men moving. French voices murmured and there was the smell of fires being rekindled.

They looked at one another.

'What do you intend to do with me?'

'You are Lieutenant Colonel Mallington's daughter.' His expression did not change and yet it seemed that his eyes grew darker and harder. 'You will be sent to General Massena's camp at Santarém until you can be exchanged for a French prisoner of war.'

She gave a nod of her head.

'You may be assured that, unlike some, we do not ride roughshod over the rules of warfare or the protection that honour should provide.' His face was hard and lean, all angles that smacked of hunger and of bitterness.

It seemed to Josie that Captain Dammartin disliked her very much. 'I am glad to hear it, sir.'

He made some kind of noise of reply that said nothing. 'If you wish to eat, do so quickly. We ride within the hour and you will leave before that, travelling with the escort of Lieutenant Molyneux.'

Side by side, without so much as another word between them, Josephine Mallington and Pierre Dammartin made their way back down into the village and the French soldiers' camp.

'What were you playing at, Pierre?' Major La Roque demanded.

Dammartin faced the Major squarely. 'I wanted his surrender, sir.'

'Foy is asking questions. What am I supposed to tell him? That it took one of my captains almost two hours to overcome twenty-five men, without artillery, holed up in a ramshackle village. Given our fifty dragoons, seventy chasseurs and four hundred infantrymen, it does not look good for you, Pierre. Why did you not just storm the bloody monastery straight away like I told you?'

'I wanted to interrogate him. I would have thought that you, of all people, would understand that.'

'Of course I do, but this mission is vital to the success of the Army of Portugal and we have lost a day's march because of your actions. Not only that, but your men failed to catch the British messengers that were deployed! Only the fact that you are my godson, and Jean Dammartin's son, has saved you from the worst of Foy's temper. Whether it will prevent him from mentioning the *débâcle* to Bonaparte remains to be seen.'

Dammartin gritted his teeth and said nothing.

'I know what you are going through, Pierre. Do you think I am not glad that Mallington is dead? Do you think that I, too, do not wish to know what was going on in that madman's mind? Jean was like a brother to me.'

'I am sorry, sir.'

La Roque clapped his hand against Dammartin's back. 'I know. I know, son. Mallington is now dead. For that at least we should be glad.'

Dammartin nodded.

'What is this I hear about an English girl?'

'She is Mallington's daughter. Lieutenant Molyneux will take her back to General Massena's camp this morning.'

'I will not have any of our men put at risk because of Mallington's brat. These hills are filled with deserters and guerrillas. We cannot afford to lose any of the men. The child will just have to come with us to Ciudad Rodrigo. Once we are there, we can decide what to do with her.'

'Mademoiselle Mallington is not a child, she is—'

But La Roque cut him off, with a wave of the hand. 'It does not matter what she is, Pierre. If you jeopardise this mission any further, Foy will have your head and there will not be a damn thing I can do to save you. See to your men. Emmern will lead through the pass first. Fall in after him. Be ready to leave immediately.' The Major looked at Dammartin. 'Now that Mallington is dead, things will grow easier for you, Pierre, I promise you that.'

Dammartin nodded, but he took little consolation in his godfather's words. Mallington being dead did not make anything better. Indeed, if anything, Dammartin was feeling worse. Now, he would never know why Mallington had done what he did. And there was also the added complication of his daughter.

Whatever he was feeling, Dammartin had no choice but to leave the house that Major La Roque had commandeered in the valley and return to Telemos.

Josie was standing by the side of the window in the little empty room as she watched Dammartin ride back into the village. She knew it was him, could recognise the easy way he sat his horse, the breadth of his shoulders, the arrogant manner in which he held his head. Condensed breath snorted from the beast's nostrils and a light sweat glimmered on its flanks. She wondered what had caused him to ride the animal so hard when it had a full day's travel before it.

He jumped down, leaving the horse in the hands of a trooper who looked to be little more than a boy, and threaded his way through the men that waited hunched in groups, holding their hands to fires that were small and mean and not built to last.

Even from here she could hear his voice issuing its orders.

The men began to move, kicking dust onto the fires, fastening their helmets to their heads and gathering up the baggage in which they had packed away their belongings and over which they had rolled their blankets. He walked purposefully towards the cottage, his face stern as if he carried with him news of the worst kind.

She watched him and it seemed that he sensed her scrutiny, for his gaze suddenly shifted to fix itself upon her. Josie blushed at having being caught staring and drew back, but not before he had seen her. Her cheeks still held their slight wash of colour when he entered the room.

'Mademoiselle Mallington, we are leaving.'

Her hands smoothed down the skirts of her dress in a nervous gesture.

He noticed that the worst of the dirt had been brushed from her dress and that she had combed and re-plaited her hair into a single, long, tidy pigtail that hung down her back. He moved to take up his baggage, then led her out into the sunlight and across the village through which her father and his men had run and fired their rifles and died.

The French dragoons around ceased their murmuring to watch her, wanting to see the woman who had defied the might of the 8th to stand guard over her dying father.

She followed him until they came to the place she had seen him leave his horse. The boy still held the reins. Dammartin handed him the baggage and the boy threw them over the chestnut's rump and strapped them into place. Beside the large chestnut was a smaller grey. He gestured towards it.

'You will find Fleur faster than a donkey.' Dammartin took a dark blue cloak from the boy and handed it to Josie. 'There was a portmanteau of women's clothes alongside Lieutenant Colonel Mallington's. I assumed that they were yours.'

Her fingers clutched at the warmth of the wool. She touched it to her nose, breathing in faint lavender and rosemary, the familiar scent of her own portmanteau and its sachets that she had sown what seemed an eternity ago on sunny days at home in England. The last time she had worn this cloak her father had been alive, and twenty-seven others with him. She still could not believe that they were dead.

'It is my cloak, thank you, Captain Dammartin,' she said stiffly, and draped the material around her.

'We have not a side-saddle.'

'I can ride astride.'

Their eyes held for a heartbeat before she moved quickly to grasp her skirts and, as modestly as she could manage, she placed her foot in the stirrup and pulled herself up on to the grey horse.

The troopers cast appreciative gazes over Josie's ankles and calves, which, no matter how much she pulled at and rearranged her skirts, refused to stay covered. Several whistles sounded from the men, someone uttered a crudity. She felt the heat rise in her cheeks and kept her gaze stubbornly forward.

'Enough,' Dammartin shouted at his men in French. 'Look to your horses. We leave in five minutes.'

Another officer on horseback walked over to join them, his hair a pale wheaty brown beneath the glint of his helmet.

Dammartin gave the man a curt nod of the head before speaking. 'Mademoiselle Mallington, this is Lieutenant Molyneux. Lieutenant, this is Lieutenant Colonel Mallington's daughter.'

Molyneux removed his helmet, and still seated firmly in his saddle, swept her a bow. *'Mademoiselle.'*

Dammartin frowned at his lieutenant.

Josie looked from the open friendliness on the handsome young lieutenant's face to the brooding severity on his captain's, and she was glad that she would be making the journey to Massena's camp in Lieutenant Molyneux's company rather than that of Captain Dammartin. Dammartin looked at her with such dislike beneath his thin veneer of civility that she was under no illusions as to his feelings towards her. Still, there were formalities to be observed in these situations, and she would not disgrace her father's name by ignoring them.

'Goodbye, Captain Dammartin.'

'Unfortunately, *mademoiselle*, this is no goodbye.'

Her eyes widened.

'You travel with us.'

'But you said…' She glanced towards Lieutenant Molyneux.

The lieutenant gave a small, consolatory smile and said, 'I am afraid, *mademoiselle*, that there has been a change of plan.' He dropped back, so that it seemed to Josie that he was abandoning her to Dammartin.

Dammartin's face was unreadable.

'Am I to be exchanged?'

'Eventually,' said Dammartin.

'Eventually? And in the meantime?'

'You are a prisoner of the 8th,' he replied.

A spurt of anger fired within her. 'I will not ride to act against my own country, sir.'

'You have no choice in the matter,' he said curtly.

She stared at him, and the urge to hit him across his arrogant face was very strong. 'I would rather be sent to General Massena's camp.'

'That is my preference also, *mademoiselle*, but it is no longer an option.'

'Then release me. I will make my own way to the lines of Torres Vedras.'

'Tempting though the offer is, I cannot allow you to do so.'

'Why not?' she demanded, feeling more outraged by the minute.

'I have my orders.'

'But—'

A drum sounded, and a second company of French cavalrymen, not dragoons but Hanoverian Chasseurs, began to ride into the village.

Dammartin shouted an order and his men began to form into an orderly column. The chasseur captain, who was dressed in a similar fashion to Dammartin, but with yellow distinctives on the green of his jacket and a dark fur hat upon his head, drew up beside Dammartin, saluting him. His face broke into a grin as he spoke a more informal greeting.

'Emmern.'

For the first time Josie saw Dammartin smile. It was a real smile, a smile of affection, not some distortion of his mouth out of irony or contempt. And it changed his whole face so that he looked devastatingly handsome. Shock jolted through her that she could think such a thing and, pushing the thought aside, she forced herself to concentrate on what the two men were discussing. They spoke in rapid French, discussing the land that lay beyond the village, and the quickest and safest method by which their men might traverse it.

'Foy is like a bear with a sore head this morning.' Captain Emmern laughed. 'The delay has not pleased him.'

'I am aware,' agreed Dammartin. 'I will have the joy of reporting to him this evening.'

'The day has started well, then,' teased the chasseur.

'Indeed,' said Dammartin. 'It could not get much worse.'

Emmern's eyes flicked to Josie and the grey on which she sat. 'I would not look so gloomy if I had spent the night in such pleasant company.' He inclined his head at Josie in greeting. 'Come, Pierre, introduce me. Surely you do not mean to keep her all to yourself? I swear, she is utterly delicious.'

Josie felt the blood scald her cheeks. She ignored the chasseur captain, fidgeted with the grey's reins, and focused on a peculiarly shaped rock high up on the hill to the side.

'She is Lieutenant Colonel Mallington's daughter.' Dammartin's eyes were cold and his jaw rigid.

Captain Emmern's brow lifted slightly with surprise. 'They said there was a woman, but I did not realise that she was his daughter. What the hell could the man have been thinking?'

'Who knows the workings of a madman's mind?' replied Dammartin dryly.

Josie's fists clenched at the Frenchmen's words of insult.

With blazing eyes she glared at them, words of defence for her father crowding in her mouth for release. Yet the suspicion that flashed across Dammartin's face served as a timely reminder that she must feign ignorance of their conversation.

Dammartin edged his horse closer towards her, his brows lowered. *'Parlez-vous français, mademoiselle?'*

Even had she not understood his language, there was no doubting the accusation in his demand. This was dangerous ground, for she realised that by showing her emotions too readily she was in danger of revealing the one advantage that she had over her captors. The Frenchmen would let down their guard and talk easily in front of her if they thought that their words could not be understood by their prisoner. Any information she could glean might be of use, for Josie had every intention of passing on all she could learn to General Lord Wellington. She straightened her back and, squaring her shoulders, faced Dammartin, meeting his penetrating gaze directly.

'I have not the slightest idea of what you are saying, sir. If you would be so good as to speak in English, then I may be able to answer you.'

Dammartin's face cracked into a cynical disbelieving smile, yet he switched to English. 'Do not tell me that you understand not one word of my language, for I will not believe such a ridiculous assertion.'

Josie did her best to appear outraged. 'Are you suggesting that I am lying?'

'You have been lying all along, *mademoiselle*...about that which you know, and that which you do not: the details of your father's men, his purpose in these hills, his messengers...'

She flinched at that and there was no longer any need for pretence; her outrage was all too real.

'You are the daughter of a senior officer; your father must have arranged your education. I believe that in England even the lowliest of governesses teach the rudiments of French.'

The heat scalded Josie's cheeks, and her chest tightened at his words. She might have been fluent in French, but that had nothing to do with governesses and everything to do with her mother. Mama and Papa had been the best of parents, yet she felt Dammartin's implied criticism as sharp as a knife.

'What time was there for schooling or governesses following my father around the world on campaign? There is more to education than such formality, and besides, my mother and father ensured that both my brother and I were educated in those matters that are of any importance.' She negated to mention the truth of the situation.

Silence followed her inferred insult.

Still she did not drop her gaze from his so that she saw his eyes narrow infinitesimally at her words. He twitched the rein between his fingers and the great chestnut horse brought him round to her side.

'Have a care in what you say, Mademoiselle Mallington. Such words could be construed by some of my countrymen as offensive, and you are hardly in a position to abuse our hospitality.'

'Hospitality?' Her eyebrows raised in exaggerated incredulity, and so caught up in her own anger was Josie that she did not notice the scowl line deepen between Dammartin's brows. 'You kill my father and his men, you lock me in a cellar for hours on end and interrogate me. Forgive me if I am surprised at your notion of hospitality, sir!'

He leaned in closer until his face was only inches above hers. It seemed to Josie that the angles of his jawline grew sharper and the planes of his cheeks harder, and his eyes darkened with undisguised fury. As awareness dawned of how much bigger he was, of his strength, his overwhelming masculinity, all of Josie's anger cooled, leaving in its stead the icy chill of fear.

'I assure you, *mademoiselle*, that I have been most hospitable in my treatment of you...so far.' His voice was the quiet purr of a predator. 'Do you wish me to prove it is so, by demonstrating how very inhospitable I can be?'

Josie's heart was thumping nineteen to the dozen. She wetted the dryness of her lips, and swallowed against the aridity of her throat. 'You are no gentleman, sir.' Still, she forced herself to hold his dark, menacing gaze.

'And you, no lady.'

She could have argued back. She could have called him the scoundrel that he was, but there was something in his eyes that stopped her, something fierce and impassioned and resolute that shook her to her very core.

'I ask you, sir, to release me,' she said, and all of the bravado had gone so that her voice was small and tired. 'You do not want me as your prisoner any more than I wish to be here. It is madness to drag me all the way to Ciudad Rodrigo. Allowing me to walk away now would be the best solution for us both.'

There was a moment's silence in which he made no move to pull back from her, just kept his gaze fixed and intent, locked upon her, as a hunter who has sighted his prey. 'Ciudad Rodrigo?' he said softly.

Her heart gave a shudder at what she had unintentionally revealed.

'What else do you know of General Foy's mission, I wonder?' His question was as gentle as a caress.

Josie dropped her eyes to stare at the ground, an involuntary shiver rippling through her.

He leaned in closer until she could feel the warmth of his breath fanning her cheek.

Her eyelids closed. The breath stalled in her throat and her fingers gripped tight around the reins, bracing herself for what was to come.

'Pierre.' Captain Emmern's voice sounded, shattering the tight tension that had bound her and Dammartin together in a world that excluded all else.

She opened her eyes and blinked at the chasseur captain, allowing herself to breathe once more.

'Captain Dammartin,' said Emmern more formally this time. He looked from Dammartin to Josie and back again with a strange expression upon his face. 'We should get moving, before the General grows impatient.'

Dammartin gave a nod in reply, then, with a small nudge of his boots against the chestnut's flank, he and the horse began to move away.

Relief softened the rigidity throughout Josie's body, so that she felt that she might collapse down against the little mare's neck and cling on for dear life. She caught her fingers into the coarse hair of the mane, stabilising herself once more now that the danger was receding.

'Mademoiselle Mallington,' he called softly.

She froze at the sound of his voice, saw him turn back to look at her.

'We shall finish this conversation later.'

She felt the blood drain from her face, and she stared at him aghast, unable to move, unable to utter a single word in response.

'I promise that most solemnly.' And with a twitch of his reins he was finally gone.

Foy's column with its cavalry detachment travelled far that day, twenty miles across terrain that was rocky and high and inhospitable. The ground was frozen hard beneath their feet and great chunks of ice edged the rivulets of streams that carved passageways down the hillsides. And in all the hours that passed, Josie could not find a way to escape the officers of Bonaparte's 8th Dragoons.

She had hoped that she might be able to fall back or just slip away unnoticed, but there was no chance of that. The 8th Dragoons were neatly sandwiched between Emmern's Hanoverian Chasseurs in front and a whole regiment of French infantry to the rear. And were that not bad enough, Lieutenant Molyneux rode nearby, offering occasional polite conversational words, checking on her welfare and ensuring that she was served the hard bread rolls and wine when they stopped to water the horses. There seemed no way out. Yet when Josie looked in front to where Dammartin rode, she knew that escape was an absolute necessity.

Dammartin did not look back at her and that was something at least for which she felt relief. His attention was focused upon his men, on the ragged drops that fell away from the sides of the narrow rough roads along which they trotted, and the precipices so high above. If a trooper wandered too close to the edge, Dammartin barked a warning for him to get back in column. If they moved too slowly, one look from Dammartin was enough to hurry them onwards.

Throughout the long hours of riding he ignored her, but his promise lay between them as threatening as the man himself. He would interrogate her in earnest. She knew it with a certainty, had seen it in his eyes. She thought of the danger that emanated from him, of the darkness, a formidable force waiting to be unleashed…upon her. She trembled at the prospect of what he might do to her, knowing that for all her bravado, for all her own tenacity, he was far stronger. He would lead her in circles until she no longer knew what she was saying. Hadn't she already inadvertently revealed that her father had known of Foy's destination? What more would she tell the French Captain?

The thoughts whirred in her head, churning her gut with anticipation. No matter her father's instruction or the promise she had made him, she knew that she had to get away, to somehow make her way back towards the British lines. She would be safe from Dammartin there, and she would ensure that the news of Foy's mission had reached Wellington. Papa would have understood, she told herself.

Having made up her mind, Josie no longer looked ahead to the breadth of Dammartin's shoulders or the fit of his green dragoon jacket across his back and, instead, focused every last ounce of her attention on a way of evading her captor.

They had reached the site of their camp in a small valley between Cardigos and Sobreira Formosa before the opportunity that Josie had been waiting for arose. Most of Dammartin's dragoons were busy pitching the tents. The air rang with the sound of small iron-tipped mallets driving narrow iron tent pegs into the frozen soil. Those troopers not helping with the tents, gathered wood and lit fires upon which they placed kettles and pots to boil, cooking that evening's rations. All along the massive camp both cavalrymen and infantrymen were orderly and disciplined and—busy. Even Molyneux seemed to have disappeared.

Josie knew that this was the best chance of escape she would get. She stood were she was, eyes scanning around, seeking the one man above all that she sought to evade, but of Dammartin there was no sign, and that could only be construed as a very good omen.

Slowly, inconspicuously, she edged towards a great clump of scrubby bushes at the side of the camp until she could slip unseen behind them. And then, hitching up her skirts in one hand, Josie started to run.

Dammartin was making his way back from reporting to Major La Roque and all he could think about was the wretched Mallington girl. She was too defiant, too stubborn and too damned courageous. When she looked at him, he saw the same clear blue eyes that had looked out from Mallington's face. A muscle twitched in Dammartin's jaw and he gritted his teeth.

The old man was dead and yet little of Dammartin's anger had dissipated. His father had been avenged, and still Dammartin's heart ached with a ferocity that coloured his every waking thought. All of the hurt, all of the rage at the injustice and loss remained. He knew he had been severe with girl. She was young, and it was not her hand that had fired the bullet into his father's chest. He had seen that she was frightened and the pallor of her face as she realised her mistake over Ciudad Rodrigo, and even then he had not softened. Now that he was away from her he could see that he had been too harsh, but the girl knew much more than she was saying, and if Dammartin was being forced to drag her with him all the way to Ciudad Rodrigo, he was damn well going to get that information—for the sake of his country, for the sake of his mission… for the sake of his father.

The dragoon camp was filled with the aroma of cooking—of boiling meat and toasting bread. Dammartin's stomach began to growl as he strode past the troopers' campfires, his eyes taking in all that was happening in one fell swoop. Lamont had a pot lid in one hand and was stirring at the watery meat with a spoon in the other. Molyneux was sharing a joke with a group of troopers.

The prickle of anticipation whispered down Dammartin's spine, for Josephine Mallington was nowhere to be seen.

'Where is Mademoiselle Mallington?' The stoniness of his voice silenced Molyneux's laughter. Lamont replaced the pot lid and spoon and got to his feet. The troopers glanced around uneasily, noticing the girl's absence for the first time.

A slight flush coloured Molyneux's cheeks. 'She was here but a moment since, I swear.'

'Check the tents,' Dammartin snapped at his lieutenant, before turning to Lamont. 'Have the men search over by the latrines.'

With a nod, the little sergeant was up and shouting orders as he ran.

Dammartin knew instinctively that the girl would not be found in either of these places. He strode purposefully towards the horses. None were missing.

Dante was saddled by the time that Molyneux reappeared.

'The tents are empty, Captain, and Lamont says that there's no sign of her down by the latrines.' He bent to catch his breath, tilting his head up to look at Dammartin. 'Do you want us to organise a search party?'

'No search party,' replied Dammartin, swinging himself up on to Dante's back. 'I go alone.'

'She cannot have got far in such little time. She is on foot and the harshness of this countryside…' Molyneux let the words trail off before dropping his voice. 'Forgive me, but I did not think for a minute that she would escape.'

Dammartin gave a single small nod of his head, acknowledging his lieutenant's apology. 'Mademoiselle Mallington is more resourceful than we have given her credit for.'

'What will happen if you do not find her? Major La Roque did not—'

'If I do not find her,' Dammartin interrupted, 'she will die.' And with a soft dig of his heels against Dante's flank he was gone.

Chapter Four

The wind whispered through the trees, straining at their bare branches until they creaked and rattled. Josie's run had subsided to a half walk, half scurry as she followed the road back along the route the French army had travelled. The track ran along the ridge of a great hill in the middle of even more hills. The surrounding landscape was hostile: jagged rocks, steep slopes and scree, with nothing of cover and nowhere that Josie could see to shelter.

She knew from the day's journey that some miles back there had been the derelict remains of a cottage and it was to this that Josie was heading. All she needed to do was to follow the road back up over the last hill and keep going until she came upon the cottage. She pushed herself on, knowing that it was only a matter of time before her absence was noticed. They might already be after her; *he* might already be after her. Her lungs felt fit to burst and there was a pain in her side. Josie willed her legs to move faster.

The light was rapidly fading and soon everything would be shrouded in darkness, making it impossible to see the rubble and pot-holes littering the road, and more importantly the cliff edge over to her right. Somewhere far away a wolf howled, a haunting sound that made the hairs on the back of Josie's neck stand erect. She knew what it was to be hunted, but it was not the wolf from which she was running.

Her foot twisted suddenly into an unseen dip on the unevenness of the road's surface, tipping her off balance, bringing her down, landing her hard. The fall winded her, but almost immediately she was scrabbling up to keep on going, ignoring the stinging in her hands and knees.

Dammartin cursed the charcoal-streaked sky. Once darkness fell she would be lost to him, and lost to herself too, he thought grimly. Little idiot, without shelter, without warmth, she would die out here. And no matter who her father had been, Dammartin did not want that to happen.

His eyes swept over the surrounding land, before flicking back to the road over the hill that loomed ahead. The French Captain's instinct told him which route the girl had chosen. Taking the spyglass from his pocket, he scanned the road over which they had travelled that day, and as the daylight died Pierre Dammartin felt the wash of satisfaction. He snapped the spyglass away.

A lone wolf's howl rent the air, urging Dammartin to move faster. He had not reached her yet, but he soon would.

Josie stopped and glanced back, her scalp prickling with foreboding, her ears straining to listen. There was only the wind and the ragged panting of her own breath. A noise sounded to her left, a rustling, a rooting. She stared suspiciously through the growing darkness, but there was nothing there save a few spindly bushes at the foot of the great rock wall. To her right a trickle of pebbles slid over the cliff edge, making her jump nervously.

She was being foolish, she told herself, these were the normal noises of the night, nothing more sinister. But as she hurried on, she remembered the stories of the bandits that roamed this land and she pulled her cloak more tightly around herself, only now beginning to see just how very dangerous her predicament was.

Come along, Josie, she told herself sternly, and she was in the middle of reciting the Mallington family motto, *audaces fortuna juvat*—fortune favours the brave—when she heard the gallop of a horse's hooves in the distance.

Dammartin.

She looked back into the deep inky blueness, her eyes examining every shadow, every shape, but seeing nothing through the cover of the night. For a moment Josie was so gripped with panic that she did not move, just stood there staring for a few moments before the sensible part of her brain kicked back into action.

It would be impossible to outrun him, he was coming this way and fast, and the few bushes around were too small to hide her. Glancing swiftly around she realised that just ahead, to the left, the sheer wall of rock and soil seemed to change, relaxing its gradient, leaning back by forty-five degrees to give a climbable slope. Her eyes followed it up to the flat ground at the top, which merged into the darkness of the other hills. Josie did not wait for an invitation; she began to run again.

A thin crescent moon hung in the sky and Dammartin could just about see the small, dark shape moving on the road ahead. He kicked Dante to a gallop to close the distance between them. One more curve in the road and she would be his, but as he rounded that last corner, with Dante blowing hard, the road was deserted.

Dante pulled up, clouds of condensation puffing from his nostrils, the sweat upon his chestnut coat a slick sheen beneath the moonlight. Dammartin was breathing hard too, his heart racing, a sudden fear in his chest that she had gone over the edge of the cliff rather than let herself be taken.

A small noise sounded ahead, somewhere high up on the left, a dislodged pebble cascading down. Dammartin's gaze swivelled towards the sound, and what he saw made his mouth curve to a wicked smile.

Josie heard the horse draw up below. Just a single horse. She could hear the rider dismount and begin to climb.

One man.

She had to know. Her head turned. She dared a glance below… and gasped aloud.

The thin sliver of moon lit the face of Captain Dammartin as he scaled the rock face at a frightening speed.

Josie redoubled her efforts, clambering up as fast as she could.

She could hear him getting closer. Her arms and legs were aching and she could feel the trickle of sweat between her breasts and down her back, but still she kept going, puffing her breathy exertion like smoke into the chill of the night air.

'Mademoiselle Mallington.'

She heard his voice too close. *Keep going, Josie, keep going*, she willed herself on, climbing and climbing, and still, he came after her, closing the gap between them.

'Cease this madness, before you break your neck.'

She glanced back and saw that he was right below her.

'No!' she cried in panic, and pulling off her hat, she threw it at him.

A hand closed around her ankle—firm, warm fingers. She felt the gentle tug.

'No!' she yelled again. 'Release me!' And she tried to kick out at him with her foot, but it was too late; Josie's grip was lost and she slid helplessly down over the rock and the dirt, towards her enemy.

Dammartin leaned out, away from the slope, so that the girl's body slid neatly in beneath his. Her back was flush against his chest, her buttocks against his groin. The wind whipped her hair to tickle against his chin. She seemed to freeze, gripping for dear life to the rock face, before she realised that he had caught her, that she was safe. He heard her gasp of shock as she became aware of her position, and braced himself.

'Unhand me at once!' She bucked against him.

He pressed into her, gripping tighter. 'Continue as you are, *mademoiselle*, and you will send us both to our deaths,' he said into her ear.

She ceased her struggles. 'What are you going to do?' Her words were quiet.

'Save your life.'

Only the wind whispered in return, but he could feel the rapidity of her breathing beneath his chest, and the tremor that ran through her slight frame.

'It is not in need of saving. Leave me be, sir. I will not return with you to the camp.'

'Then you will be clinging to this rock face beneath me all damn night, for I have no intention of returning without my prisoner,' he said savagely.

She tried to turn her head, as if to glance at what lay beyond, but her cheek touched against his chest, and he knew she could see nothing other than him.

'I do not think you so foolish as to throw your life away, Mademoiselle Mallington, no matter how tempting it may be to dispense with mine.'

There was a silence before she said, 'You climb down first and I will follow.'

His mouth curved cynically. 'We climb down together, or not at all. You cannot answer my questions with a broken neck.'

He felt her tense beneath him. 'You are wasting your time, Captain, for I will never answer your questions, no matter how many times you ask them. I would rather take my chances here on this rock face.'

Dammartin understood then why Mademoiselle Mallington had run. The lavender scent of her hair drifted up to fill his nose. 'And if I tell you there will be no questions tonight, will you come down then?'

Another silence, as if she were contemplating his words, reaching a decision, just a few moments, but time enough for his awareness of the soft curves moulded against him to grow.

She gave a reluctant nod of the head.

They stood like two spoons nestled together, the entire length of their bodies touching. And it was not anger at her escape, or the jubilation of her recapture of which Dammartin was thinking; it was not even the difficulty of the descent they had no choice but to make. For the first time, Dammartin saw Josie not as Mallington's daughter, but as a woman, and a woman that stirred his blood.

She glanced directly down, looking to see the rock face below. Her body tensed further and she clung all the harder to the rocks, laying her face against them.

He started to move.

'No, I cannot!' she said, and he could hear the slight note of panic underlying her words.

'Mademoiselle Mallington…'

'It is too high, we cannot…'

'Just do as I say.'

'I cannot…please…'

There was just the sound of the wind and the rise and fall of her breathing and the feel of her body beneath his.

'I will help you and we will reach the ground safely enough.' He became conscious of where her hips nestled so snugly and felt the stirrings of his body response.

She hesitated before giving a tiny nod.

Josie had thought of nothing other than escape on her way up the cliff, but now she was aware of how very far the ground seemed below, of the loose, insecure surface of the rocks and the wind that pulled at both her and Dammartin. In the darkness she could not see what was safe to grip with her hands, and the skirt of her dress hid her view of her feet and where she might place them. A wave of panic swept through her and she thought that she might be stuck there, unable to move either up or down, but then the French Captain said that he would help her. He edged her to movement and the panic was gone. Slowly they began to descend the rock face.

The warm press of his body and the clean masculine smell of him pulled her mind from the danger of the rocks beneath. He was gentle, encouraging her with quiet words when she struggled to place her feet, coaxing her to keep moving when she thought she could move no more. There was no anger, no harshness, no danger, and, ironically, as they risked their lives to reach the ground, she felt safer with him now than she had ever done. It did not make sense. She did not know this new Dammartin.

She heard his exhalation of breath as they made it to the ground. The cold rushed in against her back as he moved away, opening the space between them. She turned, and was able to see him properly for the first time. Words of gratitude hovered on her lips, but she bit them back, not understanding why she wanted to thank him for saving her, when in truth he was the enemy who had just destroyed her chance of escape.

For a moment Dammartin just stood there by the foot of the slope; the weak silvery moonlight exposing the dark slash of his scar, the lean hard planes sculpting his face, and the rugged squareness of his jaw. Shadow obscured half his face, making it impossible for Josie to read his expression, but there was something in the way he was looking at her, something in his stance, that made her wonder if this was indeed the same man from whom she had run. Her gaze dropped to hide her confusion and her feeling of vulnerability.

'You do not need to take me back,' she said, 'you could say that you did not find me. It is a plausible story.'

He gave a cynical laugh and shook his head. 'What part of this do you not understand, *mademoiselle*? That you would not survive out here alone, or that I do not lose my prisoners?'

The arrogance of his words rankled with her, urging her pride to deny the truth in his answer. 'I would survive very well, if you would let me.'

'With no weapon, no shelter, no means to make fire, no food or water?' he mocked. 'And what of guerrillas and bandits? You think you can take them on single-handed?'

'As a woman travelling alone, I would present no threat to any such men. They would be unlikely to harm me. I *am* British.'

'You think they care about that?' Dammartin raised an eyebrow.

Josie's indignation rose. 'I would have managed well enough.'

'You are a fool if you think so—' his eyes narrowed slightly '—and you would be a bigger fool to try a further escape.'

'You cannot stop me,' she retaliated. 'I swear I will be long gone before you are anywhere close to Ciudad Rodrigo.'

The wolf howl sounded again, and in the moonlight Dammartin transformed once more to a sinister mode. 'No, *mademoiselle*,' he said softly, 'you are much mistaken in that belief.'

All of Josie's fear flooded back at the certainty in his voice.

She looked at him, not knowing what to say, not knowing what to do, aware only that he had won, and that her failure would cost her dearly when he got her back to the camp.

There was the sound of the wind, and of quietness.

'Please,' she said, and hoped that he would not hear the desperation in her voice.

The scree crunched beneath his boots as he came to stand before her. 'I will not leave you out here.'

Her eyes searched the shadow of his face and thought she saw something of the harshness drop away.

'No more questions this night.' He reached out and, taking her arm, pulled her from where she leaned against the slope.

He led her across to the great chestnut horse that stood waiting so patiently, his grip light but unbreakable around her arm, releasing her only long enough to mount and lift her up before him. She was sitting sideways, holding on to the front of the saddle with her left hand, and trying not to hold on to Dammartin with her right

Dammartin looked pointedly at where the hand rested upon her skirts. 'We shall be travelling at speed.'

She gave a nod. 'I know,' she said.

'As you will, *mademoiselle*.'

As they reached the surface of the road, the horse began to canter, and Josie gripped suddenly at Dammartin to stop herself from being thrown from the saddle. By the time the canter became a gallop, Josie was clinging tight to the French Captain's chest, while he secured her in place with an anchoring arm around her waist.

Stars shone like a thousand diamond chips scattered over a black velvet sky. The silver sickle of the moon bathed all in its thin magical light, revealing the road ahead that would lead them back to the French camp.

For Josie there would be no escape.

Dammartin swigged from the hip flask, the brandy burning a route down to his stomach. The fire burned low before them, and most of the men had already retired for the night. He wiped his mouth with the back of his hand and offered the flask to Lamont.

'The men were taking bets on whether you would find her.' Lamont took a gulp of the brandy before returning the flask.

'Did you win?' asked Dammartin.

'Of course,' replied the little Sergeant with a smile, and patted his pocket. 'I know you too well, my friend.'

They sat quietly for a few minutes, the sweet smell of Lamont's pipe mingling pleasantly with that of the brandy, the logs cracking and shifting upon the fire.

'She has courage, the little *mademoiselle*.' It was Lamont who broke the silence.

'She does,' agreed Dammartin, thinking of Josie halfway up that rock face, and the way she had defied him to the end. He glanced towards the tents.

Lamont followed his captain's eyes, before returning

his gaze to the glow of the burning logs. 'What will you do with her?'

'Take her to Ciudad Rodrigo as I am commanded.'

'I mean, this night.'

'What does one do with any prisoner who has attempted to escape?' Dammartin poked at the embers of the fire with a stick.

'She is gently bred, and a woman. You would not...?' Lamont's words petered out in uncertainty.

There was a silence in which Dammartin looked at him. 'What do you think?'

'I think you are too much your father's son.'

Dammartin smiled at his old friend, and fitted the top back on to his hip flask, before slipping it into his pocket. 'But she is too much Mallington's daughter.'

There was the soft breath of the wind while both men stared wordlessly into the fire.

'Why did she run, Pierre? The girl is no fool; she must have realised her chance of survival was slim?'

'She was afraid.' Dammartin's gaze did not shift from the warm orange glow of the dying fire as he remembered Mademoiselle Mallington's face in the moonlight as she stood at the foot of the slope. He had felt the tremor in her body, heard the fear beneath the defiance in her words. *I will never answer your questions, no matter how many times you ask them.* He heard the whisper of them even now. 'Afraid of interrogation.'

Lamont gave a sigh and shook his head. 'There is nothing of any use she can tell us now.'

'I would not be so certain of that.'

'Pierre...' the older man chided.

'I will question her again,' interrupted Dammartin. 'But her only fear need be what answers she will spill.'

'And when we reach Ciudad Rodrigo, what then?'

'Then she is no longer my problem,' said Dammartin.

Lamont sucked at his pipe for a few moments, as if weighing Dammartin's answer. 'It is a long way to Ciudad Rodrigo.'

'Do not worry, Claude.' Dammartin gave Lamont a clap on the back. 'Mademoiselle Mallington will give us no more trouble. I will make certain of that.' He got to his feet. 'Sleep well, my old friend.' And began to make his way across the small distance to where the officers' tents were pitched.

'And you, my captain,' said Lamont softly, as he sat by the fire and watched Dammartin disappear beneath the canvas of his tent.

The girl was sitting at the little table, busy working her hair into a plait when Dammartin entered the tent. She jumped to her feet, her hair abandoned, the ribbon fluttering down to lie forgotten upon the ground sheet. From the corner of his eye he could see a white frilled nightdress spread out over the covers of his bed.

'What are you doing here, Captain Dammartin?' she demanded, her face peaked and shocked.

'Retiring to bed.'

Her eyes widened with indignation and the unmistakable flicker of fear. 'In my tent?'

'The tent is mine.' He walked over to the small table and chair.

Even beneath the lantern light he could see the blush that swept her cheeks. 'Then I should not be here, sir.' Hurrying over to the bed, she slipped her feet into her boots sitting neatly by its side, before grabbing up the nightdress and rolling it swiftly to a ball. 'There has clearly been some kind of misunderstanding. If you would be so kind as to direct me to the women's tent.'

'You are a prisoner, *mademoiselle*, not a camp follower. Besides, the women's tent is within the camp of the infantry, not my dragoons. As a prisoner of the 8th, you stay with me.'

'Then you can show me the tent in which I am to stay the night.' She stood facing him squarely, clutching the nightdress in a crumpled mass like a shield before her, ready to do battle.

'You are already within that tent.' He turned away and began to unbutton his jacket.

'Indeed, I am not, sir!' she exclaimed with force, and he could see the colour in her cheeks darken. 'What manner of treatment is this? You cannot seriously expect that I will spend the night with you!' Her nostrils flared. She stared at him as if she were some great warrior queen.

'You speak of expectations, *mademoiselle*. Do you expect to be left overnight all alone, so that you may try again to escape?'

She gave a shake of her head, and the loose blonde plait hanging down against her breast began to unwind. 'I would try no such thing. The night is too dark, and I have no torch.'

'These things did not stop you this evening.'

'There was still daylight then.'

'Hardly,' he said, and shrugging off his jacket, hung it over the back of the wooden chair by the table.

'I give you my word that I will not try to escape this night.'

'Only this night?' he raised an eyebrow.

'It is this night of which we are speaking.'

'So you are planning another attempt tomorrow.'

'No!'

'Tomorrow night, then?'

'Very well, I give you my word that I will not attempt

another escape.' She looked at him expectantly. 'So now will you arrange for another tent?'

'Your word?' He heard his voice harden as the memories came flooding back unbidden, the grief and revenge bitter within his mouth. He gave an angry, mirthless laugh. 'But how can I trust that when the word of a Mallington is meaningless.'

'How dare you?' she exclaimed, and he could see the fury mounting in her eyes.

He smiled a grim determined smile. 'Most easily, *mademoiselle*, I assure you.'

'I have nothing more to say to you, sir.' She spun on her heel, and began to stride towards the tent flap.

Dammartin's hand shot out and, fixing a firm hold around her upper arm, hoisted her back. She struggled to escape him, but Dammartin just grabbed hold of her other arm and hauled her back to face him. Her arms were slight beneath his hands and he was surprised again at how small and slender she was, even though he had felt her body beneath his upon the rock face only a few hours since. He adjusted his grip so that he would not hurt her and pulled her closer.

She quietened then, looked up at him with blue eyes that were stormy. The scent of lavender surrounded her, and he could not help himself glance at the pale blonde hair that now spilled loose around her shoulders.

'But I have not finished in what I have to say to you, *mademoiselle*.' The nightdress slipped from her fingers, falling to lie between them.

They both glanced down to where the white frills lay in a frothy pool against the black leather of Dammartin's boots.

And when he looked again, her eyes had widened slightly and he saw the fear that flitted through them.

He spoke quietly but with slow, deliberate intent, that she would understand him. 'All the tents upon this campsite are filled, and even were they not, my men have travelled far this day and I would not drag a single one from their rest to guard against any further escape attempt that you may make. So tonight, I guard you myself. Do not complain of this situation, for you have brought it upon yourself, *mademoiselle*, with your most foolish behaviour.' He lowered his face towards hers until their noses were almost touching, so close that they might have been lovers.

He heard the slight raggedness of her breathing, saw the rapid rise and fall of her breast, and the way that the colour washed from her cheeks as she stared back at him, her eyes wide with alarm.

The silence stretched between them as the soft warmth of her breath whispered against his lips like a kiss. His mouth parted in anticipation, and for one absurd moment he almost kissed her, almost, but then he remembered that she was Mallington's daughter, and just precisely what Lieutenant Colonel Mallington had done, and all of the misery and all of the wrathful injustice was back.

His heart hardened.

When finally he spoke his voice was low and filled with harsh promise. 'Do not seek to escape me again, Mademoiselle Mallington. If you try, your punishment shall be in earnest. Do you understand me?'

She gave a single nod of her head; as Dammartin released his grip, she stumbled back, grabbing hold of the chair back, where his jacket hung, to steady herself.

He turned brusquely away, pulling two blankets and a pillow from the bed and dropping them on to the ground sheet beside the bed. 'Make yourself a bed. We leave early tomorrow and must sleep.'

She just stood there, by the table, looking at him, her face pale and wary.

He did not look at her, just sat down on the bed and removed his boots.

And still she stood there, until at last his gaze again met hers.

'Make up your bed, unless you have a wish to share mine, *mademoiselle*.'

An expression of shock crossed her face and she hurriedly did as she was bid, extinguishing the lantern before climbing beneath the blankets on the groundsheet.

Dammartin did not sleep, and neither did the girl. The sound of her breathing told him that she lay as awake as he, so close to his bed that he might have reached his arm down and touched her. The wind buffeted at the canvas of the tent, but apart from that everything was silent.

He did not know how long he lay listening, aware of her through the darkness, turning one way and then the next as if she could find no comfort on the hardness of the ground. He rolled over, conscious of the relative softness of his own mattress, and felt the first prickle of conscience.

Goddamn it, she was his prisoner, he thought, and he'd be damned if he'd give his bed up for Mallington's daughter. Just as he was thinking this, he heard her soft movements across the tent, and with a reflex honed by years of training, reached out through the darkness to grab at her dress.

He felt her start, heard her gasp loud in the deadness of the night.

'Mademoiselle Mallington,' he said quietly, 'do you disregard my warning so readily?'

'No,' she whispered. 'I seek only my cloak. The night is cold. I am not trying to escape.

Swinging his legs over the side of the bed, he sat up,

guiding her back towards him, turning her in the blackness and tracing his hands lightly around her, like a blindman, until he found her hands. Even through the wool of her dress he could feel that she was chilled. Her fingers were cold beneath his before she pulled away from his touch.

'Go back to your bed, *mademoiselle*,' he said curtly.

'But my cloak…'

'Forget your cloak, you shall not find it in this darkness.'

'But—'

'*Mademoiselle*,' he said more harshly.

He heard the breath catch in her throat as if she would have given him some retort, but she said nothing, only climbed beneath the blankets that he had given her earlier that night.

Dammartin swept his greatcoat from where it lay over his bed, and covered the girl with it.

'Captain Dammartin…' He could hear her surprise.

'Go to sleep,' he said gruffly.

'Thank you,' came the soft reply.

He turned over and pulled the blanket higher, knowing himself for a fool and slipping all the more easily into the comfort of sleep because of it.

Josie awoke to the seep of thin grey daylight through the canvas overhead. Sleep still fuddled her mind and she smiled, burrowing deeper beneath the cosiness of the covers, thinking that her father would tease her for her tardiness. Voices sounded outside, French male, and reality came rushing back in, exploding all of her warm contentment: Telemos, her father's death, Dammartin. Clutching the blankets to her chest she sat up, glancing round apprehensively.

The bed in which Dammartin had slept lay empty; she

was alone in the tent. The breath that Josie had been holding released, relief flowed through her. She got to her feet, her head woolly and thick from her lack of sleep.

How may hours had she lain awake listening to the French Captain's breathing, hearing it slow and become more rhythmic as he found sleep? For how many hours had the thoughts raced through her head? Memories of her father and of Telemos. She had spoken the truth; the night was black and most of the fires would be dead; she had no torch, and she did not doubt that there would be sentries guarding the camp. Her chance of escape had been lost. He would watch her more carefully now.

A shudder ran through her as she remembered how he had held her last night, his face so close to hers that the air she breathed had been warmed by his lungs. His dark penetrating gaze locked on to hers so that she could not look away. For a moment, just one tiny moment, she had thought that he meant to kiss her, before she saw the pain and bitterness in his eyes. And she blushed that she could have thought such a ridiculous notion. Of course he did not want to kiss her, he hated her, just as she hated him. There was no mistaking that. He hated her, yet he would not let her go.

I do not lose prisoners, he had said. And she had the awful realisation that he meant to take her all the way to Ciudad Rodrigo—far away from Torres Vedras, and Lisbon and the British—and in the miles between lay the prospect of interrogation.

Her eye caught the thick grey greatcoat, still lying where he had placed it last night, on top of her blankets. When she looked at the bed again, she saw its single woollen cover. The chill in the air nipped at her, and she knew that the night had been colder. She stared at the bed, not understanding why a man so very menacing, so very dangerous, who loathed her very existence, had given her his covers.

More voices, men walking by outside.

She glanced down at the muddy smears marking her crumpled dress, and her dirty hands and ragged nails—souvenirs of the rock face and her failed escape.

She was British, she reminded herself, and she would not allow the enemy to bring her down in such a way. So she smoothed the worst of her bed-mussed hair, and peeped out of the tent flap. Molyneux lingered not so very far away. He was kind; he spoke English...and he came when she beckoned him. It seemed that the Lieutenant was only too happy to fetch her a basin of water.

'I apologise, mademoiselle, for the coldness of the water, but there is no time to warm it.' He smiled at her, his skin creasing round his eyes, and the wind ruffling the pale brown of his hair.

'Thank you,' she said, and meant it.

Taking the basin from the Lieutenant's hands, she glanced out at the campsite beyond. All around dragoons were busy putting out fires, packing up, dismantling. She recognised Dammartin's sergeant, Lamont, speaking to a group of troopers, but Dammartin himself was nowhere that she could see.

'Thank you,' she said again, and disappeared within the tent flaps.

Dammartin glanced over towards his tent, but there was still no sign of Mademoiselle Mallington. Coffee had been drunk, bread eaten, portmanteaux packed, and the girl slept through it all. At least he had had the foresight to set Molyneux to guarding his tent, lest the girl took the notion into her head to try to slip away again. And truth be told, this would be the best time to do it, when the camp was in chaos, the men's attentions distracted, and a full day of light ahead.

Lamont appeared. 'The men will be ready to leave in twenty minutes. Only the officers' tents remain. Mademoiselle Mallington...' He looked enquiringly at Dammartin.

'Shall be ready to leave with the rest of us,' Dammartin replied.

'You look a little tired this morning, Captain,' said Lamont, his gaze fixed on Dammartin's tent. 'Perhaps something disturbed your sleep?'

Dammartin gave a wry smile and shook his head at his sergeant's teasing, before walking off towards his tent.

'She is in there still?' he said to Molyneux as he passed, indicating his tent.

'Yes, Captain.'

Dammartin closed the last of the distance to his tent.

'But, sir, she...'

Molyneux's words sounded behind him, but it was too late. Dammartin had unfastened the ties and was already through the tent flap...and the sight that met his eyes stilled him where he stood. A basin of water sat upon his table; Mademoiselle Mallington stood by its side, washing, bare to her waist.

Chapter Five

Josie gave a small shriek and, trying to cover herself with one arm, reached for her towel with the other. In her panic she succeeded only in dropping the soap into the basin and knocking the towel off the back of the table. She clutched her arms around herself, acutely aware of her nakedness and the man that stood not four feet away, staring. She saw his gaze move over her, saw the darkening of his eyes as they met hers, yet she stood there gaping like a fool, staring at him in utter shock.

'Captain Dammartin!' she managed to gasp at last, those two words conveying all of her indignation.

He held her gaze for a moment longer, that second seeming to stretch to an eternity. 'Pardon, *mademoiselle*,' and, with a small bow of his head, he was gone as suddenly as he had arrived.

It was over in less than a minute, yet Josie stood there still, staring at the tent flap, before hurrying round to the other side of the table to snatch up the towel. She barely dried herself before pulling up her shift and petticoats from her waist with hands that were shaking. Humiliation set a scald to her cheeks, and a roughness to her fingers as she pulled down the hair pinned up high and loose upon her head to coil it into a tight little pile stabbed into place at the nape of her neck.

She was angry beyond belief, angry and embarrassed. 'How dare he!' she muttered to herself again and again as she stuffed her belongings back into her portmanteau. 'The audacity of the man!'

Her indignation still burned so that when she left the tent, standing outside with her cloak fastened around her, and her hair neat and tidy beneath her best hat and her fresh blue dress, she was intent on snubbing the French Captain, but Dammartin was only a figure at the other end of the camp and it was Lieutenant Molyneux who waited some little distance away.

The wind dropped from her sails.

'*Mademoiselle.*' Molyneux appeared by her side, his grey eyes soft with concern. 'I am here to escort you this day.'

Dammartin had assigned his lieutenant to guard her, thought Josie, and her anger at Dammartin swelled even more.

'If you will come this way, it is time we were upon our horses.'

'Thank you, Lieutenant,' she said, as if she were not furious and outraged and humiliated, and walked, with her head held high, calmly by his side.

It soon became clear that her supposition regarding Molyneux was correct for, unlike the previous day, the Lieutenant stuck closely by her side. In Molyneux's company the events of that morning ceased to matter so much to Josie. The young Lieutenant had such an easy and charming manner that she felt her ruffled feathers smooth and her anger dispel.

It was true that Molyneux had been in the monastery at Telemos just as much as Dammartin, but as the hours passed in his company she saw that he was like so many young men who had served beneath her father. His eyes were clear and honest and he seemed every bit the gentleman that Dammartin was not.

When the dragoons stopped to rest and eat, Molyneux sent a boy to fetch them bread and cheese, and then sat beside her on a boulder while they ate together.

'You are kind to me, Lieutenant,' she said, thinking of how much Molyneux contrasted with his captain.

'Why should I not be kind? You are a lady, alone, in a difficult situation.'

She raised her gaze to his. 'I am a prisoner.'

Molyneux's lips curved in a small half smile but there was a sadness in his eyes. 'I believe that prisoners should be well treated.'

'I do, too, as did my father.'

He gave no reply, but a strange expression stole upon his face.

'It seems that Captain Dammartin does not share our opinion, sir.'

'The Captain, he has his reasons, *mademoiselle*.' Molyneux glanced away.

'What reason could he possibly have to act as he has done?' she demanded, feeling nettled just at the thought of Dammartin. 'There is nothing that could excuse that man's behaviour.'

Molyneux's eyes returned to hers and she saw something of astonishment and pity in them. 'You truly do not know.'

'Know?' She felt the prickling of suspicion. 'What is it that I should know?'

Molyneux's gaze held hers for a moment longer than it should, then he turned away and got to his feet. 'Come, *mademoiselle*, we should make ready to ride again.'

'Lieutenant—'

'Come,' he said again, and did not meet her eyes.

And when they resumed the journey, Molyneux was quiet, leaving Josie to wonder as to exactly what the Lieutenant had meant.

Dammartin rode at the head of the 8th Dragoons crossing the bleak terrain before them, but it was not the harshness of the Portuguese countryside of which he was thinking, nor the perils of the mission in which they were engaged. Something else entirely filled Dammartin's mind—Josephine Mallington.

A vision of her standing there in his tent that morning, her clothing stripped aside to reveal her naked skin, so smooth and white and inviting that he longed to reach out and touch its silky surface. The slender column of her throat with the gold chain that hung around it, leading his eye down in invitation over a skin so pale and perfect, to the swell of her breasts.

He had seen them, just a glimpse, firm and thrusting and rosy-tipped, before his view was partly obscured. That slim arm crushing hard against them in a bid to hide herself from him, and in truth, serving only to tantalise even more in what it revealed. He could have traced his fingers over the bulging swell of that smooth white flesh, slipping them down behind the barrier of her arm to cup her breasts in his hands. To feel her nipples harden beneath his palm, to taste what he touched, taking her in his mouth, laving those rosy tips with his tongue...

Dammartin caught his train of thought and stopped it

dead. Hell, but she was Mallington's daughter. The one woman who should repulse him above all others, and all he could think of was her naked, and the sight of her soft lips, and the feel of her beneath him as they perched upon that rock face. He was already hard at the thought of her, uncomfortably so. And that knowledge made him damnably angry with Mademoiselle Mallington, and even more so with himself.

Hour after hour of a ride in which he should have been alert, aware, focused on his duty, spent distracted by Mallington's daughter. Well, no more of it, he determined. Dammartin hardened his resolve. He was here to safeguard Foy's journey to Ciudad Rodrigo—and that is what he would do. He could not refuse the order to take Mademoiselle Mallington with him to the Spanish city, and so he would take her there as he must.

And he thought again that Mallington was dead and all of his questions regarding Major Jean Dammartin's death were destined to remain unanswered for ever.

His mind flicked again to Josephine Mallington and the fact that her father had brought her with him into these hills, and her knowledge of the messengers and of Dammartin's own destination—a girl very much in her father's confidence. Had she been there at the Battle of Oporto, just over eighteen months ago? He felt his lip curl at the thought that she might have witnessed his father's murder, and his heart was filled once more with the cold steel of revenge. There would be no more distractions; Dammartin would have his answers.

Lieutenant Molyneux's pensive mood allowed Josie time to think. She spent much time pondering the Lieutenant's strange remarks, but came no nearer to fathoming of what he had been speaking. There was definitely something that she did not know, something to do with Dammartin and the hatred that he nursed.

Her eyes followed ahead to where the French Captain rode, and she thought how she had caught him looking at her several times that day with an expression of such intensity as to almost be hunger. He was not looking at her now.

She remembered his face from this morning when he had strode so boldly into her tent, *his* tent. The hours spent with Molyneux had mellowed Josie's anger and indignation. There had been an initial shock in Dammartin's eyes before they had darkened to a dangerous smoulder. The camp had been disbanding and she had overslept. And it had all happened so quickly that she doubted he could have seen very much at all.

She thought of the long, cold hours of the night when he had given her his greatcoat, and she wondered as to that small kindness. Josie had heard the stories of what French soldiers inflicted upon the towns that they took and the people who went against them. She knew of the interrogations, and the torture…and the rape. That she was an innocent did not stop her from knowing what enemy soldiers did to women. Within the Fifth Battalion of the 60th Regiment of Foot gossip reached the Lieutenant Colonel's daughter just the same as it reached everyone else. Yet for all the dislike in his eyes, Dammartin had not touched her, nor allowed his men to do so. He had not beaten her, he had not starved her when he could so easily have done so. She knew all of these things, yet whenever Dammartin looked at her, she could not prevent the somersaults of apprehension in her stomach, or the sudden hurry of her heart.

They broke for camp in the late afternoon, before the light of day was lost. Fundao—another day's march closer to General Foy fulfilling his mission, another day's march between Josie and the British lines.

Molyneux stood some distance away, talking with Sergeant Lamont, but the Lieutenant was careful to keep Josie within his sight.

Josie sat on her portmanteau, watching while the tents were erected, wondering how fast Molyneux could move if she were to make a run for it. She could not imagine him with the same harsh rugged determination of his captain.

There was something single-minded and ruthless about Dammartin, something driven. And she thought of the deadly earnest of his warning, and knew that even if Molyneux did not catch her, Dammartin most certainly would. Her eyes closed, trying to stifle the intensity of the memory. Dammartin was not a man to make promises lightly.

'Mademoiselle Mallington.'

The sound of his voice behind her made her jump. She rose swiftly to her feet and turned to face him. 'Captain Dammartin.'

He instructed a young trooper to carry her portmanteau to his tent. Everything about him was masculine and powerful. His expression was closed, his dark brows hooding eyes that were as hard as granite and just as cold.

'You will sleep in my tent tonight—alone.'

Alone? She felt the surprise lighten her face and relief leap within her. 'Thank you,' she said, wondering if she really did have the measure of Dammartin. She did not dare to ask him where he would be spending the night.

He continued as if she had not spoken. 'There will be a guard posted outside all of the night, so do not think to try to escape, *mademoiselle*. I trust you remember my warning.'

She gave a wary nod and made to move away towards the tent.

'I am not yet finished,' he said icily.

Josie hesitated, feeling his words rankle, but she turned back and raised her eyes calmly to his. 'You wish to say something further, sir?'

'I wish to ask you some questions.'

It seemed that her chest constricted and her heart rate kicked to a stampede. 'You said there would be no more questions.'

'No more questions last night,' he amended.

She held her head high and looked him directly in the eye. 'Perhaps I did not make myself clear, Captain. You will waste your time with questions—there is nothing more that I can tell you.'

'We will see, *mademoiselle.*'

She breathed deeply, trying to keep her fear in check. He could not mean to interrogate her, not now, not when she was so unprepared. 'I am tired, sir, and wish only to retire.'

'We are all tired,' he said harshly.

She clutched her hands together, her fingers gripping tight.

'You may retire when you have told me of your father.'

'My father?' She stared at him in disbelief, feeling all of her anger and all of her grief come welling back. 'Is it not enough that you killed him? He is dead, for pity's sake! Can you not leave him be even now?'

'It is true that he is dead, *mademoiselle,*' admitted Dammartin, his face colder and harsher than ever she had seen it, 'but not by my hand…unfortunately.'

She was aghast. 'Unfortunately?' she echoed. 'Our countries may be at war, but my father does not deserve

such contempt. He was the bravest of soldiers, an honourable man who gave his life for his country.'

'He was a villain,' said Dammartin, and in his eyes was
a furious black bitterness.

'How dare you slur his good name!' she cried, her breast
heaving with passion, all fear forgotten. All of her anger
and hurt and grief welled up to overflow and she hated
Dammartin in that moment as she had never hated before.
'You are the very devil, sir!' And, drawing back her hand,
she slapped his cruel, arrogant face as hard as she could.

The camp fell silent. Each and every dragoon turned
to stare.

No one moved.

No one breathed.

The audacity of Josie's action seemed to slow time
itself.

She saw the ruddy print of her hand stain his cheek,
saw his scar grow livid, and she could not believe that she
had struck him with such violence, with such hatred, she
who was his captive at his mercy.

His eyes grew impossibly darker. There was a slight
tightening of the muscle in his jaw. His breath was so light
as to scarce be a breath at all. The air was heavy with a
rage barely sheathed.

She stared in mounting horror, every pore in her body
screaming a warning, prickling at her scalp, rippling a
shiver down her spine, and she knew that she should run,
but beneath the force of that dark penetrating gaze her
legs would not move.

'I…' She gasped, knowing she had to say something,
but the way that he was looking at her froze the very words
in her throat.

Her eyes swept around, seeing the faces of all his men,

and all of the incredulity and anticipation so clear upon them, waiting for the storm to erupt.

Josie began to tremble and slowly, ever so slowly, as if she could move without his noticing, she began to inch away, her toes reaching tentatively to find the solidity of the ground behind her.

When he struck it was so sudden, so fast, that she saw nothing of it. One minute she was standing before him, and the next, she was in his arms, his body hard against hers, his mouth claiming her own with a savagery that made her gasp with shock.

Dammartin's lips were bold and punishing, exploring her own with an intimacy to which he had no right.

Josie fought back, struggling against him, but his arms just tightened around her, locking her in position, so that she could not escape but just endure, like a ship cast adrift while the lightning flashed and the thunder roared, and the waves crashed upon its deck.

He claimed her as if she were his for the taking, his lips plundering and stealing her all, his tongue invading with a force she could not refuse. And all the while the dark stubble of his chin rasped rough against her.

She felt as his hands slid around her back, one tangling within her hair, anchoring her to him, the other pulling her closer still until her breasts were crushed mercilessly against the hard muscle of his chest. This was no kiss, but a possession, an outright punishment.

And then the anger and violence were gone and she felt his mouth gentle against hers, still kissing her but with a tenderness that belied the ravishment. His lips massaged, stroked, tasted, his tongue dancing against hers in invitation. Kissing her, and kissing her until she could no longer think straight; kissing her until she no longer knew night from day.

Josie forgot where she was, and all that had just happened—Telemos and her father and just who this man was. There was only this moment, only this feeling, only this kiss—so slow and thorough and seductive. And just as she gave herself up to the sensation his lips were gone, and it was over as suddenly as it had started.

The men were cheering as Dammartin released her, the idiotic grins splitting their faces hitting her like a dowse of cold water, revealing reality in all its starkness.

Josie stumbled back, the full horror of the situation hitting her hard, knocking the breath from her lungs, buckling her legs, and she would have fallen had not Dammartin moved to support her, catching her weight against him. She looked up into the dark smoulder of his eyes, and just for that moment their gazes held, before she pushed away, and turning, fled towards the safety of his tent.

She lay that night, fully clothed, in Dammartin's tent, on the makeshift bed, alone, but for Josie there was no sleep—there was only the blood-splattered room in Telemos, and the death of her father…and the terrible weight of what she had just done.

Dammartin lay on his bed within the tent shared by Molyneux and Lamont, listening to their snores, awake, as he had been for hours, running the events of that evening through his mind for the hundredth time. The full-blown argument, her slap, and he would have let it go, done nothing, had not his men been watching.

She was a prisoner, a captive, Mallington's daughter and he knew he could not let her action go unpunished. And he wanted so very much to kiss her, to show her that she could not defy him. And hadn't he done just that? But what had started as a punishment had ended as something very different.

It seemed he could feel her against him still, so small and slender and womanly, her lips gaping with the shock of his assault. She had fought him, struggled, tried to escape, and he, like a brute, had shown no mercy. He had taken from her that which she did not know she had to give, and the taste of her innocence was like water to a man parched and dying.

He did not know what had changed, only that something had, and he found that he was kissing her in all honesty, kissing her as if she was his lover, with tenderness and seduction. And the sweetness of her tentative response, the surprise of it, the delight of it…so that he lost himself in that kiss, completely and utterly. It had taken the laughter and jeering of his men to bring him back from it, awakening him from her spell.

She was as shocked as he. He could see it in her face— shocked and ashamed and guilty.

Too late, Mademoiselle Mallington, he thought bitterly, too damned late, for there was no longer any denying what he had known these days past: he wanted her—the daughter of the man who had murdered his father. The knowledge repulsed him. God help him, his father must be turning in his grave. But even that thought did not stop him wanting to lay Josephine Mallington down naked beneath him and plunge his hard aching flesh deep within her. He wanted her with a passion that both excited and appalled.

Dammartin took a deep breath and forced himself to think calmly with the same hard determination that had driven him these past months. He might want her, but it did not mean that he would take her. More than lust would be needed to make Pierre Dammartin disgrace his father's memory. He had been too long without a woman and that simple fact was addling his brain. He would stay away from her, assign all of her care to Molyneux, and finish this journey as quickly as he could. And on that resolution, Dammartin finally found sleep.

In the days that followed, Josie saw little of Dammartin. He was always somewhere in the distance, always occupied. Not once did he look at her. And strangely, despite that she hated him, Dammartin's rejection made Josie more alone and miserable than ever.

But there was Lieutenant Molyneux and he was so open and handsome and so very reasonable. It did not seem to matter to him that she was British and his prisoner. He was respectful when there was nothing of respect anywhere else, and friendly when all around shunned her.

A hill rose by the side of the camp that evening, smaller and less jagged than those through which they had spent the day trekking. Up above, the sky was washed in shades of pink and violet and blue as the sun began to sink behind its summit. Something of its beauty touched a chord in Josie and she felt the scene call out to the pain and grief in her heart.

She turned to Molyneux in appeal. 'Lieutenant, I would dearly like to climb that hill and watch the sunset. I would not wander from the route, which is clear and within your view from this position. I give you my most solemn word that I would not try to escape and that I would return to you here as soon as possible.' Her voice raised in hope as she willed him to agree.

'I am sorry, *mademoiselle*…' his voice was gentle '…but Captain Dammartin…' His words faltered and he started again. 'I would be very happy to accompany you in your walk up the hill, if you would permit me. The sunset does indeed look most beautiful.'

She gave a nod of her head. 'That would be most kind, Lieutenant.'

'Then we should go quickly before we miss it,' he said.

Josie smiled and wrapped her cloak more tightly around her and pulled her hat lower over her ears.

Together they walked up the hill by the camp side. And when the slope grew steeper, it seemed perfectly natural that Lieutenant Molyneux should take her arm in his, helping her to cover the ground with speed.

The summit was flat like a platform specially fashioned by the gods with the sole purpose of viewing the wonder of the heavens. Josie and Molyneux stood in awe at the sight that met their eyes. Before them the sky flamed a brilliance of colours. Red burned deep and fiery before fading to pink that washed pale and peachy. Great streaks of violet bled into the pink as if a watercolour wash had been applied too soon. Like some great canvas the picture was revealed before them in all its magnificence, a greater creation than could have been painted by any mere man. And just in the viewing of it, something of the heavy weight seemed to lift from Josie's heart and for the first time since Telemos she felt some little essence of peace. Such vastness, such magnificence, as to heal, like a balm on her troubled spirit. Words were inadequate to express the beauty of nature.

Josie stood in silent reverence, her hand tucked comfortably within Molyneux's arm, and watched, until the sound of a man's tread interrupted.

Josie dragged her eyes away from the vivid spectacle before her to glance behind.

Captain Dammartin stood not three paces away. His face was harder than ever she had seen it, his scar emphasised by the play of light and shadows. He looked at where Josie's hand was tucked into his lieutenant's arm, and it seemed that there was a narrowing of his eyes.

'Lieutenant Molyneux, return to your duties,' he snapped.

'Yes, sir.' Molyneux released Josie's hand and made his salute. He smiled at her, his hair fluttering in the breeze. His eyes were velvety grey and sincere and creased with the warmth of his smile. In the deep green of his jacket and the white of his pantaloons tinged pink from the sky, he cut a dashing image. 'Please excuse me, *mademoiselle.*'

'Immediately, Lieutenant.' Dammartin's voice was harsh.

The Lieutenant turned and hurried away, leaving Josie and his captain silhouetted against the brilliance of the setting sun.

'I have tolerated your games long enough, Mademoiselle Mallington.' The colours in the sky reflected upon his hair, casting a rich warmth to its darkness. The wind rippled through it making it appear soft and feathery. It stood in stark contrast to the expression in his eyes.

All sense of tranquillity shattered, destroyed in a single sentence by Dammartin.

'Games? I have no idea of what you speak, sir.' Her tone was quite as cold as his.

'Come, *mademoiselle*,' he said. 'Do not play the innocent with me. You have been courting the attention of my lieutenant these days past. He is not a lap-dog to dance upon your every whim. You are a prisoner of the 8th Dragoons. You would do well to remember that.'

Shock caused Josie's jaw to gape. Her eyes grew wide and round. It was the final straw as far as she was concerned. He had kissed her, kissed her with violence and passion and tenderness, and she, to a shame that would never be forgotten, had kissed him back—this man who was her enemy and who looked at her with such stony hostility. And she thought of the blaze in his eyes at the mention of her father's name. He had destroyed everything that she loved, and now he had destroyed the little transient peace. In that moment she knew that she could not trust herself to stay lest she flew at him with all the rage that was in her heart.

'Must you always be so unpleasant?' She turned her face from his, hating him for everything, and made to walk right past him.

'Wait.' He barked it as an order. 'Not so fast, *mademoiselle*. I have not yet finished.'

She cast him a disparaging look. 'Well, sir, I have.' And walked right past him.

A hand shot out, and fastened around her right arm. 'I do not think so, *mademoiselle*.'

She did not fight against him. She had already learned the folly of that. 'What do you mean to do this time?' she said. 'Beat me?'

'I have never struck a woman in my life.'

'Force your kiss upon me again?' she demanded in a voice so cold he would have been proud to own it himself.

Their gazes met and held.

'I do not think that so very much force would be required, *mademoiselle*,' he said quietly.

She felt the heat stain her cheeks at his words, and she wanted to call him for the devil he was, and her palm itched to hit him hard across his arrogant face.

His grip loosened and fell away.

She stepped back and faced him squarely. 'Well, Captain, what is of such importance that you must hold me here to say it?'

'What were you doing up here?'

'Surely that was plain to see?'

His eyes narrowed in disgust and he gave a slight shake of his head as if he could not quite believe her. 'You are brazen in the extreme, Mademoiselle Mallington. Tell me, are all English women so free with their favours?'

Josie felt the sudden warmth flood her cheeks at his implication. 'How dare you?'

'Very easily, given your behaviour.'

'You are the most insolent and despicable of men!'

'We have already established that.'

'Lieutenant Molyneux and I were watching the sunset, nothing more!' Beneath the thick wool of her cloak her breast rose and fell with escalating righteous indignation.

'Huddled together like two lovers,' he said.

'Never!' she cried.

Anger spurred an energy to muscles that had not half an hour since been heavy and spent from the day's ride. All of Josie's fury and frustration came together in that minute and something inside her snapped.

'Why must you despise me so much?' she yelled.

'It is not you whom I despise,' he said quietly.

'But my father,' she finished for him. 'You killed him and you are glad of it.'

'I am.' And all of the brooding menace was there again in his eyes.

'Why? What did my father ever do to you, save defend his life and the lives of his men?'

He looked into the girl's eyes, the same clear blue eyes that had looked out from Lieutenant Colonel Mallington's face as he lay dying, and said quietly. 'Your father was a villain and a scoundrel.'

'No!' The denial was swift and sore.

'You do not know?' For the first time it struck him that perhaps she was ignorant of the truth, that she really thought her father a wondrous hero.

'No,' she said again, more quietly.

All that was raw and bloody and aching deep within

Dammartin urged him to tell her. And it seemed if he could destroy this last falsehood the Lieutenant Colonel had woven, if he could let his daughter know the truth of the man, then perhaps he, Dammartin, would be free. Yet still he hesitated. Indeed, even then, he would not have told her. It was Mademoiselle Mallington herself with her very next words that settled the matter.

'Tell me, Captain Dammartin, for I would know this grudge that you hold against my father.'

The devil sowed temptation, and Pierre Dammartin could no longer resist the harvest. 'You ask, *mademoiselle*, and so I will answer.'

Dammartin's gaze did not falter. He looked directly into Josephine Mallington's eyes, and he told her.

'My father was a prisoner of the famous Lieutenant Colonel Mallington after the Battle of Oporto last year. Mallington gave him his parole, let him think he was being released. He never made it a mile outside the British camp before he was murdered by your father's own hand. So, *mademoiselle*, now you have the answer to your question, and I will warrant that you do not like it.'

She shook her head, incredulity creasing her face. 'You are lying!'

'I swear on my father's memory, that it is the truth. It is not an oath that I take lightly.'

'It cannot be true. It is not possible.'

'I assure you that it is.'

'My father would never do such a thing. He was a man to whom honour was everything.'

'Were you there, *mademoiselle*, at Oporto?' The question he had been so longing to ask of her. 'In May of last year?'

She shook her head. 'My father sent me back to England in April.'

He felt the stab of disappointment. 'Then you really do not know the truth of what your father did.'

'My father was a good and decent man. He would never have killed a paroled officer.'

'You are mistaken, *mademoiselle*.'

'Never!' she cried. 'I tell you, he would not!'

He moved back slowly, seeing the hurt and disbelief well in her face, knowing that he had put it there. He said no more. He did not need to. The pain in her eyes smote him so hard that he caught his breath.

'What do you seek with such lies? To break me? To make me answer your wretched questions?'

And something in her voice made him want to catch back every word and stuff them back deep within him.

She walked past him, her small figure striding across the ragged hilltop in the little light that remained, and as the last of the sky was swallowed up in darkness Pierre Dammartin knew finally that there was no relief to be found in revenge. The pain that had gnawed at him since learning the truth of his father's unworthy death was no better. If anything, it hurt worse than ever, and he knew that he had been wrong to tell her.

He stood alone on the hill in the darkness and listened to the quiet burr of the camp below and the steady beat of a sore and jealous heart.

Chapter Six

Josie avoided both Lieutenant Molyneux and Sergeant Lamont and headed straight for her tent. The smell of dinner filled the air, but Josie was not hungry. Indeed, her stomach tightened against the thought of eating. She sat in the darkness and thought of what Captain Dammartin had said, thought of the absurdity of his accusation and the certainty of his conviction. His words whirled round in her head until she thought it would explode. *He never made it a mile outside the camp before he was murdered by your father's own hand.* She squeezed her eyes shut. Not Papa, not her own dear papa. He would not murder a man in cold blood.

Josie knew full well that her father, as a ruthless commander in Wellington's army, had been responsible for the deaths of many men, but that was on a battlefield, that was war, and there was a world of difference between that and killing a man who had been given his parole.

Josie could think of nothing else. She did not move, just sat as still as a small statue, hunched in her misery within the tent.

A voice sounded from the flap. *'Mademoiselle.'* It was Lieutenant Molyneux.

'Please, sir, I am tired and wish to be left alone.'

'But you have not eaten, *mademoiselle.*'

'I am not hungry.'

'You must eat something.'

'Perhaps later,' she said, wishing that the Lieutenant would go away, and then, feeling ungracious, added, 'but I thank you, sir, for your concern.'

He did not reply, but she knew he had not moved away.

'Mademoiselle,' he said softly, 'has the Captain upset you?'

She paused, unwilling to reveal the extent to which Dammartin had hurt her. Then finally she said, 'No, I am just tired, that is all.'

'He does not mean to be so...' Molyneux searched for the right word in English and failed to find it. 'He is a good man, really. He just never got over the death of his father.'

Something twisted in her stomach at his words. Slowly she moved to the front of the tent, pulling back the flap that she might see Lieutenant Molyneux.

He smiled and held out the mess tin of stew that he had collected for her.

'Thank you.' She took it, but did not eat. 'What happened to Captain Dammartin's father?' she asked, and inside her heart was thumping hard and fast.

The smile fled Molyneux's face. 'Major Dammartin was a prisoner of war,' he said quietly.

She waited for his next words.

He flushed and shifted uncomfortably. 'It was a dishonourable affair.' He cleared his throat and glanced away.

'What happened?' she prompted.

He did not look at her. 'He was killed by his English captors.'

'No,' she said softly.

'Unfortunately, yes, *mademoiselle*. It is a story famous throughout France. Major Dammartin was a very great war hero, you see.'

'Do you know who held him? Which regiment?'

He looked at her then and she could see the pity in his eyes. And she knew.

But Molyneux was much more of a gentleman than Dammartin and he would not say it. 'I cannot recall,' he said. He gave a small smile. 'You should eat your dinner, *mademoiselle*, before it grows cold.'

She raised her eyes and looked across the distance, to the other side of the fire that burned not so very far away from the tents. Dammartin was standing there, talking to Sergeant Lamont. But his face was turned towards her and she felt the force of his gaze meet hers before it moved on to take in Lieutenant Molyneux. She felt herself flush, remembering what Dammartin had said, and knowing what it must look like with her standing by the tent flap, and the Lieutenant so close outside, their conversation conducted in hushed tones.

'Thank you,' she said to Molyneux, and she let the canvas flap fall back down into place.

The morning was as glorious as the previous evening's sunset had predicted. A cloudless blue sky filled with the soft, gentle light of pale sunshine. A landscape over which drifted small pockets of mist that had not yet blown away, and which during the night an ice maiden had kissed so that everything within it glittered with a fine coating of frost.

Josie noticed none of the beauty.

She thought again and again of what the Frenchmen had said, both of them. And the thing that she could not forget was not the terrible words of Dammartin's accusation with his fury and all of his bitterness. No, the most horrible thing of all was Molyneux's kindness. *I cannot recall*, he had said, but he could and he did. She had seen the pity in his eyes, and his silence roared more potent than all of Dammartin's angry words.

She knew now why the French soldiers looked at her as they did, and understood the whispers. Yet Josie clung with every ounce of her being to her father's memory, refusing to believe her gentle papa guilty of such a crime.

Molyneux was ever present during the long hours of the day, attempting to cheer and amuse her when in truth what Josie needed was time alone to think—time away from all of the French, even Molyneux. No sentries, no feeling of being for ever watched, for ever guarded, and definitely no Dammartin, just space to think clearly.

As they struck camp that evening, Josie waited until Dammartin and his men were at their busiest before making her excuse of the need to relieve herself. It was the one place to which neither Molyneux nor his men would accompany her.

Looking up into the Lieutenant's face, she felt a twinge of guilt at her dishonesty, for Molyneux alone in this camp had tried to help her. But her need for some little time alone overcame all such discomfort.

'Come, sit down, take a drink with me.' The Major steered Dammartin back to the table and sat down. He unstoppered the large decanter of brandy and poured out two generous measures. 'Here.' He pressed one of the glasses into Dammartin's hand.

'Thank you, sir.' Dammartin took a sip.

'Snuff?' The Major extracted an exquisitely worked

silver snuffbox from his pocket and, opening the lid, offered it to Dammartin.

Dammartin shook his head. 'Thank you, but, no, sir.'

'Forget the "sir". We are alone now. You are Jean's son, and since my old friend is no longer with us, I look upon you as my own son.' La Roque took an enormous pinch of snuff, placed it on the back of his hand, sniffed it heartily up into his nose and then gave the most enormous sneeze. He lifted his own glass of brandy from the table and lounged back in his chair.

'So tell me, how are you really doing, Pierre? I've been worried about you since Telemos.'

Dammartin took another sip of brandy, and gave a wry smile to the man who had helped him so much since his father's death. 'There's no need. I told you I am fine.'

'Who would have thought that Mallington would have been holed up in that shit-hole of a village? There truly must be a God, Pierre, to have delivered that villain into our hands. I am only sorry that he died before I got to him. At least you had the satisfaction of looking into the bastard's eyes while he died.'

'Yes.' And even La Roque's finest brandy could not mask the bad taste that rose in Dammartin's throat at that memory. 'Yet I found no joy in Mallington's death.'

'Come, come, boy. What is this? At long last your father's murder has been avenged.'

'I know.'

'We both waited a long time for that moment.'

'Indeed we did.' But the sourness in Dammartin's throat did not diminish. He took another sip of brandy.

'Jean can now rest in peace, and you can move on with your life.'

'At last,' said Dammartin, but his voice was grim.

La Roque drained the last of the brandy from his glass and reached again for the decanter. 'Come along, hold your glass out, time for a top-up.'

'I need a clear head for the morning,' protested Dammartin.

'I insist,' said the Major, 'for old times' sake.' He refilled Dammartin's glass. 'Let's drink to your father. The finest friend a man ever did have and a hero for all of France.' La Roque raised his glass. 'Jean Dammartin.'

Dammartin did likewise. 'Jean Dammartin, the best of fathers.'

They drank the brandy and sat in silence for some minutes, Dammartin lost in memories of his father.

And then La Roque asked, 'What of the woman, Mallington's daughter? Her presence cannot be easy for you.'

'Mademoiselle Mallington does not affect me in the slightest,' said Dammartin, and knew that he lied. 'She is a prisoner to be delivered to Ciudad Rodrigo as you instructed, nothing more.'

'That is what I like to hear, Pierre.' La Roque smiled. 'Drink up, boy, drink up.'

Josie sat perched near the edge of the ravine, looking out over the swathe of the rugged Portuguese landscape beyond. The air had grown colder with a dampness that seemed to seep into her very bones. She did not know how long it would be before Molyneux missed her, so she just savoured each and every moment of her solitude.

The fingers of her left hand kneaded gently at her forehead, trying to ease the knotted confusion of the thoughts that lay within. From beyond the trees and bushes behind her through which she had passed came the now-familiar sound of tent pegs being hammered in the distance, and the faint chattering and laughter of the soldiers.

She breathed deeply, allowing some of the tension, which had since Telemos been a part of her, to slip. Within this light the rocks in the ravine looked as brown as the soil that encased them. A bird called from the cool grey sky, gliding open-winged on a current of air, and Josie envied its freedom. The breeze fluttered the ribbons of her bonnet beneath her chin and loosed some strands of hair to brush against her cheeks.

She thought again of Dammartin and of his accusation, and as terrible and ridiculous as it had been, at least she now understood something of the French Captain's darkness. He was a man drowning in bitterness and vengeance…and hurt. And all because of a lie.

Dammartin's father was dead, but not by her papa's hand, not by murder. Papa had been honest and steadfast, a strong man whose integrity was not open to compromise. But Dammartin believed the lie; she had seen the absolute conviction in his eyes. That knowledge explained all of his hatred, but little else.

Why had he taken her from the monastery in Telemos? For she knew now that he had never intended to honour her father's dying wishes. For information? Yet he had known of the messengers, and not from her. And why had he come after her across the Portuguese countryside? What did it matter to him if she lived or died?

She thought of his coaxing her down the rock face, and giving her his cover in the night, of his kiss that had gentled to become… Josie did not want to think of that. So many questions, to which she did not have the answers.

A twig snapped behind her, the noise of a footstep upon the pebbled soil. Josie glanced round to tell Molyneux that she was just coming. But it was not Molyneux that stood there.

* * *

'What do you mean she has not come back?' demanded Dammartin. 'Where the hell is she?'

'She wished to use the latrine,' said a white-faced Molyneux.

'And you let her go alone?'

Molyneux wetted the dryness of his lips. 'I could not expect her to attend to her…needs…in front of me.'

'No? You were instructed not to leave her side.'

Molyneux faced Dammartin with a slight air of defiance. 'She is a lady, Captain.'

'I know damn well what Mademoiselle Mallington is,' snapped Dammartin, peering into the bushes. 'Fetch your musket, Lamont, and a couple of troopers. We have not much time before the light is lost.'

Molyneux saluted and moved away.

'And, Molyneux,' Dammartin called after him. 'You'll be tracking her on foot down towards the ravine.'

A calloused hand clamped over Josie's mouth, a brawny arm fastened tight around her chest and upper arms, hauling her to her feet.

She kicked out, her boot hitting hard against the man's shin.

He grunted and, drawing back his hand, dealt her a blow across the face.

She made to scream, but his hand was already around her throat, squeezing tight, and she was choking and gasping with the need for air. She heard his words, fast and furious Portuguese, as he lifted her clear of the ground by that single hand encircling her neck.

A cracked, grubby finger with its dirt-encrusted fingernail touched against his lips, as he looked meaningfully into her eyes.

She nodded, or at least tried to, knowing that he was demanding her silence. The world was darkening as at last his grip released and she dropped to the ground, limp and gasping for breath.

More voices, talking, and she raised her eyes to see five more shabby, dark-bearded men coming out from among the bushes. They were all lean to the point of being gaunt, their clothes dirty and faded, their faces hard and hostile as they encircled her, like wolves closing in around a kill. Bandits, realised Josie, just as Dammartin had warned.

'*Inglês,*' she said hoarsely, and raked through her brain for some more Portuguese words that would make them understand. '*Não francês.*'

But the men were talking quietly among themselves, gesturing in the direction of the French camp.

'I am British,' she said, swallowing through the pain of the bruising on her throat. 'British,' she said, and tried to scramble to her feet.

The large man, her attacker, pushed her back down and crouched low to look into her face. 'I like British,' he said, and traced a thick tongue slowly and deliberately over his lips in a crude gesture that even Josie in all her innocence could understand.

'General Lord Wellington will pay well for my return,' she lied. 'W-e-l-l-i-n-g-t-o-n,' she said enunciating slowly so that they must be sure to understand, and 'g-o-l-d, much gold.'

But the bandit just leered and spoke words to the men behind him to make them laugh. He spat and something brown and moist and half chewed landed close to her leg.

Josie's heart was racing and fear flowed icy in her veins at the realisation of her situation. She skittered back, driving her heels against the ground, trying to put some space between her and the bandit, but he grabbed hold of her

ankle and with one wrench, she was flat upon her back
with the man climbing over her. She kicked and punched
and tried to scream, but his mouth was hard upon hers,
the unwashed stench of him filling her nostrils, the weight
of him crushing her down upon the rocky soil so that she
was staked out, unable to move. His hand ranged over her,
rough and greedy and grasping, ripping aside her bodice,
tearing at her petticoats and shift. She bucked beneath
him, trying to throw him off, but he smiled all the more,
and she felt him pressing himself against her, forcing his
brown-stained tongue into her mouth. The foul taste of
him made her gag, but he did not stop, not until she bit
him. He drew back then, his face contorted, his filthy hand
wiping the blood from his lower lip.

'Bitch!' he cursed, and lashed out, slapping her face hard.

The men behind him were saying something, looking
back nervously towards the dragoons' camp.

Josie knew she had only one hope. She prayed that
Dammartin would come, and unleash all of his darkness,
and all of his fury, upon these bandits. *I do not lose prisoners*, he had said. In her mind she called out his name
again and again, as if that mantra would summon the devil
to deal his revenge and save her.

But the bandit's hands were at her skirts, bunching them
up, ripping at them, clawing to reach beneath so that she
could already feel his ragged fingernails raking the soft
skin of her thighs. The others gathered closer to watch,
smiling with lust, and cruelty and anticipation.

Josie's hope weakened and began to wither, and just
as it had almost died, she heard the French war cry, and
knew that Dammartin had come.

Dammartin saw the ruffians gathered round, and he
knew without seeing what they were watching. He sig-

nalled to his men, sending Molyneux and a trooper silently through the undergrowth to cover one side, and Lamont with a second trooper to the other. And even while they moved into place, he was priming his musket ready to fire.

He roared the war cry, the sound of it echoing throughout the hills and down across the ravine.

The bandits reacted with a start, some reaching for their weapons, the others trying to run.

He saw the flash of exploding gunpowder and the shots rang out, deafening in their volume. Three of the bandits were downed, but Dammartin was not focusing on them. He looked beyond to where the man was scrabbling up from a woman's prostrate body, saw him snarl at her as he turned towards Dammartin, his hands raised in the air in submission.

'Surrender! Surrender!' the bandit shouted in garbled French.

Dammartin did not even pause in consideration. His finger squeezed against the trigger, and the man dropped to his knees, a neat, round, red hole in the middle of his forehead, his eyes wide and staring, before he crashed facedown to the ground.

When Dammartin looked again, Josephine Mallington was on her feet, clutching what was left of her bodice against her breasts, and standing over the bandit's body. She was staring down at the gore the dripped from his head, her breast heaving, her eyes flashing with barely suppressed emotion.

'Villain!' she shouted, 'Damnable blackguard!' and delivered a kick to the dead man. 'Rotten evil guttersnipe!' Dropping to her knees, she lashed out, hitting again and again at the body. 'Wretched, wretched brute!'

'*Mademoiselle*,' Dammartin said, and tried to guide her from the corpse, but she just pushed him away.

'No!' she cried. 'Leave me be!' She struck out all the harder.

'Josephine.' Dammartin stayed her flailing arms, pulling her up, turning her in his encircling arms so that her face looked up to his.

And all of her anger seemed to just drop away, and in its place was devastation. Her eyes met his then, wide and haunted. Beneath the smears of dirt, her face was so pale as to be devoid of any colour, save for beginnings of bruises where a fist had struck, and the thin trickle of red blood that bled from the corner of her mouth.

'He was going to…'

'I know.' Dammartin felt his outrage flare at the thought.

'Like a rutting animal…' And her voice was hoarse with distress and disgust. 'Like a great, filthy beast.'

'Josephine—' he tried to calm her '—he is dead.'

'And I am glad of it!' she cried in her poor, broken voice, 'So very glad! Me, a Christian woman, my father's daughter.' Her eyes squeezed shut and he thought that she would weep, but she did not. Her head bowed so that she stood, resting her forehead lightly against his chest. And he could not imagine the strength with which she held back her tears. Within his arms, he felt the rapidity of her breathing and the tremble that ran through her.

'I prayed that you would come,' she said so quietly that he had to strain to catch her words. 'I prayed and prayed.'

Dammartin stroked a gentle hand against her hair, and held her to him. 'You are safe now, *mademoiselle*,' he said, 'safe, I promise.'

He stood for a few moments and the wind blew, and the sky grew darker, and he was overwhelmed with the need to protect her, to make all of her terrible hurt disappear.

And then Molyneux moved, Lamont cleared his throat, and Dammartin forced himself to think straight.

'Mademoiselle Mallington,' he said softly, and stripping off his jacket, wrapped it around her. 'We must return to the camp.'

She focused down at the ground. 'Of course.' There was nothing left of resistance, nothing of the fight she had so often given in the past.

He kept his arm around her waist, supporting her, as she walked by his side.

In silence and with grim expressions upon each of their faces, Dammartin and his men made their way back to their camp.

Dammartin sat her down on the chair at the table within his tent, speaking fast words of command over his shoulder, to Molyneux or Lamont, she supposed, but she did not look to see. She could not, for all that her eyes were open and staring. She was frozen, unable to move from beneath the terrible, heavy emptiness that weighed her down.

There was the trickle of water, a cloth being wrung out over a basin. The water was warm, his touch gentle, as he cleansed away the blood and the dirt, carefully wiping and dabbing and drying her face and hands, while his jacket hung warm and protective around her shoulders.

She looked at him then and there was nothing of bitterness in his eyes, only compassion.

'I told him I was British,' she said, and the words crawled like glass through the rawness of her throat. 'And it made no difference, just as you said.'

'Josephine,' he said softly. 'I should have guarded you better.'

She shook her head. 'I was not escaping.' It seemed

important to make him understand and she did not know why. 'I just wanted some time alone, some place where I might sit and think of all you had said…of my father.'

They sat in silence and the flicker of the lantern danced shadows upon the canvas walls. Outside all was quiet.

She felt the touch of his fingers, as light as a feather, against the bruising at her throat and the tenderness of her mouth.

'He hurt you very badly, *mademoiselle*—for that I am sorry.'

And his gentleness and compassion almost overwhelmed her.

'But you are safe now, I swear it.'

She looked deep into the darkness of his eyes, and saw a man who was resolute and strong and invincible, and she believed what he said.

The smallest of nods. And she sat there, dazed and battered and not knowing anything any more.

And when he unlaced her boots to ease them from her feet, and laid her down upon the bed beneath the blankets, she let him.

'Do not leave me alone,' she heard her lips murmur.

He gave a nod and returned to sit upon the chair. 'I will be here all the night through. You can sleep safe.'

She could hear his breathing, the creak of the chair at his small movements, and every so often she opened her eyes just by the slightest to check that he was still there. Checking and checking until finally the blackness of sleep stole over her.

But sleep brought no refuge, only more horror, so that she could smell the stench of the villain and feel the claw of his hands upon her, and hear again the thunder of Dammartin's musket shot. The wound in the bandit's skull gaped, leaking the dark, rich liquid to drip into an expanding pool. So much blood. Just like in Telemos.

Blood and more blood. Upon the bandit, upon the men of the 60th and her father, upon herself as she hit out at the bandit's dead body. One blow and then another, and as she reached to strike him a third time the bandit sat up with an evil grin. She felt her heart flip over, for in his hand was the musket that had shot her father, all sticky and dark with blood. The barrel raised, the bandit took aim directly at Josie's heart. Death was certain. She cried out, pleading for him to stop.

'Mademoiselle Mallington. Josephine.' Dammartin's voice was close and quiet, his hands on her arms, dragging her from the nightmare. She stared through the darkness, reaching out to find him.

'Captain Dammartin,' she whispered, and on her tongue was the saltiness of tears and in her nose was the congestion of weeping.

'It is a bad dream, nothing more. I am here. All is well.' He stroked a hand against her hair. 'Go back to sleep.'

But when he would have left, she caught at his fingers, unable to bear being alone. 'Stay,' she said.

He stilled in the darkness.

'Please.'

In answer he lay down beside her, and covered them both with the weight of his greatcoat. He was warm even through the blankets that separated them and she could feel the linen of his shirt soft against her cheek and smell the clean, masculine smell of him. With his strong arm draped protectively over her, holding her close, the nightmare receded and Josie knew, at last, that she was safe.

As Dammartin rode the next day his thoughts were all with Josephine Mallington. She had been seconds from being raped. In his mind's eye he could still see the bandit lying over her, and the memory made his blood run cold so that he wanted to smash the butt of his musket into the man's face again and again. Death had come too quickly for the bastard.

He remembered her anger, and her devastation, and the way she had clung to him in the night. *I prayed that you would come*, she had said. Him. Her enemy.

And he thought of Lieutenant Colonel Mallington firing the shot into his father's body, just as he had thought of it every day for over the last eighteen months. She was the murderer's daughter, his flesh and blood. He had every right to hate her, but it was no longer that simple. She had not known of her father's crime, and she did not deserve what had happened to her, not in that room in Telemos, not his contempt, nor the assault by the bandits. Lamont had been right. She was a woman, a woman who had watched her father die, who was alone and afraid and the captive of an enemy army.

But there was still the matter of what Mallington had done, and Dammartin could not forgive or forget. The wound ran too deep for that. If he could have understood the reasons underlying Mallington's crime, perhaps then there might have been some sort of end to it all, a semblance of peace. But Mallington had died taking his answers to the grave, leaving Dammartin with his anger and his bitterness…and his desire for Josephine Mallington.

As Lamont had said, it would be a long way to Ciudad Rodrigo, a long way indeed.

Josie rode silently by Molyneux's side that day. The Lieutenant had been kind and understanding, trying to make the journey as comfortable as he could for her, but she could see that he did not know what to say to her. Even Sergeant Lamont had brought her a cup of hot coffee when they stopped to rest and eat, his gruff expression belying the small kindness. She could see the way they looked at her, with pity in their eyes, and Josie hated it. Their contempt would have been more welcome. She did not want to be vulnerable and afraid, an object of sympathy, and she resented the bandit even more that he could have made her so. And she knew what the bandit would have done had not Dammartin arrived.

Saved by the one man she had hated. It was under his command that her father and his men had been killed. He could be nothing other than her enemy. But Josie thought of the hole that his bullet had made within the bandit's head, she thought of how he had taken her in his arms and held her. He had washed away the dirt and the stench and the blood, and stayed with her the whole night through, and lain his length beside her when she had begged him to stay. She had begged him. And that thought made Josie cringe with shame, yet last night, in the darkness the fear had been so very great that there had been no such embarrassment. Last night she had needed him, this man who hated with such passion.

Your father was a villain and a scoundrel, he had said, and she thought again of the terrible accusation he had made. Dammartin believed in it with all his heart. And she wondered why he should ever have come to think such a thing. How could he be so misled? There was only one man who could answer her questions.

Yesterday she would not have considered entering into a discussion with Dammartin over his accusation, but much had changed since then, and she knew that, for all the darkness and danger surrounding him, he would not hurt her. For all else that Dammartin was and for all else that he had done, he had saved her, and Josie would not forget that.

She rode on in silence, biding her time until evening when she would speak to the French Captain.

Chapter Seven

It had been a long day, long and cold and hard, and the dust of it still clung to Dammartin's boots. Smoke drifted from the newly lit fires and the men busied themselves with cooking pots and rice and beans. The air was filled with the smell of wood smoke and the damp air of impending night.

'We head for Sabugal tomorrow,' he said to Lamont. 'The maps show that the mountains do not grow less and Foy is demanding we speed our current pace.'

'Men will be lost if we push them too hard.'

'More of Massena's men are lost with every day that we delay.' Dammartin rubbed wearily at the dark growth of stubble that peppered his jaw. 'Our army is dying in this damned country for need of reinforcements.'

Lamont's gaze focused over Dammartin's right shoulder before swinging back to meet the Captain's. 'I think perhaps the *mademoiselle* wishes to speak with you. She keeps glancing over here.'

Dammartin's expression remained unchanged. 'I am busy. There remains much to be done this evening.' He had no wish to speak to Mademoiselle Mallington. Matters concerning the girl were already too complicated for his liking.

Lamont sniffed and scratched at his chin. 'After last night, I thought…'

Dammartin forced the images from his mind. 'I would not wish what happened last night upon any woman, but she is still Mallington's daughter, Claude. I cannot allow myself to forget that.'

Lamont said nothing for a few moments, just looked at his captain before giving a nod. 'I will see to our evening meal.' And he walked off.

Dammartin nodded over at Molyneux, and began to move towards his lieutenant. A woman's step sounded behind him and there was the scent of lavender.

'I wondered if I might speak with you, Captain Dammartin.' There was a slightly awkward expression upon Mademoiselle Mallington's face; she seemed almost embarrassed, and he knew that she was remembering last night, just as he was.

He opened his mouth to refuse her, noticing as he did the tendrils of fair hair that had escaped her bonnet to feather around her face and the shadow of the bruise that marked her jaw.

'Concerning my father.'

Mallington. And he knew he would not refuse her after all. 'Very well, *mademoiselle*.'

'Perhaps we could talk somewhere more private.'

He felt the register of surprise, along with a sliver of excitement at the prospect of what it could be that she wished to tell him.

'If that is what you desire.'

He saw Molyneux standing not so far away, the Lieutenant's gaze darting between the girl and Dammartin.

'There is a river down through the woodland.'

She nodded her agreement.

Dammartin headed towards the trees, leaving Molyneux staring after them.

They walked in silence through the woodland, down the slope that ran towards the river, with only the tread of their boots over soil and the snapping of twigs between them, until they left the clearing where the 8th Dragoons were camped some distance behind at the top of the gorge. Slightly to the east they could hear the sounds of the infantry's camp, but it was not close enough to challenge their privacy.

He led her to the edge of a fast-flowing river, to where great boulders of rock clustered along its bank.

'We shall not be overheard here,' he said, and, leaning easily against a giant rock, looked out over the river.

Back up through the trees, from where they had come, he could just about see the carmine-coloured lapels of his men's jackets as they moved about the camp. Had the red lapels not been there, the green of their uniform would have made an effective camouflage even though the woodland was bare and barren. Beyond the great stones the water flowed fast despite the lack of rain. In the fading light it was a deep greeny grey that foamed to white where the water splashed hard over its rocky bed. The noise of it was so loud and gushing as to be almost a roar.

Josie turned from the river to face him, feeling suddenly nervous. 'There is not much time, Captain Dammartin. The daylight shall soon be gone and I would prefer to be back at the camp before it is dark.' She took a deep breath, squared her shoulders and prepared to speak the words she had come here to say.

He did not look round, just stayed where he was. 'You are recovered from last night, *mademoiselle*?'

The question unsettled her, reminding of things best forgotten: bandits and nightmares and the warmth of Dammartin's body sharing her bed. 'Yes, thank you, sir.'

His eyes met hers, and they were a clear honey brown, rich with emotion that she could not name—compassion, affinity, protectiveness. 'I am glad.'

And to Josie there was an intensity about the moment that set the butterflies fluttering in her stomach so that she had to look away.

The water rushed on. Somewhere in the distance was the thumping of axes splitting wood, and through the trees ahead she could see the sun was setting: a vibrant red halo surrounding the dark branches of the trees, as if a fire had touched against them, deep and hot and burning.

Still leaning his elbows on the stone boulder with the rosy pink light softening his face, he appeared to Josie ruggedly handsome. 'What is it, then, that you wish to say?'

She turned her mind from its observations, reminding herself of why she had come here. 'I wished to ask you of this…this accusation that you level at my father.'

He resumed his study of the river scene before him. 'It is no mere accusation, *mademoiselle*, but the truth.' And there was a weariness in his voice.

'That is your belief, but it is not correct, sir.'

'And this is what you wished to tell me?' He stopped leaning against the rock and turned to face her, and she could see that anything of softness had vanished, that he was once again the dark and dangerous French Captain who had stormed the monastery in Telemos.

'I did not come here to argue,' she said quickly.

'Really?' He arched an arrogant eyebrow.

She glanced away, suddenly very aware that they were alone down here. 'Did you witness your father's death?'

There was only the sound of the river in reply.

She thought she saw the flicker of pain in his eyes, so brief that she could not be sure.

The muscle in his jaw clenched. 'I did not.'

'But you were there, with him, at Oporto?'

'Unfortunately, no.'

The smallest of pauses, before she asked gently, 'Then how do you know the manner of his death?'

'Mademoiselle,' he said with the hard cynical breath of a laugh, 'all of France knows what your father did to him!'

She bit back the retort that sprang to her lips. 'Then, there were witnesses…to the crime?'

'Yes, there was a witness,' he said harshly. 'An honourable man who is beyond reproach, if it is his word that you are seeking to discredit.'

His words stung at her. 'What is there of honour in dishonesty?' she replied.

A twig snapped close by, and Josie jumped. Both of them peered in the direction of the trees from whence it had come.

There was only silence and the dying light and stillness.

'It is nothing,' said Dammartin dismissively. 'There is nothing to be gained in this, *mademoiselle*, we should return to the camp. The light begins to fade, and you said yourself that you are in a hurry to be back there.' He made to move.

'No, wait.' She stepped forwards, blocking his path, needing to show him that he was wrong. 'Before he died my father told me that you were an honourable man. He bade me trust you. If your accusation is true, I do not understand why he would say such a thing. When he saw you…when you came into that room in the monastery… when it was all but over, there was nothing of guilt or regret or fear in his eyes. He looked at you with respect. Given what you say, sir, how do you explain that?'

'I cannot, but it does not mean that he was innocent.'

'But will you not at least admit that his was not behaviour in keeping with a man that is guilty?'

'It was not in keeping with what is expected of a man that is guilty,' said Dammartin carefully.

'He was dying, for goodness' sake!' she said, and the pain stabbed in her heart. 'Do you really think that he would have bothered with pretence at such a time? What would have been the point?'

'As you said, Lieutenant Colonel Mallington was dying, and leaving his beloved daughter alone with the son of the man he had murdered. I think he had every reason to behave as he did.'

'You did not know him,' she said quietly, and stared up into his now-shadowed face. 'He was not such a man.'

'You are his daughter. Of course you do not wish to believe the unpleasantness of the truth.'

'No, you are wrong.' But with the denial came the first whisper of doubt in Josie's mind.

'You were not there. You can never really know what happened in Oporto last year, can you, *mademoiselle*?'

She bent her head, pressing the tips of her fingers to the tightness across her forehead. The thought came to her in a flash, and she wondered why she had not realised it before. Her father's journals—a log of all that had happened to Lieutenant Colonel Mallington and his men over the years—recorded by her papa's own hand in book after precious book. She raised her chin, staring at him with renewed confidence, feeling the excitement of her realisation flow through the entirety of her body.

'Oh, but you see, I can, sir,' she exclaimed. 'Every detail of every day.' She smiled her relief.

It seemed that Dammartin's lungs did not breathe, that his heart did not beat. 'And how might that be, *mademoiselle*?' he asked in a deathly quiet voice.

His very stillness alerted her to her mistake. 'I…' She swallowed, and glanced away, searching her mind frantically for a safe answer and finding none. She backed away. 'You were right; we should be returning to camp. It will soon be dark and the trees—'

His hand snaked out and caught gently around her wrist, preventing her escape. 'No, no, *mademoiselle*,' he said softly, 'our discussion, it begins to grow most interesting.' The angles of his face seemed to sharpen and his eyes darken, as he became the hunter once more.

'Captain Dammartin—'

'Every detail of every day,' he said slowly, repeating her words. 'Where might you learn that, I wonder?'

She tried to free her wrist, but Dammartin's hold was unbreakable. The thudding of her heart was so loud that she could no longer hear the river. Her breath was shallow and fast.

Foolish, foolish tongue, she cursed, to almost reveal what had remained hidden for so long. Her words had been too few, she told herself; he could not know, he could not. The journals would be safe.

Dammartin slowly pulled her closer, so that they were standing toe to toe within the twilight. 'From your British newspapers of the time?' His face tilted so that he was staring down at her.

'I meant nothing by my words. You are mistaken…' She tried to step away, but Dammartin secured her other wrist, locking her in place.

His head lowered towards hers so close that she could feel his breath, warm and soft against her face, and see the passion and determination within the darkness of his eyes. 'From your father's friends?' he asked.

She felt the jolt that jumped between them as his mouth brushed against her cheek, light and transient.

'Or perhaps from your father's journals?' he whispered softly into her ear.

The breath froze in Josie's throat. The blood in her veins turned to ice. She could not suppress the shiver. 'This is madness,' she breathed at last. 'My father kept no journal. Take me back to the camp at once.' She pulled her face back from his, staring up at him.

'Where are they, *mademoiselle*?' Darkness had crept to cover the sky, but she could still see him through the dim silver moonlight.

'You are quite, quite mistaken, sir.'

'We can stay here all night and play this game. Or perhaps you prefer to tell me now where the journals are kept, so that we may eat something of our rice and beans.'

There was silence in which neither moved nor spoke.

'At home, in England,' she said at last, knowing that it was not the journals' existence that was the secret to be protected, but their location. She thought of the irony of the journals' true hiding place. 'I will read them when I return to Winchester and then I will know exactly what happened between your father and mine in Oporto.' She stared at him defiantly, knowing that she could not allow one shred of fear to show. 'And I will warrant that it is not the lie that you French have told.'

He looked at her with his dark, penetrating stare, and it seemed to Josie that he could see into her very soul.

For too long their gazes held, as if locked in some kind of strange battle of wills, and if battle it was, then Dammartin was the loser, for it was he who looked away first.

'Let us return to the camp, *mademoiselle*,' he said, and,

taking her hand in his, he began to lead her back towards the woodland.

She let her fingers lie where they were, warm and comfortable within his own, despite knowing that she should be fighting his touch. But the night was dark and their route through the woodland steep and uneven, and her sense of relief and of triumph was greater than anything else.

Hand in hand, without a further word between them, Josie and Dammartin walked through the trees that would lead them back to the camp of the 8th Dragoons.

The campaign portmanteau which contained all of Josie's worldly possessions sat opposite her makeshift bed within Dammartin's tent. It was made of brown leather, battered and scratched from its many miles of travel following her father.

Josie unbuttoned the top of her dress and let the woollen material fall back to expose the chain that hung around her neck. Its golden links glinted within the soft light of the lantern. Her hand disappeared down her dress. From just above her breasts she retrieved what had been threaded to hang upon the chain: a small brass key. Kneeling down upon the groundsheet, she leaned forward towards the portmanteau, neatly turned the key in first one lock and then the other. The fastenings opened easily beneath her fingers. She opened the lid and rested it carefully back.

Inside were piles of neatly folded clothes. They were, in the main, garments that had been purchased with the practicalities of life on campaign in winter in mind. There were two woollen travelling dresses, a sensible pelisse, scarves, a shawl, gloves, a pair of sensible shoes that could be worn instead of her boots, and of course, a large pile of plain white warm underwear, the warmest that she had had.

There were stockings and two nightdresses and ribbons and hairpins. Near the top there was a tiny silver and ivory set that included a comb and brush and hand-held looking glass. But Josie was interested in none of these things.

She moved with deliberate care, removing the items one by one, laying them in tidy bundles across the ground-sheet, until at last the portmanteau was empty, or so it seemed. Then she pressed at the rear left-hand corner of the portmanteau and smoothly lifted away the false floor. Beneath it, spread in neat piles over the entirety of the base of the portmanteau, as if a single uniform layer, were notebooks.

Each book was backed in a soft paper cover of a deep pinky-red coloration; some were faded, others stained. Josie picked one from the closest corner and opened it. The white of the pages was scarcely visible beneath the pale grey pencil script that covered it. She checked the date at the top right-hand side of the page—21st June 1807—closed the book, set it back in its place in the pile, moved on to the next, until she found the book that contained the date for which she was searching.

The false floor was slotted back into position. The bundles of clothes were returned in neat order to the portmanteau, as was every other item that had been removed. The lid was carefully closed, the key turned within the locks and the straps rebuckled. Only then did Josie make herself comfortable upon the wooden chair and sit down at Captain Dammartin's little table to lay the notebook upon its surface. She adjusted the direction of the light within the lantern and, taking a deep breath, began to read her father's journal for the Battle of Oporto.

Josie could barely concentrate on Molyneux's chatter the next day, for thinking of the words that her father had

written. Dammartin had been correct in saying that his
father had been captured by hers. It was true, too, that the
French major had been paroled, but that is where any similarity between the two stories ended. Lieutenant Colonel
Mallington's telling of the two men's meeting could not
have contrasted more sharply with Dammartin's.

Her papa had written of respect and admiration between
two men who happened to be fighting on opposite sides
of a war. Those faded grey words conveyed an underlying
sense of something bordering on friendship.

Why should there be such a discrepancy between the
two accounts? It made no sense. The more she thought
about it, the more she became convinced that there was
something very strange about such a blatant contradiction.
And she longed to question Dammartin more on his story.

Who was the man who claimed to have witnessed the
murder? Someone honourable, who was beyond reproach,
Dammartin had said.

She glanced ahead to where the French Captain rode,
her eyes skimming his broad shoulders, and the sway
of the long, black mane of horsehair that hung from his
helmet. She wanted to show him the journal entry, to prove
to him that he was wrong, to show him that her father was
indeed an innocent man, but she could not.

Trust was a fickle thing, and Dammartin was still the
enemy. Even had she torn that single page from its binding so that he might have read only that and nothing else,
then he would have known that the journals were in her
possession and she knew that Dammartin would not stop
until he had them from her.

Her teeth worried at her lower lip, and she knew that
she dare not approach him again, no matter how many
questions still burned unanswered. Last night had been
too close for comfort, in more ways than one. The memory

of his face so close to hers, of his breath warm against her cheek, of the dark, dangerous look in his eyes…and how very close he had come to discovering that all of her father's journals were here under his very nose.

'Your thoughts are elsewhere this morning, *mademoiselle*.' Molyneux smiled that kind smile of his, making Josie feel guilty at her inattention.

'Forgive me, Lieutenant, I am but a little tired.'

'You did not sleep well?' he enquired with concern.

She gave a small shake of her head. 'Not since Telemos.'

'I am sorry, *mademoiselle*. I did not mean to raise such distressing memories.' His smile was small and wry. 'We should talk of happier times, especially as I, too, am feeling a little sad this day.'

Josie glanced up at him with questioning eyes.

'I confess to you alone, *mademoiselle*, and you must keep a very great secret, that I am missing my wife most dreadfully.'

'I did not know that you are married, sir,' said Josie.

'I do not often speak of Mariette. It makes me too emotional, and that is not good for a lieutenant in the Emperor's army.'

Josie felt her heart soften for the poor lieutenant. 'I think it is most commendable that you miss her.'

'We have been married for three years,' he said, 'and we have two fine sons.' He smiled at that.

'Would it be of help if you were to speak of your family, sir?'

'I think, perhaps, *mademoiselle*, that it might.'

So Molyneux told her of his boys and how he missed them. He told her of Mariette and how he had courted her despite her father's disregard for a mere military man. They laughed over the antics that two-year-old Louis got up to, and then Lieutenant Molyneux grew sad when he spoke of how tiny the baby, Dominique, had been when last he had seen him, and how in the months that had since passed that the baby would have grown beyond all recognition. He was trying to keep his emotion in check, but she could hear the wistful longing in his voice and it tugged at her heartstrings.

Impulsively she reached over and briefly touched her hand to his sleeve. 'You must not be sad, sir. Your family would not wish it so and I am sure that you will see them soon.'

'Yes.' But there was nothing of hope in the word. He gave a sigh and then seemed to pull himself from his reverie. 'Now you understand, *mademoiselle*.' He forced a smile to his face.

She could see the slight sheen of tears in his eyes and knew that he would not want the embarrassment of having her see them. 'Indeed, I do, sir,' she said. 'Perhaps we should speak of other matters.' She smiled. 'The weather has been uncommonly fine of late. Do you think that it will hold?'

He laughed at that and she could see that the sadness had left his eyes. 'You English always speak of the weather. It is a national interest, I think.'

'Yes,' she agreed, 'I think it probably is.'

They rode in companionable silence for a little, and Josie was just thinking how pleasant Lieutenant Molyneux was when a small and rather daring idea popped into her head. 'Would you mind if I were to ask you something of a rather delicate nature, Lieutenant?'

'But of course, you must ask,' he replied.

'It concerns the death of Captain Dammartin's father.'

Molyneux's face betrayed a fleeting surprise. 'What is it that you wish to know, *mademoiselle*?'

'I understand that there is a man who claims to have

witnessed the—' She broke off and quickly revised her words. 'To have witnessed Major Dammartin's death.'

'That is the case.'

'I was wondering if you knew the identity of that man.'

Molyneux's grey eyes met hers. There was the jangle of harnesses, and the steady clop of horses' hooves. 'Why do you ask such a question?'

'I wish to know the name of the man who is responsible for falsely accusing my father of murder.'

'Mademoiselle,' said Molyneux softly.

'My father is innocent, Lieutenant, and he is dead,' she said in justification of her request. 'There is no one else to defend his name.'

Concern and pity welled in Molyneux's eyes, and all she could think of was showing Molyneux that such pity was unjustified, that her father really was innocent. 'Do not think that I am misled because he was my father. He is innocent, sir, and I have the evidence that will prove it.'

Molyneux stared at her.

'Will you tell me the man's name, Lieutenant?'

Molyneux looked away and with a gentle sigh, shook his head.

'You do not trust me?'

'It is not that,' Molyneux said quietly.

'Then what?'

He looked back round at her. 'I fear that you will find only sadness if you follow this path.'

'No,' she said with determination, 'you are quite wrong in that.'

He gave a wry smile, and they continued on in silence.

Dammartin saw the way in which Mademoiselle Mallington looked at Molyneux, saw too the brief touch of fingers against his arm before he turned away again. She was

Mallington's daughter, a prisoner, so what did it matter to Dammartin if she flirted with his lieutenant? he thought. Did he not want to be rid of her in Ciudad Rodrigo as soon as was possible? She was nothing to him, just as he had told La Roque.

But Dammartin was not fooling himself. He wanted her, and though he was adamant that he would not act upon it, nothing that he did seemed to alter that desire.

He longed to cup those pale, perfect breasts, to span his hands around the narrowness of her waist, to slide his fingers over the swell of her hips. And those lips…so ripe for the tasting, and he remembered the kiss, and how it had served only to stoke his hunger for her higher. The feel of her long hair beneath his fingers, the clean lavender scent of her, her very softness…

Last night, in the darkness by the river, with her wrists imprisoned in his, he had come close to kissing her again, to claiming her sweet mouth with his own. His lips had been so close that they tingled to kiss away the pain of her bruises. It had been an enormous effort of willpower not to succumb to temptation.

He thought of the excitement that had stirred in his blood when she had said that she wanted to speak to him of her father. The flair of hope that she would tell him what he so longed to know: the workings of a madman's mind. But Josephine Mallington had wanted only to argue her father's innocence, and he supposed that that was an admirable thing.

She was young, her father's only daughter, and he thought what she had told him of following her father around the world, of the death of her mother. It could not have been easy to learn the truth of her father, that he was not the beloved hero she thought him. No wonder she fought so hard for the old man. Dammartin knew he would have done the very same for his own father.

He wondered what Mallington had written in his journal about Oporto and Jean Dammartin. And he wondered, too, as to Josephine Mallington's reaction when he had asked about the journals. What was she so frightened of revealing if the journals were safely stowed in England? Dammartin thought of his own current campaign journal locked within the drawer of his small campaign desk, and of his journals from previous years stored at the bottom of his portmanteau…and he smiled at Mademoiselle Mallington's audacity.

Chapter Eight

It was after they had stopped for a lunch break that the rain started. It was not like English rain that came on slowly enough to give a person time to hurry to cover, or put an umbrella above their head. This was Portuguese rain and it was as if God had decided to operate a pump stand in the heavens. The rain poured suddenly upon them in a great deluge and that is the way it stayed for the next few hours. Molyneux offered her the great cape that covered over him and his horse, but Josie refused it.

The rain penetrated everywhere and at a speed at which she could never have guessed. She had never seen such a torrential downpour from the heavens in all of her life. Josie's hat was soon a sorry, sodden affair that dripped water down her face. Her gloves were wet and her hands were so cold that she ceased to feel her fingers. She could feel the water trickling between the toes of her stockings within her boots. But she made no complaint, just kept her thoughts focused on the strange mystery surrounding Dammartin's father's death. When her mind was fixed on that, Josie felt infinitely better, for then she could not dwell upon what had happened in Telemos, or the bandit's attack, or her worries over what would become of her.

Water dripped from her nose, ran in rivulets down her cheeks, and blurred her vision, and through it all, Josie thought on the words in her father's journal. The road became muddy and great puddles appeared that slowed the horses' progress. Troopers' shouts sounded from the rear of their column, an animal's scream of pain, and with an exchange of looks, both Dammartin and his lieutenant disappeared to investigate—leaving Josie alone. What she would have given for such a situation only a few days ago, but much had happened since then, and any chance of escape had long gone. They were too far into hostile countryside, too far from the British and too close to bandits. And aside from all of that, she knew now with an absolute certainty that Dammartin would not rest until he had hauled her back.

The French escort struggled on, and the only sound was the slop of hooves against the mud, and the constant lash of rain and wind.

They had not yet reached Sabugal when they pitched the tents, but the men could go no farther even though the rain's intensity had lessened. Josie sheltered beneath some trees and watched the speed and efficiency with which Dammartin's dragoons operated even after a day's march through the worst rainstorm imaginable. The men were cold and wet, and completely disciplined. Josie watched in amazement. She had never felt less disciplined in her life. Her clothes clung to her like a heavy, cold shroud, and there was not one vestige of warmth left in the whole of her body. Her nose was running and even the handkerchiefs from her pocket were sodden. She longed for shelter, for dry clothes, for warmth. Overhead the sky was dark with cloud and the promise of more rain. Night would come early.

Across from her tent there seemed to be some kind of altercation. Two dragoons were talking, gesturing with their hands. Dammartin was frowning and firing questions at the men, with Molyneux seemingly involved. Sergeant Lamont stood looking on from the background. There was much pointing at Josie's tent, then back at the place where the mules were clustered. The men looked over at where Josie stood, and she knew that whatever they were discussing involved her.

The dragoons went about their business, and Dammartin began to walk across the field towards her. His caped greatcoat was so long that it touched to the ground. The grey wool was dark and saturated. The long, black crest of horse hair of his helmet hung sodden and lank. Water dripped from his face, and around his face his hair clung dark and wet. She could hear the squelch of his boots in the mud, and his scar etched dark and deep against the pallor of his cheek.

Dread gathered in her stomach and she knew that something was wrong.

'Captain?'

'Mademoiselle.' His face was grim.

Her stomach clenched tighter. 'What is it? What is wrong?'

'I am afraid that there is a problem. Your portmanteau, it cannot be found.'

She stared at him, hardly fathoming the import of his words. 'But it was attached to the officers' mule train. Two of your troopers took it this morning as normal. I saw them load it myself.'

'It is not there now. I have instructed my men to search again through all of the baggage, but I am not hopeful.'

The realisation of what he was saying hit home. The breath stilled in her throat, her eyes looked up at him wide and round. 'No, it cannot be.'

'I am afraid it is true.'

She bit at her lower lip. 'It has been stolen.'

'We do not yet know if that is the case.'

'Of course it has been stolen,' she cried. 'What other explanation could there be?' And she thought of her father's journals stacked so neatly within their hiding place within the portmanteau...now in French hands.

'Oh, God!' She felt a horrible sick sensation heavy in her stomach.

'Mademoiselle,' he said.

'What am I to do?' she whispered, as if to herself. 'What on earth am I to do?' She clutched a hand to her mouth.

'We shall find you some dry clothing and blankets.'

'No, no!' She shook her head. 'You do not understand!'

'Calm yourself, Mademoiselle Mallington.'

But Josie barely heard him, for all she could think of was that she had lost the one thing that remained of her father, the thing that she had been entrusted to keep safe, lost to the enemy. And she could say not one word of the truth of it to Dammartin.

'Thank God that I—' She broke off. 'Please excuse me, Captain,' she said, and turning, ran to her tent, before she could betray herself any further.

Josie sat for what seemed a long time at the small table within the tent, trying to tell herself that there was every likelihood that the thief would not find the hidden compartment within her portmanteau. The journals might be lost, but that did not necessarily mean that the French had found them. She focused on that one small hope and sat motionless upon the wooden chair, just breathing, until all of her panic had gone.

Only when she was calm did she notice that she was shivering. The rainwater from her sodden cloak had seeped through her dress and underwear to touch damp and cold upon her skin, and Josie knew she must try to dry and warm herself. With a sigh she began to peel off her clothing. First came the woollen hat pulled so unflatteringly on her head, next, her woollen mittens and finally her leather gloves. Her fingers were stiff and slow to move, so she took her time, peeling the saturated leather covers off each finger with patience. Her cloak and pelisse followed, being dropped onto the growing pile of sodden material that was gathering by the tent's flap. Her boots took some time to unlace as her fingers would not bend well and she could scarcely untie the knots in her laces, but she persevered and soon the boots and stockings, too, lay on top of the pile.

She then unfastened the tent flap, knelt by the opening and worked her way methodically through the pile of clothes wringing out each item as dry as she could make it. When she had finished she closed the flap, stripped off her dress, petticoats and shift and hid her nakedness beneath her newly wrung-out cloak. She then repeated the wringing operation with her dress and undergarments. She wrung out her hair, and emptied her boots. Finally she slipped back into her shift and dress, and spread the rest of her clothing out across the floor so that it might have some chance of drying. She had just finished this when a woman's voice sounded outside the tent flap.

'Señorita Mallington?'

'Yes.' Josie moved to open the flap. 'I am Josephine Mallington.'

The woman that stood there was of similar height and build to Josie. But she was as dark as Josie was fair, and her face showed that she was perhaps five years older. Her hair was hidden in the main by the great hood of the plain brown cloak that she wore, but around the edges of her face a riot of dark brown curls clustered. Her eyes were soft and brown and tinged with quite the longest lashes that Josie had ever seen. Her lips were full and luscious, her face barely lined and a warm honey colour within the light of the lantern. Her expression was neither friendly nor hostile, but her eyes flickered over Josie and the interior of the tent, appraising and summing up in a matter of seconds.

'Captain Dammartin, he say you need clothes. I give you mine.'

The two women looked at each other for a minute before Josie gave a nod. 'Please come in.' Josie stepped back. 'It is kind of you to lend me a dress. My portmanteau is missing and my own clothes are rather wet.'

'Wet, yes,' said the woman and flicked a glance over the garments spread the length of the floor.

Josie's eyes followed the woman's. 'I thought perhaps the clothes might dry a little.'

The woman looked at her with the same unruffled expression. 'They no dry in here. Too cold, too wet.'

'You are probably right,' said Josie, 'but it seemed better than leaving them in a pile in the corner.'

Whether the woman understood Josie did not know, for she gave no reply.

'Please sit down, take off your cloak.' Josie pointed a hand towards the table and chairs.

At first she thought the woman would decline, but then she pushed back her hood and sat down on one of the small wooden chairs.

'*Gracias.*'

Josie looked at the woman. She was beautiful, with

her wet hair pinned up and its escaping curls tumbling down the sides of her face and across the bareness of her shoulders. Her skin was smooth and unblemished. She did not look as if she had spent the day marching or sitting on a donkey for hours in the rain. No, the woman that sat in Josie's tent looked damp but untroubled. Her cloak might be of coarse homespun wool, but everything in her bearing was fiercely, almost violently proud.

'For you.' The woman held out a bundle of red-and-black material.

'Thank you.' Josie took it.

'I am Rosa,' said the woman.

Josie gave a small smile. 'Thank you, Rosa.'

Rosa unfastened the ties of her cloak and pushed the garment back, flicking off droplets of rainwater as she did.

Josie's eyes slid down to the dress that Rosa was wearing. It was of a red-and-black material that flattered the olive hues of her skin, cut in the style of Spanish ladies and worn over a white chemise. But it was not the colour that brought a widening to Josie's eyes—that was readily accomplished by the tight-fitting bodice and extreme décolletage of the white chemise that she wore beneath.

The sleeves were pushed off her shoulders. Unlike the high waistlines that were so fashionable with the ladies of Britain and France, this dress was reminiscent of the style of an earlier time, with its waist set lower and pulled in small and tight before the skirt swept out with a fullness of material. The dress revealed much of Rosa's figure and left little to the imagination.

Oh, my! thought Josie and, finding that she was staring, hastily averted her gaze.

'You wish me to help you dress?'

'No, thank you.' Josie could feel a slight warmth wash her cheeks. 'I can manage.' She hoped that the dress that was folded so neatly in her hands was not a match for the one that Rosa was wearing.

There was a moment of silence before Rosa said, 'You are the English Lieutenant Colonel's daughter.' Her eyes were dark and bold.

Josie prepared herself for a defence. 'Yes.'

'The one who murdered the Captain's father.'

'My father did not murder Major Dammartin.' Josie's hackles rose. She eyed the woman angrily. 'The story is a lie perpetrated by the French.'

Rosa shrugged her beautiful bare shoulders in an insolent gesture.

'Thank you, Rosa,' said Josie icily, 'I shall return your clothes as soon as my own are dry.' She got to her feet, signalling to the woman that their conversation was at an end.

'No return,' said Rosa. 'Captain Dammartin, he give me money. You keep clothes.'

'Captain Dammartin paid you?'

Rosa nodded, and her lips curved to a seductive smile. 'Yes, he pay me money. He is very kind.'

A horrible suggestion made itself known to Josie. She blushed at the thought of just what kind of relationship Captain Dammartin might have with this woman. 'You are not a prisoner of the French, are you?'

'A prisoner?' Rosa seemed almost to be laughing at her. 'No, *mademoiselle*, I am not a prisoner… Nothing is simple in love and war,' said Rosa, pulling the hood back up over her head. '*Adios*, Señorita Mallington,' she said, and left the tent.

Dammartin sat his helmet in the corner of the tent and raked a hand through his hair, pushing the sodden strands back from his eyes. The tent was empty. He stood there, relishing the few minutes of solitude. He was tired and cold. His bones were aching and he was hungry. Nothing different from any man that served beneath him. That was not what was bothering Dammartin. He rubbed damp fingers over the rough growth of stubble that had appeared on his face with the progress of the day, and released a sigh. Uneasiness sat in his gut. He sighed again and rubbed harder at the stubble. A noise from the tent flap alerted him. Sergeant Lamont entered.

'Captain.' The small man nodded. 'Rosa has taken the clothes to Mademoiselle Mallington.'

'Good. Thank you, Lamont. You gave Rosa the money?'

'Yes. I told her she should not accept it, sir, but she wants to save.'

'For your future together?'

Lamont laughed. 'She will not stay with an old man like me. Soon she will be off.'

'No, my friend,' said Dammartin. 'I do not think so. You saved her from an ordeal abhorrent to any woman. She will not forget.'

'I demand nothing from her.'

'And that is why she stays. Following the drum is not easy for any woman. There must be something here that makes her wish to stay,' Dammartin said teasingly.

Lamont shrugged as if he did not know, but Dammartin knew better.

'The *mademoiselle*'s portmanteau, it has not appeared?'

'All the baggage, including the women's, has been searched, every tent. It is not to be found.'

'It could not have fallen,' said Lamont.

The two men looked at one another.

'And,' said Lamont, 'a portmanteau is not so easy to steal from the officers' mule train during a day's march.'

'You do not ask the question as to why anyone would want to steal an Englishwoman's portmanteau?' said Dammartin.

'It was not the women. Rosa knows everything that goes on with them. They do not like the *mademoiselle*, but they would not dare to steal from the officers' train. They did not take it.'

'No, the women are not behind this, Claude. Even had they wanted the portmanteau, they could not have lifted the damn thing.'

'There is another possibility, sir.'

Dammartin waited for what the Sergeant would say.

'Mallington is a much hated man and there is no one in this company that does not know she is his daughter. The rain has poured from the skies. She is cold. She is wet. And now she has no dry clothes to change into? Perhaps they play a petty trick to make the *mademoiselle* suffer.'

'Perhaps,' said Dammartin, but in his heart he did not believe that to be the case. If he guessed right, Lieutenant Colonel Mallington's journals lay behind the theft. 'Ask around the men, informally. A portmanteau cannot just disappear. Someone must have seen something.'

'Yes, sir.' said Lamont. 'The food is almost ready. Do you want me to take a tray to Mademoiselle Mallington?'

'I will do that myself. I wish to speak to her.'

Lamont looked at his captain and there was just the suggestion of a smile upon his lips.

'Do not give me that look, Lamont. If I wanted female company of the sort you are thinking, then I would find it in the baggage train. I am not likely to forget who Mademoiselle Mallington's father was.' But even as he said it Dammartin knew that it was not true. He had never used a woman from the baggage train, and as for the other, he had already come too close to forgetting about Mademoiselle Mallington's father.

Lamont laughed and walked off, leaving Dammartin to see to Josephine Mallington.

Josie had just finished lacing the bodice of the dress.

'Excusez-moi, mademoiselle.' The voice from the other side of the tent flap was unmistakably that of Captain Dammartin.

She looked down at just how much that the neckline of Rosa's chemise revealed, and winced. 'A moment, please.' She glanced around the tent in panic, scanning for something with which she could preserve her modesty. There was nothing save the wet clothes spread across the floor or the covers of the makeshift bed. She nipped over to her makeshift bed, whipped off the top blanket and hastily pulled it around her shoulders.

'Mademoiselle Mallington?' he said again and, without waiting further, let himself in through the tent flap.

'Captain Dammartin.' She spun to face him, ensuring that the blanket was firmly in place.

He was no longer wearing his greatcoat, but just his green jacket with its decorated brass buttons. His head was bare, and his dark hair had been slicked back from his face. 'Your dinner.'

Her eyes dropped from his face, lower, to the tray that he held between his hands and the mess tin and half-skin of wine and tumbler upon it.

He sat the tray upon the table.

'Thank you, Captain,' she said, and darted him a glance, suspicious that he had brought the food himself.

He gestured to the table.

She sat down on one of the chairs.

Dammartin sat down in the other.

Josie's heart began to beat a warning tattoo. 'You have news of my portmanteau?' she said slowly.

'Unfortunately, no.'

She waited.

He unstoppered the wine skin and filled the pewter tumbler that sat by its side, clearly intent on staying. 'Eat...' he gestured to the mess tin '...before it grows cold.'

Josie gave a nod and, lifting the spoon, began to eat the watery stew.

She saw his gaze sweep down over the blanket around her shoulders to the full red-and-black skirt covering her legs. 'Rosa brought you the dress, then.'

Another nod.

Dammartin's scar stood prominent and dark against the pallor of his skin. His eyes were dark, but showed nothing of either his intent or his mood. A strange tension sat around him, a stillness almost, as if he were poised, as if he were waiting, and her stomach fluttered with anticipation. She wondered why he was here and what this undercurrent was that flowed between them.

She focused her gaze upon her dinner as her spoon scraped against her tin, the noise seeming too loud in the silence that filled the tent. 'I will return the clothes as soon as I can.'

'There is no need,' he said. 'Rosa has been recompensed for her loss.'

'So I have been told.' Josie looked up at him then, and in her ear whispered the beautiful dark-haired woman's words seemingly taunting her naïvety. For the first time she saw him not as the French Captain who had stormed the monastery at Telemos, nor an officer of Bonaparte's man, not even as her enemy—but just as a man.

She realised that she knew scarcely anything of Dammartin, other than the story of his father. Whether he was married. Whether he had children. Whether he took the beautiful Rosa to his bed at night. Josie did not know why she found the thought of him with the Spanish woman so discomforting. It should not have mattered one iota to her, but, as she sat there in Rosa's dress, she knew that it did matter, very much. She did not want to think of Rosa.

She took a swig of wine. 'Are you married, Captain Dammartin?'

Surprise registered in his eyes. He hesitated before answering. 'I am not married, *mademoiselle*.'

Her heart beat a little faster. She fortified herself with some more wine. 'Rosa is not a prisoner of the French.'

A single dark eyebrow raised at that. 'No, she is no prisoner.' And he looked at her with that too-perceptive gaze.

Silence, and the tension within the tent seemed to tighten a notch.

Josie regretted her impulsiveness. He was the enemy. She was his prisoner. What did it matter what he did? Why was he even here in the tent with her?

'Rosa is Sergeant Lamont's woman,' said Dammartin.

Another silence. Awkward. Tense.

'I just thought…' Josie sipped at the wine and started again. 'I am surprised, that is all, given that she is Spanish.'

'Lamont saved her from being raped and flogged by a group of Spanish guerrillas near her village.'

Josie felt her stomach tighten with shock and the memory of her own experience at the bandit's hands. She pushed the thought away, forced herself to concentrate on Rosa. 'Why would her own people do that to her?'

'They thought she was fraternising with the enemy.'

'And was she…fraternising?'

'She was innocent of the charges, but passions run high

when it comes to our army in Spain. She would have been killed had she returned to her village.'

'So she has travelled with your army ever since.'

'She follows Lamont, and only Lamont,' he said.

'Because he saved her.' And the breath was shaky in her throat as she looked into his eyes.

'Yes.'

They stared at one another, knowing that the subject had come much closer to something that touched them both.

It was Josie that looked away.

'Thank you for bringing me the dinner,' she said, moving the empty mess tin upon the tray. She stood up, hoping that Dammartin would take the hint and leave.

Dammartin lifted the wine skin and refilled the tumbler.

'It has been a long day, sir. I am tired and—'

'Sit down, *mademoiselle*,' he said quietly.

Despite the flair of alarm in Mademoiselle Mallington's eyes, Dammartin knew he could defer his questions no longer. She had eaten, they were both tired…and he had to know for sure.

'You were most distressed by the loss of your portmanteau.'

'I was,' she admitted, but he could hear the note of caution in her voice.

'Clothes can be replaced.' His eyes dropped to the thick, grey blanket draped around her shoulders, knowing that it hid the low-cut Spanish dress beneath.

A slight nod as her gaze wandered over the empty mess tin, the cup and the tray.

'I find myself wondering over your reaction to your missing baggage.' He watched her very carefully.

'I do not understand what you mean, sir.' Still she did not look at him, but her fingers began to toy with the spoon.

'You were distraught, panicked, afraid.'

She forced a dismissive smile. 'I was cold and wet, and I had just learned that all of my possessions had been stolen. What reaction did you expect, Captain?'

'For how long have you followed your father, Mademoiselle Mallington?'

'Most of my life.' He could see her trying to fathom his line of questioning.

'How many years have you, *mademoiselle*?'

'I am two and twenty years old,' she replied. Her fingers played against the spoon's handle.

So young, Dammartin thought. Too damned young to be caught up in this situation. He thought again of Lieutenant Colonel Mallington's utter selfishness. 'Then you know well the rigours of campaign life?'

'Yes, but…' she frowned '…I do not understand what this has to do with my missing portmanteau.'

'I ask myself why Mademoiselle Mallington, who has shown such bravery, such resilience, should be so very upset by a few missing clothes.'

She sat very still.

'And the thought comes to me that perhaps the lady has within her portmanteau something more precious than clothes.'

The colour drained from her cheeks.

'Something that she wishes very much not to fall into French hands.'

Her grip tightened around the spoon.

'Might that be the case, *mademoiselle*?'

Her gaze stayed on the spoon, and he saw how white her knuckles shone.

He let the silence stretch, increasing the tension that was already wound taut between them.

'I begin to think of what is most precious to Mademoiselle Mallington.'

Her breath held.

'And I find the answer is her father.'

There was the slightest widening of her eyes.

He leaned forward, bringing his face closer to hers. 'Lieutenant Colonel Mallington's journals were within your portmanteau.'

The spoon dropped with a clatter. Her gaze swung to his, showing all of her shock and her hurt and her anger. 'It was you!' she whispered, and then she was on her feet, the chair falling over behind her. 'You stole my portmanteau!'

'Mademoiselle Mallington.' He rose.

But she backed away, increasing the space between them, staring at him with outrage blatant upon her face. 'And now that you cannot find what you seek, you come back to me to discover…' She touched her knuckles to her mouth, as if to stopper the words and her breath came in loud ragged gasps.

He moved towards her.

But she trod back farther, shaking her head, warning him away. 'Not once did I think that it might have been you.'

He stepped closer. *'Mademoiselle.'*

'Leave me alone,' she said, and her face was powder white.

His arms closed around her, pulling her against him.

She tried to push him away, but he just held her closer, aware of the tremble through her body.

'Listen to me.'

'No.' She shook her head and pushed harder at his chest. 'Leave me!'

'Josephine.' He gazed down into her eyes, needing to reach her, needing to make her understand. 'I did not steal your portmanteau. What need had I to do such a thing? Had I wanted to search it, do you not think that I would have come in here and done just that?'

Josie looked up into Dammartin's eyes, and his words permeated the mist that had clouded her brain. The air she had been holding tight and still within her lungs escaped in a single fast breath.

He was right. Dammartin would have emptied her whole portmanteau before her very eyes without the slightest compunction.

'I...' She shook her head, unwilling to betray her father further by admitting the existence of the journals. Dammartin was still French. He was still her enemy. 'You are mistaken, Captain, there were no journals within my portmanteau.'

'Perhaps,' he said, but she knew that he was not convinced.

'I would just like to have my possessions returned to me, that is all.'

He looked deep into her eyes. 'A portmanteau is not so easy to hide on the war trail. If it is here, then it shall be found. I will discover who is behind this, *mademoiselle*.'

He *was* French. He *was* her enemy. But in that moment she believed what he said. And now that the panic had gone she became aware that she was still standing in the French Captain's arms, and that he was staring down at her with an intensity that made her shiver.

'You are cold,' he said quietly.

'No,' she whispered, conscious that she was trembling. She should have pulled herself free, for the grip of his hands had gentled. But Josie just stood there.

His hand moved up and she felt the stroke of his thumb

brush against her mouth and her lips burned where he touched.

There was only the sound of their breath between them.

'*Mademoiselle,*' he whispered, and not once did the intensity of his gaze falter. His eyes had darkened to a smoulder that held her so completely that she could not look away. It seemed as if she were transfixed by him, unable to move, unaware of anything save him, and the strange tension that seemed to bind them together.

Her eyes flickered over the harsh, lean angles of his face, over the straightness of his nose, over the dark line of his scar, down to his lips. And she was acutely conscious of the hardness of his chest and hip and, against her, the long length of his legs. The breath wavered in her throat, and she was sure that he would hear its loud raggedness.

'Josephine,' he said, and she could hear the hoarse strain within his voice. 'God help me, but you tempt me to lose my very soul.'

His hand moved round to cradle her head. His face lowered towards hers, and she knew that he was going to kiss her. Slowly Josie tilted her face up in response, and the blanket slipped from her shoulders to fall upon the groundsheet.

A noise sounded from outside: a noisy tread over the grass, a man clearing his throat.

They froze.

'Captain Dammartin,' a man's voice said.

The spell was broken.

The truth of Josie's situation hit her. One of Dammartin's hands was threaded within her hair, the other rested against the small of her back. Her blanket lay upon the floor, showing Rosa's dress and just how much it revealed. Their bodies seemed to cling to together.

Dammartin released her and moved towards the tent

flap, opening it by the smallest crack so that whoever stood there would not have a view of Josie.

There was the soft, fast lilt of French voices. They spoke so low she had to strain to hear them. She did not catch every word, but she heard enough of them to know why Sergeant Lamont had seen fit to interrupt his captain. The lantern within the tent created the perfect lighting for a shadow show. The Captain's actions and those of Mademoiselle Mallington were clear to see for anyone outside the tent…and their actions were not going unnoticed by the men. Josie's face scalded with heat.

If Dammartin was embarrassed, there was no sign of it upon his face as he let the tent-flap drop and faced her.

'Pardon, *mademoiselle*…I must go.'

She bit at her lip, uncertain of what to say, knowing what they had been on the brink of doing.

He gave her one last look before he turned and was gone.

Chapter Nine

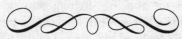

In view of Lamont's words, Josie extinguished the lantern before undressing for bed. She kept on only Rosa's shift and laid the blankets on to the bed once more before climbing within.

She lay there in the darkness, and the silence. Her heart was beating with a strong, steady thud, and her body tingled with awareness of what would have happened had not Lamont interrupted. Dammartin would have kissed her and she would have kissed him back. She was sure of it. Not a kiss that had started as a punishment, not a kiss to humiliate her before his men, but a real kiss between a man and a woman.

Her fingers touched to her mouth, exploring gently just as Dammartin had done. She knew that she had wanted him to kiss her—Captain Pierre Dammartin, the man responsible for her father's death, her enemy. It was a sobering realisation, and one that brought a wave of guilt and shame. Lord help her, what would her father have said? She was supposed to be fighting the enemy, not fraternising with him. And she remembered what Dammartin had said of Rosa and the terrible consequences of the accusations against her.

She groaned and whispered into the darkness, 'Papa, forgive me.' She lay there for a long while, contemplating what she had come so close to doing, and the madness of it and the badness of it.

Josie had been around soldiers and the army for most of her life. There had been many officers who had been friendly towards her, there had been some who had taken her hand, but not one had ever tried to kiss her. Men did not see Josie in that light. Not even during that awful year in England when she had been dangled before every young man in the hope of catching her a husband. Josie, who could ride a horse faster than most men and shoot a rifle with accuracy, and make good of the hardship of the campaign trail, had floundered and stumbled beneath the ridicule. The men had thought her gaucherie something to be laughed at; the women had been more spiteful.

Dammartin was different: he did not laugh at her; he did not make her feel foolish or inept. Indeed, he made her feel alive and tingling and excited; he made her want to press her lips to his and feel his strong arms surround her. With him she forgot all else—the journals and her papa and the bandits and Telemos. There was only the French Captain and the prospect of his kiss…and the realisation both shocked and appalled her.

Her eyes peered though the darkness as if she could see through two layers of canvas, into the neighbouring tent, which housed Lamont and Molyneux and…Dammartin. A tingle ran down Josie's spine just at his name. She closed her eyes and prayed for the strength to resist her own wanton nature.

But Dammartin was not in the nearby tent. Only Molyneux sat in there. Dammartin and Lamont stood across the field beneath a copse of trees that, while being distant from the tents, showed a clear view of them. Lamont was smoking his long clay pipe, drawing the tobacco in the pipe head to glow like a small orange spot in the darkness. The sweet scent of tobacco smoke surrounded them. Occasional droplets still dripped from the tree's bare branches, remnants of the day's downpour.

Lamont sucked at his pipe and seemed content to stare up at the dark grey cloud that covered the night sky above them.

There were no stars. The brightness of the moon was masked by the dense cover. The night was dark and gloomy.

Lamont sniffed. 'You want her, the English *mademoiselle.*'

Dammartin stared over at his tent which now lay in darkness. 'She is the daughter of my father's murderer; she bears the family name that I have for so long lived to hate. She is British, my very enemy, the one woman of all that should repel me.' His mouth curved in a crooked smile filled with irony. 'And none of it is enough to stop me.' He glanced round at his sergeant. 'That is a problem indeed, Claude.'

'Some problems are easily solved.'

'Not this one.'

Lamont said nothing.

'Where Mademoiselle Mallington is concerned, it seems that I can no longer trust in my own resolve. Had it not been for your interruption…'

'I am sorry to have spoiled things, but I thought that you would wish to—'

'You did right.' Dammartin cut him off. 'I am grateful that you stopped me.'

'Are you really?' Lamont turned his gaze upon his captain.

Dammartin looked right back at him. 'Do you think I want to insult the memory of my father?'

'I know what his murder did to you, Pierre.'

Dammartin turned his gaze back to the tent.

'What of the girl? From what I saw tonight, she is not averse to your interest.'

Dammartin thought of the softness in Josephine Mallington's eyes, of the parting of her sweet lips as her face tilted up to his, of the way she had stood within his arms, so trusting. 'It makes no difference. It is all of it still wrong.'

'There has been something between the two of you from the very beginning, a spark, an attraction, call it what you will. You cannot fight such a powerful desire, for it will always win in the end. If you truly do not wish to have bedded her before we have reached our destination, then there is only one thing you may do: send her into another's care—Emmern, La Roque or one of the infantry officers, it does not matter who, just as long as she is no longer here with you. Otherwise…' He shrugged. 'It is your choice.'

Dammartin rubbed at the stubble on his chin. 'I am sure that she still holds information regarding Mallington that may be of use. If I let her go, then I lose my last hope of understanding why Mallington killed my father.' He looked at his sergeant. 'And there is another matter to consider, Claude.' He thought of the journals. 'The loss of Mademoiselle Mallington's portmanteau is perhaps not as straightforward as it seems. I suspect she had her father's journals hidden within some kind of secret compartment within the portmanteau.'

'I understand now why the *mademoiselle* was so upset to hear the portmanteau was gone. So how did the thief know of the journals?'

'I do not know. Mademoiselle Mallington is not foolish enough to speak of them to anyone here. There was a mention made of the journals when I walked with her the other evening, but we were some distance from the camp and we were alone. I suppose that there might have been an eavesdropper.'

Lamont looked grim. 'Were that the case, it would have to have been one of our own men.' He sucked harder on the pipe. 'I do not like it.'

'I am not enamoured of the idea myself.'

Lamont's small, beady eyes glittered in the darkness. 'There is something uneasy in the air, Pierre.'

'I sense it too.'

They sat in silence. Pipe smoke drifted up and disappeared into the night sky. 'What will you do with Mademoiselle Mallington?' asked Lamont.

The two men looked across the field to Josie's tent.

'I do not know, my old friend, I really do not know.'

The next morning was grey, but without rain. For all its absence the ground was still sodden.

Josie awoke feeling surprisingly calm. Last night, with Dammartin, had been an aberration, a temporary madness that would not happen again. She had been drenched through and exhausted. She had suffered the loss of all her possessions and her father's precious journals. And Dammartin had guessed the truth of the journals. It was little wonder she had been rendered…susceptible… to strange fancies. But morning was here and Josie was strong again, strong enough to face the French captain.

'Mademoiselle Mallington?'

She jumped, her heart suddenly racing, for the voice that called her name came from immediately outside her tent.

'It is I, Lamont.'

She scrabbled from beneath the blankets, wrapping one around her shoulders.

'Mademoiselle,' he said again, and she recognised the Sergeant's accented tones.

'Sergeant Lamont,' she said quickly, trying to forestall his entry. 'I am coming.'

But Lamont was not like Dammartin; he merely stood by the door and waited.

'The Captain, he sends me with food for you.' He passed a mug and mess tin into her hands.

The heat rose in her cheeks. 'Thank you, sir.'

Swirls of steam rose from the mug. The smell of the coffee and warmed bread spread with honey caused her stomach to growl. 'I do not understand…'

The little Sergeant looked at her knowingly.

Her cheeks grew hotter as she remembered just what Lamont and all the rest of Dammartin's men had witnessed last night.

'The fires, they are put out,' Lamont said by way of explanation. 'We leave soon. Captain Dammartin has sent me to collect your bedding and wet clothing to be transported. I will wait here until it is ready, *mademoiselle.*'

She gave a nod and disappeared back inside the tent to hurriedly dress herself in Rosa's dress and woollen stockings before returning with her own clothing, neatly folded and still damp, on top of the blankets and pillow.

Lamont said nothing, just took the pile from her and walked back across the field, leaving her standing there in the stark morning light in the revealing Spanish dress and her hair flowing long and loose around her shoulders.

She watched him go, her focus shifting to look beyond him across the field. There, in her line of vision, was Captain Dammartin talking to a trooper. He was dressed just as he had been last night in full uniform, the green jacket neatly brushed, its carmine collar clean and bright, the long curved sabre hanging down by his left leg. He was without his helmet, his hair being ruffled by the breeze; his stance was relaxed and easy. As her gaze rested upon him, he looked up and for a moment their eyes met across the field.

Josie, her cheeks burning hotter than ever, retreated quickly into the tent. With shaky hands, she drank the coffee and ate the bread and eventually her heart slowed enough to allow her to fix some semblance of order to her hair. The trudge of boots sounded outside, troopers' voices—Dammartin's men come to dismantle the tent. Grabbing her damp woollen cloak and her small leather satchel, she squared her shoulders and walked out to face the day.

In the light of Lamont's words the previous evening, Dammartin was taking great care to stay well away from Josephine Mallington, but although he had sent his sergeant to collect her clothing, as he would have him deliver it again this evening, it was his own portmanteau into which Dammartin packed the clothes.

There has been something between the two of you from the very beginning, a spark, an attraction, call it what you will. You cannot fight such a powerful desire, for it will always win in the end. The words haunted him. But Dammartin would fight it and, contrary to Lamont's warning, he would win…he had to, for the sake of all that he believed in, for the sake of his father.

The luxury of Major La Roque's tent made Dammartin's look like something fit for a peasant. Normally the Major preferred to take over some local's house when he camped. Tonight, in the middle of the mountains with no buildings as far as the eye could see, he had had no choice but to sleep under canvas the same as the rest of his officers and men. Canvas is where the similarity ended.

Firstly, the Major's tent was enormous, with partitions that separated it into two rooms. Secondly, it was decorated with fine rugs and a few items of furniture. Within the impromptu dining room where the Major was hosting dinner there was also a long dining table on which a white tablecloth, matching napkins, china plates, bowls and crystal glasses had been set. Along the longitudinal midline of the table were three silver-branched candelabras, in which beeswax candles burned extravagantly. Decanters of red and white wine sat on a small tray, their cut-crystal bodies sparkling in the glow of the candles. The brandy would not be brought out until later. There were ten guests for dinner, all of them commissioned officers.

Each man's jacket was spotless, the blue of France's liberty or the green of her dragoons and chasseurs, the uniforms decorated with cording and frogging, sashes and epaulettes. Spirits were good, and the Major was in generous mood as usual. The dinner, served by the Major's staff, made the men's mess taste like pig swill, and not for the first time Dammartin wondered that a meal of such superior taste and quality could be prepared in a field kitchen with provisions that had been carried by mules for days across country.

They spoke of their mission and that soon they would reach Ciudad Rodrigo. They spoke of Bonaparte and of Paris. They spoke of the whores that followed the army. They ate. They drank. They smoked cigars. They took snuff. The waxing moon was high in the sky when the Major drew a close to the evening, each man deep in his cups, and each one happier for having spent the evening in Major La Roque's company.

Dammartin let the others leave first, waiting until they had all gone before he spoke. 'I wondered if I might talk to you, sir...in an informal capacity.'

'Of course, of course, Pierre.' La Roque clasped a friendly arm across the young captain's shoulders. 'Come, boy, sit down. Let us have a drink together, mmm?' He poured some brandy into two glasses and handed one to his godson. 'So, how are things with the 8th Dragoons?'

'They are well.'

'The presence of your prisoner is not causing any problems?'

'None,' replied Dammartin, wondering if the Major had come to hear of last night.

'Good, good. I am glad to hear it. I had thought that the fact she is Mallington's daughter might affect your sensibilities.'

A vision of Josephine Mallington in that revealing dress with her fair hair all tumbling down across her shoulders and her lips parted and moist, ready for his kiss, swam into his head. 'Nothing I cannot deal with,' he said with a great deal more confidence than he felt.

With a leisurely, lazy action La Roque swirled the brandy around his glass. 'Does she know what Mallington did?'

'She refuses to believe it.'

'I suppose that is to be expected.'

'Mademoiselle Mallington's portmanteau was recently stolen.'

La Roque swigged his brandy. 'I am not surprised that her presence has roused dislike among the men. Everyone knows who her father was.'

'I do not think that it is that simple. It is this of which I wished to speak to you.'

La Roque raised his brows in surprise.

'I believe that she may have had hidden some of her father's campaign journals within the baggage. I cannot be certain.' Dammartin thought of Josephine Mallington's reaction in his tent last night. 'But I am convinced that it is so; I think that the portmanteau was stolen for the journals.'

'But why would *she* be carrying her father's journals?'

Dammartin shrugged. 'Because they would not be looked for in the baggage of his daughter?'

'Pierre, you are too much focused on Mallington. You grow obsessed over him. You do not even know that these journals were in the portmanteau. It is more likely that one of your troopers took the portmanteau as a prank because she is Mallington's daughter. I am only surprised that it has taken so long for something like this to happen. She is, after all, a most hated woman.' La Roque sighed, and leaning forward, placed a hand on Dammartin's shoulder. 'Pierre, Mallington is dead. You must put this behind you and move on, for the sake of your father.'

'Perhaps you are right.' Dammartin sighed and turned his gaze to the brandy glass. The meniscus did not move. The pungent aroma drifted up to fill his nostrils amid the fading smells of cigar smoke and food and low-burning candles.

'Maybe it would be better to send Mademoiselle Mallington to travel in my company. At least then she would not be around to stir up such painful memories,' said La Roque.

Dammartin thought of Lamont's advice and for a moment he was tempted to accept his godfather's offer, but that would mean an admission of Josephine Mallington's power over him, and Dammartin was not about to admit any such thing. 'Thank you, but no. I can handle Mademoiselle Mallington.'

The Major drained the rest of his brandy and the glass hit the table with a clumsy thump. He rose from his seat. 'If you change your mind, you need only say the word. You know I only want to make things easier for you.' He swayed rather unsteadily on his feet and kissed Dammartin's cheeks. 'Goodnight, Pierre.'

'Goodnight, sir.' Dammartin made his way out into the freshness of the cool night air.

La Roque stood by the tent flap and watched him go, raising a hand to bid him good-night. He stood there a long time after Dammartin had disappeared from sight, still looking as if he could follow the Captain's trail through the blackness of night. The smile slipped from his face, and his gaze was hard and thoughtful.

Josie woke with a start, her heart beating too fast within her chest, her throat tight with emotion. She lay very still and let the image of the room in the monastery at Telemos slowly fade. She forced her breathing to slow from the ragged pant, wiped the tears from her cheeks and blew her nose.

The night was unnaturally quiet. It seemed that the silence hissed within her ears.

She pulled the blanket higher so that it tucked beneath her chin.

The moon was bright outside, casting a hint of light through the thick canvas of the tent to lift something of the pitch from the black. She forced her eyes to stay open, would not let them shut until the last of the nightmare had left her. But it seemed that nothing would stop the thoughts in her head. Even with her eyes staring up at the canvas above her head, she could see the bullets that annihilated the door within the monastery, wood splintering as if it were feeble with rot. Without mercy the nightmare pulled her once more into its clutches. Her eyes closed.

The stench of powder and blood surrounded her. The line of six men crouched across the room, her father on her left side, the bare wall on her right. It was almost as if she could feel the weight of the rifle pulling at her arms, and the terrible slowness of its loading. Her fingers did not move fast enough, snatching at bullets, fumbling with powder, and she could feel the terrible frustration at her own dull speed. The noise all around was deafening and she knew that the attack would not fail. But it was not the French who were firing through the door, it was the bandits.

Smith took a bullet in the thigh and kept on shooting. Cleeves fell without so much as a whisper, a round red hole in the white of his forehead. The men's muskets were firing twice as fast as Josie's. She heard her father's shout, *We will not surrender!* But as she looked through the disintegrating wood of the door she saw the face of the bandit laughing.

Josie sat bolt upright, suddenly, quickly awake. The blankets fell back, and, grabbing one up, she ran to the mouth of the tent, unfastening the flap with shaking fingers to stumble out into the brightness of the night.

The fat moon hung shining and high in the sky and stars were scattered as tiny jewelled pinpricks. The air was so icy as to make her gasp as she stood there, outside her tent, not moving, looking up at the sky, glad of the harshness of the cold, feeling the cleansing purge of the chilled night air enter her lungs. Out here, in the open, the drowsy drug of sleep had no power. She was awake in the here and now, and the nightmare seemed far away. So she stood with the blanket wrapped around her and let the peace enfold her.

She had no idea of what time it was, but she knew by

the empty state of the camp and the burned-down fires that it was late. The men were all in their tents asleep. Everywhere was silent.

She had only been there some few minutes when she heard the footsteps come across the grass from the direction of the horses. She turned towards her tent, then instinctively glanced back at the presence she sensed.

Dammartin was standing at the other side of what remained of the fire, the flicker of tiny flames lighting his face from below, making him appear dangerous.

A shiver swept across her stomach. She gave a small nod of her head to acknowledge his presence and turned her face back to the tent. Her fingers closed around the flap, drawing back the heavy canvas.

His feet moved. 'Mademoiselle Mallington.' His voice was as soft as a caress, and when she looked round again, he was standing right behind her.

She let the canvas slip through her fingers and turned to face him. 'Captain Dammartin,' she whispered.

He looked devastatingly handsome.

Warning bells began to ring in her head. She took a step back and felt the brush of the tent against her shift. The chill of the ground rose up through the soles of her bare feet.

'You could not sleep?' he said quietly.

'No.' A little shake of her head, and the long tresses of her hair fluttered pale and loose in the moonlight. He was looking at her with that same intense expression as last night within the tent, before Lamont's interruption. And for all that she knew that she should not, Josie could not help herself from looking right back.

They stared at one another in the silence of the surrounding night, without words. A tension that was taut between them holding them there, that neither seemed able to break.

He stepped closer, so that there was nothing to separate his long cavalry boots from the hem of her shift.

Nervousness fluttered through Josie. She glanced away, breaking the gaze that seemed to lock them together, knowing that she should not be standing here in the middle of the night talking to this man who was her captor, this very man responsible for the deaths of her father and his men. She had to go now, walk away while she still could.

'I should go.' She lowered her gaze to the polished black sheen of his boots, and made to move.

'No.'

She felt the warmth of his hand catch gently at her fingers, and glanced back up.

The moon touched a silver frosting to his hair, and revealed each and every plane that sculpted his face.

Josie stood where she was, captured by the magic of the moonlight and the man.

The fingers of one hand entwined with hers, anchoring her to the spot, while the other hand caressed her cheek, sliding down to her chin. Slowly, with a touch that seemed too light, too gentle to be from the tall, strong man that stood before her, he tilted her face up to his.

'Mademoiselle Mallington,' he said softly. 'Josephine.' And his eyes were filled with a depth of emotion she had not seen before and such promise.

She knew that he would kiss her, and, Lord help her, but she wanted him to, so very much.

His mouth lowered towards hers.

She stood on tiptoe and reached her face up, her lips parting in expectation.

He took her with such gentle possession as to wipe everything else from her mind, and it seemed to Josie as if she had waited all her life for this moment, this wonderful, amazing sensation that was so much more than just a kiss.

His arms stretched around her, holding her to him, his palms warm and enticing against her back, stroking her, caressing her. She ran her hands up the wool of his coat, feeling the strength of the muscle across his back. And amid the warmth of him, the smell of him, the brandied taste of him, was the feeling that this was meant to be, that she had met her destiny, and nothing had ever felt so right.

She did not remember that he was the enemy. She forgot all about her father and the terrible events of Telemos and the bandits. She lost herself in his kiss and for Josie, in that moment, there was nothing else.

He kissed her gently, undemanding, revelling in the sweetness of her. She tasted of innocence, of all that was goodness and light, and her purity cleansed the darkness from Dammartin's soul.

For so long he had thought of nothing other than wreaking vengeance upon the man who had murdered his father. And now that man's daughter was in his arms, and there was in her something so incorruptible and pure that she filled his very mind and there was no room for thoughts of his father or hers, no room for any other thoughts at all.

He wanted her, all of her, every last bit of her, all of her warmth, all of her softness, all of her comfort. She was like a fine down pillow on which a man might lay his head and never wish to rise. He wanted her and his body ached with the need.

She met his mouth with encouragement, but in it he knew her innocence. The small, soft movements of her hands against his back and the press of her body against his warmed his blood to a fire so that it seemed that he was not in the barren winter plains of Iberia but somewhere else altogether. Dammartin had never known a feeling like it, and he wanted it never to stop.

His hand slid beneath the blanket, feeling the curves of her woman's body through the thin linen of her borrowed shift, knowing that only it separated him from her nakedness. He cupped her buttocks, pressing her closer to his hardness as his tongue entwined with hers in such erotic play to leave him breathless with desire.

'Josephine,' he whispered, and gentled the kiss against her lips so that he might look down into her eyes. He stroked the silk of her hair, stroked the softness of her cheek, felt the raggedness of her breath against his fingers.

'Captain Dammartin,' she said, and he heard his need mirrored in her breathy words.

'Pierre,' he said, 'my name is Pierre.'

'Pierre,' she whispered as his mouth closed again on hers.

He wanted her, wanted her more than life itself.

A noise sounded. He glanced towards the tent that he shared with his lieutenant and sergeant—movement, the sleepy clambering of a man with a need in the night.

He reacted in an instant, pushing her within the flap of her tent and moving quickly round to the other side of the fire to retrace the steps he had taken not so very long ago, pretending that he had only just returned.

Molyneux appeared at the mouth of the tent, his hair ruffled, his expression sleepy. 'Captain?' He yawned.

'I hope you have not stolen my bloody blankets again,' said Dammartin.

'Not this time,' said Molyneux, and, crawling from the tent, pulled his boots on and made his way across the field to the latrines.

Dammartin said nothing, just entered the tent, and stripped off his clothes as best he could in the dark. As he lay down in his bed, he could still taste her sweetness on his lips. And he knew that this battle with his desire for Josephine Mallington was going to be a great deal more difficult than anticipated.

Josie lay flat on her back in her tent, the blankets loose around her. For once she was not cold. Her whole body tingled with warmth, and her lips felt hot and swollen where Captain Dammartin had kissed her. She touched a finger gently to their surface, as if she could not believe what had just passed between herself and the French Captain. And in truth she did not. Yet even as she lay there with her heart still thudding and her blood still rushing, her eyes slipped to the canvas wall on her left-hand side through which was the tent in which Dammartin slept, so close that she could have called his name in a soft voice and he would have heard her.

A strange kind of vibrancy flowed through her and it seemed to Josie that she had never felt more alive. She forgot all that had gone before, all of the bandit's attack, all of the anxiety of the 60th's sacrifice, all of the horror of Telemos. For the first time since that terrible day, Josie felt glad to be alive. She would not sleep, she told herself. Her body hummed with wakefulness and something that was almost joy. She closed her eyes, and sleep surrounded her like a warm woollen cloak. Josie sank into it without even knowing that she did so. She was cosy and cosseted within its dark comfort, and her sleep was untroubled.

'You say that he kissed her?' Major La Roque narrowed his eyes and peered at the man before him.

'Yes, sir, and with a great deal of passion.'

'And there have been no other incidents of this nature?'

'No, sir, apart from those of which you already know:

when he kissed her in punishment for her slapping him, and in his tent the other evening he had her in his arms. Had not Lamont interrupted them, I believe that he would have kissed her then.'

'And the night they left the campsite together, you are sure there was nothing then?'

'Nothing other than talk.'

'And what talk! The journals will prove most useful. You have done well so far. Your loyalty will not go unrewarded.'

Lieutenant Molyneux smiled and took the proffered glass of brandy from Major La Roque's hand. 'Thank you, sir.'

'So, there is something between Captain Dammartin and Mallington's daughter. What do you think of that?'

Molyneux sipped the brandy from the glass that he had been given and looked cagily at his superior officer. 'I confess I find it most surprising, sir, given the history of their fathers.'

'It is a damnable abomination, that's what it is.' La Roque poured the rest of the brandy down his throat and set the glass down hard upon the table. 'What is she like, this Mademoiselle Mallington? Is she pretty? Does she have a figure to drive a man's senses from his head?'

Molyneux cleared his throat, unsure of how much to reveal.

'Come, come, Molyneux, do not be shy. Tell me, do you find her distasteful?'

The Lieutenant swallowed hard. 'No, she is…a most attractive woman.'

'Good.'

Molyneux glanced up quickly, the surprise clear across his face.

'Captain Dammartin does not know what he is doing. The shock of meeting Mallington has affected him. But he will disgrace himself if we let him continue as he is. This Mallington woman will turn him into a laughingstock. The next thing we know, he will be crawling between her legs. What would the Emperor say to that? Jean Dammartin's son ploughing Mallington's daughter!'

Molyneux kept quiet.

'Jean would turn in his grave,' said La Roque. 'Dammartin was my friend. I saw what that bastard Mallington did to him. And I've still got the scars of what he did to me.'

Molyneux nodded, placatingly.

'It is up to us to protect Captain Dammartin.'

'Yes, sir. Perhaps you could forbid him from seeing her, move her into the care of another company.'

'You have much to learn of human nature, Molyneux. If I take her from him, all I shall succeed in doing is to make him want her all the more. No, we must be a little more clever than that…'

Molyneux took another sip of brandy.

'I have another little job for you, Lieutenant.'

'Sir?'

The Major smiled. 'It might not be all that bad if you try to forget who she is, and you did say that you found her attractive.'

Molyneux looked across at La Roque.

'I have heard that you have quite a reputation with the women, Lieutenant, so I am sure that what I ask will not be beyond you. We must all do what we can for the good of our country, must we not, Lieutenant?'

'We must, sir.'

'Good, for here is what I want you to do…'

Josie awoke the next morning in a panic, her eyes springing open immediately.

She could hear the milling about of soldiers. Footsteps,

chatter, clank of mess tins, the smoky aroma of coffee and of burnt wood. Daylight shone bright through the paleness of the canvas.

There was only one thought in her head and that was the French Captain's kiss. Dammartin had kissed her and she had kissed him back with just as much vigour, and with every bit as much wanting. She gave a groan and buried her face against the pillow.

She had kissed him! He was French and her captor. He was the captain of the force that had destroyed her father and his men. He was the man that believed her father guilty of a heinous crime. Josie clutched a hand to her forehead. *Fraternising with the enemy*—the phrase seemed to taunt her.

What was this madness that seemed now to overcome her in Dammartin's presence? Nothing could excuse it. Her behaviour was worse than reprehensible. She was a disgrace to the British, a disgrace to her father and the men of the 60th that had died. And yet if Dammartin strode into her tent this very moment and took her in his arms, she could not trust her foolish, selfish, traitorous heart that she would not kiss him again.

She got to her feet, pulled on her borrowed clothes and began to fold up her bedding.

'Pardon, Mademoiselle Mallington.'

The voice from the tent flap made her jump and she thought for a moment that it was Dammartin. Her heart began to race and the blanket that she had been folding slipped from her fingers. She turned to face him.

But it was not Dammartin that stood there.

'Lieutenant Molyneux.' She was caught unawares, her thoughts still lingering with Dammartin. 'Is there any news of my portmanteau?' she asked, smoothing back her hair with a flustered hand and wondering why the Lieutenant was here. Only Dammartin strode straight into the tent.

'Unfortunately not, *mademoiselle*. It is not easy to lose all of one's possessions.'

'No, but Rosa has been kind enough to lend me some clothing.' Josie suddenly remembered that she was, at this very minute, wearing the red-and-black dress, and without the protection of her cloak. She darted a rather horrified glance at the Lieutenant, but he was looking at the bedding she had been folding and his expression was kindly. Molyneux was too much the gentleman to stare at what the dress revealed.

'The Captain has sent me to collect your possessions to be transported this morning, *mademoiselle*.'

'Of course, Lieutenant. I am afraid that my clothes are still damp.'

'There has been little chance for them to dry.'

She sat the clothing on top of the blankets and pillow and passed the pile to Molyneux.

'At least it does not rain this morning.' He smiled. 'You see, you are making me like the English with all this talk of the weather,' he teased.

Molyneux's kind lightheartedness dispelled her tension. She felt herself smile in response as she opened the tent flap for him to leave. Across the field, Dammartin was talking to Lamont. The smile fled her face. Her heart began to race as her eyes met his. The expression on his face was hard and angry. All of the darkness was back, and she wondered that he could be the same man who had kissed her with such passion and tenderness last night. And as she looked, he coldly turned his gaze from hers.

Dammartin, together with half his men, watched Molyneux leave Mademoiselle Mallington's tent, the Lieuten-

ant's arms piled high with her clothing and bedding. He
saw, as did the men, the way she held the tent flap open
for him, and smiled so sweetly. His eyes noted how very
well the fully exposed red-and-black dress showed off her
figure. The men's tongues were practically hanging out
over the sight of her as she stood so boldly in the entrance
of the tent.

The tent flap had barely closed before Molyneux managed to drop half her clothing upon the wetness of the
ground; when he had gathered it back up again, Mademoiselle Mallington's shift was clearly displayed on the
top, while one of her stockings dangled precariously from
the side.

'Captain,' said Molyneux, when he reached him. 'Mademoiselle Mallington asked me to carry this.'

'Then carry it,' said Dammartin coolly.

From among the troopers someone laughed.

'See to your horses,' he snapped at them, and the men
exchanged glances as they moved to follow his command.

It was late afternoon when they had set up their camp
for the night near Hoyos. The light had gone by the time
the meal was ready, paltry as it was—a thin stew of onions
with the odd lump of meat. Supplies were running low
and the foraging parties had come back with little. Having
finished the dregs of the insubstantial meal, Dammartin
was sitting at his desk within the shared tent, writing his
report. The men would go hungry again tonight. He had
just dipped his pen into the ink when Lamont appeared.

'Sir.'

Dammartin glanced up at him, and, seeing the expression on his sergeant's face, laid the pen down within its
holder. 'What is it, Claude?' he asked quietly.

Lamont's voice lowered. 'Lieutenant Molyenux is within your tent with Mademoiselle Mallington.'

'They are alone together?'

Lamont nodded.

Dammartin quirked an eyebrow. 'It is up to Mademoiselle Mallington how she conducts herself.'

'There is something that you should see, sir.'

Dammartin stilled. Lamont would not have come to fetch him if it were not necessary. He gave a grim nod and followed the older man outside.

He could hear the men's appreciative murmurs as they stared. His gaze followed round to what their attention was so riveted upon. His tent was light and illuminated, the canvas the perfect screen on which the silhouettes of those within were projected. Josephine and Molyneux were standing close. They were talking, and Josephine had taken Molyneux's hand up between hers. Her head was bent as if she would kiss his hand. It was a most intimate gesture and one that roused a fury in Dammartin.

He had thought her an innocent. He had thought that the attraction that had exploded between them was unique and special. The shadow show playing out on Mademoiselle Mallington's tent showed him that he had been wrong. His lip snarled in disgust at his own weakness. She was Mallington's daughter, in truth.

He became aware of his men's attention, that they were watching to see what he would do. And his pride burned sore. He wanted to go in there and pulverise Molyneux's perfect handsome face. He wanted to call Josephine Mallington the whore that she was.

'Captain.' Lamont's voice was low, his hand touched lightly against Dammartin's arm to stay him.

'The men are expecting a show, Claude. It would be a pity to disappoint them.'

'Pierre,' Lamont whispered with urgency. 'Think how you do this.'

'Do not worry,' said Dammartin, and his mouth curved to a hard cynical smile. 'I shall not give them quite the show they are expecting.' And with that he walked towards his tent.

Chapter Ten

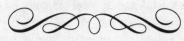

Josie was adjusting Molyneux's hand within her own directly beneath the bright hanging light of the lantern to peer closer at his palm.

'I feel so foolish to bother you with such a trivial complaint,' said the Lieutenant sheepishly.

'I am afraid that I still cannot see it properly, sir.'

'The light, it is poor and I fear I have driven the wretched thing deeper when I tried to pull it out. I would not ask, but I fear the infection will grow.' He looked up at her, anxiety clear in his velvet grey eyes. 'It is my sabre hand.'

'Do not worry, I will fetch the splinter out for you.' She smiled wryly.

'Perhaps you think me less than a man to worry over such a small thing, but I watched my good friend die because of a dirty splinter of wood. He thought it nothing, and left it where it was. Two months later, he was dead from a poisoning of the blood.'

Josie's heart softened at his words. 'I am sorry that you lost your friend.' Her eyes met his briefly in compassion before she turned her focus to his hand once more. The small sewing needle between her fingers glinted in the light. 'Now hold still and I will soon have the splinter out.'

He smiled at her.

She bent her head and concentrated on a delicate probing of the Lieutenant's hand with the needle. It was strange to notice that, as she held on to Molyneux's hand, his touch elicited none of the same reactions that she had experienced with Dammartin. Had it been Dammartin's hand held so gently between her own…

'Mademoiselle Mallington and Lieutenant Molyneux.' There was no mistaking the steel beneath the quiet control of the voice.

Josie gave a gasp and jumped, inadvertently pricking Molyneux with the needle.

Dammartin stood within the tent. The line of his jaw was hard and uncompromising, and his eyes filled with a deadly darkness.

Molyneux paled and drew his hand swiftly from Josie's grasp.

'Captain Dammartin,' she said, her heart suddenly racing. 'You startled me.'

'So I see, *mademoiselle*.' His voice was harsh.

Outside the murmur of voices had gone; the camp was in total silence.

'Lieutenant Molyneux has a splinter in his hand. I am in the process of removing it. If you do not mind, I shall have it out shortly.'

'Please, go ahead. Do not allow my presence to stop you,' said Dammartin. 'I am content to wait.'

Josie ignored his sarcastic tone. She reached for Molyneux's hand, conscious of Dammartin's scrutiny.

'It is no matter, *mademoiselle*.' Molyneux stepped away, looking awkwardly at Dammartin. *'Capitaine,'* he said, and, with a salute, hurriedly left.

Josie was alone with Dammartin.

She stood unmoving beneath the lantern light, the small needle flashing silver in her hand. She could sense his tension. It was latent, coiled, ready to spring, the calm before the storm. She did not know what had happened to make him so angry, yet she had the unassailable notion that it was related to Molyneux and her removing the splinter. Very carefully, she set the needle down upon the tabletop.

'Is there something wrong, sir?' She forced her voice to stay calm and low.

He walked towards her and stopped where Molyneux had stood.

Josie's heart was thudding so hard it seemed to echo within the silence that surrounded them.

He glanced at the table to where the needle lay. 'You were removing a splinter?'

'Yes. What else did you think that I was doing?'

Every angle of his face sharpened. His eyes narrowed ever so slightly. The scar was livid against his cheek. Everything about him was dark and predatory and dangerous. 'What else indeed might a woman standing so close to a man and holding his hand within her own be doing? Every dragoon in this company has been asking himself that question this evening. The lantern, it lights your silhouettes so well.'

She flushed scarlet at his implication. 'I have done nothing improper.' Even as she said it, the realisation of just how her actions might have been misconstrued was dawning on her. But beneath Dammartin's cold, arrogant stare she was not about to admit any such thing. 'And if the lantern has shown my actions so clearly to all, then every man here should know that.'

His eyes were on her, hard and disbelieving, razing all of her defences. She made to move, but as she did so he reached up above their heads and quickly extinguished the lantern. The darkness was sudden and complete.

Josie gasped, and froze where she was. 'What are you doing?'

'I do not mean to continue the night's entertainment for the men.'

The thick blackness that surrounded them hid him from her, but every inch of her body tingled with awareness of his proximity.

'This is madness. You cannot mean to continue a conversation in the dark.'

'I do not mean to continue a conversation at all, *mademoiselle.*'

The skin at the nape of Josie's neck prickled. The drum of warning beat through her veins. She licked her lips nervously, and whispered, 'Then you should leave.'

She heard him move closer.

'But I am not yet finished with you, *mademoiselle*,' he said quietly.

A shiver rippled through her, and she felt her nipples harden as if a rush of cold air had blown through her. 'If you will not go, then I will,' she replied and, thrusting out her arms before her, she began to step hesitantly through the darkness towards where there was some light at the entrance of the tent.

There was the tread of his boots, and the sensation of movement. As the panic began to rise, she quickened her steps and reached out towards the tent flap.

His arm fastened around her waist and Josie knew that there would be no running away from this.

'No,' she whispered, but whether it was to Dammartin or herself, she did not know.

He came up behind her, pulling her closer until her back was snug against him, her buttocks at his groin. She felt his palm splay over her abdomen, holding her in place, while his other hand closed over her breast.

While his hands imprisoned her, she felt the moist touch of his mouth on the skin at the side of her neck, where her pulse throbbed so violently. The touch became a kiss, a slow tantalising kiss that grew hungrier and hungrier until his lips were sucking her and his tongue was lapping her as if he would draw the very lifeblood from her veins. And as his kiss possessed her, his hand slid lower down her belly, stroking and teasing it went, creeping ever closer to that most secret of her woman's places. His fingers roved over one breast as if the cotton of Rosa's chemise were not there, feeling her, claiming her, circling her taut and straining nipple.

She gasped aloud, amazed both at his audacity and the sensations flowing within her. Somewhere on the outer recesses of her mind a faint voice whispered that this was wrong, that she should stop, but Josie barely heard it. She was quivering beneath his touch, trembling with the need for it never to cease. And when his fingers loosed her buttons, and freed the pins from her hair, she barely noticed, just turned to him and let him take her, kissing his lips, breathing his breath.

He pulled the bodice of her dress and chemise down, his hands cupping her breasts though the linen of her shift, stroking them, petting them, rolling her hardened nipples between his fingers as his mouth moved against hers. And just when she thought the pleasure could not be any greater, he dropped to his knees, pulling her down with him, to lay her beneath him. She heard his breath as ragged as hers, felt the urgency that strained throughout the entirety of his body as his mouth traced lower to close hot and wet over her breast, devouring her through the thin material.

The sensation was so overwhelming, so ecstatic that she was endlessly gasping. There was the sound of linen tearing, and her shift separated them no more. He suckled her bare breasts, first one and then the other, his mouth ranging over their mounds until it fastened upon her nipples, to suck and lick and tease. Josie groaned and arched beneath him, threading her fingers through his hair, pressing him to her that he might never stop. And still it was not enough, still she wanted more of him.

'Oh, Pierre!' she moaned, feeling him nudge her legs open while his mouth stayed busy against her breast.

Then he seemed to catch himself, to stop. She felt his face come up to hers, his breath hot against her mouth.

'No,' he whispered in disbelief. He was panting hard and she could feel the slight tremor that ran through him.

Through the darkness she sensed his face move back to stare at her. 'God help me.' His voice was low and gritty and filled with agony.

Gentle fingers stroked her cheek as he collapsed down to lay by her side, holding her gently against him as his lips dropped small, isolated kisses to her forehead.

'God help us both, Josephine Mallington,' he said softly into her hair, and Josie lay in his arms, knowing that his prayer was futile.

Her tight, sensitised nipples still moist with his saliva and her unsated desire were the evidence. She craved his kiss. She needed his touch. Josie had stepped beyond redemption. Pierre Dammartin was no longer her enemy, but her temptation, and it made a mockery of the sacrifice in Telemos, of her father's death and those of the men of the 60th; it made a mockery of everything in which Josie believed.

Dammartin's men saw him leave the English *mademoiselle*'s tent. They saw, too, the harshness of his face and they wondered what had happened within those canvas walls. Would the Captain be prepared to share the woman with his lieutenant? From his face it did not seem so. The men began to take bets on the outcome.

The first thing that Dammartin saw on leaving Josephine Mallington was Molyneux sitting over at the farthest side of the fire. The two men's gaze met and held for a few seconds until the Lieutenant looked away.

Dammartin strolled to stand by the fire directly opposite to where Molyneux sat near to Lamont.

Lamont quietly slipped away to stand by some troopers.

Molyneux got to his feet, looking nervously across at Dammartin. He cleared his throat. 'She offered to remove a splinter from my hand, sir.'

Dammartin said nothing.

'She was most insistent. I did not wish to be rude. She fetched the needle and before I knew it…' His voice trailed off.

Still Dammartin said nothing, just looked at Molyneux as if he would tear the Lieutenant's head from his body.

'I did not realise that she…that you…' Molyneux cleared his throat again.

Dammartin paused long enough to make Molyneux squirm. 'What are you still doing within my line of vision, Lieutenant?'

A moment's hesitation and then Molyneux saluted and walked quickly away.

Dammartin stood there alone for a few moments, staring into the flames of the fire, then he turned and headed towards the stables, and not long after, the sound of his horse was heard galloping away into the night.

Josie had slept little, but she was up and ready early, sitting on the chair by Dammartin's table within his tent. Her stomach was churning, and she both dreaded and desired to see Dammartin again. What had occurred between them last night had shocked her. She had not known herself capable of such…such wantonness. She thought again of his mouth, hot and hard against her breast. Her nipples tightened at the memory and her cheeks flushed warm. Beyond redemption indeed.

For all of her determination, for all that he was and had done, when he was near, when he touched her, when he as much as looked at her, she could not help herself from wanting his kiss. She was within his power, and yet last night there had been the sensation that it was he who was within hers. Dammartin did not want this any more than she did. There had been anguish and torment in his voice. *God help me*, he had said, *God help us both*.

This craving that linked them together was beyond both their controls, and it frightened her to think where it would lead, so Josie did not allow herself to think. One day at a time, she told herself, one hour, one minute, one second. She could not hide for ever. With her cloak wrapped around her, she stepped out to face the aftermath of the night.

Lieutenant Molyneux was sitting outside altering some tack for his horse. He nodded good morning, but did not speak.

Dammartin was over speaking to a small group of dragoons. He gave no sign of having seen her.

Josie stood there.

Molyneux kept his head bent, concentrating on his task in hand. Men arrived and began to remove the furniture and baggage, first from the officers' tent and then from her own. They cast looks of overt interest towards her and their lieutenant, but what they said was a low murmur and could not be heard. She walked over and waited by her horse. All around her men worked to deconstruct their camp, to ready themselves and their mounts. No one spoke to her. She waited alone, the men leaving a wide space around her.

Josie adjusted the strap of the leather satchel that still hung around her. It did not need to be adjusted, but she felt so uncomfortable, just standing there, that it made her feel better to pretend to be doing something. The satchel was adjusted and lay against her hip. And still Josie waited.

At last Molyneux came to set up his mount. She caught his eye, but he just murmured, '*Mademoiselle,*' and looked away.

A little seed of dread sprouted in her stomach. For all of the discomfort of facing the men of the 8th this morning, of facing Molyneux, she knew something far worse was coming. She could feel it in her bones. She turned her face to the little horse, and taking off her gloves, began to stroke its smooth neck. Her fingers rubbed at the soft muzzle.

'Fleur,' she whispered softly, and was glad when the mare blew softly against her fingers and licked at her hand. She did not look again at Molyneux or the men around her, but kept her focus fixed solely on the little horse. Something brushed against her shoulder, warm breath blew against her, and something moist nuzzled against her neck. Josie gave a yelp of surprise.

'Dante!' She turned to find Dammartin's great war-horse at her shoulder. He stood tall, perhaps seventeen hands high, his chestnut coat glossy in the sunlight, quite dwarfing Josie and the little mare by her side. The horse was trained for battle: long, muscular legs to carry his rider with speed in the charge towards the lines of British infantry, strong hooves that would rear and smash a man's skull, and a mouth taught to bite hard and mean.

Dante had heard the drums beating for war many times, he was not afraid of the roar of cannons or the screams of men. He knew what he was to do. He was a killer every bit as much as the man that sat upon his back. But not this morning.

The saddle and stirrups had not yet been fitted to his back. He wore the thickly sewn sheepskins that Dammartin covered him with through the cold of the night. His eyes were dark and soft and soulful and he was determined that Josie would feed him the nuts that his master normally brought. But Josie had nothing to give him. He nosed at her stomach, inadvertently pushing her back against Fleur. Then he nibbled at the tie to her cloak and knocked the hat from her head

'Dante!' Dammartin's voice sounded close by, and then the big chestnut horse was being pulled away from Josie.

'Captain Dammartin.'

'Mademoiselle Mallington. Did he hurt you?' He kept his face impassive.

She looked very small and slender this morning, and his heart had skipped a beat when he saw her pressed between the two horses. One move and Dante would have her crushed. Dammartin had made his way swiftly over. And now Dante was at his back and Josephine Mallington before him, her eyes a vivid blue within the pale oval of her face. Some of her pins had been loosened and a few long strands of hair had escaped to hang down the side of her face, their pale trail stark against the bodice of her own high-necked, dark blue dress, and he thought of the red-and-black Spanish dress that he had stripped from her breasts last night. He saw the colour rise in her cheeks. Desire tightened his gut.

'No. He is just looking for his treat.'

They looked at each other in the bright light of morning,

before Dammartin stooped to retrieve her hat from where Dante had knocked it to the ground. He handed it to her.

'Thank you.' Their fingers brushed, gloveless, bare, and he felt her jump before he drew his hand away. Her blush deepened.

He told himself again that what he was doing today was for the best. This thing between them had been released in earnest and would never be recaptured. It would not be hidden or suppressed. It would not be ignored or broken. Its strength was far beyond anything of willpower. It was a living, growing thing, spiralling out of control...and it would destroy them both if he let it.

She fixed the hat back on her head and fitted the gloves on to her hands. She no longer looked at him, but the scald still marked her cheeks.

He would tell her now. He had to, for they would come for her soon. 'Josephine,' he said softly. 'What happened last night, what has been growing between us...this attraction...' He groped for the best words to convey his meaning. 'It cannot be allowed to exist, for the sake of our fathers, for the sake of our honour. And so, because of this, there has been a change of plan.'

She glanced up at him and he could see the question in her eyes.

He forced himself to continue. 'From today you no longer ride with the 8th. You shall be in the care of the 47th Regiment of Line and Major La Roque.' He held her gaze. 'You asked me once of witnesses to my father's murder. Major La Roque was my father's closest friend. It was he who was with him at Oporto when my father died.' And he wondered if he was telling her this as some kind of reparation to make up for the fact that he was sending her away.

'Thank you for telling me.'

He gave a small nod of acknowledgement.

Silence and awkwardness stood between them.

'It is for the best that you must go,' he said.

'Yes.'

Dammartin's hands itched to pull her into his arms. His fingers gripped together behind his back. There was nothing more he could say.

'When do I leave?'

Dammartin was struck anew by her courage and her dignity.

The sound of horses' hooves sounded in the distance.

They both glanced towards the road. They both knew who was coming.

'Now,' he said.

Two infantry officers of La Roque's first company came into the field and dismounted. They were being directed to where Dammartin stood with Josie.

She saw them coming.

'You may take Fleur.' Another salve for the wound.

'Thank you.' She was watching the officers in their blue coats and black shakos cross the field towards her. When they had almost reached her, she turned to him and said, 'Did you take my portmanteau?'

'No, Josephine, I did not.'

Then the officers of the 47th were there saluting him. He moved to help her climb up on to Fleur, but she stepped quickly and pulled herself up without the need for his hand.

'Goodbye, Captain Dammartin.' She looked at him for one last time and what he saw in her face stilled the breath in his throat and made him want to pull her back down from the horse and send La Roque's men away empty-handed.

'Goodbye, Mademoiselle Mallington.'

She twitched her heels and the small grey moved off, flanked by the two larger mounts of the officers. Her back was ramrod straight as they moved slowly across the field, breaking into a trot when they came close to the road. Dammartin stood and watched until Josephine Mallington disappeared from sight.

Josie followed the officers down the road at the side of the camp to where the infantrymen had pitched their tents. She could see another small party of officers ahead on horseback, and took a deep breath, steeling herself for what was to come.

She knew La Roque before he even spoke. His jacket was of the Emperor's blue with white facings and gilt buttons. On his left shoulder he wore a full epaulet and on his right, a contre-epaulet without the fringes; both were gilt and a fine contrast to the red collar and cuffs upon his jacket. Around his neck, fitting snug beneath his collar, sat his metal badge of office—a gilt gorget—and at his left hip hung his sword with its golden tassels around the hilt. The pure white of his breeches and the shine on his riding boots struck Josie as strange, given that they had spent the past days riding through such hostile terrain. On his head he wore a black bicorne hat as befitted his rank, complete with a white pompom and a small circular tricolour in the centre and tassels of gold at either corner.

He was not as old as she had expected. His hair was dark slashed with silver, his face full from too much good living. Across his top lip sat a large moustache. He would have been what was termed a handsome man in his youth, and the semblance of it could still be seen in him. She met the gaze of those pale silver-grey eyes, and knew that this was the man who had lied about her father and something twisted in her stomach.

He smiled and his teeth were white and even.

When he spoke, his voice held the heavy accent of his country. 'We meet at last, Mademoiselle Mallington.'

'Major La Roque,' she said, but she did not return his smile.

'You come into my care now.'

She said nothing.

'The *47e Régiment d'Infanterie de Ligne* shall convey you in safety. We do not harm our prisoners.'

The unspoken accusation hung between them. She knew that he was baiting her.

She gave no reply.

'Do you know that I met your father once?'

'So I have heard,' she said.

He arched a silver brow. 'Perhaps Lieutenant Colonel Mallington spoke of me?'

'He did not.'

'Or of Major Jean Dammartin, the man that he murdered.'

She bit back the response that she would have given him, taking her time to fashion some civility into it. 'My father was no murderer.'

The Major looked round at the officers surrounding them, smiling as if she had just cracked a joke. 'Her loyalty is admirable.'

'My father did not kill Jean Dammartin.'

'I saw him with my own eyes, *mademoiselle*. Perhaps you do not know that I was with him when he died, or that your father tried to kill me too.'

'I know that is the story that is told.'

She could almost hear the sudden intake of breath from the surrounding group of officers.

But La Roque just smiled. 'What can you be implying, Mademoiselle Mallington?'

'I am implying nothing,' she said. 'But I know that my father did not kill Major Dammartin.'

La Roque shook his head sorrowfully. 'Poor child. How difficult it is to face the truth.'

Josie bit back what she would have said.

'I trust Captain Dammartin treated you well?'

'He did, thank you.'

'He is very like his father, you know—a fine man and a good soldier for France. Such a shame that your father murdered his in the most dishonourable of ways. How he must hate you, *mademoiselle*.'

Once there had been hatred between her and Dammartin, but not any more. Josie lowered her face to hide the truth.

La Roque leaned forward in his saddle and said quietly, 'It is little wonder he makes a whore of you.' He sat back and smiled again. 'You will be escorted today by Lieutenant Donadieu. Such a pleasure to welcome you to our company, *mademoiselle*.' The Major turned his horse around and, together with his officers, made his way slowly up the side of the thick column of infantry.

One man stayed behind, a young man with fairish hair and a soft pink complexion—Lieutenant Donadieu—a man-boy, hardly old enough to be out of his school gown. But Josie barely noticed him. She was watching the retreating figure of Major La Roque, and hearing again the cruelty of his words.

'Mademoiselle Mallington.'

She turned her eyes slowly to Lieutenant Donadieu.

He was looking at her with undisguised disgust.

She met his gaze and held it defiantly, daring him to say the words that his face so clearly expressed.

Donadieu averted his eyes and led off.

Josie had no choice but to follow.

The sky above was blue and clear. The sunlight was bright and white. Birdsong sounded over the noise of horses' hooves. But to all of these things Josie was both blind and deaf. The column of French infantry moved forward.

In the day that followed Josie came to realise what being a prisoner of the 47th Regiment of the Line meant, and, try as she might to remain unaffected, she found herself growing more and more miserable. None of the officers or men spoke to her. They looked at her plenty, their expressions ranging from curiosity to pity to blatant dislike. Lieutenant Donadieu was not like Lieutenant Molyneux. He rode close to her, but that was all. He did not bring her anything to eat or drink. He did not make conversation or strive to turn her mind away from the misery of the march to lighter things.

Donadieu was at her side. Four officers and Major La Roque rode ahead. Four hundred men formed the column of the 47th. Before them rode one-hundred-and-twenty cavalrymen, and Captain Dammartin. Over five hundred men. And amidst them all Josie was alone.

La Roque rested the men halfway through the day's march. As with Dammartin's dragoons, there was no time to cook a meal; instead, bread and hard biscuits were distributed. The men ate and drank the water from their canteens, sitting spread on the ground in uneven clusters, some resting, some even sleeping.

Donadieu left her in the middle of a group of his fusiliers, a clear space of ground separating her from the infantrymen in their imperial-blue coats with their distinctive white facings and cross-belts, and matching dirty white pantaloons. Like La Roque, their collar and cuffs were red. Most of them had taken off their shakos as they lounged, leaving their hats lying on the ground beside their knapsacks and rolled greatcoats. They watched her with interest. She could hear their conversations quite clearly, for they did not think that she could understand, and they did not care. Some called her the murderer's daughter, some speculated as to why Dammartin had kept her for a week before sending her to La Roque. Most of the comments were so crudely obscene as to send an angry blush to her cheeks.

She sat alone, and pretended that she could hear none of them. Yet still she listened and she learned that the French thought La Roque a hero and that they anticipated that they would reach Ciudad Rodrigo late the next day. Only twenty-four hours. She had endured much more. She could endure this.

Chapter Eleven

That night Lieutenant Donadieu delivered her to the large tent that was erected for the women of the baggage train. The women, who were for the main part French, remained distant. They knew who she was judging from the ferocity of their comments, yet not one woman said anything to her face; they just looked at her with cold eyes and sullen mouths. These were the women who were wives to the ordinary soldiers and non-commissioned officers. These, too, were the women who were whores to whatever man would pay for their services.

She knew some of the women's faces from having seen them come into the 8th's camp, and she knew Rosa, the only woman who displayed any vestige of friendliness towards her. It was Rosa who gave her a mess tin and spoon, and Rosa that made sure that Josie had food and water that evening. And for that Josie could only be glad.

The two women ate their stew.

'Will you stay travelling with the French?' Josie chewed at a small, fatty lump of meat.

Rosa lifted a suspicious face. 'Why do you ask?'

'I just wondered.' Josie thought of what Dammartin had told her of Rosa's history.

Rosa seemed to accept Josie's answer. 'Where Claude goes, then I go too.'

'And after the war?'

She shrugged. 'Still then I follow him. There is nothing in Spain any more for me, there is only Claude.'

'Do you love him?'

'Yes.' Rosa smiled at that. 'Do you love, *señorita*?'

'I loved my parents and my brother.'

'And Captain Dammartin,' Rosa said, and her dark beautiful eyes seemed too knowing to Josie. 'Do you love him?'

'No!' she exclaimed. 'Of course not. He is my enemy. It is because of him that my father and all of his men are dead.' But as she said it, there was the small, insistent thought in her head that her words were not true. Dammartin had given them more than enough chance to surrender. He had wanted Lieutenant Colonel Mallington taken alive. It was her father himself who had signed all their death warrants—so that the information might reach Wellington.

Rosa's eyebrows raised by the smallest degree. 'That is no difference if you love him. I see his eyes on you, and I see, too, your eyes on him, *señorita*.'

Heat scalded Josie's cheeks scarlet. 'I do not love him!' She did not understand this thing between her and Pierre Dammartin, but it was not love, it could not possibly be love.

'You say no too many times, too loudly. Who do you try to convince, *señorita*, me, or you?'

Josie's eyes widened. 'You are mistaken, Señora Rosa,' she said coolly.

The hint of a smile touched to Rosa's lips, but she said nothing more.

They sat in silence for a few minutes, Josie feeling angry and embarrassed, Rosa seemingly contented. It was Rosa who recommenced the conversation.

'What will they do with you at Ciudad Rodrigo?'

'Send me back to Santarém, to General Massena,' said Josie, relieved at the change of subject from Dammartin. 'He will exchange me for a French prisoner of war held by the British—I hope.'

'And then?'

And then? It was the question that Josie had not yet dared to ask herself. What would happen? 'I suppose I will be sent back to England.'

'To your mother?'

'My mother is dead.'

'I am sorry.'

'She died four years ago.' Josie scraped her spoon at some invisible contents of the mess tin. 'My brother was in the cavalry. He was killed two years ago. There is no one waiting for me at home.'

'You have an aunt, an uncle, cousins?'

'No one.'

'Then where will you go?'

Josie set the mess tin and spoon down, and did not look at Rosa. 'My father's friend and his wife were kind enough to let me stay with them last year. They might be willing to help me arrange a position of some sort—a ladies' companion, perhaps.' But she held little hope and much dread.

She had no skills that would be of use in genteel life in England. She was useless to the point of being inept at any formal social occasion. She could not sing or play music, or paint or embroider. Her voice had been commented upon as being dull and her conversation even duller. Before the ladies of the *ton* Josie's mind was sure to go blank. She knew not one thing that would be of any interest to such women. It would be that dreadful year all over again, being forced into a society into which she did not fit. The prospect of such a future seemed unbearable. Josie looked up suddenly at Rosa, unaware that all her fears showed in her eyes.

Rosa touched a hand to Josie's arm in a token of comfort. 'You and I, we are the same. Without father or husband, without home.'

Josie averted her gaze.

But Rosa continued just the same. 'But we are strong. We survive. Claude, he save my life. Captain Dammartin, he save yours. There is nothing in Spain for me, there is only Claude. For you it is England and another man.'

'Rosa, no—'

'We are sisters.'

Josie left her words unspoken.

The two women looked at one another, a bond of friendship forming.

'Thank you, Rosa, your kindness means much to me.'

Later that evening Rosa left the women's tent to go to Lamont. Josie stayed alone, sitting cross-legged on the blanket bed, trying to repair her torn shift. One stitch sewn and she remembered Dammartin's hands ripping the shift from her body. A second stitch and the image flashed in her head of his mouth upon her breast. She felt the breath catch in her throat, felt the flush rise in her cheeks and the press of her nipples against her underclothes. No. She shook her head as if by so doing she could deny the thoughts and pretend they did not exist.

Dammartin had been right to send her away, for, Lord

help her, she could not stop this fire that burned in her for him. She wanted his kiss, his touch, his taste upon her tongue. It was like some kind of madness that robbed her of all rational thought so that not the memory of her father, nor the war, nor all that had happened, could quench her desire.

Dammartin had acted for duty and for honour in sending her away. La Roque had been wrong; it was not Dammartin that had made her a whore, but Josie herself. She swallowed down that hard realisation, and felt the misting of her eyes. She blinked the tears away, scorning her own weakness and set the shift and its memories aside.

One hand reached and extinguished the lantern before she rose silently to stand by the tent's entrance.

The night sky above was a deep, dark velvet. Stars glittered small and bright. The moon had grown larger so that it was a fat three-quarters full. The air around her was cold and filled with the dampness that always came with night. Her breath smoked in small puffs of condensation. And as she stood there, under the great vastness of the sky, and the settling silence, Josie thought of her father and of Dammartin's, and of the lies that had been told of them...and of La Roque, a man that Dammartin had said was his father's close friend.

La Roque had woven a web of lies to destroy Lieutenant Colonel Mallington's reputation across all of France, that much was clear, but the question was why. The only person who could answer that question was La Roque himself. She glanced over to where the two infantrymen lounged that had been set to guard her, knowing that, whatever she said, they would not let her leave the tent.

A group of three women, wearing dresses so low cut as to appear positively indecent, pushed past her. Josie stepped aside to let them pass, pulling her cloak tightly around her and watching them go. No one stopped their progress. They moved forwards unaccosted, their laughter and teasing voices loud across the field. An idea slipped into Josie's mind.

She turned and, back inside the tent, found the clothes that Rosa had given her. And then from within the leather satchel she had carried with her so closely she removed the thin precious book she had guarded for so long. Within the darkness she changed into the Spanish dress, hiding the book in the safest of places and unlacing the top of the chemise like she had seen the other women doing. Instead of her cloak she wrapped a shawl around her shoulders. Quickly she pulled the pins from her hair, mussing it with her fingers to lie long and wanton. She hesitated by the tent's doorway, darting a nervous glance across at the guards.

One deep breath and she hesitated no more. Josie walked out into the night, feeling the breeze chill the tops of her breasts and the wind stir through her hair. She held her head up and walked out with the same sway of the hips mimicked from the women, and the same air that she knew exactly where she was going.

She had almost made it across the field when the fusilier stopped her.

He stared at her suspiciously. *'Madame?'*

Josie's heart was thudding fit to leap out of her chest. She forced herself to smile at the man. *'Monsieur,'* she said in as sultry a tone as she could manage and let the shawl that she held wrapped tightly around her fall open. The light of the man's flambeau danced across the bareness of her skin that Rosa's dress revealed. 'I am afraid that I already have an appointment for this night. Perhaps tomorrow...' Her French was flawless and without the trace of an English accent.

The man no longer looked at her face. He addressed the rest of his comments to the neckline of the dress at the place where her breasts rose and fell. 'I am Antoine Nerin and I would be very pleased to accommodate you tomorrow, *madame*.'

He was still staring.

Josie suppressed the urge to wrap the shawl as a shield around her.

'You will come?'

'Naturally,' she said, and gave what she hoped sounded like a trill of laughter. Then she turned to go and jumped as she felt the man's hand stroke across her bottom.

'Until tomorrow.'

She nodded.

And finally she was on her way and pulling the shawl tight around her.

It was not difficult to locate Major La Roque's tent. It was large and set slightly apart from the others. She saw him standing by the opened flap, looking out, watching, as if he were waiting for someone, and then he moved back inside and she saw him no more.

A fusilier looked at her suspiciously. She let the shawl gape and looked away.

He saw the nature of her business and approached no farther, allowing her to continue on her way towards the Major's tent.

There was a campfire to the right with a group of blue-coated men sitting around it. She saw to her consternation that one of them was Donadieu, so she skirted away, going round the other way to come at La Roque's tent from behind. She began to walk towards the tent flap.

A flambeau mounted on a stand burned near the front. On the inside of the tent a lantern illuminated the figure of La Roque lounging in a chair at his table.

Footsteps sounded and she saw the figure of Lieutenant Molyneux approaching. She ducked down out of sight and waited for him to pass. But Molyneux did not pass; instead, he reported to the Major's tent. Josie crept back behind the tent, wondering why Dammartin had sent his lieutenant to La Roque at this time of night. She crouched low as if she were lacing her boot.

La Roque's French words sounded clear from within. 'Brandy?'

'Thank you, sir.'

There was the sound of glass chinking against glass, and the fall of liquid. 'You have done well, Molyneux. What have you to report tonight? Has he made any mention of the girl?'

'No sir. Not a one.'

'Then it seems that our plan has worked. You must have convinced him most thoroughly of her perfidious nature.'

'Indeed sir, Mademoiselle Mallington was most easily manipulated.'

Josie felt her blood turn to ice. Shock kicked her hard so that she held her breath, poised and waiting for what was to come.

'Did you manage to search her person for the missing journal?

'Unfortunately the Captain arrived before I could progress to that stage. I must confess I was rather disappointed.'

La Roque laughed. 'Why so, Molyneux? If you want the girl, you may have her.'

Josie bit hard at her lip, disbelieving the words that she was hearing.

'But she is a lieutenant colonel's daughter and, as such, will be returned to the British. If she makes allegations...'

'You worry too much, Molyneux.' She heard the smile in La Roque's voice. 'The British do not even know that Mademoiselle Mallington is still alive. They will believe her killed with her father. You may do what you like with her and no one will mind in the slightest.'

Josie's stomach constricted to a small, hard ball.

'Captain Dammartin will mind,' said Molyneux. 'He was looking at me last night as if he would kill me.'

'Leave Captain Dammartin to me,' said La Roque. 'You concentrate on the journal. It cannot be mere coincidence that Mallington's journal for Oporto is the only one missing. The girl must have it. Take her tonight. Seduce her. Strip her. Search between her damn legs if you have to. I want that journal. You did well to find me the others, but it is this one that we need—for Pierre's sake.'

Josie's eyes widened. Her mouth gaped open.

'I will try my utmost, sir.'

'I like a man that can be trusted. You'll go far in this army, Lieutenant Molyneux, far indeed, if I have anything to do with it.'

She knew then the true extent of Molyneux's treachery.

They started to speak of various women of the baggage train, but Josie had heard enough. She felt sick to the bottom of her stomach, sick and angry and disgusted. Molyneux was La Roque's spy. The shock of what he had done and what he planned to do made her stomach heave and her legs shake. Josie swallowed hard and breathed deeply before rising and moving swiftly from her crouched position by La Roque's tent.

She did not retrace her steps back to the women's tent. Instead, Josie hurried through the campsite towards Bonaparte's 8th Dragoons, and the man that commanded them—Captain Pierre Dammartin.

Dammartin and Lamont were sitting by what was left of the fire.

'So, the problem of Mademoiselle Mallington is no more.'

Dammartin rubbed at the stubbled growth of his jawline and gave no reply. What could he say—that even now he could not stop thinking about her, that he wanted her, that a part of him regretted sending her to La Roque?

'Then, what happened in the tent with Molyneux made up your mind?' Lamont puffed at his pipe.

'No,' said Dammartin, 'it was what happened afterwards.' He thought of her beneath him, of his mouth suckling upon her perfect breasts, of the raggedness of her breathing and her low seductive moan of heated desire.

Lamont wisely said nothing.

'You saw her with Molyneux. The whole bloody camp saw her. And even that did not make a difference. I would have had her, taken her right there, had I not come to my senses in time.' Dammartin shook his head. 'I think I have been too long without a woman, my friend, that I am so willing take Molyneux's leavings.'

A cloud of tobacco smoke released from Lamont's mouth, filling the air with its sweet aroma. 'I could not help but overhear about the splinter.'

Dammartin smiled cynically. 'Ah, yes, the splinter.'

'The girl's interest is in you, Pierre, not Molyneux. God only knows why, given who she is and what happened in Telemos...and the fact that you have hardly been gentle with her.' He sniffed and gave a philosophical shrug. 'But then, I suppose, there is nothing of reason in the affairs of the heart...or of the breeches.'

Dammartin stared sullenly into the dying flames. 'What game is our lieutenant playing at, I wonder?'

'Who can know? But at least now she is with La Roque it will be an end to the matter.'

Dammartin said nothing.

'Goodnight, Captain,' said Lamont, and, getting to his feet, made his way to his tent.

'Goodnight, Sergeant,' came the reply.

Dammartin sat for only a few moments more, before he, too, retired for the night, leaving the dragoon camp deserted.

The night was quietening down as Josie made her way through the line of camps. She did not know when Molyneux would leave and she had no wish for him to discover her on the road. Three times men made advances to her. Three times she told them she already had an appointment. One of the men clasped his arm around her waist and pulled her close to him, his foul breath hot against her neck. 'Let me persuade you otherwise, *madame*,' he had said, and pulled a handful of coins from his pocket.

Josie pushed him away, but he would not release her. She held the panic that threatened to break loose in check. 'I tell you, I have an arrangement with an officer. Now release me, sir, or you will have him to answer to.'

'Let her go, Thomass,' his friends said. 'We don't want any trouble. This bloody forced march is bad enough without being pulled up over a whore.'

The man, Thomass, sneered, but eventually he threw her away, and spat noisily after her.

Josie quelled the urge to run. She walked away, pulling the shawl tight around her, refusing to look back. But her heart was thrumming fast and the blood was pounding in her ears, and she could not rid herself of the notion that Thomass was following her.

Eventually she came to the dragoons' camp and the tents that belonged to their officers. A fire burned low in the foreground, but the tents themselves were in darkness, and for one fearful minute she wondered if they would be empty and that her journey would have been in vain.

This camp was quiet. The two identical tents sat before her and she realised that she did not know which was Captain Dammartin's and which was that of his officers. She dare not make the mistake, especially if Molyneux had returned.

Looking around her, she found a small stone upon the ground. She stooped and caught it up, then, taking careful aim, she threw the stone at the tent pitched farthest to the right-hand side. There was a soft thud as the stone found its target against the canvas.

She waited, but there was nothing. Another stone. Another hit.

This time a man appeared at the tent flap. He was garbed in an unfastened shirt, breeches and hastily donned boots. Even in the low light from the fire that stood between Josie's hiding place and the tents, she could see quite clearly that it was Pierre Dammartin.

He looked out into the night, peering across to the bushes where Josie crouched. She heard him treading about by the tent until he eventually went back inside. A quick glance around and then she rose and silently crossed the ground that separated them.

Dammartin did not climb back into bed upon his return to his tent. Instead, he slid his sabre quietly from its scabbard. Awareness tingled and he could not rest. The sound had most likely been one of his men fooling about, but Dammartin's instinct told him otherwise, and through the years Dammartin had learned to listen to his instinct. On the war trail it was often the only thing that kept a man alive. So he stood there and listened to the silence of the night, and eventually he heard the soft pad of footsteps cross the soil to his tent. He stuffed his pillow beneath the blanket on the bed so that it would vaguely resemble the bulk of a figure. Then his fingers closed around the sabre's hilt. The weight balanced in his hand and he moved forwards noiselessly to stand at the side of the tent flap. Whoever was stealing into his tent would find Dammartin, but not quite as they expected.

His mouth was hard, his eyes narrowed. He wondered as to the identity of the intruder, knowing that it had to be someone from within Foy's escort. Maybe Molyneux in retaliation for what had happened between them over Josephine Mallington.

Someone was untying the fastenings of the tent flap. His body tensed. The canvas that made the tent's door drew back and the figure stepped inside into the black within that was slightly darker than the black without. Too small and slight for Molyneux. Silently, the intruder moved towards the bed.

Through the darkness Josie could just make out the mound of Dammartin's figure within the bed. She stepped forwards and felt a sudden press against her back. An involuntary gasp escaped her, and she did not need to look round to know the touch of a blade.

'Turn around slowly,' he said in French. His voice was quiet and low, but she knew that it was Dammartin. Relief swamped her. She released the breath that she had been holding.

'Captain Dammartin…Pierre.' She spoke as quietly as he.

The pressure dropped from her back. The sabre blade hissed as it was plunged back into its scabbard. 'Josephine?' There could be no mistaking his shock. 'What the hell—?'

'Thank God!' She turned and slipped into his arms. 'I had to come, I had to warn you…'

Releasing her, he caught up a lantern, intent on lighting it.

'No.' She stayed his hand. 'No one must see me here. It is not safe.'

'The men are abed. There is no one to see.'

'There is Lieutenant Molyneux,' she whispered, knowing that even as she spoke Molyneux was probably looking for her in the women's tent.

'He also has retired,' he said coldly.

'Believe me, Molyneux is abroad this night.'

'Josephine, what are you—?'

'No, you must listen to me. There is not much time. Molyneux will soon realise that I am gone and La Roque will be alerted.'

'Mademoiselle Mallington,' he said more sternly.

'Captain Dammartin,' she countered, catching at his hands through the darkness. 'Please just listen.'

Dammartin felt the urgent press of her fingers against his and knew that what had been achieved by sending Josephine Mallington to his godfather had just been undone. She had come to him and he knew by the coursing of his blood and the strength of his desire that he could fight no more this night.

'Very well.' The scent of her teased beneath his nose. He wrapped his arms around her waist, pulling her closer.

'No,' she pushed him away, and he could hear the slight breathlessness in her voice. 'I must tell you…'

'Then speak.'

'I went in search of Major La Roque's tent. I intended to go in, to talk to him, to ask him why he had lied about my father…and yours.'

'Josephine—' he started to chide, but she cut him off.

'But Lieutenant Molyneux arrived before I could.'

Dammartin's eyes narrowed. Molyneux.

'I heard them talking through the canvas.'

'Molyneux and La Roque?'

'Yes.' Her breaths were fast and shallow, her anxiety barely suppressed. 'Molyneux is spying for him.' He felt her fingers touch gently to his wrist. 'He is spying on you, Pierre.'

He let her words drop between them, feeling a spurt of anger at what she sought to do. Quite deliberately he moved from her touch, smiling a sardonic smile through the darkness. 'You must try harder, *mademoiselle*, to think of something more convincing. The story of the splinter and your flirtation with Molyneux was a much better effort.'

'What are you speaking of?' The pitch of her voice rose with incredulity.

'Do you think that you can so easily cause trouble between us?'

'It is the truth, I swear!' she gasped. 'La Roque used Molyneux to make you send me away. And Molyneux is the Major's spy. It was they that stole my portmanteau… and my father's journals.'

'You admit, then, that the journals were in the portmanteau?'

'Yes,' she said simply, no longer pretending any denial. 'They were hidden beneath a false floor. La Roque has them now.'

'Does he indeed?' he asked quietly.

A pause.

Dammartin rubbed his fingers against the roughness of his chin as he remembered La Roque's dismissive attitude to Dammartin's own suspicions regarding the journals and the portmanteau. She had to be lying. She was Mallington's daughter, an English prisoner, his enemy. La Roque was his senior officer, his godfather, a man who had been like an uncle to him since childhood. And then it dawned on him what he had been missing.

'*Vous parlez français, n'est pas?*' he shot at her.

'*Oui,*' she said, then reverted to English. 'It was the one advantage that I had. I could not let you know of it.'

'Then your story of following your father around the world, without schooling or governesses, was a lie too.'

'It was the truth,' she said.

There was a silence. Still, Dammartin did not believe what she was saying, and yet… He raked a hand through his hair.

'How did you get here? There are sentries posted at all the camps. Did no one stop you?'

Josie thought of the men that had done precisely that. She thought of Thomass and the cruelty of his grip and the anger in his face. There was no need to tell Dammartin of such things. 'I am in disguise. They did not see an English prisoner.'

He grabbed hold of her wrist and dragged her to the tent flap, opening it so that he could look on her in the moonlight.

'No!' She tried to resist.

'I see no disguise, *mademoiselle*.'

'*Vraiment?*' she whispered furiously. '*Regardez-moi de près, monsieur.*'

Dammartin's gaze drifted to her hair that was flowing long and wanton over her shoulders, then down lower to the thin shawl. The skin of Josie's throat was exposed. He could see it, pale and smooth through the light of the moon. Anger flashed in her eyes as she yanked open the shawl that was wrapped around her. The low-cut bodice and unlaced chemise presented a very full view. Her breasts swelled pale and smooth and inviting. Dammartin remembered too well how they had felt, how they had tasted. He swallowed as his gaze skimmed down over the red-and-black dress that fitted so neatly to her figure. Its skirt was overlapping his left leg.

'Am I not *une femme française*?'

'Your accent…' He stared at her, understanding now why the sentries had believed her so readily.

She stared right back before the anger seemed to wash from her and she glanced away, a distant look in her eyes. 'My mother was French,' she said quietly.

Dammartin felt the shock like a kick in the gut. He stared all the harder, feeling that the foundations of his beliefs of Mallington and the woman before him had just been shaken. He let the tent flap fall back into place.

'You risked much to come here, *mademoiselle*. Why?'

She did not move, just stood where she was, so still that he did not think that she would answer. 'To warn you,' she said.

He felt his heart beat a little faster.

'To let you know what manner of man this La Roque is. He is spying on you, Captain. That is hardly conducive with a man whose word as a witness is above reproach.'

He understood now, and he smiled that he could have believed anything else. His voice hardened. 'You are lying about La Roque in an effort to persuade me of Mallington's innocence.'

'My father was innocent, he *is* innocent. I have no need to lie about La Roque.'

'You have every need,' he said curtly.

She sighed. 'I did not come here for this.'

'Then what *did* you come here for, Mademoiselle Mallington?'

Silence.

'For this?' He reached for her, hauling her into his arms, pressing her body to his.

'Or this?' He slid a hand round to capture one breast, his fingers raking beneath the unlaced chemise.

'Or perhaps this, *mademoiselle*?' His mouth closed harshly over hers, kissing her with the hunger that had gnawed at him all the long day through.

She fought him, but he did not release her, just deepened the kiss, until she softened against him, and yielded the fight. But unlike before, she did not return his kiss.

He ceased his onslaught and rested his forehead against hers. 'I am sorry, Josephine.' The tightness of his grip loosened. One hand slid up to cradle her face as he felt the brush of her eyelashes against his. 'You did not deserve that.' Her breath was warm against his mouth. He skimmed a caress down the length of her back.

'I came because La Roque has told Molyneux he may have me…tonight. I…I thought that you would help me.'

He stilled. He drew his face back slightly as if he could see into her eyes through the darkness.

A minute passed, and then another, in which there was only the hush of their breaths, the beat of their hearts.

When he spoke his tone was grim. 'Stay here,' he said. 'I will be back soon.'

'No.' She gripped at him. 'You cannot go to La Roque. He will be enraged. It is too dangerous.'

'Your concern touches me,' he said, 'but it is unwarranted.' He smiled and dropped a kiss to her cheek. 'Try to get some sleep. You will find the bed most comfortable.' He pulled his jacket on and was gone.

Major La Roque pressed the full glass of brandy into Dammartin's hand. 'Mademoiselle Mallington seeks to turn us against each other. Such a scheming little vixen for one so young, but then we must remember who sired her. Mallington's poison runs in her veins. She hates us French just as her father did before her.'

'Her mother was French.' Dammartin tasted the brandy and set the brandy glass on the table before him.

'Mallington's wife?' La Roque stiffened before relaxing back into his chair. 'The girl told you that?'

Dammartin gave a nod.

'It is probably another lie spun to garner your sympathy.'

Dammartin thought of the Josephine's fluency in French. 'I do not think so, Frederic.'

'Pierre, Pierre…' La Roque sighed. 'The girl is dangerous. She watches you kill Mallington and his men. Then you tell her the truth of her beloved precious father, that he is a murdering bastard. There is no honour in the killing of a paroled officer; even Mademoiselle Mallington must know that. So she hates you, and she sets about finding a way to destroy you…with seduction and lies.'

La Roque's words made sense. Dammartin knew that Josephine Mallington had every reason to hate him. But there had been nothing of hatred in her kiss, or the response of her body to his.

'Are you saying that Molyneux did not report to you this evening?'

La Roque set his glass down on the table and looked at Dammartin. 'I will tell you the truth, Pierre. You are my godson; I care for you, and your mother and your brother very dearly. You know that. When I heard something of this Mademoiselle Mallington, the way she was with you, I began to worry. And so I asked Molyneux to keep an eye on her, to let me know what she was up to. That is all, Pierre, I swear, nothing more.'

'You might have told me of your concerns rather than have my first lieutenant spy upon me.'

La Roque shook his head. 'There was nothing of spying in it. I was concerned for you. She is the spawn of that monster and you…' he sighed with heavy sadness '…you are still affected by your father's death. Had I tried to warn you of her, you would have resented me for it, so I thought I would just keep a gentle eye on things myself.'

'Frederic…'

'Perhaps I was wrong to do so, but I am proved right about the girl. With her slyness she has caught you like a worm upon a hook. You want her, even knowing who she is.'

Dammartin said nothing, just downed a mouthful of brandy, focusing on the heat burning its way down into his chest.

'I am right, am I not? You want Mallington's daughter in your bed.'

Again Dammartin ignored the assertion spoken with its disgust. 'What of her portmanteau?' he said instead. 'What of the journals?'

'I told you before. I know nothing of her damn portmanteau, and as for Mallington's journals, we have only her word that they even exist. Do you think I would have that demon's journals in my possession and say nothing of it to you? Do you not think that I want to know just as much as you why Mallington did what he did that day? If we had his journals, we might have the answer to the questions that we both have asked for so long.' La Roque rose from his seat and walked round to stand before Dammartin. 'I have known you since you were a boy,' he said. 'I have watched you grow to a man. You, Marie and Kristoffe are in my heart, along with the love I bore your father. Do you believe the word of a murderer's daughter over mine, Pierre?'

Dammartin shook his head. 'Forgive me, Frederic.'

La Roque reached a hand across and touched to Dammartin's shoulder. 'I understand how hard this has been for you.'

'She said that you would give her to Molyneux.'

'The girl is playing you, Pierre. She is here because you asked me to take her. Molyneux has nothing to do with it.'

Dammartin thought of the way that Josephine had clung to him, her relief at finding him spontaneous and overflowing. He thought of her standing so quietly before him. *I thought that you would help me*, she had said, and he had seen the unspoken fear in her eyes. Such an adept liar, such persuasive acting. Logic and all that Dammartin had believed in told him that La Roque was right, yet a stain of unease marred his soul.

'I envy her her loyalty to her father. Had I but an ounce of it, I would not be in this damnable mess.'

'Pierre.' La Roque's hand gripped at Dammartin's shoulder. 'I know how hard you have fought against this... this appetite she has whetted within you. But maybe you are using the wrong tactics; maybe it would be better if you just took her and be done with it. Use her. Ride her like the whore that she is. Eat until you are sated, and perhaps then the hunger shall be no more.'

'Perhaps you are right,' said Dammartin. He knew that no matter what La Roque said, no matter whether Josephine Mallington had lied or not, once he was alone with her, all of it was inconsequential. He was like some animal, wanting her, needing her so much that he could no longer think straight...so much that he thought not of his father or of his duty or even of honour, but only of Josephine Mallington.

He had thought that sending her to La Roque would be an end to it, but it had only been an accelerant. Now she was in his tent, and before the night was out she would be in his bed.

Chapter Twelve

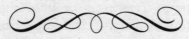

Josie heard the footsteps and saw the movement of the tent flap. Her heart began to pound as she wondered if it really were Dammartin returning. If something had happened to him, if it were Molyneux that had come in his stead… Her hands clenched by her sides. She rose swiftly to her feet, turning from the little table to face the tent flap, waiting, poised, ready.

'Captain Dammartin…' she breathed her relief '…it is you. I thought…' She gave a little smile and let the words fall unsaid.

'You thought what, *mademoiselle*?' he asked, and she could see that his eyes were dangerously dark and that something had changed since he had left. And she knew then that La Roque had destroyed any belief that Dammartin might have had in her.

The smile flitted from her face. 'It does not matter,' she said, and wrapped her shawl more tightly around her.

He lit the lantern and closed all of its shutters save for one. 'La Roque denies your accusations. He says that you are trying to cause trouble between us.'

'Of course he does,' she exclaimed. 'You did not think he would admit the truth, did you? Molyneux was *there*. I know what I heard.'

'Molyneux *was* there, but it is not how you think.' She saw the shadow of something flicker in his eyes.

'I have told you the truth, Captain Dammartin. It is Major La Roque who is lying.'

'It is your word, *mademoiselle*, against his. You are the daughter of the man who murdered my father. La Roque is a hero to all of France. He is a senior officer in the Emperor's army, a friend to my family; he is my godfather. Were you in my position, who would you believe?'

'La Roque is your godfather?' she said, and gave a mirthless laugh. 'Then I never had a chance of your belief.' She looked at him. 'Are you sending me back to him?'

His eyes held hers. 'No.'

The silence hissed between them.

'And what of Molyneux?'

'Molyneux is of no consequence.'

'You would keep me here, and yet you believe not a single word that I have said, not of La Roque or of Molyneux or my father. Why?' In that single questioning word there was disappointment and dread…and anticipation. She fixed her eyes on him, hoping that she was wrong.

'We both know why, Josephine,' he said, and began to unfasten his jacket.

She swallowed hard, feeling the sudden skitter of her heart. She shook her head as if to deny it, but she recognised too well the smoulder in his eyes and the familiar heat that ignited in response low in her belly.

'No,' she said, and shook her head again. 'I will not let you kiss me.'

He walked the few steps towards her, not stopping until

the skirt of her dress was brushing the toes of his riding boots.

She felt his warmth across the small distance that separated them, and smelled the scent of him.

He raised a hand and traced a finger lightly against her cheek.

Josie bit at her lower lip and resisted the sensation. 'Would you force me against my will?'

'No.' His voice was as gentle as his caress.

'Do not kiss me,' she pleaded, not trusting herself to resist him if he did. 'Please do not.'

The dim flickering light shadowed his face, and softened his eyes. He stared at her for a moment longer, and then he turned away and moved to sit down in the same chair in which Josie had been seated upon his arrival. He sighed and raked a hand through his hair.

'What am I then to do with you, Josephine Mallington?'

She sat down in the other chair, to his left, resting her hands gently upon the table's smooth wooden surface.

There was only the quietness of the night.

'I wish there was some way I could make you believe the truth,' she said quietly.

'We will never agree on what is the truth.' His hand slid over hers, even though he did not look at her, but faced straight ahead, watching the tiny light of the lantern.

They sat there, not moving, not speaking, with only the warmth of his hand resting on hers.

'I will ask you just one question, and then no more. *Were* your father's journals within your portmanteau?'

'Yes.'

'Then I can never know what was in your father's mind in Oporto. The one chance that I had is lost.'

Josie knew then a way that she could convince Dammartin of the truth. The cost was high, traitorous even;

once she would have died rather than pay it, but things had changed since then, much more than she ever could have known.

He was still looking in front of him, staring at the canvas, and it seemed that there was a despair about him. Her eyes traced the outline of the scar running down his cheek, the harsh lean planes of his face, the sweep of the dark lashes, the straightness of his nose, the hardness of his lips. A man that seemed invincible, and yet he hurt as she did. He had lost a father, like her.

'It is not lost,' she said softly. And her hand rotated beneath his so that their palms touched together and their fingers entwined. 'There is something I have not told you, Captain Dammartin.'

Slowly he turned his face to her.

'My father's journal for Oporto was not amongst the others in my portmanteau.'

She saw the hope leap in his eyes.

'It was the night that we walked together by the river. I took it out to read and did not replace it.'

His gaze clung to hers like a man drowning clings to life. 'You have this journal?'

'Yes. It is the reason La Roque was sending Molyneux to me tonight. He wanted the journal.'

'Josephine,' he whispered, 'do not lie to me of this above all things.'

'It is the truth. I have read my father's words from Oporto and there is nothing of murder in them. He writes of admiration and respect for your father, of their issuing invitations to visit each other's homes after the war. His are not the words of a man who would kill that same officer when he was paroled.'

His thumb stroked against hers. 'How am I to believe you, that man's daughter?'

She looked deep into his eyes and she saw the darkness of his pain and anguish, and the hope that her words had lit.

'Show me the journal, Josephine,' he said quietly. 'Let me read the words with my own eyes.'

'You will tell La Roque. He will take it like he took the others.'

'No, I promise.' He moved, his hands slipping up to cup her face. 'Please, Josephine. I will beg if that is what you want.'

Seconds seemed to stretch to minutes, and minutes to hours, in which they sat there like that—until at last Josie nodded.

She moved away, turned her back to him and began to unlace her dress.

Dammartin watched across the small distance between them while Josephine loosened her dress. For a moment he thought she had misunderstood, that what she would offer him was something quite different from the journal, but something that he wanted just the same. He felt himself harden at the thought, but then he realised that she was not stripping off the clothes, but seeking beneath and within, and he knew that she had not lied about the journal.

He waited, unable to take his eyes from her, anticipation spiralling within, until at last she fixed her clothing back in place and turned towards him.

She brought the notebook to the table and laid it down before him like some precious offering.

His eyes slid down to the small, battered book with its deep red covers all blotched and warped.

She sat down in the empty chair. 'The rain soaked through the leather of my satchel to reach its pages, but the writing is still legible.'

He stared at it, knowing that this was it, at last—

Mallington's voice from the past; Mallington's thoughts on Jean Dammartin.

His heart was beating fast now, and he could feel the prickle of sweat upon his palms. It was feeling that came before battle. That time of tense stillness, when fear churned in every man's gut, and his nostrils filled with it and his fingers grew numb with it, that time when one could scent his own death and the urge to run to safety was strong. The worst time, when men could do nothing but endure until with relief the order came to charge, or to fire, or to move, and the waiting was over. It was the same now.

'Read it,' she said.

He took a deep breath and with infinite care opened the book's covers, feeling them still warm with the heat from her body. Within, the pages were stained a pinky red where the dye had seeped from the covers. But it was as Josephine had said, the pencilled flowing script with its small, neat letters and its words crammed close together was still clear enough. Mallington had filled the page one way, and then turned it upside down and continued his writing in the spaces between his original lines.

His skin tingled as his fingers touched the paper. He turned the delicate pages, one by one, until he came at last to the date he was looking for: May 1809.

His heart was racing, his blood pumping hard. He held his focus on the date and breathed before allowing it to slip along the line and read the words that Lieutenant Colonel Mallington's hand had written.

He read the entries for the days from 12th May 1809 onwards, from the time that Wellington had routed the French from Oporto. His eyes raced over the words, pausing over the pertinent ones: *Dammartin...a most worthy adversary...confess to liking the fellow heartily...regret that fate has seen fit to place us each on opposing sides of this war...La Roque is scarcely to be noticed beside Dammartin...the two officers will be paroled...I bid adieu to Major Dammartin...agreed that should we survive this war then when peace is instilled we should become friends... invited me to his villa in Evran...I made a reciprocal invitation that he should come to Winchester...I returned their swords and provided them with weapons with which they might defend themselves against attack...it is the first time I pray that an enemy's journey shall be safe...having witnessed Dammartin's and his men's bravery and met the man himself...I can do nothing else as a gentleman.*

Dammartin closed the journal and sat back in his chair. There was a curious numbness within. All that he had believed these past months, all that he had done, were contrary to what was written in these few fragile pages. Mallington wrote of respect and honour and admiration. Josephine had been right: they did not sound to be the words of a murderer.

Upon the table her fingers wrapped gently around his. 'I am sorry,' she said gently.

'Why should you be sorry?' He tried to smile, but the curve of his lips was bitter. 'You have achieved what you wanted.'

'No.' She bit at her lip and looked at the flame's flicker within the lantern. 'I never wanted any of this.'

He lifted her hand, still entwined with his, and touched it to his mouth before placing it back down upon the table. 'Fate has played a cruel game with us.'

Her eyes met his. 'What are we to do?'

He shook his head, feeling empty and set adrift from all that was real. 'I do not know, Josephine. I honestly do not know.'

There was such a note of despondency and despair in

his voice that it seemed to Josie that a hand had reached into her chest and squeezed upon her heart.

She reached to touch his arm, patting a comfort.

And when he looked round at her, she could see the teardrop that ran down his ravaged cheek.

'Oh, Pierre,' she whispered, and went to him, wrapping her arms around him, cradled his head against her breast. She rocked him gently, soothing him, dropping small kisses to his hair. And with every breath she felt his pain, so raw and bleeding, as he wept silently into her heart. She held him for what seemed like hours, until the tight tension had gone from his body, and anguish had left, leaving in its place an empty quietness.

All was silent.

He rested against her, his arms around her waist, his cheek against her heart. Her fingers were threaded through his hair, massaging a slow rhythm. He raised his face and looked up into her eyes, and she knew in that moment that nothing would ever be the same again.

Gently she cupped a hand against his scarred cheek and moved her mouth to his. She kissed him with all that was in her heart, seeking to take away his pain, to heal the wound he had been dealt. And as she kissed him, she felt his lips awaken beneath hers, and he was kissing her back, his mouth sliding against hers.

He pulled her on to his knee, kissing her harder, with the same urgency that was rising within Josie. Their tongues danced together, teasing and moist. He kissed her and licked her and sucked her, while his hands worked at her dress's laces until her breasts were free beneath his fingers.

She knew what he would do, and she wanted it, wanted to feel his tantalising caress, wanted to feel his mouth roving over her breasts.

Her nipples were heavy and sensitive as he rolled them

between his fingers, plucking at them to make her pant with a desire that could no longer be suppressed. And when he licked at those hardened, rosy peaks, she closed her eyes and almost drowned in the ecstasy of it, arching her back, driving herself deeper into him.

He carried her to his bed, laid her down within the blankets. Stripping off his boots and his jacket, he discarded his shirt, until only his breeches remained. Beneath the low lantern light his naked skin was honey-gold, his body lean and hard with muscle. She reached up and trailed her fingers down the taut plane of his stomach, feeling the twitch of his muscles beneath her touch. His eyes closed momentarily and he groaned before his hand closed over hers and he lifted it to his mouth.

'Josephine,' he pleaded, and his voice was low and guttural as if in pain.

'Not Josephine,' she said, 'but Josie.'

'Josie.' Her name was like a caress from his lips.

He kissed the tip of her smallest finger before taking it into his mouth and sucking gently upon it.

The heat in Josie's thighs burned hotter.

He did the same to her ring finger and the finger next to it.

She dragged the air noisily into her lungs.

By the time he had reached her forefinger, her eyes were closed and she wanted to beg him to do whatever it was that her body was crying out for.

And then came her thumb.

'Pierre!' She arched upon the bed, thrusting her nipples into the air so that he would take them again. But he did not. He lowered himself over her and kissed her mouth. He kissed her face, her hair, her neck. He kissed every inch of each pale breast, teasing round their rosy summits, but his tongue stopping agonisingly short of taking them. 'Pierre!' she cried again, and tried to guide his mouth to suckle.

He raised his face to look into hers, the intensity of his gaze searing her. 'Josie,' he said, and seemed to stare into her very soul. *'Mon amie.'* He lowered his mouth and kissed her, deeply, passionately, giving all as she had done. She revelled in it, and felt his hand move beneath her skirts, his fingers sliding against the bare skin of her thighs, creeping ever up towards her most secret of places.

His face drew back and he looked into her eyes as he touched her.

Josie gasped loud.

'Sweet Josie,' he murmured and, holding her gaze with his, he began to caress her, sliding against her moist heat, slowly at first, then a little faster, building to a rhythm. She arched her neck, panting, feeling the blush of heat spreading throughout the entirety of her body. And still, he gazed into her eyes and she into his, as he stroked her in her most intimate of places. There was nothing of shame, nothing of embarrassment, only the most pressing of needs, escalating, urging his fingers to move faster, to never cease their magic.

'Pierre!'

He threaded the fingers of his left hand through the fingers of her right, pressing her hand into the softness of the pillow above her head. And all the while his other fingers worked busily.

Through the pleasure was a desperation, a need so utterly overwhelming that she could not help herself reaching for it. She needed him, needed him more than life itself. And the urgency was so great and the pleasure so strong that she could not help herself panting faster and faster as she strained towards it. Her eyes shuttered with the intensity of it. She felt his mouth close over her nipple, sucking

at it, laving it, and at this final touch that she had so craved
the world seemed to explode in a myriad of pleasure. She
cried out loud as a thousand sunbeams danced throughout
her body and a wave of total bliss rippled out from the
warm pulsating centre between her legs.

Dammartin's hand was no longer moving, his fingers
cupped her still, warm and gentle as they lay there.

She opened her eyes to find that he was watching her.

He smiled. 'My sweet girl.' Then he lay down by her
side, curving his body around hers so that she could feel
the strong steady beat of his heart against her back, and
he held her.

And Josie knew that she had given herself to him completely, holding nothing back. She was his. She did not
think of what the future would bring, only of here and
now, of Pierre Dammartin...and how she loved him.

'She is not to be found because she is with Dammartin.
There has been a change of plan.' La Roque swilled the
brandy around the glass. 'He knows that you have been
watching the girl for me.'

Molyneux's eyes bulged. 'He will kill me!'

'He will not. Captain Dammartin understands that you
were acting under my orders and that it was for his own
good.'

'He is a hard man, sir, a cold-hearted, ruthless killer
who—'

La Roque raised his eyes from the brandy glass. 'He is
my godson, Lieutenant.'

Molyneux stared down at the ground. 'I apologise,
Major.' There was a pause before he looked back up. 'Then
Mademoiselle Mallington is to stay with the Captain?'

'For now.' La Roque smiled and pulled at his moustache. 'Do not worry, Molyneux. Dammartin will soon tire

of shagging her. And when he does, you must be ready to act. The journal must be found…and the girl, Lieutenant, will be yours.'

'What if Dammartin finds the journal first? Do I still get her?'

'Dammartin knows nothing of the missing journal, and he is the last person that Mademoiselle Mallington will reveal it to. You, on the other hand, Molyneux, must be a little more persuasive. Do whatever it takes to get me that journal. Make the most of her in Ciudad Rodrigo, for we will leave her to General Gardanne's men when we return to Santarém. Then maybe Mallington's influence will be destroyed and my godson can resume his life once more.' La Roque filled Molyneux's glass with brandy. 'To Ciudad Rodrigo and all that awaits.'

The glasses chinked, and the two men drank in silence.

Dammartin sat by the rekindled fire and watched the beginnings of the new day dawn as over in the east the darkness of the night sky began to pale. The tin mug was warm between his hands, the steam from the coffee within rising up as wisps of smoke to drift into what was left of the night.

He needed time to think, even though he had lain awake most of the night hours doing just that. Could the man who had written such words of Jean Dammartin within his journal then have killed him? It was not impossible, he supposed, but the Mallington that the journal conjured was the same Mallington that had given his daughter into Dammartin's keeping as he lay dying within a cold monastery room. The scene from Telemos was etched upon Dammartin's mind. He had replayed it a hundred times in his head, studying each of Mallington's words, his every nuance. *He was a most worthy opponent*, Mallington had said. *I do not need to ask that you treat her honourably. I already know that, as Jean Dammartin's son, you will do nothing other.*

More than eighteen months of hatred, eighteen months of planning a revenge…against a man who it now seemed was not guilty. It had to be Mallington. La Roque had witnessed the murder, La Roque had seen his father die by Mallington's hand. Could his godfather have been mistaken? Could he be lying as Josie had said? Lying about his father, lying about the journals, and about Molyneux? Major Frederic La Roque—a man that he had known all of his life, a man that had kissed his father's cheek, and dangled his brother upon his knee, who had laughed with his mother, who had eaten at his parents' table and slept beneath their roof. The thought was anathema.

Maybe Mallington had not pulled the trigger, but there had to be some reasonable explanation as to why La Roque had thought it was so. Or maybe Mallington had truly been insane and killed the man he had written so warmly of, avoiding a record of the crime to spare his daughter the truth. Maybe Mallington really was guilty after all.

He heard the soft tread behind him and did not need to look round to know that she stood there.

'Pierre?' she whispered.

She was standing with a blanket wrapped around her, the crumpled red-and-black skirt visible below. Her eyes were wide and cautious, as if she doubted what she would find in him this morning. An image of her beneath him flashed in his mind, her face flushed with passion as his fingers slid within her secret silken folds. And he thought how he had entered his tent last night so intent upon taking her to satisfy only himself, and how differently the night had unravelled. He had wanted to pleasure her, to show what heady delights there could be. He had needed to give to her as she had given to him, just to give, not to take. That his own passion, his own desperate need, had gone unslaked did not matter.

There was such selflessness within her as to wrap around him like a quilt of the warmest softest down. No one, save his father, had ever seen beyond the armour that he wore in this life, until last night. Josie had witnessed the full extent of his weakness, looked upon his despair, vulnerable and raw, and she had gathered up the shattered pieces of his soul and fitted them back together—the daughter of the man he had so hated.

He was ashamed of his weakness, and that she had witnessed it. But his shame was all the greater for knowing how harshly he had treated her for a crime that he was no longer sure that Mallington had committed. Last night had been of despair and guilt and gratitude. None of it was Josephine Mallington's fault.

He held out his arm to her in an encompassing gesture, and she came to him, sitting down beside him, as he snuggled her in close by his side.

'You could not sleep,' she said.

He shook his head gave a wry smile. 'Coffee?' He offered her his mug.

She accepted the cup from his fingers.

'You said that your mother was French.'

She nodded and sipped at the coffee. 'My parents met when *Maman* came to England in 1784, the year after the last war had ended. She was very young and very pretty.'

'Like you,' he said.

She smiled. 'Her parents did not wish the marriage, for my father was English and a military man. He was also older than her—sixteen years, to be precise. But she loved him, and he loved her, and so she defied her parents to marry him.'

He looked into her eyes, noticing the way that they seemed to light up when she spoke of her parents. 'Then your father was a lucky man.'

She smiled again and passed the coffee back to him. 'My mother followed him all around the world with the army and I never once remember hearing her complain of it. First they were in North America, but I remember little of that. Then my father was sent to the West Indies—to Jamaica. That is were my mother died. Yellow fever, the doctor said. There was nothing that could be done for her.'

His arm tightened around her to pull her closer as they sat side by side before the small, weak flames of the fire.

'You stayed alone with your father.'

'And Edward, my brother. Papa was eventually recalled to England before being sent to Ireland. Edward joined the 20th Light Dragoons and was posted to Portugal. I accompanied my father when he was sent here too.'

'Where is your brother now?'

'He died at the Battle of Vimiero; he was three and twenty years old.'

'I am sorry, Josie. You have suffered too much loss.'

'We both have,' she said, and lifted the back of his hand from her waist to briefly touch against her lips. 'May I ask you of your father?'

He nodded, even though he had no wish to reveal any more of his pain.

Her question was worse than he could have anticipated. 'How exactly did he die?'

Something of the old bitterness welled up as it ever did when he thought of what Mallington was supposed to have done. 'Are you sure that you wish to hear this?'

'I think that I must hear it.'

'Very well.' He took a breath and told her. 'My father and Major La Roque were captured by Lieutenant Colonel Mallington at Oporto. They were his prisoners before being released with their parole. Not a mile after they left his camp he came after them, alone. And when he found them he came in close, levelled a musket and fired. The bullet killed my father instantly. Mallington reloaded and shot again. La Roque had no choice but to ride for his life. Mallington's bullet skimmed his arm. He was still bleeding when he reached the French lines; he was lucky to survive. So now you know the full extent of it.'

He had expected shock, denial, even distress from Josie, but not the wide-eyed revelation that he saw there.

She turned to him, gripped at his arm. 'The man that La Roque saw could not have been my father.'

'Josie,' he said quietly, 'the journal does not touch upon what happened after La Roque and my father left.'

'No, you do not understand,' she said urgently, and he could sense an underlying fervour within her. 'My father was injured at Vimiero, a sword blade across the fingers. He healed well enough to grip the hilt of a sword, but he could not pull back the hammer of a flintlock or release the trigger to fire a bullet. You see, if Major Dammartin was shot, it could not have been by my father's hand; that would have been a physical impossibility.'

An image flashed in his head of the little room in the monastery at Telemos, of the dead bodies of men with their rifles by their sides, of the one woman that faced them still, her rifle aimed at his her heart. He thought of the grey-haired old man and the sword that had fallen from his hand. What use was a sword against a barrage of bullets? Even his daughter had used a rifle, but Mallington himself had not.

And it all began to make sense. 'Then La Roque was mistaken in thinking that the officer was Mallington.'

'Perhaps the man had a look of my father about him.'

'A similar uniform, one of his officers, maybe.'

'No.' Josie shook her head. 'Whoever the villain was, he was not a rifleman. You said he used a musket. The Fifth of the 60th Foot are a rifle battalion. They are issued with rifles, not muskets. And as rifles are so much more accurate over distance, the killer would not have had to approach your father so closely had he used one.'

Dammartin nodded, knowing that everything she said made sense. There was a silence in which he let the thoughts settle. He did not know whether to be sad or glad. He did not know for sure whether she had proved to him at last Mallington's innocence. But the cold, heavy sensation sat upon him that he had persecuted an innocent man and all because La Roque had made a mistake.

'I am never going to know the true identity of the man who murdered my father, am I?'

She slid her hand around his waist, and dropped a small kiss to the side of his arm closest to her face.

They sat in silence, together, and watched as day drew back the dark curtain of night.

Somewhere in the distance a crow cawed. There were stirrings from the tents.

He drained the last of the coffee. 'Come, we should make ready.'

They got to their feet.

'Last night…' she said.

He touched a gentle finger to her lips to stay her words and, taking her hand in his, they walked back to the tent.

In the pale morning light she could see the crumple of his bed, that she had so recently vacated, and across from it the smooth surface of the table, empty save for the burned-out lantern.

'The journal…' She glanced round at him, feeling the sudden flurry of her heart. 'Pierre!'

'It is safe.'

'Where?'

'It is better that the journal stays with me, Josie.'

Her heart skipped a beat. 'You said that you would not take it from me; you promised.'

He took hold of her hand again and pulled her gently to him. 'I said that I would not tell Major La Roque.'

Her stomach seemed to drop to the soles of her feet. 'It is not yours to keep.' She stared at him. 'I let you read it in good faith.'

'Josie.' His thumb soothed a caress against her palm. 'I promise it is safe.'

'I trusted you,' she said, and the ground upon which she had built that trust seemed to tilt.

She saw the slight flinch at her words, there and then gone so quickly. His eyes were dark and unreadable as they met hers.

'You are a British prisoner in a French camp. Already your portmanteau has been stolen. I will ensure both your and the journal's safety until you can be returned to Lisbon.' She saw the flicker of his muscles as he clenched his jaw. 'It is the least I can do for your father.'

Their eyes held.

And in her heart was gladness that at last Dammartin believed in her father's innocence, and a terrible sadness, an ache almost. Papa was dead and Jean Dammartin's murderer would never be found…and soon Josie would be back with the British.

She nodded a small acknowledgement and looked away.

Nothing could change what had happened.

The war and the ghosts of their fathers stood between them.

Chapter Thirteen

The day's march was long, and Dammartin kept Josie by his side for every hour of it. There was no let up in the pace as Foy pushed the men relentlessly on, knowing that they were so close to their destination. Dammartin felt fatigue heavy in his muscles, and the gnaw of hunger in his belly. He glanced again at Josie, knowing that if he felt this bad, then she must be feeling it a hundred times worse. The grey blanket enveloped her as she sat looking straight ahead. He studied her profile.

The shadows beneath her eyes were dark against the pallor of her skin. Although she sat her saddle well, he could see the slight droop in her shoulders, and the weariness about her.

It was ten days since Telemos, ten days since he had watched Mallington die and taken Josie as his prisoner. He remembered her standing there, in that blood-splattered room in the monastery with the rifle in her hand, standing before her father, guarding Mallington against him and his men. One woman against them all. Defiant. Fearless. It was a sight he would never forget. So small, so slender, and yet so strong. He had both hated her and respected her. Only ten days later and it was not hate that he felt for the woman riding by his side.

He remembered the feel of her body pressed against his, her softness, her strength, the beat of her heart beneath his cheek. And the thought of her warmed him against the damp cold of the day, and prevented the chill wind's cut.

Above the sky stretched to an unending white-grey, but Dammartin did not notice. Ahead lay Ciudad Rodrigo.

A massive medieval wall enclosed the city. They marched through the fortified gateway, the horses' hooves clopping loud against the cobblestones that lined the streets. Josie looked up through the twilight to see an ancient castle nestling on the hill just above the town. She was so tired that she was almost slumped in Fleur's saddle, her fingers too numb to know if the reins were still within them. The little mare followed Dante and Dammartin.

She was aware of lights and of buildings, the hum of voices and soldiers dressed in Bonaparte's blue everywhere. The 8th did not stop until they reached the stables. Josie just sat there, knowing that this was the end of the journey. General Foy would go on to Paris, but of Dammartin's fate and her own, she did not know.

'Josie.'

She heard his voice, soft with concern, felt his hands helping her down. And then he took his baggage and placed a supportive arm around her waist, not caring that his men saw. Together they walked out of the stables to face what awaited them in Ciudad Rodrigo.

The room in which Dammartin had been quartered was small but clean and tidy. He could only be thankful that he and Josie had the room to themselves and did not have to share. With five thousand Frenchmen in the town, he knew that he was lucky indeed.

His portmanteau lay abandoned on the floor. Josie sat perched at the edge of the bed.

'What will happen now?' She was glad that her voice sounded calm.

'General Foy will go on with a smaller fresh escort, to Salamanca and Valladolid. We rest here and await our orders to return to Santarém along with Ciudad Rodrigo's garrison and that of Almeida.'

'And what of me?'

'You stay with me until I can return you to Wellington at Lisbon.'

She breathed her relief.

He dropped a kiss to the top of her head. 'Get some sleep, Josie. I must speak with Major La Roque, but I will be back soon. Lock the door behind me and keep it locked. There are too many Frenchmen about this night in search of a beautiful woman.' He pressed his lips to hers in a hard passionate kiss that was over too quickly. 'And I intend to keep you all to myself.'

'Come, come, Pierre, this is not like you. You have let the woman get under your skin, and now she is tormenting you with her lies.' Major La Roque dismissed his servant and refilled both his and Dammartin's glasses of wine before resuming his attack on the pile of chicken that lay on his plate.

Dammartin rubbed unthinkingly at the edge of his jaw. 'But think about it; if Mallington's hand injury meant that he could not fire a musket—'

'Are you doubting my word?' La Roque stopped eating.

'Of course I am not. But I am suggesting that you might

have been mistaken in the identity of the man that fired the shot. The shooter may have looked like Mallington—'

'The shooter damn well was Mallington. He was twenty yards away. I saw the bastard clearly with my own two eyes. Were it anyone else making such an accusation, I would place my sword at their throat.'

Dammartin raked a hand through his hair, his fingers leaving a ruffle of dark fingers in their wake. 'Frederic—'

'You wound me, Pierre, deeply.' La Roque pushed his plate away.

'Forgive me. It was never my intention.'

'I dread to think what your mother would say.'

Dammartin sighed. 'I meant no insult. It is not you that I doubt, but who you think that you saw pulling that trigger. I do not believe that it was Mallington.'

'What can have brought about such a madness in your mind?' La Roque's face paled. His eyes glittered as he stared at Dammartin, intent on his godson's answer.

Dammartin thought of Mallington's journal; he thought, too, of his promise to Josie. 'There is nothing in particular. I have been questioning Mademoiselle Mallington, and her answers have made me think.'

'What has the little bitch been saying?'

'She spoke in defence of her father's character.'

La Roque flushed. 'She is a liar, Pierre, a conniving, manipulative little liar, and the sooner you see it the better. You would do well to remember who she is, and who I am too.'

Dammartin looked into La Roque's now-ruddy face as his godfather made an effort to call back the anger of his words.

'I am sorry, Pierre, but I cannot forget what I saw Mallington do to your father, and I cannot forget that I was forced to ride away and leave him there dead. My feelings run high on the matter; they always will. When I look at Mademoiselle Mallington and see how she has turned your mind from the truth, I am enraged and, at the same time, beyond despair.' La Roque clenched his teeth and blinked away the moisture from his eyes.

'Frederic, Frederic...' Dammartin rose and pouring a large glass of brandy passed it to La Roque.

La Roque sniffed. 'I thought if you bedded her it would destroy her influence over you.' He took a generous swig of brandy.

'I am not influenced by Mademoiselle Mallington.'

'But I am afraid, Pierre, that you are, and it breaks my heart to see what Mallington's daughter has done to you.'

Dammartin took his farewells of his godfather and made his way back to Josie. He heard the echo of La Roque's words, and of his own.

La Roque was convinced that Mallington had fired the bullet that killed Jean Dammartin, and he had been there, witnessed the whole thing. Did what Mallington had written in his journal really change that? Could Dammartin even trust what Josie had said of her father's inability to fire a gun?

He had told La Roque that he was not influenced by Josie, when in truth it was she that filled his mind, his every walking hour. He craved her. He needed her. She influenced him beyond measure, whether he willed it or not. And the realisation of the extent of her control over him made Dammartin uneasy. Far from clarifying matters this night, he seemed only to have made things worse.

Josie was lying half dozing when she finally heard the tap at the door. She slipped from beneath the covers of the bed, shivering as the chill of the night touched her body through the thin linen of her shift.

'Pierre?' Only when she heard his reply did she turn the key within the lock to let him enter.

He smelled of damp night air and brandy, and the wool of his sleeve was cold beneath her fingers. The night was clear and moonlight flooded through the small window to bathe him in its strange silver light and its magic.

Outside the cathedral clock sounded eleven chimes.

She knew immediately that his meeting with La Roque had not gone well. His expression seemed strained, his face harshly handsome, his scar sinister.

'You are cold,' she said, brushing her fingers against his, the words so trivial beside everything that she really wanted to say.

'And tired.' He rubbed at the stubble of his chin. 'We should sleep.'

She retreated to the bed, snuggling beneath the covers over at the side closest to the window, lying there, watching him while he stripped off his clothing.

The contrast of moonlight and shadows played upon his body, revealing the taut rippled muscles of his abdomen, his chest, his shoulders and arms. She felt his weight tip the bed as he sat down upon its edge to ease off his boots and his stockings. His hands moved to free the fall on his breeches and he rose to his feet once more. Josie looked away, feeling her heart beating too fast, and the sudden flash of excitement within her belly. Her mouth was dry; she wetted her lips. She heard the soft thud of his breeches hitting the floor and then the mattress tilted once more as he climbed in beside her. She lay still, anticipating his touch, the feel of his hands upon her. But Dammartin made no move.

He lay there on his back, saying nothing, eyes open and staring up at the ceiling, waves of tension emanating from him.

Apprehension gripped at her and she knew that something was wrong.

The silence strained between them, hissing and loud, until she could bear it no more.

'How was your meeting with Major La Roque?'

She heard him swallow. 'There is nothing to speak of,' he said in a quiet voice devoid of emotion. 'The hour is late, go to sleep.'

'What is wrong, Pierre?' Dread tightened her stomach to a small, hard ball. She wondered what La Roque had said to make him this way.

'There is nothing wrong.' He sighed and turned away from her, to lie on his side.

She felt the sting of his rejection, and shivered. All of the warmth, of what had bound them together, had gone, and she did not understand why. Pride would not let her ask him again. She rolled to her side, close to the edge of the bed, and gazed out of the window.

At Telemos the moon had been a slim crescent, now it loomed huge and full outside, too big to be real, too bright for the night. So much had happened in those days in between. Her father was dead, his good name despoiled, and Josie's innocence lost. She had hated Pierre Dammartin, hated him more than she had thought it possible to hate, but somehow in their journey hate had turned to love. She could not say where, or how or even why. She should hate him still, but her heart was a traitor to all logic. And fool that she was, she had believed that he felt something of it, too, this ridiculous, accursed, forbidden love. But now…now she was no longer sure.

The ice crept from her feet up through her legs, from the tips of her fingers up through her arms. Josie did not shiver; rather she embraced the chill, praying it would soon reach her heart and numb the ache within.

Dammartin fixed his eyes upon the door, the wall, the crooked picture that hung upon it, anything in a bid to resist the temptation to turn to the woman who lay behind him. He could hear the soft sound of her breathing, feel her small movements as she curled on her side. Her faint scent of lavender water touched his nose. He tried to stay strong, to resist, determined that he, Pierre Dammartin, would not be so easily under the influence of any woman, but he could feel the insistent prick of guilt at the callous words he had uttered. And his mind was filled with her: whether she was hurting, whether she was cursing him, the sight of her standing by the door in her shift with the flimsy material revealing the protrusion of her nipples and contours of her hips. His skin tingled at the memory of that brief brush of her fingers.

Dammartin could resist no more. He rolled onto his back. 'Josie.'

She ignored him, lying there so still as if she were asleep.

He moved to her, curving his body around hers, warming her chill with his heat. His arm curled around her, anchoring her in, his hand finding hers and closing over it.

'Forgive me, Josie,' he said softly against her ear. He felt her hand move within his. 'I did not mean to hurt you.'

She turned in his arms, rolling round to look up into his face.

'I should not have spoken to you as I did.'

'You are tired,' she said, making excuses for him.

'No.' He shook his head. 'I am a fool...' he stroked her hair, gliding his hand down to gently cradle her face '...a thousand times over.' He lowered his face, and pressed a kiss to her forehead. 'There is something between us, Josie, you know that, do you not?' His lips lightly traced

the line of her nose to place a kiss upon its tip. 'I have tried
so hard to fight it.' His mouth reached hers and lingered
so close above, his breath brushing warm against her lips.
'Harder than you can imagine.' Their lips entwined, her
mouth responding to his with such sweet tenderness that
he almost could not break the kiss to pull back and look
deeply into her eyes. 'I want to kiss you and never stop.
I want to love you for an eternity. I need you, Josie Mallington. I need you like I have never needed anyone.' His
thumb caressed her cheek, slowly, sensually, conveying
with that small movement what his words could not. 'But
if you do not want this…if—'

She touched the tips of her fingers to his lips, cutting off
his words. 'I need you too. I know I should not. It is against
all sense, all logic, everything that is right. My father, and
yours, and the war…'

He saw in her eyes the same agony, the same desperation and fight as were in his soul. And he knew that Josie
was as powerless in all of this as he; that desire had made
slaves of them both. Her eyelids briefly closed and she
shook her head, and when her eyes opened again, she
reached up and touched her lips to his in a single kiss as
light as a butterfly's landing.

They were wrapped around each other, so close that
Josie could feel the beat of his heart where her hand rested
against his chest, strong and steady like the man himself.

She sighed.

'Josie,' he whispered, and one hand massaged a caress
against her back where he held her, while the other tilted
her face up until his mouth lowered to find hers. And he
began to kiss her again, slowly, gently, filled with tenderness and love.

He kissed her and kissed her, the stubble upon his chin
scratching her skin pink, until their mouths began to move

harder and faster, and their lips grew moist and needful. The kiss was everything to Josie. It clouded the pain of the past and obscured the fear of the future. There was only here and now and Pierre Dammartin. Her heart was thudding, but not with fear. Desire flowed through her veins. Her breasts tingled with it. Her thighs grew warm with it. She wanted the kiss never to end.

His hands moved down to caress her breasts, his thumbs teasing across their pebbled peaks. The thin linen of her shift strained against their sensitivity as Josie arched, thrusting herself into his hands, aching for his touch, wanting more.

Then his hands were pulling at the shift's neckline. 'Take it off,' he whispered.

She sat up and did as he bid, as eager to rid herself of the barrier between them as he was. But when she lay back down, he caught hold of the blankets before she could cover herself again.

'Let me look at you. I want to see you, every inch of you.'

She lay there, naked and exposed as the dark smoulder of his gaze travelled over her. He reached to touch her breast.

'I—I wish to see you too,' she said, amazed at her own boldness.

He smiled at that and climbed from the bed to stand before her. The moonlight paled his skin, and revealed every detail of his tall, athletic frame.

Josie stared, amazed at how different his body was to hers. He was all hard and lean and muscular, nothing of softness, nothing of curves. Her eyes skimmed the breadth of his shoulders, the strength of his arms, the dark, flat nipples of his chest, down lower to the regimented pattern of muscles that sat in lines across his abdomen, and lower still…to the nest of dark hair and his manhood that sprang from it, so large and rigid. Her cheeks flushed hot and her gaze dropped rapidly down his strong muscular legs to his feet.

'Do I pass muster, Mademoiselle Mallington?' he asked with a wry grin.

She cleared the dryness from her throat, feeling her cheeks grow hotter still. 'I have never looked upon the male form before.'

'That I am glad to hear.'

Then he reached his hand to her and pulled her up to him.

They stood there, naked in the moonlight. And Josie no longer noticed the coldness of the room, but the contrast of his skin as it caressed hers, and how big and honed and strong he was. She traced her fingers up his arm, across the tight, hard muscle of his chest, up his neck to reach his jaw, feeling the dark shadow of stubble rasp rough beneath her fingers. Her hand crept farther up to lay gently against the scar that ravaged his left cheek.

He stood very still, his eyes glittering and dark in the moonlight.

Then, standing on her tiptoes, she reached her face up and kissed the top of the scar. One kiss and then another and another, tracing down the long line of the scar until all of it had been kissed.

From outside in the streets came the sound of men's voices, French, drunk, the clatter of their boots against the cobbles, and of women's laughter, deep and throaty. But neither Josie's nor Dammartin's gazes shifted. They stayed steady, trained on each other.

He moved his knuckles to gently stroke the outer edges of her breasts. She sucked the breath hard into her lungs.

'You are beautiful,' he whispered, the backs of his fingers thrumming against her taut nipples, 'so beautiful.'

He dropped to his knees before her and she gasped, feeling the excitement shimmer within her as his lips grazed the skin of her stomach. His breath was hot, searing a path up to her ribs. Her breasts were heavy with need, ripe for his touch. Her nipples, standing to attention, hard and ready within the cool night air.

She did not look, just stood there waiting, while in her mind she was urging him to do it, begging his mouth to suckle upon her. And as his mouth closed over one breast, his tongue flicking over its most sensitive tip, she sighed her relief. He sucked her and the warmth low in her belly ignited. She looked then, saw his head so dark against the pallor of her breast, and the sight of what he was doing to her caused her thighs to burn. Her fingers threaded through his hair, pressing him closer, inviting him to feast all the more.

But he pulled back, his dark smouldering gaze flicking up to hers, as his mouth slid lower, retracing its path to where it had started. She felt him hot against her stomach, his tongue circling around her navel before travelling on down. Josie gasped as he kissed the curled fair hair of her mound, his hands moulding to her buttocks, guiding what he wanted to his mouth.

'Pierre!' She gasped in shock.

But he was between her legs and she found herself opening instinctively to him. She groaned as his tongue stroked her most intimate of places, and the unexpected raw pleasure of it shimmied through her. He kissed her there and the need within her spiralled. He sucked her and the need stoked hotter and hotter until she was burning with it. His tongue flicked and licked at her and the need raged, unbridled and wanton, and she was panting and her legs were trembling.

He rose then, scooped her up into his arms and laid her on the bed, climbing over her and pulling the blankets to cover them both.

She felt his manhood against her belly, probing and firm, while elsewhere their bodies barely touched.

He stroked her hair, stroked her cheek, looked deep into her eyes and there she saw such love that it took her breath away.

'Pierre,' she whispered his name into the stillness of the night. 'Pierre.' And she knew only the depth of her love for this man and the depth of her desire.

He moved, and his manhood was between her legs, touching where his mouth had been, sliding with such slow enticement against her wetness. She wanted him. She needed him. Such overwhelming love could not be wrong. Her hips moved against his instinctively, sliding herself along the length of his shaft, gasping with the pleasure it wrought.

'Josie,' he whispered into her ear, and there was a pause before he thrust into her, filling her with himself. There was the smallest of pains, but he was kissing her again and their breaths mingled and their bodies were unified, and the pain was forgotten. As he began to move inside her, Josie knew that this was meant to be—nothing had ever seemed so right.

They were as one, a man and his woman moving together in the most intimate of sharings—a physical expression of their love, two souls entwined. With each thrust Pierre claimed her as his own. She writhed beneath him, feeling the pleasure riotous and wanton, knowing that this bond would bind them for eternity. She looked up into his face, and it was dark and shadowed despite the brightness of the moon high in the sky outside, and the intensity in his eyes was scalding. Someone groaned, moaned, gasped and she did not know whether it was Pierre or herself from whom the sounds issued.

She loved him, loved him absolutely, overwhelmingly. She clutched at him, moving faster with him, clinging to him, crying out his name for this merging of souls until, with one last thrust, all the barriers broke, and her whole being exploded in a myriad of ecstasy. Such bliss. Such euphoria. Such love. The joy of it pulsated through every inch of her being, every corner of her mind.

She was his, and he was hers. They were as one.

Josie could see that the strength of love transcended everything; all else was tiny in comparison with its vastness. Love was all. War and power and politics were as nothing. All that had been and all that lay ahead was, in that moment, irrelevant. She loved him; they had shared that love in a union of their bodies, and nothing else mattered.

They clung together in the darkness, even when Pierre arranged the covers over them that they might not grow cold through the night. She clung to him and there was no need for words. She did not think of the past nor of the future. There was only now, this precious moment with the man that she loved, and the glorious wonder of it. And eventually she slept.

Major La Roque sat up late. He had finished the best part of a bottle of brandy and it still did not make matters any better. It was all Josephine Mallington's fault. How he rued the day that they had chanced upon Mallington and the girl in Telemos. *Then* it had seemed like a godsend. Mallington's death should have freed him from the constant torment the past months had brought. But he had not reckoned on the girl.

What kind of madman took his daughter to war? What was she even doing there in that goddamn monastery? She should have been killed there, like her father. La Roque still did not understand how she could have walked out of the monastery alive.

Damn her, and the spell she had woven over his godson. Because of her, Pierre was asking too many questions. Because of her, Pierre doubted his own godfather's word. Jean Dammartin was dead, and La Roque's heart was still heavy with the grief of it, but at least there had always been Pierre. But now Pierre no longer believed Mallington's guilt and that knowledge shook the very foundations of La Roque's defences.

He stared at the empty brandy glass, tracing his finger slowly around its rim—such a delicate balancing act, just like life itself, he thought. He had involved Molyneux for Pierre's own good, trusting in his own instinct that the girl might cause trouble, but not for one moment had he imagined just what her presence might lead to.

Pierre should have been repulsed by her, he should have hated her as La Roque now hated her. But Pierre had wanted her, and now it did not matter how quickly he tired of bedding her. He could cast her aside tomorrow and it would be too late; the damage had already been done, the spectres raised.

La Roque unstoppered the bottle and emptied the last of the brandy into his glass.

There was nothing else for it, nothing else he could do. What damn choice did he have if he wanted to survive? The agony that he had endured in these months seemed trivial in comparison to that which lay ahead, but La Roque would bear it; he had to. It would be the best for them all in the end. All the risk had to be destroyed. He sat alone, sipping his brandy, and made his plans for tomorrow.

* * *

Dammartin woke, and for the first time in such a long time there was a contentment about him, a calmness, a warmth. He felt the weight of Josie's legs entwined in his and he smiled. Last night had been wonderful; this morning was wonderful; Josie Mallington was simply wonderful.

The light was still murky with the night, but there seemed to be a slightly golden quality about it, a strange brightness within the dark. He dropped a kiss to Josie's head and, taking care not to wake her, climbed from the bed. Fetching up his discarded jacket from the chair, he draped it around his shoulders against the chill and moved to stand quietly at the window.

At one side the sky was lit with a warm, golden hue, while across the way still lay the mid-inky blue of night. And as he watched the glow intensified and spread, warm and ethereal. Across the city the rooftops were covered with a glittering white frost, and from a few chimneys smoke curled wispy into the air. Dawn moved across the sky, lightening its blue, opening up a new day. A bird was singing, while others chirped, and it seemed to Dammartin the most glorious of mornings to be alive.

His mind slipped once more to the woman sleeping in the bed behind him, and his heart seemed to fill with joy and he found that he was smiling. If this was lust, it was like no lust Dammartin had ever known. La Roque might say what he would, but Dammartin had no intention of giving up Josie. He wanted to hold her in his arms for ever, to keep her safe from all harm, to make her happy. He smiled again at the thought of it.

'Pierre?' Her voice sounded sleepy and unsure.

He turned from the window and went back to bed,

snuggling into her, ignoring her protestations that he was cold.

'I will soon make you warm again, *ma chérie*,' he whispered against her ear. And he kissed her, and, with such gentle tenderness, loved her all over again.

The streets were busy with voices and footsteps by the time that Dammartin finally left the bed to hurriedly wash, shave and dress.

Josie was sitting up in the bed, the covers pulled high, hugging her knees. Part of her feared to ask the question, not wishing to destroy what last night and this morning had brought, but the other part knew that she must.

'Pierre…' She hesitated, before continuing, 'What did Major La Roque say last night that was so very bad?'

The blade within Dammartin's hand nicked the edge of his chin. *'Merde,'* he muttered beneath his breath, and pressed the towel to stem the blood.

'I am sorry,' she said, 'I should not have asked.'

Dammartin sighed. 'You have every right to ask, Josie, but I do not think that you will like the answer.' He finished scraping the beard growth from his face before splashing the water up to cleanse away the stubble-peppered soap lather. Only when he had finished and was drying his face did he turn to her.

'La Roque was only twenty yards from the man that shot my father. He is adamant that the man was Lieutenant Colonel Mallington and no other.'

'But you know that is impossible. You have read my father's journal. You know about the injury to his hand.'

'I am afraid that neither are conclusive proof of his innocence, Josie.'

'But you believed me before.' She threw aside the covers

and climbed out of the bed to stand there naked beside it. 'Are you saying that you no longer do so?'

Dammartin's gaze swept briefly down over her body. 'I think that your father did not murder mine, but—' his eyes came back up to meet hers '—the truth is, I can never be absolutely certain of it.'

The hurt welled up in her, gushing and disbelieving. 'Then you do not truly believe me at all,' she said, and all of the magic of the night and the morning shrivelled and died.

'That is not what I am saying, Josie.' He pulled the shirt on over his head, and lifted his breeches from where they lay on the floor.

'It sounds like that to me,' she retorted.

'I do not have time to argue with you over this, this morning. We will speak of it later, I promise.' He fastened the fall on his breeches and fetched his cravat and waistcoat from the chair.

'What of La Roque stealing my father's journals? What of his giving me to Molyneux that he might find the missing journal? Do you believe the truth of that?' She watched him, holding her breath, waiting for his answer.

'Josie,' he chided.

'Tell me,' she said from between gritted teeth.

She heard his sigh. He finished tying the cravat in place and looked round from the mirror. 'If La Roque had the journals, I would know of it. What need has he to lie? Your portmanteau was probably stolen and dumped without the journals ever having been recovered.'

'And Molyneux?' she demanded.

'You are a beautiful woman, Josie, and Molyneux can hardly keep his breeches up at the best of times.'

'That is not true; he is married with two small sons.'

He gathered his boots and sat upon the chair to pull

them hard upon his feet. 'Molyneux is not married, and as to children, who knows what he has left behind. He was spinning you a story, Josie, that he might crawl beneath your skirts.'

She flinched at his baseness. 'He was acting on La Roque's orders.'

Dammartin eased himself into his jacket, fastening each button with speed. 'La Roque may well have encouraged Molyneux's interest as he so disapproves of mine. He loved my father and sees…our friendship, as a betrayal.'

Josie looked down at her nakedness, to her breasts peaked hard with the cold, and the bloodsmears that stained the pale skin of her inner thighs. She had given herself to him, body and heart, and still he did not believe her. And she could have laughed bitterly at the irony of his talk of betrayal.

'You do not believe anything that I have told you,' she said, and could not hide the anger and hurt from her words.

'*Chérie.*' He came to her, pulling a blanket from the bed to wrap around her, rubbing his hands over her to chase away the chill. 'You misinterpreted what you overheard of La Roque's and Molyneux's conversation.' His hand stroked against her hair. 'Now get dressed before you are frozen completely.' He pressed a brief kiss to her lips. 'I am already late, I have to go, but we will talk of this later, yes?'

'No,' she said firmly, 'I do not wish to talk of it later.'

'I have not the time for this now, Josie.'

'No, for you have had what you wanted—my father's journal and my body in your bed,' she said bitterly.

The light fled from Dammartin's face. He stilled, just stood there for a moment and stared at her.

She had said the words to hurt him just as he had hurt her, and she could see in his eyes that she had done just that. But the feeling was not one of victory; it did not make her feel better; her own hurt was not lessened by the cruel retaliation. She opened her mouth to tell him that she was sorry, that she had not meant it, but he turned and was gone. The door closed behind him and his footsteps echoed along the passageway towards the stairs, leaving Josie more alone than ever.

Dammartin departed La Roque's office in a hurry, the small leather document wallet tucked securely within his jacket. He already knew which men he would select for the mission—those that were trustworthy, and fast, whose aim was true and whose courage was great...and Molyneux, of course, since Dammartin could not trust that Josie would be safe with the Lieutenant around.

He spoke to Lamont first, making sure that his sergeant understood why he was being left behind. 'There is no one that I trust more to guard her. Do this for me, my friend, and forgive me that I do not take you with me.'

Lamont nodded.

'Have a care, Pierre. The road to Valladolid is a dangerous one for any Frenchman, and I grow too long in the tooth to be taking orders from a new puppy of a captain.'

Dammartin smiled and clapped his friend on the arm. 'You will not be rid of me so easily, Claude. Keep the brandy ready for my return.'

They laughed, but both of them understood the risk involved in travelling through Spain with such a small escort.

'Ready the men. There is something I must do before I leave.' Dammartin made his way back up to his room.

Chapter Fourteen

Josie was sitting in a chair by the window, bathed in sunlight and stitching a tear in one of Pierre's shirts when he arrived.

He came in, leaving the door open behind him and picked up his portmanteau. 'I am for Valladolid with an urgent message for General Foy. I have come to take my leave of you.'

Her heart plummeted at his words. The sewing was set hastily aside as she jumped to her feet. 'You are leaving now?'

He gave a nod. 'We are under orders to pass a letter to Foy before he departs for Paris.'

He could not go now, she thought, not when there was so much that she needed to say to him. She felt as if the rug had been pulled from beneath her feet. Her fingers touched to her forehead. 'How many men travel with you? Are there not bandits on the road?'

'Go to Lamont if there are any problems. Rosa shall keep you company during the days, and if you are afraid at night, I am sure that she would stay. All being well, I should be back some time next week.'

He was going and she was not fool enough to dismiss the danger of his journey.

'Molyneux, he comes with me, so you need not worry over him, but Ciudad Rodrigo is filled with men. Keep the door locked. Do not venture out alone.' He produced a purse from his pocket and threw it on to the bed. 'There should be enough money in there to buy yourself food, clothes, whatever you need.'

She looked at the purse, feeling her heart beating very fast, and then up at Dammartin. 'You are leaving no guard; you are giving me money and freedom. Are you not afraid that I will escape?'

'I can no longer hold you against your will, Josie. If you wish to leave me, I will not stop you.'

Their gazes met and held.

The sunlight glinted against the darkness of his hair and lightened his eyes to a clear warm amber.

She did not understand what this meant. She wanted him to want her. She wanted him to fight for her, to hold her in his arms and kiss her and love her as he had done so often. But everything had changed. Cruel words spoken in haste lay between them; cruel words and a lack of faith.

They looked at each other across the little room for a moment longer, and as he turned to go, she knew that she could not let him leave like this.

'Pierre.'

He stopped, looked back at her.

'The words that I spoke to you this morning, I…I did not mean—'

The shuffle of booted feet sounded outside the door, a man clearing his throat before he knocked.

Josie bit at her lip, all explanations and apologies left unspoken.

He gave a nod of acknowledgement. '*Au revoir*, Josie.'

And she wanted to tell him, wanted to shout the truth out loud to him, but the door swung wide and Lamont was standing there, his little black eyes watching them.

'Captain,' he murmured. 'The Major wishes to see you before you leave.'

Dammartin nodded. 'I am coming, Claude.'

One last look and then he turned and walked away, closing the door behind him as he went, leaving only the sound of brisk booted footsteps that receded into nothing.

Josie stood by the window and watched Pierre ride out with only twenty-five of his dragoons, knowing that there was a very real risk that he would not come back.

After he had gone she sat in the chair and stared out of the window, thinking and thinking some more, as the sun moved across the sky.

Only twenty-five men to secure his safety when Foy had taken twenty times that number. And she thought what he might face—Spanish armies, disgruntled locals, murderous bandits, all of whom had a reason to hate Bonaparte's men. The horrible stories of what they did to the French soldiers that they captured made her shudder. If Pierre were to suffer, if he were to die… She closed her eyes to the thought, unable to bear it. Such cruel imaginings to torture herself with, not knowing for days whether he was safe, whether he still lived.

She thought of their parting: awkward, stilted, with so many barriers between them. And she had not had the chance to tell him that she regretted her harsh words, that they were spoken only out of hurt and anger, that she had known that they were not true. He had gone carrying those same words with him, not knowing the truth that she loved him.

The sky stretched unending in a clear, pale blue silk, and as she stared at it, she knew that was her biggest regret of all. She loved him, and she had not told him so. She loved him, and he might die without knowing it.

He did not believe her, she reminded herself, but what was that in comparison to losing him? Whether he believed her or not now seemed of little consequence. Was it so bad that Pierre should have some measure of loyalty to his godfather? He had wanted to speak of it this evening, but Josie and his orders had ruined that. He was gone, and her heart had gone with him.

Dammartin scanned the surrounding rocks while his men rested and the horses took their fill from the stream. He swigged from his canteen, wetting his parched throat and leaned back against the boulder behind him.

'Anything?' he shouted across at the trooper who had been posted as lookout.

His man shook his head. 'Nothing, Captain.'

Molyneux approached, his face sheepish. 'Captain, I wonder if I might speak with you.'

Dammartin gave a slight nod.

'I wished to apologise for what has happened between us. One evening when I was visiting the women's tent, Major La Roque called me in and explained that he was concerned for you because of Mademoiselle Mallington. He is a most important man, and your godfather, and so when he asked me to keep him informed of matters concerning Mademoiselle Mallington, I could not refuse him. I was not permitted to tell you, sir, and for that I am sorry.'

'I understand the position you were put in, Lieutenant.' Dammartin stoppered his canteen and placed the strap across his body, fixing the container back into place by his hip.

Molyneux visibly relaxed.

'What did the Major offer you in return for your…help?' Dammartin's eyes met Molyneux's before the Lieutenant glanced away.

Molyneux cleared his throat and would not meet his gaze.

'Come, come, Molyneux, do not be shy. Tell me,' Dammartin said quietly, with the barest suggestion of a threat about the words.

'He offered me the girl.' Molyneux glanced fearfully up at his captain.

Dammartin frowned. 'Mademoiselle Mallington?'

Molyneux nodded. 'I would not have hurt her.'

'Just taken her against her will,' said Dammartin dryly. So Josie had not misunderstood. She had known exactly what was going on, and if she had been right about that… 'And the journal?'

Shock flitted across Molyneux's face. 'You were not supposed to know about the journal. The Major said—' He stopped himself in time.

'What *did* the Major say, Lieutenant Molyneux?' Dammartin's eyes narrowed.

But Molyneux just shook his head.

A hollow feeling of dread rose in Dammartin. 'La Roque was sending you to retrieve the journal from Mademoiselle Mallington by means of rape.'

'It would not have been like that. She trusted me. She would have given it over to me. I would have been gentle with her, for all that La Roque said I might do.'

Dammartin's lip curled, he glanced away, and gave a subtle shake of his head, and as he looked back, he stepped forwards and landed his fist hard against Molyneux's jaw. The force of the blow sent Molyneux sprawling.

'Stand up, Lieutenant.'

Molyneux got to his feet, dabbing a hand gingerly to the blood that trickled from his lip. He did not cower, just faced Dammartin squarely. 'I suppose that I deserve that.'

'When Mademoiselle Mallington came to me, what then?' demanded Dammartin, thinking fast.

'The Major said you would soon tire of her, and then...'

'You would have her.'

Molyneux nodded. 'He wants the journal.'

Dammartin's face hardened. 'If he wants it so damn badly, he is not going to sit and wait for us to come back from Valladolid, is he? He thinks Josie has it, and he will go to her to get it.'

'He would not—' Molyneux stopped, and his gaze met Dammartin's.

'I think perhaps we both have underestimated my god-father, Molyneux.'

'But she just needs to give him the journal and she will be safe.'

'She cannot give him the journal,' Dammartin said in a cynical voice, 'when it is in my possession, can she? I am going back to Ciudad Rodrigo. You must deliver the letter to Foy.'

Molyneux stared in disbelief before he nodded.

Dammartin put his hand into his pocket to retrieve the document wallet with its letter just as the lookout shouted...and the shots began to fire.

Josie was still sitting in the chair by the window when the knock sounded at the door. Rosa, the thought flashed in her mind and she went to let the Spanish woman in, pausing by the door before she opened it.

'Rosa, is that you?'

There was a silence before the reply sounded.

'Mademoiselle Mallington.'

Josie recognised the voice and her scalp prickled with the knowledge of who stood there. 'Major La Roque,' she said through the wood of the door.

'Open the door, *mademoiselle*.'

She remembered that night crouched outside his tent, and of the words she had heard. She made no move, just stood there quiet and waiting.

The door handle rattled beneath La Roque's hand, making her jump back.

'I bring bad news of Captain Dammartin.'

She felt the sudden dip in her stomach at his words. It had to be a trick. La Roque would not come himself to tell her of anything. She glared at the handle, part of her willing him to go away, the other small part scared that he was telling the truth. Lamont would know, she thought, he would come to tell her of any news.

There was silence and as the minutes ticked by she wondered if La Roque was still out there. Maybe he had gone; maybe she was safe.

There was a wrenching sound, the splitting of wood; the door vibrated beneath its force. Josie backed away, her eyes scanning the room for a weapon, but it was too late. The door swung quietly open and La Roque walked slowly in. In his hand was the long knife with which he had levered the door to burst its lock.

He pushed the door behind him, closing it as best he could against the splintered frame. 'There is much we have to discuss, *mademoiselle*, and it so much easier to speak face to face, do you not agree?'

She could feel her throat grip tight to her breath, feel

her mouth dry in an instant. Her eyes looked to the knife in his hand.

'Do not let this worry you, at least not yet.' He slipped the knife inside his jacket. 'And you need not fear that the Spanish doxy shall interrupt us; I have ensured that she will be kept busy for some time.' He smiled, but his eyes were like ice.

She wetted her lips nervously. 'What do you want?'

He laughed. 'I like a woman that gets straight down to business.'

She backed away to stand by the window, her eyes flicking to the partly open door.

La Roque positioned himself between Josie and the door, blocking her in, covering the exit. 'I want Lieutenant Colonel Mallington's journal for Oporto.'

'I do not have it,' she said.

La Roque raised his eyebrows. 'Oh, but I know that you do, *mademoiselle*.' He looked at her with those pale eyes of his.

'You are mistaken, sir.' She forced herself to sound calm.

'Then where is it?'

She bit at her lip, feeling the fast trip of her heart within her chest, the thrum of her pulse in her throat, knowing that she could not tell him.

'It has to be with you as it was not with the others at the bottom of your portmanteau,' he said.

Her mind was whirring, frantically seeking a way to escape him.

'You are not surprised, I see, *mademoiselle*, by my knowledge of the journals. I wonder to whom you might have been listening.'

And for one awful moment she thought that he knew

of her eavesdropping…but that was not what La Roque meant.

'Did Molyneux tell you? He cannot think any higher than what hangs between his legs.'

She balked at his vulgarity.

'I want that journal, Mademoiselle Mallington.' His hand slipped within his jacket, and when it came out again, it was holding the knife. 'And I will do whatever it takes to have it from you.'

Her eyes widened. She backed away until her legs were pressing hard against the chair, her gaze frantically seeking a way she might reach the door; but La Roque stood between her and that route of escape.

'By the time that I have finished with you, *mademoiselle*, you will be begging me to take the journal from you.' He smiled and moved towards her.

One look at his face told her he was in deadly earnest, and yet still she could not tell him the truth, for she feared what he would do if he knew that Pierre had hidden the journal from him. 'I burnt the journal, Major La Roque, for fear that it would fall into French hands like the others.'

'A clever attempt, *mademoiselle*,' La Roque sneered, 'but I do not think that you would destroy the only evidence of what happened in Oporto that day.'

The silence hissed between them as the penny dropped in her mind. Her eyes met his. 'You know,' she said as if she could not quite believe it. If La Roque knew her father to be guilty, then why would she not destroy the evidence that could prove it was so. But La Roque's words revealed that he knew otherwise. She stared at him aghast as she understood the implication of his words. 'You know that my father was innocent. That is why you want the journal,' she said slowly, 'not to protect Pierre, but to hide the truth.' The sickness welled in her stomach at the realisation that followed, for there could be only one reason why La Roque wished to hide the truth.

Something of it must have shown in her face, for La Roque stepped closer. 'I see that you have guessed my little secret.'

'What secret is that, sir?' She tried to feign ignorance.

'Come now, *mademoiselle*, it is written all over your face.'

'I do not know what you mean.'

'Oh, but I think that you do,' he said, as his hand closed around her wrist. 'An English woman alone amidst an entire French garrison and not just any English woman— the daughter of one of the most hated men in all of France. It is hardly surprising that some loyal soldier shall take his revenge.'

She tried to pull away from him, but he squeezed his fingers and held her tighter. 'Pierre shall know what you have done.'

'No, Mademoiselle Mallington, he will never know.' He looked her directly in the eye. 'You see, I was not lying when I said that I brought bad news of Captain Dammartin.'

The fear was churning in her gut, but none of it was for herself. Her lips felt cold and stiff, making it hard to force the words out through them. 'What do you mean? What has happened to Pierre?'

'He will not be coming back,' he said quietly.

'How can you know that?'

La Roque just looked at her with his cold, dead eyes, and she knew.

Her legs began to shake with the dread of it. The breath was uneven within her throat, and her fists clenched. All of the pieces fell into place. 'It was you that ordered Pierre to ride to Valladolid with the letter for General Foy.'

'The letter that he carries is unimportant; it was merely an excuse to get him away from Ciudad Rodrigo.'

The chill was spreading throughout her body, and the pulse was hammering in her head. 'Why would you do that?'

'Why do you think, *mademoiselle*? Pierre and his men will be attacked by guerrillas. The letter will be stolen, and no French survivors left, no loose ends.'

'Oh, dear Lord!' She shook her head as if she could not believe what he was saying. 'Why? He is your godson, for pity's sake!' she cried.

She saw the pain crease his face. 'Do you think it does not kill a part of me to have to do this? It is like ripping out my own heart.'

'Then do not do it. Please!'

He shook his head. 'I must.' His mouth contorted and she could see the hostility blazing in his eyes. 'The fault is all yours, *mademoiselle*.'

She stared at him in horror.

'Everything was going so well until you came along. Pierre and his brother and his mother looked up to me. I took the role that had been Jean's: hero, father, protector. All of France respected me. And all because Jean was dead by the hand of the evil Lieutenant Colonel Mallington. Do you know how much Pierre hated your father? Do you know that in all of the months since Jean's death, Pierre thought only to look into your father's eyes as he killed him?'

'He believed the lie that my father had murdered his.'

'He did.' La Roque's mouth twisted up at that and the smile was filled with pain and bitterness and anger. 'Until Mademoiselle Mallington inveigled herself into his life and, with her charms…' he swept a glance down over her body '…captured him.'

The smile had gone and his expression was grief-stricken. 'Pierre is too like Jean. Once he was no longer convinced of Mallington's guilt, there was a very great risk that he would discover the truth. I have known Pierre all his life, watched him grow from a boy to a man. I love him as if he is my own son.'

'And yet you would kill him!' she cried.

'I have no choice!' She saw the tears well within his eyes. 'I could not let him know what I had done. Thanks to you, *mademoiselle*, he questioned my word. Everything between us has changed.'

It was she who had unwittingly signed Pierre's death warrant. 'No, you are wrong, sir. You are his godfather. Pierre looks up to you. He respects you. He does not believe my protestations of my father's innocence.'

'Indeed?' La Roque looked cynical. 'And yet he has kept you against all of my advice, Mademoiselle Mallington—the daughter of the man he is supposed to believe murdered his father. He craves you in a way I have never seen Pierre act over a woman. I begin to fear the worst—that there is more between the two of you than just lust.'

She felt the heat rise in her cheeks. 'Call off the attack, please. I am begging you. I will do anything that you want. I will give you anything that you want.'

'You will do that regardless, *mademoiselle*.' And when he looked at her, she could see the cold hatred blazing in his eyes. 'Besides, it is too late. What has been set in motion cannot be stopped. Indeed…' he glanced out at the sun's position in the sky '…the deed should be long done. There can never be any going back.' He smiled and it was filled with a melancholic bitterness. 'As you are so committed to revealing the truth, Mademoiselle Mallington, I will tell you a little truth that you do not know.' He leaned forwards so that his face was close to hers.

Her fingers gripped the chair behind her.

'Molyneux told me that you are unaware of the fate of your father's messengers.'

She grew very still.

There was a pause before he continued. 'They did not reach Wellington. We found them, and we shot them like the dogs that they were.'

Josie felt the words hit her like bullets. 'No,' she whispered. 'They were not caught.'

La Roque just stood there and looked at her.

'No!' she said again. 'You're lying; you're lying now just as you lied about my father.'

He smiled a small, icy smile that made her shiver. 'It is because of you that I have sent Pierre to his death, and broken my own heart and that of his dear mother in doing so. Now you will suffer as I suffer. I wish to God that you had died in Telemos that day, Josephine Mallington.'

The tears streamed silently down her face. Her father had sacrificed himself and his men in vain. The man that she loved was dead. She had nothing left to lose, and all of the fear left her, and her devastation was so great that it seemed to Josie that she felt nothing at all. She looked at the man who had started the whole cycle of destruction with the murder of his friend.

'Why did you do it? Why did you kill Jean Dammartin?' As she looked, she saw that hatred and fear had eaten away at him to leave only the shell of a tired old man who had killed those he loved best.

'Does it matter?'

She opened her mouth to reply, but the door suddenly thumped back hard, reverberating against the wall.

'Yes, it damn well matters!' said Pierre Dammartin as he strode into the room.

'Pierre?' Josie heard La Roque utter his name with incredulity.

She did not know how much of the conversation Pierre had overheard, and she did not care. She stared at him, not quite believing that he was really here in the little room with her, and not dead by La Roque's traitorous order miles away in the desolation of the Spanish countryside. She was unsure whether he was real or a ghost or a vision willed by her imagination. The tears were still welling in her eyes, dripping down her cheeks. She scrubbed them away, stared at him all the harder. The steel of his blade hissed as he drew it from its scabbard. Then he glanced over at her, his gaze meeting hers momentarily, and his eyes were dark and simmering with something that Josie had never seen in them before.

'Has he hurt you?'

She shook her head, not trusting her voice to answer.

He gave a tiny nod of acknowledgement, then turned his attention back to La Roque. 'Drop the knife.'

The knife clattered to the floor.

'P-Pierre, you should be on your way to Valladolid,' said La Roque. 'The letter for General Foy—'

'We were attacked by guerrillas and many good men were lost, but then you already know that, Frederic, do you not? Their leader squealed like a pig with my blade at his throat, and told me of the French major who had paid him to kill his own French dragoons.'

'The villain was lying. I would never—' La Roque began.

'Do not waste your breath,' said Dammartin. 'Now, Major La Roque, you were about to explain why you murdered my father.'

La Roque's face had turned ashen. 'I—I...' He seemed

to stumble over the words and looked at Dammartin beseechingly. 'You are mistaken—'

The sharp edge of Dammartin's sabre raised to point at La Roque. 'Your explanation, if you would be so kind, Major.'

La Roque moved his eyes from the blade to his godson. 'It is not as it seems.'

Dammartin just stared at him in stony silence. He did not utter one word. He made not one movement. Just stood there, with his blade pointed at La Roque, and his very stillness was more threatening than if he had slashed and shouted and swore.

'You would not kill me, Pierre,' said La Roque slowly, 'after all that we have been through together. A lifetime, your mother, your brother…'

Dammartin moved and the sabre blade touched ever so gently against La Roque's heart.

'Very well.' La Roque inhaled a shaky breath and gave a nod. 'I suppose that you, of all people, have a right to know.' He cleared his throat nervously and began to speak. 'I worked hard all my life, harder than anyone else I have known, harder by far than Jean, and as a result I was good at many things. Good, but never quite as good as Jean. It was always that way—as boys and as men. Jean always won the race while I always came second—even with Marie.'

'Leave my mother out of this.'

'I loved her, but it was Jean that she chose to marry, not me. He had the woman that I wanted. He had the sons that should have been mine. He had a bigger house, more money. He outranked me in the army. And then there was the Battle of Oporto when we were captured by Lieutenant Colonel Mallington. I saw the way that even his enemy looked at him—with respect, with admiration, as a friend.

Mallington barely looked at me at all. I knew then that beside Jean I would always be nothing, no matter how hard I tried.

'Mallington gave us our parole and we rode away. Jean was in front of me, as always, and…' he swallowed '…and—I shot him. I could not help myself. There was just one minute when the idea came to me, one minute to make a choice to change a lifetime.

'I had a chance to escape from his shadow, a chance that people might actually see me for once, and I took it. And I was right. Marie needed me. You and Kristoffe needed me.' He stopped talking and looked at Dammartin.

'I shot myself in the arm—a minor wound that amounted to nothing. You know the rest.' He stopped again. 'I am so sorry, Pierre.'

'Not half as sorry as I am.' Dammartin's voice was low and filled with deadly promise.

La Roque's face crumpled in entreaty. 'Forgive me.'

Dammartin gave a hollow, mocking laugh. 'You killed my father and sent me for vengeance against an innocent man. You lied to me and would have had my lieutenant rape Josie, and you think that I will forgive you?' Dammartin's lip sneered as he pressed the blade hard and made to slash.

'No, Pierre!' The words tore from Josie.

'You know what he has done, to your father and to mine, to you and to me. How can you tell me to stay my hand?'

'If you kill him, you will be court-martialled and executed.'

'I do not care.' His eyes, still focused on La Roque, were hard and ruthless. She saw how hard his blade pressed against La Roque's chest.

'But I do,' she said. 'I have lost everyone, do not make

me lose you too.' She paused. 'I love you, Pierre. I should have told you that this morning.'

He looked round at her and as he did so La Roque moved, throwing himself away from the blade and towards Josie. The Major wrenched her back hard against the front of his body and drew his sword.

'I think you might want to drop your weapons, Pierre,' La Roque said as he pressed the edge of his sword to her throat.

'Do not! He will kill you regardless,' she managed to shout before the cold touch of the blade became an unbearable pressure that threatened to choke her.

'Do it!' urged La Roque in a coarse whisper, and she gasped as he began to tilt the blade edge towards her skin.

Dammartin's gaze met Josie's, and she saw the agony in them and heard the clatter of his sabre and pistol hitting the floor. 'Release her.'

La Roque smiled. 'Kick them over here.'

Dammartin watched La Roque like a hawk watches its prey, his eyes locked on those of his godfather's, as he did as he was bid. 'This is not about Josie. Let her go.'

La Roque gave a chuckle. 'On the contrary, this is very much about Mademoiselle Mallington. She has destroyed everything for which I worked so hard.'

He began to walk towards Dammartin, driving Josie before him as a shield.

She could barely breathe for the blade, which seemed to press ever harder. He was going to kill Dammartin, she knew it, and there was nothing she could do, and still Dammartin just stood there, letting La Roque close the distance, and she wanted to cry out to him to run, that La Roque would kill her anyway. Dammartin must have known that, too, but there was nothing on his face save the cold hunger of a hunter.

Just as they reached Dammartin, La Roque threw her away, before he lunged with his sword at Dammartin.

She landed hard beneath the window. Her ears were filled with a scream and she did not know that it was her own voice that cried. Everything seemed to slow: movements, words, time itself as La Roque's blade headed directly for Dammartin's heart.

To Josie there was no way he could evade the death-blow and she was yelling, her eyes widening with horror, scrambling to her feet—all too slow, too useless. And just as she thought the blade would strike she saw Dammartin react, sidestepping to come in so close to La Roque that their faces were almost touching, jerking La Roque's wrist until the sword dropped to lie upon the floor. Then the two men were fighting, with fists and feet, kicking and punching, so that their blood began to splatter as each hit thumped home—flesh pounding against flesh, the sheer ferocity awful to watch.

Josie tried to reach Dammartin's sabre and pistol, or La Roque's knife where they lay, but the two men were moving around the room so much that she could not get to them. She glanced around for anything that could be used as a weapon, anything to help Pierre. But there was nothing. When she looked again, Dammartin was punching and punching at La Roque, harder and harder, until his cuffs were soaked with La Roque's blood, and La Roque lay limp upon the floor.

Only then did Dammartin look at her.

He stood there with his face cut and bruised and bleeding, and his coat torn and stained dark with blood, and in his eyes was such intensity that it took her breath away.

He came to her then, walking slowly, and, reaching down to where she stood, pulled her up to him. 'I did not believe you.'

'It does not matter.' He was alive, alive, and she was dizzy with the relief of it.

'I am sorry,' he whispered, and feathered kisses to the top of her head, her eyebrows, the tip of her nose. 'So very sorry, for you and for your father.'

She could feel that her cheeks were wet, and taste her tears mixed with his blood as his lips brushed hers.

'My love.' He caressed her face as he kissed her again and again, his eyes imploring her forgiveness. 'My sweet Josie.'

His arms wrapped around her, crushing her to him as if he would never let her go, as if he would merge their two bodies together.

'What he said about your father's messengers was a lie told to hurt you. We did not catch them, *chérie*.'

Josie clung to him, as he clung to her, and in his caress, in his kiss, in his very touch he offered her all of his comfort, all of her strength, all of his love, and she accepted them wordlessly, weeping silently against his chest.

They stayed that way until, at last, her eyes grew dry.

Dammartin summoned two men to carry La Roque from the room. Only then did he leave to set in motion the accusation that would tell the world the truth of La Roque.

The grey light of day had begun to fade by the time Dammartin returned to the bedchamber. He could see that the blood had been cleaned from the floor and walls and the room tidied.

Josie was standing by the window when he entered, just as she had been when he had left for Valladolid earlier that day. Only a few hours had passed, and yet, in that small time, everything that was important in his life had changed. Nothing was the same.

Her silhouette showed a slim figure; although she was

looking at him, the fading light cast her face into shadow. His woman. His love.

'It is done. La Roque is arrested. He is denying all, saying that you have driven me mad.'

'But he confessed.' He saw the worry on her face.

'Only to us.'

'There is my father's journal.'

'It alone does not prove La Roque's guilt,' he said.

'He cannot murder your father and just get away with it.' She stepped towards him, away from the window, and as she did so the dying light lit her face and he could see the outrage upon it.

'He will not get away with it, Josie. The provost marshal shall have the sworn word of Jean Dammartin's son of La Roque's confession. The Spanish guerrilla leader will point out the man who paid him to kill my dragoons and me'

'You brought him back with you?'

'I could not leave such good evidence behind. There is also your father's journal from Oporto, witness statements from my men that in Telemos your father could not fire a musket even when his daughter's and his own life depended on it, and...' he paused '...Molyneux's testimony of the Major's actions these past days.'

'Molyneux will stand against him?'

'Oh, yes. La Roque arranged for him to be killed along with the rest of us. That, together with the fact that he now understands exactly why La Roque was so determined to obtain the journal, has persuaded him most thoroughly. The evidence should convince a military court, but even if it does not, it is enough that people will know the truth of La Roque. All of France will know it and that, not death, is the greatest punishment for a man like him.' He smiled a small smile. 'Your father's name will be cleared, Josie.'

She looked at him and he could see the sparkle of moisture in her eyes. 'Thank you.'

'It is I who should thank you.' His eyes scanned hers.

'Then we are even,' she said, and her voice sounded husky. 'What will happen now to us…to me?'

'Your father asked that I keep you safe until I could return you to the British. I have failed on the former.'

'You did not fail—I am safe, am I not?'

Sorrow and regret weighed heavy upon him. 'I exposed you to La Roque, and…' he thought of his interrogating her, of his kissing her, bedding her '…my treatment of you has hardly been honourable.'

She sighed and shook her head. 'Pierre.'

'I should take you to Lisbon, give you into Wellington's keeping.' He walked forwards, only stopping when there was no space between them. 'And I will do it…if that is what you want.' He waited, and Dammartin was truly afraid. He felt the beat of his heart and the throb of the pulse in his throat. He waited because he loved her and it was her decision to make.

Her gaze clung to his. 'And if that is not what I want?'

He smiled and took her hands in his. 'Marry me, Josie.'

He saw the surprise and joy light her face.

'Marry me because I cannot face my life ahead without you, because I want you in my bed each and every night. Marry me because I love you, Josie Mallington.'

'Yes,' she said, and she was smiling with overflowing joy. 'I will gladly marry you, Pierre Dammartin.'

'I will speak to General Gardanne's chaplain in the morning; we will be married before the week is out.'

And then she was in his arms and he was kissing her, kissing her with all the love and tenderness that was in his heart.

He lifted her into his arms and carried her over to lay

her on the bed and as the sun set low in the sky, he showed her just how very much he loved her, again and again and again.

Afterwards, they wrapped the blankets around their nakedness and stood together in comfortable, sated silence by the window, looking up at the clear white disc of the moon and the glitter of the scattered stars.

Dammartin's voice sounded through the quietness. 'Next week, we march with the convalescents and the garrison of Ciudad Rodrigo to meet up with the main French army.' He paused. 'We are for Santarém. We are part of Massena's reinforcements.' The moonlight showed the planes of his face all stark and angular, and the gouge of his scar and the concern upon his face. She saw the intensity of his gaze. 'You know what that means, do you not you, Josie?'

'That you will be fighting against the British when you reach your destination.' She gave a small, involuntary shiver.

'My love,' he whispered. 'I know the position in which this places you.' He touched his hand to her cheek. 'It would be safer for you in England.'

'There is nothing left for me there.' She turned her face to kiss the palm of his hand. 'My place is with you, now. I followed the drum for my father, I will follow it the same for my husband. And if it is a different drum that beats, then so be it. That is all I can do for the man that I love.'

'Chérie,' he whispered, and kissed her.

And Josie thought that out of the darkness of war and enmity, out of revenge and jealousy and murder, out of sacrifice and loss, had come love, and that one thing alone shone as a light in the darkness, and with its joy, made all of the grief and the pain and the suffering bearable. Love alone was enough. She marvelled at the knowledge, and snuggled in closer to the warmth of Dammartin's body.

Epilogue

France—August 1816

The sky was a cloudless blue that seemed to stretch to an eternity, lit by bright golden sunlight. Josie closed her eyes and felt the sun warm upon her face through the dappled shade of the trees. Up above, the birds were singing, and she could hear the droning buzz of the bees amidst the lavender, and smell the perfumed scent of the nearby roses.

She opened her eyes and looked down over the lawn to where a tall, handsome man was absorbed in playing with a small boy. Both the man and the boy had the same dark hair and eyes. The man's face was filled with love for his son and the sight of it made the happiness well up throughout Josie. The little boy looked round and saw her watching.

'Maman, maman!' he cried, and ran to her, clambering up on to her lap.

Her husband came, too, and sat down by her side, draping his arm across her shoulders, and dropping a kiss to her cheek.

'Pierre.' She smiled.

As he leaned in to kiss her again, a little wail began from the basket that sat on the bench at the other side of her. He smiled and lifted the tiny baby to him, stroking a finger gently against his daughter's soft downy cheek.

And Josie's happiness was complete.

* * * * *

His Mask of Retribution

MARGARET McPHEE

Chapter One

Hounslow Heath, London—1810

It was the perfect day for a wedding.

The October morning was crisp and filled with sunshine. The sky was a cloudless blue. Hounslow Heath was a rich green, and the surrounding oaks and beeches that peppered the heath had turned the prettiest shades of red and gold. But as the solitary dark liveried coach sped across the heath Lady Marianne Winslow noticed nothing of the beauty.

'We had better pray that Pickering is still waiting in the church. I would not be surprised if he has suffered a change of heart and gone home. And who could blame him? He has his pride, after all. What on earth were you doing in your bedchamber for so long?' George Winslow, the Earl of Misbourne, pulled his watch from his pocket and flicked open the gold casing.

Marianne wondered what her father would say if she told him the truth—that she had been staring into the peering glass for the last two hours, wondering how she might bring herself to marry a man she had met only twice, was almost as old as her father and scrutinised her as if she were a prize filly. But her father did not wait for an answer.

'Forty-five minutes late and we have yet to reach Staines.' He snapped the watch case shut and returned it to his waistcoat pocket. 'Good lord, girl! We cannot risk losing Pickering after the fiasco with Arlesford.'

'Papa…marrying Mr Pickering…I am not at all sure that I can…'

'Marianne, as your mother has already told you, what you are feeling is nothing more than wedding-morning nerves, which are perfectly normal in any young lady. We have been through all of this before.'

'Yes, but…'

'But?'

'I thought when Mr Pickering and I were first betrothed that I would grow used both to him and to the idea of marriage. But I need more time. It is barely a month since he gave me his ring.' She glanced down at the heavy signet ring upon her finger.

'A month is more than adequate for a betrothal, Marianne.'

'But, Papa, I barely know him.'

'You will come to know him soon enough and Pickering is not a demanding man. He will be kind to you.'

The gold of Pickering's ring glinted in the sunlight.

'I can understand that he may not be the most appealing of bridegrooms,' said her father, 'but he is steady and solid and reliable. Not only is Pickering's fortune vast and he highly esteemed within the *ton*, but he is a man of influence and power. No one can question the sense of the match.' He paused. 'The wedding must go ahead. You will say no more of it and do as you are told, my girl.'

She stared down at the wedding posy clutched in the

clamminess of her hand, at the pale pink roses delivered fresh from a hothouse in the country that morning and the tiny white babies'-breath flowers. She knew all of her father's arguments and knew, too, that they were right. Yet it did not make the prospect of marrying Charles Pickering any more palatable.

The coach took a bend in the road too fast and Marianne reached up for the securing strap to stop herself from sliding across the seat, her posy tumbling to the floor in the process.

'Papa, please, can we not at least travel a little more slowly?'

'The time is too short, Marianne. If Pickering walks away from this, there will be the devil to pay.' He glanced away, a strange expression in his eyes. His mouth tightened as she watched and then he seemed to remember himself and continued. 'John Coachman is under instruction to make up the time. Besides, Hounslow Heath is hardly a place to be dallying, even in daylight.' Her father retrieved her posy from where it rolled in the dust and returned it to her.

Marianne gave a little shiver. 'You cannot think that the highwayman—'

But her father cut her off. 'Neither sight nor sound has been had of the highwayman for over two months. Now that the Horse Patrol has been put in place to catch him he has likely taken himself elsewhere. And even were he still around, the hour is yet early. He would be lying drunk in some tavern, not waiting upon the heath especially for us. I will not risk losing Pickering.'

'It always comes down to my marrying,' said Marianne with a heavy heart and looked away.

'Marianne.' Her father gave a sigh and took her

hand between his own. 'You know you mean the world to me, do you not?'

She gave a nod.

'That I would only ever do what is best for you?'

'Yes, Papa.' It was the truth.

'Then believe me, my dearest, when I tell you that marrying Pickering is for the best.'

She nodded again. She would marry Mr Pickering because her father had arranged it and it was the right thing to do, even though the thought of becoming the man's wife filled her with dread.

The carriage slowed to a crawl to cross a narrow bridge and the sunlight shone through the window, illuminating her father's face as he smiled at her. She could see the specks of dust floating in the sunbeams, could see the gentleness of her father's eyes. His hands were warm around hers. Everything in the world seemed to quieten and calm. The wheels fell silent. Even the birds ceased to sing. It was a moment of pure tranquillity in the golden light.

And then the shot exploded and all hell broke loose.

The grooms were shouting and the coachman yelled a curse before a loud thud sounded. The horses whinnied. The coach lurched, then stopped. Something hard and big hit one panel, making her jump. She stared at the side from which the noise had emanated and, from the corner of her eye, saw the dark shadow move across the window. There was galloping and screaming and running feet. Then silence.

Her father scrabbled for his pistols in the pocket of the door and sat ready, a pistol primed in each hand, his eyes flicking nervously from one door to another, waiting.

She could hear the thud of her own heart and the heaviness of her father's breathing.

'The highwayman…' she whispered. 'It must be.'

Her father's jaw was clamped tight. He gave no response.

'Give me one of the pistols, Papa. Please.'

'Do not be so foolish, Marianne,' he snapped and his knuckles were white where he gripped so tight at the pistols' handles.

They waited, and there was nothing.

They waited, and the seconds dragged; the fear and the dread were almost overwhelming. Her father must have felt it, too, for he muttered beneath his breath, 'Come, show yourself.' But whoever, or whatever, was outside did not heed him.

Nothing moved. Not even a flicker. The air was so thick with tension that she felt she might choke with it. Time held its breath as surely as Marianne.

Nothing happened.

She wondered if their assailant had fled, whether they were alone. Her father must have thought the same, for he looked across at her and gave a slight shake of the head, she knew that he meant for her to remain silent and say nothing. She nodded and watched him edge towards the door…just as it swung open.

Her father's pistol fired, a deafening noise within the confines of the coach, so loud that her ears hurt from it and her eyes watered from the cloud of blue smoke. The stench of it was acrid, filling her nostrils, catching in her throat. She made to move, but her father's hand caught hard at her wrist, thrusting her back down on to her seat.

'Stay where you are, Marianne!'

The silence in the aftermath of the pistol shot

seemed almost as loud as the shot itself. It hissed in her ears and seemed to vibrate through her very bones. Through the smoke she saw a shadow flit across the open doorway and heard the taunt of a man's harsh whisper.

Her father fired at the shadow with his second pistol and launched himself out of the open doorway.

There was a thud against the carriage panel at the side of the door and the coach rocked as if something had been thrown against it. She heard a grunt of pain and then an ominous silence that made her stomach drop right down to her shoes.

'Papa?' She checked the door pockets for a spare pistol, but her father had taken no such precaution, so she hoisted up her skirts and scrambled to the door, trampling on the pink-and-white posy in her desperation to save her father. The smoke was clearing and the scene was quite clear before her as she jumped down from the coach.

The horses had been cut loose. Of the coachman, grooms and footmen there was no sign. Her father was leaning back against the side of the coach, his face powder-white, a trickle of blood seeping from the corner of his mouth, staring with angry black eyes filled with the promise of violence. Marianne knew that the highwayman was there, knew that he must be watching her at that very moment, but she could not look. Her heart was thudding hard; the fear was pounding through her blood and she was afraid to look, even though she knew that she must. Taking a deep breath to control her rising panic, she slowly followed her father's gaze to the tall dark highwayman.

He was dressed in black, wearing a long shabby greatcoat and, beneath it, a pair of buckskin breeches.

His boots were scuffed, the leather cracking in places with age and wear. Even his gloves were dark and old, well worn. On his head was an old-fashioned tricorn hat; it too was black to match the rest of his outfit, and under it she could see his unfashionably long hair, the colour of rich dark mahogany. All of this she absorbed in an instant, with barely a glance, for her focus was fixed firmly on the dark kerchief that was tied across his lower face, hiding his identity.

Her stomach was clenched small and tight, and beneath the ivory-and-pink-patterned silk of her skirt her legs were trembling. Her eyes lingered on the piece of cloth for a moment, then she screwed her courage to the mast and, with slow deliberation, she raised them to meet his.

The highwayman's eyes were not cruel and pale, but a warm honeyed brown, and his gaze was steady and strong and compelling, holding hers so that she could not look away. She felt her heart miss a beat and a shiver shimmy all the way down her spine. She did not know whether it was from shock or relief or fear, or a combination of all three.

'What the hell do you want?' her father snarled at him.

The highwayman glanced away, releasing her gaze, and only then did she realise that he had a pistol in each hand and both were aimed at her father's heart.

She knew that he smiled at the question, even though she could not see his mouth behind the kerchief. He smiled, but there was nothing of mirth in his eyes as he looked at her father.

'Stand and deliver.' The man's voice was quiet and harsh, as if half-whispered.

'You'll rue the day you picked me to thieve from, you scoundrel.'

'I think not.' He cocked his pistols.

'My daughter is on her way to be married.' If her father had thought to reason with the highwayman then he was mistaken, for the man's eyes did not so much as flicker. His gaze remained hard and relentless.

'I have a purse of money.' Her father scrabbled in his pockets, pulling out the small brown-leather pouch. 'Here.' He threw it in the direction of the highwayman. 'Take it and be gone.' The purse landed on the grass between them.

The highwayman did not even look at the purse, heavy and bulging with coins though it was. 'I do not want your money,' he said in his harsh half-whisper, his eyes fixed unblinking on Misbourne's.

Her father looked at the highwayman for a moment, as if unable to comprehend the man's answer, before speaking again. 'There is my diamond cravat pin and my watch; both are gold.' Her father's fingers were trembling slightly as he unpinned the diamond and threw it down to lie on the grass by the side of his purse. The stone glinted and sparkled in the sunlight. Then he took the watch from his pocket, unfastened the fob and offered the watch and its dangling chain to the highwayman.

But the villain made no move to take it.

'Marianne, take off your pearls and throw them down by my purse,' her father commanded, adding beneath his breath, 'Pearls before swine.' But for all his bravado, his brow glistened with sweat as she reached for the clasp.

The highwayman shook his head. 'Nor your jewellery, Misbourne.'

Her fingers stilled, then dropped away, leaving the pearls intact around her neck.

Her father frowned and she could see the suspicion and fear that flitted across his face. 'You know my name?' His voice was sharp.

'I know a lot more than that.'

The two men watched one another. The silence was heavy, pregnant with foreboding.

'Then what *do* you want?' asked her father at last.

There was a pause before the highwayman spoke. 'We'll come to that in time, but for now I'll take from you the same I took from the others—that which is most precious in the world to you.'

Every last trace of colour washed from her father's face. His beard and moustache, grizzled and grey, stood stark against the pallor of his skin. Across the heath a blackbird was singing, and in the background was the gentlest whisper of the wind. Nothing else stirred.

Her father forced the semblance of a laugh. 'You mean to kill me?'

'No!' Marianne stepped forwards in alarm. 'Do not harm him! I beg of you! Please!'

The highwayman's eyes met hers and they looked almost golden in the morning light. 'Rest assured, Lady Marianne…' how shocked she felt to hear her name upon his lips '…both your father and I know that it is not his life of which I speak.' His voice was that same stony half-whisper, devoid of all emotion, but the look in his eyes was cold and hard as the deepest winter and filled with such implacable determination that she shivered to see it. He turned his focus back to her father. 'Don't you, Misbourne?'

'No.' Her father's voice was little more than a croak.

The denial was weak and something about his expression made her think he knew exactly what was meant.

The highwayman made a small movement with the pistol in his right hand. 'I will kill you if you do not give me what I have come for. And once you are dead I will be free to take that which you seek to protect… without reprisal.'

'Papa, please, if you have any knowledge of what this villain wants, I beg you to deliver it to him. Do not risk your life.'

Both men looked at her. Her father's face was strained and haunted—he seemed to have aged a hundred years in those few moments—and the highwayman's eyes held the strangest expression.

'Run, Marianne,' her father said, and there was agony in his voice. 'Run, and do not look back.'

She shook her head. 'I will not abandon you to him.'

'Do as I say and run, damn you, girl!'

And she understood in that moment what it was that the highwayman wanted even before he said the words.

'For what does a father love best in all the world, but his only daughter?'

'You are wrong,' she said. There was her mother and her brother. But she knew in her heart that he spoke the truth. Her father had always loved her best.

'You shall not take her from me, you fiend!' Her father threw himself at the highwayman, but the villain was taller and stronger and younger. In an instant his pistols were uncocked and out of sight. He caught Misbourne's punch as easily as if it were that of a weakling and, in return, landed a hard fist to his face and then his stomach. When her father gasped and doubled over, clutching at his belly, the highwayman pushed him away and he stumbled back, hitting the side of the coach. He collapsed on to his knees, his right arm still wrapped around his belly. Blood was seeping from a cut on his cheek and his face was already beginning to swell.

'Papa!' Marianne made to rush to him, but the highwayman was quicker. He caught her around the waist and hauled her to him. 'No!' She kicked and punched and fought for all she was worth, but her captor was too strong. In an instant he had her held in his grip and facing her father.

Misbourne scrabbled to his feet from where he knelt in the dirt, the blood trickling down his poor injured face to darken and matt the grey hair of his beard. She tried to go to him, but the highwayman's arm was firm around her upper arms and *décolletage*, restraining her, pulling her back until her spine tingled with the proximity of him, even though their bodies were apart.

'What will you give for her safe return, Misbourne?'

'Anything you wish.'

'Anything?' The highwayman's voice was low and grim.

Her father nodded. 'Money. Gold. Silver. Jewels. Name your price.'

Behind her she felt the highwayman move, although his grip upon her did not slacken. He threw a folded sheet of paper to land on the ground before her father. 'My price, Misbourne.'

Her father retrieved the paper and opened it, and Marianne watched his expression contort with sudden shock and horror. He made not one move, spoke not one word, just stared at the piece of paper as if he could not believe the words written upon it. His eyeballs rolled up and he swayed before stumbling backwards. Only the panel of the coach door kept him upright—

that and his stubborn will-power as he leaned, visibly shaken, against it.

'Papa!' She struggled, but the highwayman's grip did not yield. 'Papa!'

So much sweat beaded on her father's forehead that his hair was damp from it. His face was ashen as a corpse. He looked old and weak, all of his usual strength and vitality exposed for the fragile mask it was. Yet the highwayman showed no mercy.

'The exchange will be today, Misbourne. Be ready.'

Marianne felt his arm drop to her waist and then the world turned upside down as he swung her up and over his shoulder, balancing her there as if she weighed nothing at all. She wriggled and tried to kick, but the blood was rushing to her head and his grip tightened, securing her all the more.

'No! Do not take her from me! Please!' her father cried and collapsed to his knees as he tried to stagger towards them. 'I beg you, sir. I will give you what you want.' She had never heard her father plead before, never heard his voice so thick with emotion.

But the highwayman was unmoved. 'Yes, you will,' he said. 'Watch for my message.' Then he whirled around and, in the blink of an eye, was upon his horse, sliding Marianne to sit sideways on the saddle before him. The huge black beast reared, impatient to be off, and she found herself held hard against his chest, gripped so tightly that she could not move.

'Who sent you? Was it—?' her father shouted and she could hear the fear and trembling in his voice. But the highwayman cut him off.

'No one sent me.'

'Then who the devil are you?'

The highwayman's arm was anchored around her

waist as he stared down at her father. 'I'm your past come back to haunt you, Misbourne.' The horse reared again and then they were off and galloping at full tilt across Hounslow Heath, leaving behind her father, white-faced and bleeding, the horseless coach, and the battered remnants of her wedding flowers blowing in the breeze.

Chapter Two

Rafe Knight pushed the horse hard, all the while keeping a careful hold of his most precious cargo. He could smell the sweet scent of violets from the girl's hair and feel the soft curves of the slender body pressed against his. He regretted that she had to be any part of this, but she was Misbourne's one weakness: the only hope of finding what he sought.

It would not be long before the coachman, groom and footmen reached the inn and summoned help. He did not have much time. He headed west, as if travelling on towards Staines, until he was out of Misbourne's sight, then he left the road and doubled back across the wild heath land towards Hounslow and London.

Callerton was waiting exactly as planned, hidden from view within the derelict farm buildings on the outskirts of the town. The doors of the great barn were wide open and Knight rode straight inside, slid Marianne Winslow down to his friend and servant, and dismounted.

The highwayman's masked accomplice placed Marianne inside a dark coach that waited within the barn, then assisted the highwayman in harnessing his horse as part of the team. Her throat was so dry that it stuck together, making it difficult to swallow. Within her chest her heart beat in a frenzy and every muscle in her body was racked tight with tension. The fear was so great that her breath shook from it and her palms were clammy. She squeezed her eyes shut and slowed her breaths, counting them to control the panic. When she looked again, the men had a flask and a rag and were washing the distinctive white flare from the horse's muzzle. They were focused, hurrying, intent on their task. Marianne gathered the remnants of her courage. A deep breath in and out, then she curled her fingers round the door handle.

Her blood was still rushing, her heart beating loud as a big bass drum. The door opened without a sound, letting her slip noiselessly to the ground and edge towards the rear of the coach. Once there she stood, her back pressed against the empty boot, while her eyes scanned desperately for an escape route or hiding place. She held her breath, ragged and loud as it had become, fearing they would hear it, fearing they would notice at any moment that she was gone.

Time seemed to slow and in that tiny moment of waiting every sense seemed sharpened and more intense. She could smell hay and horse sweat and leather tack, and the damp scent of autumn and brambles. She could hear the jangle of the harness and the shuffle of hooves as the horses grew impatient. Against her face the air of the shadowed empty barn was cool. There was nowhere to hide: not one hay bale, not one cart. Her heart sank. She knew that she was going to have to take her chance. Taking a deep breath and lifting her skirt clear of her ankles, she eyed the great, wide, opened barn doors. Outside the sky was blue and clear, the sun lighting the heath land as if in invitation. She hesitated no longer, but ran for her life.

Three paces and there was a yell and a sudden swift movement and Marianne gasped aloud as strong arms enclosed her. Within a second the highwayman had her backed against the coach door, both wrists secured behind her back, as his eyes glowered down into her own.

'Not a good idea, Lady Marianne,' he breathed, in that harsh half-whisper of his.

He was so close that with every breath she took she could feel the brush of her bodice against his chest, so close that she could smell the scent of the sandalwood soap he had used to wash with. She had not realised that he was so very tall, or how much he would dwarf her. She felt overwhelmed, by him, by shock, by fear. For a moment she could not speak, could not even breathe as she stared up into his eyes. Her heart was pounding, her mouth dry. She forced herself to think of what he had done to her father, forced her anger to override her fear.

'Scoundrel!' she hissed. 'What did you expect? That I would just sit there waiting for you to come and beat me as you beat my father?'

'I do not beat women.' His eyes were hard and angry as they held hers.

'Only old men who have done you no wrong.'

'You know nothing of the matter, Lady Marianne.'

'You did not need to hit him! You did not need to make him bleed!'

'Misbourne got off lightly.'

'What has my father ever done to warrant such treatment?'

'Your father is a thief and a murderer.'

She shook her head in disbelief, stunned by the declaration. 'And you are a madman, or drunk on wickedness.'

'I am as sane and sober as you are, my lady.'

His gaze bore down into hers and in the shadowed light of the barn his eyes were the colour of her father's best tawny port and clear and lucid as he claimed, and when she looked into them she could not prevent the shiver that ran through her. He was still holding her in place against the door, her wrists secured in his grip, his body too close to hers. There was an aura of such danger surrounding them she could scarcely breathe.

'It is you who is the thief. And, for all I know, a murderer too.'

He stepped closer, his eyes intent on hers, and she saw the flare of fury in them. 'It is true I have thieved, but as for murder? When your father grovelled in the dirt before me I could have done it, Lady Marianne, so very easily. I confess I was tempted.' His hushed voice was so harsh and so filled with anger that she caught her breath to hear it. 'An eye for an eye is what the Bible says. But murder...' He shook his head. 'That is your father's game, not mine. I'll settle to see him brought to justice in a hangman's noose.' The force of his words flayed her. Then, as suddenly as he had captured her, he released her, stepping back to open up a space between them.

'My quarrel is with your father. You need have no fear. I shall not hurt you.'

She moved away from the coach and rubbed her wrists—not because he had hurt her, but because they still tingled from the feel of his skin against hers. 'Then what are you going to do to me?' Her heart was thumping fast and hard. Her lips were stiff with fear but she asked the question even though she was so very afraid to hear the answer. She waited with legs that trembled, but she did not let herself look away from that razing gaze.

The silence seemed to stretch between them and tension knotted her stomach.

'Keep you until your father gives me what I want. He has something belonging to me. Now I have something belonging to him. It is a fair exchange.'

'And what is it that you want?' The words were little more than a whisper. She remembered too clearly her father's reaction when he had read the highwayman's demand and the shock and worry she had felt to see it.

'Too many questions, my lady. We can delay no longer.' Not once did his gaze shift from hers and she quivered from the intensity of it. She knew what he was and, despite his reassurance, what he could do to her.

'You shall not get away with this.'

'Indeed?' And there was such arrogant certainty in that one word.

'You are despicable, sir.'

'I am what your father has made me, Lady Marianne. Pray to God that you never find out the truth of it!' He opened the door and gestured her into the coach.

Marianne had no option but to hold her head high and climb inside.

She had her father's eyes. Black as midnight, wary, and watching him with that same contempt Misbourne used on those around him. Little wonder she was the apple of her father's eye. Little wonder he guarded her as if his pampered daughter were as precious as the crown jewels. In the rest of her face she favoured her mother. Her shapely lips pressed firm and her small nostrils were flared. His gaze swept over the blonde tendrils that framed her face, so soft and pale beside the strong darkness of her eyes. But the eyes, it was said, were windows to the soul. He wondered whether Marianne Winslow's soul was as black as her father's. He pulled the curtains closed and the stiffening of the girl's body, the sudden fear in her face, spurred a twinge of irritation within him. As if he would ravish her, as if he would even touch her. Misbourne was the blackguard in this, not him.

'I have told you that you have nothing to fear from me,' he snapped. 'Given your propensity for escape, you will understand the need for preventative measures.' He produced a short length of rope.

'And if I refuse?' She raised her chin a notch.

'You have no choice in the matter, my lady.'

She stared at him as if he were the devil incarnate. 'You are a villain.' Her voice was high, her face pale.

'Yes, I am,' he said. 'And you had best not forget it, Lady Marianne, especially if you have any idea of resisting me.'

Her eyes widened, but she did not suffer an attack of the vapours or hysteria as he had expected of Misbourne's coddled daughter. Indeed, she did not cry or plead or scream. Everything about her was contained and careful. She just eyed him with a quiet defiance and more courage than many a man as he bound her wrists behind her back, checking that the rope was not too tight.

He turned his attention away from the woman and slid open the dark wooden panel beneath his seat to remove the small travelling bag from within. He took his time, yet his actions were slick and smooth, well practised. From the bag he took a pair of highly polished riding boots, a new hat and a pair of the finest black-leather gloves. Then he removed the pistols from his pockets, checked they were safe and laid them at the bottom of the bag. He shrugged out of his greatcoat, rolled it into a ball and thrust it on top of the pistols. The tricorn hat, his shabby gloves and the old boots followed, before the bag was stowed out of sight once more. He glanced up to find Marianne watching him. Their eyes met through the dim grey light and that same *frisson* of awareness rippled through him, just as it had before. And the thought that he could feel any measure of attraction towards Misbourne's daughter sent anger licking right through him.

She turned her face away, fixing her gaze on the dark curtains drawn across the window.

He kept his eyes on her as he slid his feet into the smart black boots, scraped his hair back into a low tidy queue at the back of his head and tied it in place with a black ribbon from the pocket of his tailcoat. But the woman was not stupid; she did not look at him again. Not once. Not through the little country towns of Brentford or Hammersmith or even the village of Kensington. He slipped his hat and gloves in place and the rest of the journey continued in silence, the tension between them seeming to wind tighter with every mile closer they travelled through London. Eventually, Callerton thumped the carriage body and Knight knew they were nearing St Giles Rookery. He looked at Misbourne's daughter.

'Time to move, Lady Marianne.'

She glanced round at him then. A small steady movement as controlled as everything else about her, yet he could sense the sudden escalation of distrust and see the flash of fear in those large dark eyes. He felt his conscience stir at what he was doing, but her gaze flitted momentarily away and when she looked back at him it was as if she had drawn a veil across her eyes and the only expression on her face was one of contempt. She looked so like Misbourne that any doubts he might have harboured vanished instantly.

Knight reached for her arm and moved to execute the next stage of his plan.

In the study of his town house in Leicester Square, the Earl of Misbourne lay on a daybed covered by a cream woollen blanket and listened to the carriage sounds from the street outside.

'He is gone.' Francis Winslow—or Viscount Linwood, as he was otherwise known—Misbourne's son and heir, stood by the window and watched Pickering's carriage until it turned the corner and headed away from the square. 'Do you think he believed us?' Linwood's eyes were as dark and venomous as his father's as he came to stand by the daybed.

Misbourne gave a nod.

'It will be more difficult tomorrow when he returns and wishes to visit his betrothed. Although the story of our "carriage crash" being all over tomorrow's newspapers should help. I've ensured the news is already being whispered in the clubs.' His son was good at taking care of such details, but Misbourne offered no thanks; his mind was on other matters.

He slipped the crumpled sheet of paper from the pocket of his dressing gown and smoothed it out that he might stare at it again. The hand was bold, the words, few as they were, angular and angry. A place. A year. And the highwayman's demand.

1795, Hounslow Heath

The document that was taken—in exchange for your daughter.

He was thinking, and thinking hard. There was only one other person that knew of the document and Misbourne had eyes and ears stationed in every main port in the south watching for his return. It was possible that Rotherham had evaded detection, that he was back in England already. Misbourne's blood ran cold at the thought and he shivered as if someone had walked over his grave.

'Father?' Linwood was staring down into his face and he could see the concern and agitation in the eyes that were so like his own.

'Let me think,' Misbourne snapped. It made no sense. Whatever else Rotherham was, he was a man of his word and one who liked everything done exactly to the letter. There was still time left before he would come. Time enough for the wedding between Marianne and Pickering.

Misbourne lounged back against the pillows of his bed and read the words again. The criminal fraternity had a way of talking even when they'd been sworn to silence. A boast in the tap room of a public house, a whisper in the ear of the buxom wench beneath them. Thank God for illiteracy. He wondered how much the highwayman could possibly know.

'You are not well, Father. Let me deal with this in your stead,' said Linwood.

'Don't fuss so, boy, I tell you I'm fine.' An idea was taking shape in Misbourne's mind.

'And I disagree,' said Linwood without a flicker of emotion.

'You always were a stubborn little sod.'

'Chip off the old block, so they say.' Linwood held his gaze.

Misbourne gave a smile and shook his head. 'And they're not wrong.'

'Then let us go to the brotherhood,' said Linwood without returning the smile, speaking of the secret society of which both he and his father were members. 'Seek their assistance in this.'

'No!'

'It's different now that Hunter is the Master. He'll help us and—'

'I said, no, damn you, boy!' Misbourne felt a stirring of panic and knew he had to convince his son. 'We manage this ourselves. This is family business; it does not go outwith this room, no matter what else you might think.'

Linwood's face was angry and defiant.

'I will not risk Marianne's reputation. I will not risk your sister's safety. Do you understand?'

Linwood gave a sullen nod. 'What is this letter from fifteen years ago that he wants?' It was the question that Misbourne most dreaded to hear.

'None of your damned business.'

'Will you give it to him?'

There was a pause before Misbourne replied, 'Yes, I'll give it to him.' His scowl deepened and he pinched at the bridge of his nose, a sure sign that he was trying to control his temper. 'The day progresses and still we hear nothing.'

'We will.'

'What the hell is taking him so long?' Misbourne's upper lip curled in a snarl.

'He means to make sure we take him seriously—

and no doubt he wants to twist the knife a little. Whoever he is, he certainly does not like you.'

'And, by God, I'll give him good reason not to! By the time I've finished with him he won't know what he likes and what he doesn't.' Misbourne was only slightly mollified by the thought.

A knock sounded at the study door. The butler entered, holding a silver salver with a single letter laid upon it.

'Just delivered, m'lord, by an urchin.'

'Does the wretch wait for a reply?'

'No, m'lord. The boy ran off.'

Misbourne saw the servant's gaze take in his tender swollen cheekbone and felt a spurt of annoyance. He took the letter and dismissed the man with a flick of his fingers. The seal broke easily, but his hands were trembling with impatience and fear as he unfolded the letter and read its content before passing the note to his son.

'Aldgate High Street where it meets Fenchurch and Leadenhall,' said Linwood. 'He's chosen well. It's a busy junction at the best of times; it will be pandemonium there at three o'clock. And with its links to so many roads and alleys it will be difficult to cover the whole area.'

'Difficult, but not impossible,' said Misbourne. 'Once Marianne is safe…'

'Once Marianne is safe, we'll hunt him down like the villain that he is,' finished his son.

From the rooms above came the sound of a baby crying and a man and woman arguing, shouting and swearing at full volume. An old man was singing a drunken bawdy song and outside, in the street, a dog was barking. Marianne sat very still on the single wooden chair and waited, just as she had waited through all the previous hours. It was the sole piece of furniture in the room. Her eyes ranged again over the pile of filthy covers in the corner that served as a bed. Mould grew on the walls and the floorboards were bare. Two buckets sat behind the door—one held water, and the other was so stained with filth that she did not want to contemplate its use. There was no coal on the fire, no pots or pans. Not so much as a cup to drink from. The dirt encrusted upon the windows made the light hazy and hid her view of the rookery beyond.

'Who lives here?' she asked. The filthy bed of rags in the corner gave lie to her denial that anyone could live in such squalor.

'A family with five children,' replied the highwayman's accomplice from behind his pale mask.

'All in this one room?'

'Aye, lass. But he'll pay them more than they get in a year just for the use of this room for a few hours. He helps where he can.'

'I did not know such poverty existed.' She had never seen a place the like of this, with its maze of streets and alleyways crowded with ramshackle houses. 'The children are so ragged and thin, with eyes that seem too old for their faces, and their mothers…' She thought of the women with their rotten teeth and low, revealing bodices, and how they had fanned their skirts high when they had seen the highwayman and his accomplice.

'For some, it is the only way they can feed their bairns.'

She was horrified to learn it.

The light was a dull grey and the air was so ripe with rotting rubbish—and worse—that she wondered if she would ever clear the stench of it from her nose.

Something small and brown appeared from beneath the mound of blankets and scuttled across the floor.

'It'll not be much longer,' the accomplice assured her. 'He'll be here soon and then we'll have you back with your pa.'

'You seem to be a kind man. Why are you helping that villain?'

'He's not the villain in any of this, m'lady, for all that you think him. And I'm helping him because he's a good man and he fought his way across a battlefield to save my life. Don't judge him so harshly. He's only doing what he must, to set his demons to rest.'

The words were spoken with such sincerity that she could not doubt that the accomplice believed them. And she thought again of the tall dark masked man with amber eyes that made her shiver. 'Why does that involve my father?'

But the man shook his head. 'I've already said too much. Pardon me, my lady, but that is not my question to answer.'

When the clock struck three, Knight was nowhere near Aldgate High Street. He was drinking champagne in the bow window of White's Gentleman's Club with Bullford, Devlin, Razeby and Fallingham, and making sure the *ton* of London knew that he was there. He knew the boy he had paid would wait for Misbourne to arrive before passing him the note.

'What d'you make of the story of Misbourne's carriage crash?' Bullford was asking.

'Maybe Pickering's getting cold feet,' said Devlin. 'After all, she's hardly good *ton* at the minute. It will take a while longer before Misbourne lives down the embarrassment over Arlesford. And it's not as if Pickering needs the money.'

'Lucky escape for little Lady Marianne, if you ask me.' Fallingham swigged at his champagne. 'Pickering's so old that he's in danger of dying on the job, if you know what I mean.'

All the men except Knight laughed.

'What do you think, Knight?' asked Bullford, draining his glass.

He should not give a damn about Marianne Winslow, but he did not wish to think about her lying beneath Pickering. 'I think it's time we opened another bottle of champagne,' he said. 'I've got better things to do with the rest of my day.' Callerton should have the girl well in place by now.

'Would that involve keeping a certain widow satisfied?' Devlin asked.

Knight smiled, but said nothing.

'Lucky bugger!' said Razeby. The rest of the men chortled in appreciation.

'Maybe you should be laying off the champers in preparation for tomorrow's four-in-hand race. Do you think you'll beat Hawick?' asked Bullford.

'Why? Are you thinking of wagering against me?' drawled Knight. His eyes slid across the room to the grandfather clock in the corner.

'Wouldn't dream of it, old man,' said Bullford.

'We like to make money, not lose it,' agreed Fallingham.

The champagne arrived. 'A monkey on it that no one can down the bottle in one,' said Devlin.

'Prepare to pay up,' said Fallingham, lifting the bottle and placing it to his lips. He began to drink while his friends stamped their feet and chanted their support around him.

Knight waited until another two bottles of champagne had been opened before he slipped away.

'If this is a direction to yet another street...' warned Misbourne, grabbing the letter from beneath the apple cart in Cutler Street. 'This is the fourth note. He's had us on a wild goose chase all over London. The villain's intent on making fools of us.'

'He's intent on making it as hard as possible for us to track him...and Marianne,' corrected Linwood.

'Give the document to the boy by the organ grinder. Lady Marianne will be delivered to your home.' Misbourne read the words aloud. 'Are the men still following us?' he added beneath his breath to Linwood, who gave a subtle nod and lifted his wolf's-head walking cane from where it rested on the ground.

'Then let us hope the boy leads them straight to the villain's lair.'

'You should let me go,' said Linwood.

'Having you running through the streets will attract too much attention. No, it is better this way.' Misbourne slipped a folded and sealed document from his pocket and walked over to the fair-haired boy by the organ grinder. The boy saw him coming and Misbourne understood from the expression on his face that the boy knew what to expect. He took the document without a word and disappeared into the crowded street. And the two men lounging in the mouth of the alleyway behind Misbourne slipped into the crowd after him.

* * *

Knight took the document from the boy. 'You're sure you lost them?'

'Easy as pie. I passed it to Jim, who passed it to Dodger, who passed it to me. We led 'em a merry dance all the way down to the dockland just as you said and left 'em there.'

'Good.' Knight slipped the coins into the boy's grubby hand.

'Pleasure doing business with you, gov, as always.' And the boy disappeared again.

Knight's heart was thumping hard. The folded paper was fragile and yellowed with age. He could see the shadow of writing shining through its thinness. His mouth dried with anticipation. The question had haunted him every day of the last fifteen years—now he held the answer in his hands. He took a breath and carefully unfolded the document.

His eyes scanned the faded ink. The document was dated for June 1795 and was a letter from a senior government minister of the time to Misbourne. Several sensitive topics were discussed and it was clear, from both the tone and the detail revealed, that the two men were on friendly terms. It was a letter that many might have paid to read, the stuff of petty scandal, but Knight crushed it within his hand as a red mist descended before him.

Marianne heard the footsteps outside in the alley-way before the highwayman's accomplice did. The highwayman strode into the room wearing the same long dark coat he had worn upon Hounslow Heath, but his hat was the smart beaver she had watched him don in the coach, and beneath the coat she caught a glimpse of the fine white shirt and dark waistcoat. The mask tied around his face had moulded to his features and his boots left a trail of footsteps through the dirt of the floor.

After all these hours of waiting, he had finally come to return her to her father. Her stomach tightened with anticipation. Then she met his eyes, and they were not golden and light but dark and dangerous and filled with such a cold hard rage that she knew, before he even spoke the words to his accomplice, that it had all gone wrong.

'Misbourne played us false.'

'He didn't deliver the document?' The accomplice sounded as shocked as Marianne felt.

'Not the right one. Does he think me so much a fool that I would not notice?'

'You said he was a blackguard but, even so, what manner of man risks his own daughter?' the accomplice whispered, but she heard him just the same.

'No!' Marianne leapt to her feet so suddenly that the chair tipped back and clattered on to the floor. 'You're lying! My father must be confused. You cannot have made it clear what you wanted.'

The highwayman walked right up to her and his eyes were dark and deadly. 'Your father knows exactly what I want, Lady Marianne.'

'No,' she whispered, shaking her head, knowing that what the highwayman was saying could not be true. 'He would not leave me here with you. He would do everything in his power to save me.' She knew it with all her heart.

Something of the rage diminished in the highwayman's eyes and the way he was looking at her made his words ring true more than any angry assertions could have done. 'I am sorry, Lady Marianne.'

'There must be some mistake.'

The harshness of his whisper softened. 'There is no mistake.'

'You're lying,' she said again and her voice was very quiet and controlled, in such contrast to the terrible frenzied thud of her heart. Of course he was lying. He had to be lying.

He said nothing, just stood there and looked at her, and she could not bear to see the pity in his eyes.

'You're lying!' she shouted it this time. 'You just want more from him!'

'Lady Marianne.' Gently he tried to take her arm.

'No!' She flinched and pushed him away. 'Do not touch me!'

'We have to move,' she heard his accomplice say in the background. 'What do we do with the girl?'

The highwayman did not take his gaze from hers as he answered, 'We take her home with us.'

The accomplice gestured the highwayman aside. They talked in hushed tones, but Marianne could hear some of what they were saying.

'Maybe we should just let her go. If Misbourne isn't going to give up the document…' The accomplice was arguing to release her.

'We keep her until he does.' The highwayman was so adamant that she knew his accomplice would not persuade him. He meant to keep her and heaven only knew what he would do to her. He glanced round, saw she was listening and pulled his accomplice further away, turning his back so that she would not hear their words. They were so intent on their conversation that they did not hear the sound of feet and voices, children's shouts and a man's growl. The door opened and four children ran in, and behind them, a man and a woman carrying a puppy wrapped in a filthy shawl.

The children did not seem fazed to find the highwayman, his accomplice and Marianne.

'All right, governor?' The oldest fair-haired boy sauntered across the room and gave the highwayman a nod.

'Tom,' the man snapped at the boy, but the boy was not cowed in the slightest. 'Beggin' your pardon, sir,' said the man to the highwayman. 'We thought you would be gone. Excuse us and we'll leave you to your business.' And then in roughened tones to the children, 'Out, the lot of you.' His head gestured to the still-open door.

One of the boys emitted a harsh hacking cough and the puppy began to whine. The family smelled of dampness and dog and unwashed bodies.

'Our business is done for today,' replied the highwayman. 'Here…' He slipped his hand into his pocket and she saw the glint of gold. The children gathered around him like flies round a honeypot. Her gaze slid to the open door and the woman standing beside it. All eyes were on the highwayman's gold. Marianne did not hesitate. She hitched up her skirts and she ran.

'Stop her!' She heard the highwayman's shout. 'Marianne, no! This place is danger—' But she slammed the door shut behind her and did not look back.

She hurled herself down the close, through the gaping main door and out into the street. The clatter of her shoes was loud against the stones, seeming to echo against the crowding walls all around. Shabby clothing hung on washing lines strung high between the houses, flapping dark and grey and damp. Marianne dodged beneath them and kept on running, ignoring the sharp press of the cobbles through her thin leather soles. A quick glance behind and she could see his dark figure further down the street, running so fast that the tails of his greatcoat were spread and billowing behind him like great black wings.

'God help me!' she whispered and, ignoring the stitch in her side, pushed herself to run faster, knowing that she could not afford to let him catch her. The paving was uneven and covered in filth. A dog snapped at her heels and a woman sitting in a doorway swigging from a bottle shouted something at her and laughed, but she kept on running. She stumbled, almost sprawling her length as she caught her foot in a hole in the road, but righted herself without slowing. Round the corner, she dived up a narrow alleyway to her right and the next one on her left, crisscrossing, desperate to find a way out, but every turn just seemed to take her deeper into the forest of houses.

The streets were growing narrower and darker, the buildings taller and more rickety; the people she passed were more sharp-faced and beady-eyed. Her breathing was so hard she could taste blood at the back of her throat, so loud that it masked the sounds around her. She knew she could not keep going, that she was spent. She dodged into another narrow street on her right and shrank back against the wall, closing her eyes and gasping air into her lungs. Her side ached like the stab of a knife blade with every breath.

There was no sound of the highwayman's footsteps. No sound of anything except the distant hum of everyday life and her own panting breath. She had lost him. She had escaped. She breathed her relief.

And then the scent of tobacco smoke drifted to her

nose and Marianne knew that she was not alone. She opened her eyes and looked around her. A little further up the street, three men lounged completely motionless against the fronts of the houses. Their clothing was all browns and greys, merging with the stonework of the buildings. Two sucked on long thin clay pipes. All three watched her with sharp hungry faces.

And for all that Marianne had sought to escape the highwayman, she knew these men were different. They would give her no assurances. Their fight was not with her father.

Her stomach dipped with dread. She made no sudden movement, even though every muscle was primed and tensed to flee. She glanced to her right towards the mouth of the street. Another two men were taking up the breadth of it, silent in their drab dirty clothes, and blocking her exit. There was a hollow sickness in her stomach and her heart was pounding in the base of her throat. She looked to her left, wondering if she stood a chance of running past the men, but a thin-faced man with a scar down his cheek was watching from the shelter of the close and another man, a great big bear of a man, was sitting on the step. And she was afraid, more desperately afraid than ever. Moving slowly, calmly, as if they were a pack of wolves, she edged away from the wall.

The thin-faced man stepped out of the close into the narrow street and it seemed to be a signal, for the other men moved to gather behind his lead.

She took her chance and whirled, trying to dodge past the two that guarded the exit of the street, but there was no way past them and she was forced back.

'Don't be in such a hurry to leave,' one of them said. 'There's plenty of fun to be had for a pretty little thing like you.' She saw his eyes rake her body before returning to rest upon her face. He licked his lips slowly, meaningfully, with a fur-coated tongue. Marianne glanced behind her at the advancing group of men.

'No way out, darlin',' said the man who had spoken before. 'Smile at me and I'll be gentle with you.' And he laughed.

She knew what they were going to do to her. She knew, and there was nothing that she could do to stop them. Nothing was going to stop them. She opened her mouth to scream—and then she saw the tall dark figure step into the mouth of the street.

Chapter Three

Marianne knew it was the highwayman, but he was alone and there were seven men around her. He walked forwards and the expression of darkness and ferocity on his face made her stomach flip. The ruffians began to close with eagerness upon him, but he did not hesitate, just kept on walking.

One of the villains gave a mocking laugh. 'You think we're scared because you're wearing a bleedin' mask?'

She did not hear the highwayman's answer. There was only the sickening sound of bone crunching against bone and the villain laughed no more. A hand closed tight around her upper arm and the thin-faced man looked down into her face.

'Unhand me!' She struggled to free herself, but the thin-faced man only smirked at her efforts.

She could not see the highwayman properly, but she could hear every fist that landed, could hear the grunts and the gasps and the curses from the ruffians. There was such menace about him that it made that of the villains pale to insignificance. The men before him seemed to crumple. One was thrown against a wall, slithering down to lie in a limp and bloodied heap. Another turned tail and ran away. She had never seen such power, such strength, such utter ruthlessness. It shook her to the very core. And it shook the thin-faced man too. With a snarl of disgust he gestured the biggest, heaviest-set of his men towards the highwayman. The villain was a giant of a man, his fists huge and scarred, and as Marianne watched he slipped a wicked-looking hunting knife from his pocket.

'Come on, darlin', me and you've got some business together. Fitz'll take care of the distraction.' The thin-faced man manhandled her towards the mouth of the close.

'No!' She struggled against him, straining for release, and her eyes met the highwayman's across the carnage just for a moment. Something passed between them, something she did not understand. He was her enemy and yet he was also her only hope. He was different from the men in the rookery. He was different from any man that she had ever seen. His gaze shifted to focus on the men between them. She watched it harden, and darken, and she shivered just to see it. She stared in awe, wanting both to run to, and away from him. The thin-faced man's fingers bit all the harder into her arm as he wrenched her so roughly that she lost her footing and went down on her knees. He yanked her up and dragged her towards the building in which she had first seen him. And behind her she could hear the sounds of the fight intensify.

They were just inside the close when the scream pierced the air. A scream of pain and of terror. A scream that made her scalp prickle and her blood run cold. Then there was silence. She strained her neck and saw the big villain lying curled on the ground sobbing like a baby. And the highwayman was still coming: relentless, unstoppable.

Knight saw Marianne Winslow being dragged towards a house by a thin-faced man. Her eyes were fixed on his and in that moment he saw her with all of her armour and pretence stripped away: her soul, bared in such honesty, and vulnerable. She was not Misbourne's daughter now, but a woman in her own right—one who was in grave danger because of him. He felt the extent of her fear, felt her unspoken plea reach in and touch him in a place he had thought lost long ago. Something inside him seemed to boil up and spill over. There were two men between him and Marianne. Knight knew that time was running out.

'Come on then, mate,' taunted the stockier of the two. 'Show us what you've got.' The black-toothed ruffian moved his fingers in a beckoning gesture. 'We don't fight with Queensbury rules he—'

Knight smashed his fist as hard as he could into the ruffian's nose. The man dropped and did not get up.

The sole remaining villain was backing away with his hands raised in surrender. 'You can 'ave 'er.' The man's face was pale beneath the grime. 'Just don't hit me, mate.' A telltale wet patch spread across the fall of the man's trousers as he spoke. Knight hit him anyway and kept on moving into the close.

From above came the sounds of the struggle. A door slammed, muffling the sounds. He took the stairs two at a time, up to the first floor, hearing the struggle grow louder as he ran. He kicked open the door and saw Marianne backed against the wall watching in terror while, in the middle of the room, the villain unfastened his trousers. Both faces shot round to him.

'What the hell…?' The villain scrabbled at the open fall of his trousers, his shifty grey eyes taking in Knight's highwayman clothes and the kerchief that still masked his face. 'Piss off and get your own.'

'She's mine,' said Knight.

'This is my territory—that makes her mine.' The thin-faced man pulled a razorblade from the pocket of his jacket and brandished it at Knight. 'Now piss off. Three's a crowd.'

'I agree.' But instead of retreating, Knight walked straight for the man. His left hand caught the wrist that swiped the razor at Knight's neck; his right grabbed the back of the half-mast breeches and, before the villain could react, ran him headlong out of the window.

When he turned back to Marianne she had not moved one inch; just stood there frozen, spine against the wall.

'You killed him,' she whispered.

He let the lethality fade from his face. 'I doubt it. We're only one floor up. Probably just broke a few bones.' He paused. 'Did he hurt you?'

Her gaze clung to his. 'No.'

Thank God!

Her voice was quiet and calm, but her face was pale as death and he could see the shock and fear that she had not yet masked in her eyes.

Someone outside started to scream.

'We have to leave here. Now.'

But she still made no move, just stared at him as if she could not believe what was happening.

'Lady Marianne,' he pressed, knowing the urgency of their predicament. He took hold of her arm and together they ran from the room.

* * *

The kitchen of Knight's house in Craven Street was warm and empty save for the two men that sat at the table. The stew that Callerton had prepared earlier was still cooking within the range, its aroma rich in the air. There was the steady slow tick from the clock fixed high on the wall between the windows. The daylight was subdued through the fine netting that Callerton had fitted across the window panes, lending the room an air of privacy.

'You were out of sight by the time I got out of there. And I knew you wouldn't go back to the room,' Callerton said. He unstoppered the bottle of brandy sitting on the scrubbed oak of the kitchen table between them and poured some into each of the two glasses.

Knight gave a nod. They both knew the arrangements if something went wrong.

'How is she?'

'She's resting.'

'You got to her in time?'

Knight gave another nod. 'Just.' Marianne Winslow's virtue had hung by a thread within that rookery. He wondered what he would have done had he not arrived in time. Killed the blackguard in the room with her. Blamed himself for all eternity.

'Thank God for that.' Callerton downed his brandy in one. 'You've got to give her back.'

He knew that. He also knew that he had come too far and could not give up Misbourne's daughter just yet. 'That's what Misbourne's banking on. We keep her…for now.' In his mind he could still see those dark eyes of hers, holding his with such brutal honesty, and the look in them that would not leave him.

Callerton rubbed at his forehead. His face was

creased with concern. 'The letter he sent is from the right date. And it's definitely something that Misbourne would not want towncried. You're sure it's not the right one?'

'Positive.' He did not let himself think of the woman. This was about Misbourne. It had always been about Misbourne.

Callerton grimaced and shook his head. 'It doesn't make sense. Why give us something we could use against him if it's the wrong document?'

'Maybe he's testing us to see if we know the right document.'

'And once he knows there's no hoodwinking us he'll give us the genuine article.'

'There's only one way to find out.'

'How do we send him the message?'

'Remember the night before Viemero?'

Callerton raised his brows. 'You're not serious?'

'Never more so.'

'It's too risky!'

'It will show him that we mean business.'

'Aye, it'll do that, all right.' Callerton played with his empty glass. 'But I wouldn't want to be in your boots tonight.'

Knight grinned. 'Liar.'

Callerton laughed.

Within the darkened bedchamber that was her prison Marianne stood by the mantelpiece and stared into the flame of her single candle. The shutters were secured across the windows and despite the chill of the early evening, no fire had been lit upon the hearth.

The thoughts were running through her head, constant and whirring. Of the highwayman in the rookery.

Of their journey back to the shuttered room. It seemed like a daze, like something she had dreamt. She knew only that the highwayman's arm had been strong and protective around her and that the villains lurking in the shadows of the narrow streets had watched him with wary eyes and had not approached. No one had moved except to scuttle out of their way. Her family and her servants had always provided a barrier between her and anyone who did not move in her own small, vetted circle, but this was different. This was like nothing she had ever experienced. Men looked at the highwayman with a curious mix of hostility and deference, women with a specific interest they made no effort to hide. He had intruded into their world, snatched her right from their grasp. They had not liked it, but not one of them had moved to stop him.

He had kept her moving at a steady pace, twisting and turning through the dark maze of narrow lanes until, eventually, the lanes had widened to streets and light had started to penetrate the gloom. The streets had grown busier, but no one had entered the space around Marianne and the highwayman; everywhere they went a path had opened up through the crowd before them. Even in her dazed state she had known the reason: they were afraid of him, every last one of them.

And by his side, Marianne Winslow, who for the past three years had been scared of her own shadow, Marianne Winslow, who had more reason than any to be afraid, had walked through the most dangerous rookery in London, past villains and thieves, unscathed and unafraid. She was still reeling from it, still seeing the different way they looked at her because she was with him. And that sense of freedom, of power almost, obliterated the terror of the rookery.

She should have been shaking. She should have been sobbing and weeping with fear and with shock. She stared at the candle flame without even seeing it, knowing that the calm she felt was natural and not the result of counting her breaths and slowing them, or drinking a preparation of valerian. He was a man more dangerous than any other, yet with him she had felt safe. It made no sense.

The flame began to flicker wildly. Her attention shifted to the tiny stub of candle that remained and she knew it would not last much longer.

She lifted the candlestick and, holding it high, glanced around the bedchamber. It was a woman's room, but one that was not used, if the quiet, sad atmosphere was anything to judge by. The walls appeared a yellow colour and were hung with a few small paintings. A large still life, depicting an arrangement of exotic flowers, was positioned on the wall above the mantelpiece. She crossed the floor to search the dressing table. There was a vanity set, bottles of perfume, jars of cream and cosmetics, a box of hairpins, a casket of jewellery and two candelabra, both of which were empty. None of the drawers held any candles. She glanced towards the bed—large and four-postered, its covers and pillows a faded pale chintz, the colour of which was indefinable in the candlelight. At one side was a small chest of drawers and on the other a table. Neither held any candles. Nor did the small bookcase. There was nothing behind the gold-chinoiserie dressing screen in the corner. The candle stub guttered, making the flame dance all the wilder and the wick burn all the faster and the first snake of fear slithered into her blood.

Her fingers scrabbled at the shutters closed across

the window and found the catch, but no amount of prising would release it. It took her a few minutes to realise that they had been secured with nails.

There were two doors within the bedchamber: one in the wall against which the head of the bed rested, and the other to the left, opposite the window. She hurried to each one in turn, trying the locks, twisting and pulling at the handles. But both were locked, confirming what she feared—that she was trapped in here, with nothing to do save wait for the candle to extinguish. The knowledge made her stomach knot.

She had been safe in the rookery with him, but this was different. Now she was his prisoner. Alone in a bedchamber. And she knew how dangerous he was and how very angry he was with her father for not delivering the mysterious document. But her mind flickered back to what would happen when the candle burned out. He had said she had nothing to fear from him. She glanced again at the candle. It should have been the highwayman that terrified her, but it wasn't. She closed her eyes and counted her breaths, slowing them as she ever did when she was afraid, making them deeper to allay the mounting panic. And when she had calmed herself, she knew what she was going to have to do.

'All done.' Callerton finished brushing the last speck of dust from the shoulder of Knight's midnight-blue tailcoat.

'The boy should have delivered the note to Misbourne by now. We'll—' The banging started before Knight could finish the words. He raised an eyebrow. 'What the hell…?'

'It sounds like she's using a battering ram against the door,' said Callerton. 'Do you want me to tie her up?'

Knight shook his head. 'I'll deal with Lady Marianne.'

'You're due at Devlin's for dinner in five minutes.'

'Then I'll be late; Devlin will expect nothing else.
It pays to cultivate a habit of unreliability. Besides,
I've no stomach for the after-dinner entertainment.'

'More lightskirts?'

'He's hired Mrs Silver's girls for the night.'

'Again?'

'Again,' said Knight.

Callerton gave a whistle. 'You'll be late back, then.'

Knight scowled at the prospect. 'I'll have to make
a show of it, but I'll be back in time.'

'Most men would love a chance to play the rake.
Come to think of it, most men would be living the
dream rather than faking it.'

'I'm not most men.'

'No, you're not,' agreed Callerton more quietly.
'Most men would have left me to die in Portugal.'

The two men looked at one another, feeling all of
the past there in the room with them. The only sound
was of something being thudded hard against wood,
coming from above.

'We'll get him,' said Callerton.

'Damn right we'll get him. And in the meantime I'll
silence his daughter.' Knight slipped the black silken
mask from his pocket, tied it around his face, grabbed
a branch of candles and strode up the stairs.

The ivory-and-tortoiseshell hairbrush splintered
into three from the force of being hammered against
the door. Marianne threw it aside and continued her
assault with her fists and her feet, not caring about
the pain.

The panic was escalating and she feared that she would not be able to keep a rein on it for much longer if he did not come soon. She banged at the door so hard that her blood pounded through her hands and she could feel bruises starting to form. She glanced round at the mantelpiece and the dying candle upon it. The light was already beginning to ebb. Soon it would be gone. Her stomach turned over at the thought. She bit her lip and banged all the harder.

She did not hear his footsteps amidst the noise. The lock clicked and then he was there in the bedchamber with her.

'Lady Marianne.' His half-whisper was harsher than ever. 'It seems you desire my company.' He stood there, holding the branched candlestick aloft, and the flickering light from the candles sent shadows darting and scuttling across the walls. His brows were drawn low in a stern frown and the shadows made him seem taller than she remembered, and his shoulders broader. He was dressed in expensive formal evening wear: a dark tailcoat, white shirt, cravat and waistcoat, and dark pantaloons. Beside all of which, the mask that hid his face looked incongruous. No ordinary highwayman.

'My candle is almost spent.' Her pride would let her say nothing more. She glanced across to the mantelpiece where the lone candle spluttered.

'It is.' He made no move, just looked at her. His gaze dropped to the broken hairbrush that lay on the floor between them. 'Not very ladylike behaviour.'

'Highway robbery, assaulting my father and abducting me on the way to my wedding are hardly gentlemanly.'

'They are not,' he admitted. 'But as I told you before, I am what your father made me.'

She stared at him. 'What has my father ever done to you? What is all of this about?'

He gave a hard laugh and shook his head. 'Have I not already told you?'

'Contrary to what you believe, my father is a good man.'

'No, Lady Marianne, he is not.' There was such ferocity in his eyes at the mention of her father that she took a step backwards and, as she did, her foot inadvertently kicked a large shard of the handle so that it slid across the floor, coming to a halt just before the toes of his shoes.

She saw him glance at it, before that steady gaze returned to hers once more. 'My mother's hairbrush.'

She looked down at the smashed brush, then back up at the highwayman and the fear made her stomach turn somersaults. She swallowed. 'Does she know that her son is a highwayman who has terrorised and robbed half of London?'

'The newspapers exaggerate, Lady Marianne. I have terrorised and robbed six people and six people only, your father amongst them.'

Her heart gave a stutter at his admission.

'And my mother is dead,' he added.

She glanced away, feeling suddenly wrong-footed, unsure of what to say.

He carried on regardless. 'Were you trying to beat the door down to escape or merely destroy my possessions?'

'Neither,' she said. 'I wished to…' she hesitated before forcing herself on '…to attract your attention.'

'You have it now. Complete and undivided.'

She dared a glance at him and saw that his eyes were implacable as ever.

'What is it that you wish to say?'

The smell of candle smoke hit her nose and she peered round at the mantelpiece to see only darkness where the candle had been. A part of her wanted to beg, to plead, to tell him the truth. But she would almost rather face the terror than that. Almost. She experienced the urge to grab the branch of candles from his hand, but she did not surrender to the panic. Instead, she held her head up and kept her voice calm.

'All of the candlesticks are empty.'

His gaze did not falter. She thought she saw something flicker in his eyes, but she did not understand what it was. He stepped forwards.

She took a step back.

He looked into her eyes with that too-seeing look that made her feel as if her soul was laid bare to him, as if he could see all of her secrets, maybe even the deepest and darkest one of all. She knew she should look away, but she did not dare, for she knew that all around them was darkness.

The silence hissed between them.

'I would be obliged if you would fill them. All of them.' She forced her chin up and pretended to herself that she was speaking to the footman in her father's house, even though her heart was thudding nineteen to the dozen and her legs were pressed tight together to keep from shaking.

His eyes held a cynical expression. He turned away and headed for the door, taking the branch of candles with him. She heard the darkness whisper behind her.

'No! Stop!' She grabbed at his arm with both hands to stop him, making the candles flicker wildly. 'You cannot...' She manoeuvred herself between him and the door, trying to block his exit, keeping a tight hold of him all the while.

His gaze dropped to where her fingers clutched so tight to the superfine of his coat sleeve that her knuckles shone white, then back to her face.

She felt her cheeks warm and let her hands fall away. 'Where are you going, sir?' She was too embarrassed to meet his gaze. Her heart was racing hard enough to leap from her chest and she felt sick.

He raised his brows. 'I may be mistaken, but I thought you requested candles. I was going to have my man bring you some.'

Her eyes flickered to the branch of candles in his hand, then to the darkness that enclosed the room beyond. 'But...' The words stopped on her lips. She did not want to say them. She could not bear for him to know. Yet the darkness was waiting and she knew what it held. She felt the terror prickle at the nape of her neck and begin to creep across her scalp.

'Lady Marianne.'

Her gaze came back to his, to those rich warm amber eyes that glowed in the light of his candles. *Please*, she wanted to say, wanted to beg. Already she could feel the tremor running through her body. But still she did not yield to it, not in front of him. She shook her head.

'If I were to leave the candles here...'

'Yes,' she said, and the relief was so great that she felt like weeping. 'Yes,' she repeated and could think of nothing else. The highwayman passed her the branch of candles. Her hand was trembling as she took it; she hated the thought that he might see it, so she turned away. 'Thank you,' she added and sank back into the room, clutching the candles tight to ward away the darkness.

There was silence for a moment, then the closing of the door and the sound of his footsteps receding.

She stared at the flicker of the candle flames and thought again that, in truth, he was no ordinary highwayman.

The clock in the corner on the mantelpiece chimed midnight. Misbourne left his son and his wife in the drawing room and made his way to his study. He needed time to think, needed space away from his wife's incessant weeping, because his heart was filled with dread and his stomach churning with fear over the gamble he had taken.

'Had he released her she would be here by now,' Linwood had whispered and Misbourne knew that his son was right. Yet he could not admit it, even to himself. He needed a brandy to calm his nerves. He needed time to gather his strength and hide his fears.

But everything changed when he opened the door to his study. For there, on the desk that he had left clear, lay two pieces of paper like pale islands floating on the vast sea of dark polished mahogany. One was a smooth-cut sheet of writing paper, and the other was a crushed paper ball. His heart faltered before rushing off at a gallop. He hurried across the room to the desk. The writing paper bore his own crest, but it was not his hand that had penned those three bold letters and single word.

IOU Misbourne.

The ink glistened in the candlelight. His hand was shaking as he touched a finger to it and saw its wetness smear. He whirled around, knowing that the words had only just been written. Behind him the curtains swayed. He wrenched them open, but there was no one there. The window was up and the damp scent of night air filled his nose. He leaned his hands on the sill, craning his head out, searching the night for the man who had the audacity to walk right into his home to leave the message. But not a single one of the lamp posts that lined the road had been lit. The street was dark and deserted. Not a figure stirred. Not a dog barked. And of the highwayman there was no sign.

He knew what the crumpled ball of paper was before he opened it. The letter he had sent to the highwayman. A letter that could have been used against Misbourne. A letter that could cost him much in the wrong hands. Crumpled as if it were worthless. The villain knew what the document was. He knew, and there was only one man left alive with that knowledge. Misbourne felt sick at the thought. It was everything he had guarded against. Everything he had prayed so hard to prevent. He shut the window and closed the curtains, knowing it would do little good; the highwayman had been in his home, the one place that should have been safe.

He filled a glass with brandy, sat behind his desk and drank the strong warming liquid down. His eyes never left the words written upon the paper. Misbourne was more afraid than he had ever been, both for himself and for Marianne. He knew there was only one thing to do when the highwayman next made contact. *If* the highwayman next made contact.

Chapter Four

Marianne sat perched on the edge of the bed. The fire that the highwayman's accomplice had set last night had long since burned away to nothing and the air was cool. The early morning light seeped through the cracks of the window shutters, filtering into the bedchamber. The bed was only slightly rumpled where she had lain awake all night on top of the covers. She had not climbed within the sheets, nor had she worn the nightclothes that the accomplice had left neatly folded upon the dressing table. She had not even removed her shoes.

It had been the first night in almost three years that Marianne had spent alone. And she had barely slept a wink. All night she had waited. All night she had feared. But the highwayman had not come back to hurt her. Instead, he had filled the room with candles to light the darkness of the night. Eventually, as night had turned to dawn, her fear had diminished and all she could think of was the highwayman in the rookery and the look in his eyes as they had met hers. She thought of the villains quailing before him, of the wary respect in their eyes, of how he had kept her safe.

He was tougher, stronger, more dangerous than any villain. And she remembered how, last night, she had physically accosted him, clutching at him in her panic, even barring the door so that he would not leave. She closed her eyes and cringed at the memory. He knew. She had seen it in his eyes. Yet he had not said one word of her weakness, nor used it against her. She slipped off her shoes and moved to sit on the rug in the bright warmth of the narrow beam of sunshine. And she thought again of the man with the hauntingly beautiful amber eyes and the dark mask that hid his face, and the strange conflict of emotion that was beating in her chest.

When Knight opened the door to the yellow bedchamber his heart skipped a beat. The words he had come to say slipped from his mind. He stared and all else was forgotten in that moment as he watched Marianne hurriedly rising from where she had been sitting upon the floor. The room was dim, but small shafts of sunlight were penetrating through the seams of the closed shutters. She was standing directly in the line of a thin ray of light so that it lit her in a soft white light. There was an ethereal quality to her, so soft and pale with such deep, dark, soulful eyes.

He realised he was staring and pulled himself together, entering the room and setting the breakfast tray that he carried down on the nearby table. Her cheeks were flushed and she looked embarrassed to have been caught sitting in the sunbeam. His eyes dropped down to the stockinged feet that peeped from beneath her skirt, then travelled slowly up the wedding dress, all crumpled and creased from sleep, to the smooth swell of breasts that rose from the tight press of the bodice.

Her hair was a tumble of white-blonde waves over her shoulders, so long that it reached almost to her waist. She looked as beautiful and dishevelled as if she had just climbed from a lover's bed.

His gaze reached her face and he met the darkness of her eyes with all of their secrets and steadfast resilience. And that same ripple of desire he had experienced when he first looked at her whispered again. He closed his ears to it, denied its existence. Her blush intensified beneath his scrutiny and she stepped away, twitching at her rumpled skirts and shifting her feet to try to hide her stockinged toes.

He wanted to ask her why a twenty-year-old woman was so terrified of the dark. It seemed much more than a spoiled girl's foible. He knew how hard she had fought to hide her fear from him, and were he to ask the question she would, no doubt, deny all and tell him nothing.

'From Pickering?' He gestured towards the heavy ornate pearls around her neck.

She nodded. 'You knew that I was on my way to be married before my father told you, didn't you?' Her eyes looked different today. Lighter, a rich brown, and the contempt had gone from them. Something of her armour was back in place, but he had a feeling she had not pulled down her visor. Her manner was still guarded, but less hostile than it had been.

'It is a society wedding of interest throughout the *ton*.' He shrugged as if it were nothing of significance and did not tell her that he had made it his business to know all there was to know of Misbourne, or that he had been waiting and watching these two months past for an opportunity to take her from her father.

'And yet still you held us up.' He could sense both her curiosity and her condemnation.

'You think me ruthless. And when it comes to your father I cannot deny it.'

'You should not have hurt him,' she said and he saw her eyes darken with the memory of what had happened upon the heath.

Yet he could not apologise. He could not say he regretted it. Or that he would not have done the same, or more, again. 'I regret that you had to witness such violence.'

'But you do not regret what you did.'

He shook his head. 'Your father deserved much more.' It was a harsh truth, but he would not lie to her.

She swallowed and something of the defensiveness slotted back across her face. No matter what he knew of Misbourne, he admired her loyalty to her father—the courage with which she stood up to a highwayman to defend the bastard so determinedly. His eye traced the fine line of her cheek, the fullness of her lips. He caught what he was doing and felt the muscle clench in his jaw. With a stab of anger he averted his gaze and began to walk away. She was Misbourne's daughter, for pity's sake! He should not have to remind himself.

'There were seven men in that alleyway,' she said in a low careful voice, 'and you are but one man, yet you did not use a pistol.'

Her words stopped him, but he did not look round. 'A pistol shot would have brought more of the rats from their holes.'

'Why did you help me?'

The question, so softly uttered, cut through everything else.

He turned then, and looked at her, at the temptation she presented: those eyes, so soft and dark as to beguile a man from all sense.

'Why would I not?'

'You hate my father.'

Hate was too mild a word to describe what he felt for Misbourne. He paused before speaking, before looking into the eyes that were so similar and yet so different to her father's. 'Regardless of your father, while you are with me I will keep you safe.'

Safe. It had been such a long time since Marianne had felt safe. There had been times that she had thought she would never feel safe again, no matter how well guarded and protected she was by her family. She studied his face. In the shaft of morning light his eyes were golden as a flame. He was a highwayman. He had beaten her father and abducted her. He was holding her prisoner her against her will. She had watched the most brutal of London's lowlife cower before him. He could be anyone behind that dark silken mask. But whoever he was, he had not used her ill, as he could have. He had brought her candles to light the darkness. And he had saved her. He had saved her—and he had bested seven men to do it.

She met his gaze and held it, looking deep into those amber eyes, trying to glean a measure of the man behind the mask. He was not lying. A man like him had no need to lie.

The expression in his eyes gentled. His hand moved as if he meant to touch her arm, except that he stopped it before it reached her and let it drop away.

'Are you all right?' he asked.

She stared up into his face and could not look away. And the highwayman held her gaze.

'Yes,' she said at last and nodded. 'I am fine.' She

had said those words so many times in the past three years, but only this time, standing there in a shuttered bedchamber with a masked man who had abducted her, was she close to telling the truth. 'The letter that you think my father holds.'

He gave no response.

'I know you believe he understands…' She saw the flicker of something dangerous in his eyes, but it did not stop her. 'Will you ask him again and tell him exactly what it is that you seek?'

'I have already done so.'

She gave a nod and relaxed at his words. 'I heard you and your accomplice talking about a document… He will give it to you this time.' Her father would give whatever it took to redeem her. 'I will stake my life upon it.'

The highwayman said nothing. He just looked at her for a moment longer and then walked away, leaving her locked alone in the bedchamber.

Five minutes later Marianne heard the thud of the front door closing and the clatter of a horse's hooves trotting away from the house. She knew that it was the highwayman leaving. The accomplice's footsteps sounded on the stairs; she heard him come along the passageway and go into a nearby room. There was the noise of cupboards and drawers being opened and closed, then the accomplice unlocked her door, knocking before entering.

'If you will come this way, my lady, I am under instruction to show you to another room in which you might spend the day. One in which the shutters are not closed.'

He took her to the bedchamber on the opposite side

of the passageway. The daylight was light and bright and wonderful after the dimness of the yellow chamber. She blinked, her eyes taking an age to adjust. The walls were a cool blue, the bedding dark as midnight and the furniture mahogany and distinctly masculine in style. Over by the basin she could see a shaving brush, soap and razor blade, all set before a mirror, and she knew whose bedchamber this was without having to be told. Her heart began to pound and butterflies flocked in her stomach. She hesitated where she was, suddenly suspicious.

Something of the apprehension must have shown in her face for all she tried to hide it, for the accomplice smiled gently, reassuringly.

'He thought you would prefer the daylight. The sun hits the back of the house in the afternoon.' He paused for a moment. 'You need not have a fear, lass. I am to take you back to the yellow chamber before he returns.'

She looked round at the accomplice and the grey mask loosely tied to obscure his face. 'Could you not simply have removed the nails from the shutters?'

'No, Lady Marianne.' The accomplice glanced away uneasily.

'Because it is at the front of the house,' she guessed, 'and you fear that I would attract attention?'

'It is rather more complicated than that. The shutters must remain closed. Those in the master bedchamber too.'

'The yellow bedchamber...' She hesitated and thought of the hairbrush. 'It was his mother's room, was it not?'

The accomplice gave a hesitant nod.

'And this is his house.'

He looked uncomfortable but did not deny it. 'I must go,' he said and started to move away.

'You said he was a good man.'

The accomplice halted by the door. 'He is.'

'What he did to my father on Hounslow Heath was not the action of a good man.'

'Believe me, Lady Marianne, were he a lesser man, your father would be dead. Were I in his shoes, I don't know that I could have walked away and left Misbourne alive.' He turned away, then glanced back again to where she stood, slack-jawed and gaping in shock. 'For your own sake, please be discreet around the window. Being seen in a gentleman's bedchamber, whatever the circumstances, would not be in any young unmarried lady's favour.'

He gave a nod of his head and walked away, locking the door behind him.

What had her father ever done to deserve the hatred of these men? Her legs felt wobbly at the thought of such vehemence. She needed to sit down. She eyed the four-poster bed with its dark hangings and covers—the highwayman's bed—and a shiver rippled down her spine, spreading out to tingle across the whole of her skin. She stepped away, choosing the high-backed easy chair by the side of the fireplace, and perching upon the edge of its seat.

Marianne glanced at the window behind her and the brightness of the daylight. The accomplice was right. Especially given it had been little more than a year since the Duke of Arlesford had broken their betrothal. The scandal surrounding it still had not completely died away. One word of her abduction, one word that she had spent the night in a bachelor's house without a chaperon—no matter that she was being held alone in a locked room—and her reputation would be ruined to such an extent that none of her father's influences could repair it. The irony almost made her laugh. Especially when she contemplated the darkness of the truth. Even so, she rose to her feet and walked to the window.

The view was the same as that of a hundred other houses in London—long, neatly kept back gardens separated by high stone walls, backing on to more gardens and the distant rear aspect of yet more town houses, all beneath the grey-white of an English autumn sky. There were no landmarks that she recognised. The catch moved easily enough, but the window was stiff and heavy and noisy to open. She did not slide it up far. There was little point, for there was no hope of escape through it. The drop below was sheer and at least twenty-five feet. She closed the window as quietly as she could and turned to survey the room around her.

It was much smaller than the yellow bedchamber and almost Spartan in its feel. Aside from the bed there was a bedside cabinet upon which was placed a candle in its holder. Against the other walls stood a dark mahogany wardrobe, a wash-stand and a chest of drawers with a small peering glass and shaving accoutrements sitting neatly on top. A dark Turkey rug covered the floor, but there were no pictures on the wall, no bolsters or cushions upon the bed. There was no lace, no frills, nothing pretty or pale. It was the very opposite of Marianne's bedchamber at home. It was dark and serious and exuded an air of strength and utter masculinity, just like the man who owned it.

His presence seemed strong in the room, so strong that it almost felt like he was here. And she had the strangest sensation of feeling both unsettled and safe at once. Her blood was flowing a little bit too fast.

She needed to search the bedchamber, to discover any clue to the highwayman's identity that she might tell her father when she got home. So she turned the key within the tall polished wardrobe and the door swung open. Sandalwood touched to her nose, a faint scent but instantly recognisable as the highwayman. Goose-bumps prickled her skin and a shiver passed all the way through her body. There was something attractive, something almost stimulating about his scent. The rails were heavy with expensive tailored coats and breeches, undoubtedly the clothing of a gentleman, and a wealthy one at that if the cut and quality of material were anything to judge by. It did not surprise her for, despite his disguise, she had known almost from the first that he was no ruffian.

Check the pockets, she heard the voice of common sense whisper in her ear. She reached out her hand, then hesitated, holding her breath, suddenly very aware of where she was and what she was doing. Slowly she touched her fingers to the shoulder of the nearest tail-coat.

The midnight-blue wool felt as smooth and expensive as it looked. Her eyes scanned the breadth of the shoulders. She let her fingers trace all the way down one lapel and it felt as daring as if she were stroking a tiger, as daring as if the highwayman was still wearing the coat. That thought made her heart skip a beat. She slid her hands within, checking the inside for hidden pockets, skimming down the tail to the pocket that was there, but nothing was to be found in any of them. She checked each coat in turn; the feel of his clothing beneath her fingers and the scent of him in her nose made her heart thud all the harder and her blood rush all the faster as she remembered the strength and hardness of the arm she had gripped so frantically last night and the weight of his hand around her arm in the rookery. And she wondered if this was what it would feel like to lay her hand against his shoulder, his lapel, his chest...

She gave a shaky laugh at the absurdity of her own thoughts. She did not like men, especially those who were dangerous. She closed the wardrobe door and, quietly and systematically, began to search the rest of the room.

The soap in the dish held the scent of sandalwood. She touched his badger-hair shaving brush and the handle of his razorblade, wondering that he had left such a weapon at her disposal. But then she remembered him in the rookery and knew that he had nothing to be afraid of. And another shiver rippled all the way from the top of her head down to the tips of her toes.

Everything was neat and tidy, everything in its place. Waistcoats, shirts, a pile of pressed linen cravats...and a black-silk kerchief. She hesitated, feeling strange to see it folded and pressed so neatly within the drawer. It seemed so harmless, so inconsequential, unlike the man who wore it.

There were two pairs of riding boots and three pairs of black slippers—all large. She did not look through his unmentionables, only closed the drawer so quickly that she wondered if his accomplice had heard the noise. Then she sat herself down in the easy chair by the fireplace, properly this time, and considered what she had gleaned of the highwayman from his room and possessions.

He was a gentleman, tall and broad-shouldered and strong. A man who wore a black-silk kerchief across his face. A man from whom one glance made her shiver, and of whom his scent alone made her heart beat too fast. A man for whom she felt both wariness and fascination. Nothing in the room had told her anything more than she already knew.

Knight did not return to his town house until dinnertime that night.

'Did you win?' Callerton asked, serving up the stew he had prepared.

'Your money's safe,' replied Knight.

'Nice to know I made a bob or two without leaving the house.' Callerton grinned. 'Shouldn't Rafe Knight, gentleman and rake, be out celebrating his victory?'

'They have arranged an outing to a gaming hell tonight.'

Callerton screwed his face up.

'If I don't go there'll be questions. And we don't want questions.'

Callerton shook his head. 'Especially not this night.'

'Is Lady Marianne in the yellow bedchamber?'

'Took her back through at four just to be on the safe side. Thought I heard her having a rummage earlier in the day, but there was nought for her to find. I made sure of that before I put her in there.'

Knight gave a nod of gratitude. She had not succumbed to tears or tantrums. With a calm logic, of which he himself would have been proud, she had undertaken a search of his room.

'Been a long time since you had a woman in that bedchamber.'

A vision of Marianne sprawled naked in his bed popped into his mind, her blonde hair splayed across his pillows, her bare breasts peeping from between the rumpled sheets to tease and torture him. He pushed the image away and clenched his jaw, knowing that he could not afford to think of her in that way.

'Maybe too long.' Definitely too long if he was having inappropriate thoughts about Misbourne's daughter. He forced his mind to think of tomorrow and all that lay ahead. Once Misbourne gave him the document he would not see her again. And that could only be a good thing. He would not allow his thoughts to stray to her again.

'Let us run through the plan again. We'll not have another chance. And then we'll send the boy with the meeting place and time to Misbourne so that he has not enough time to think up anything clever.'

Callerton gave a nod. 'Even Misbourne isn't bastard enough to risk his daughter a second time.'

'I hope you're right,' Knight replied, unrolling the crudely drawn map. For his own sake, and for Marianne Winslow's. He did not wish to consider what he would do if they were wrong.

The two men bent over the map and began to talk in earnest.

The morning was still dark when the highwayman's accomplice led Marianne out of the back door and across a few streets. They travelled on foot, keeping to the mews and alleyways, so that she did not recognise where they were or the direction they took. In a narrow alley that ran down the side of what looked to be a hospital building, a black coach was waiting. They hurried over to it and she thought they meant to climb inside, but the coachman jumped down and she saw that it was the highwayman in his greatcoat and hat. His accomplice climbed up to take his place.

'God keep you safe, friend,' he said to the highwayman.

'And you,' replied the highwayman and glanced to the sky. 'Dawn is breaking. It should be light enough by the time I am seen being trundled home three sheets to the wind.'

The accomplice nodded and with a flick of the reins was gone, leaving Marianne standing alone with the highwayman.

'Are you ready, Lady Marianne?' he asked.

She nodded, and he took her arm and guided her out on to the street. There was the smell of a dye house in the air. The houses were small and a little shabby, but this was not some rookery, and even if it had been she felt safe with the highwayman by her side. Ironic, she thought, but true.

They did not speak, just walked in silence. Even though the hour was early, the air stirred; London was awakening. A cart rattled by and two dodgy-looking characters passed from whom she averted her gaze. She was glad of the highwayman's proprietorial grip on her arm.

They kept a steady pace heading onwards. It was only when they passed the great church that she realised they were going to the burying ground.

He led her through the gate and wove a path through the stones that marked the graves of the dead. The wind that howled across the ground was sharp, nipping at her cheeks and catching her hair, blowing strands of it across her eyes. Overhead, the sky was grey and dismal and the air ripe with dampness and the promise of rain. They walked on, their pace so brisk that she found herself slightly out of breath, walked on until they reached the larger stones and monuments erected by the wealthy. And then, quite suddenly, he led her behind a tiny mausoleum built in the style of a classical temple, the stonework of which was blackened by age and the smoke from London's chimneys.

'This is the place,' he murmured, sliding a hand inside his greatcoat to produce a pocket watch. He flipped open the casing and checked the time. 'Ten minutes,' he said and the watch disappeared from sight once more.

Ten minutes and then she would be free. Ten minutes and all of this would be over. She would be back with her father and she would never see the highwayman again. Never know who he was behind that mask. She leaned back against the wall of the mausoleum and watched him.

'For what it is worth, I am sorry that you had to be a part of this, Lady Marianne. But you were the only way I could reach your father.' His eyes held a sincerity she had not expected to see.

'This document that you seek must be very important to you.'

'More important than you can imagine.'

'What is it?' She asked the question with little expectation of a reply.

He was silent for so long that she thought she had been right, but then he spoke. 'It is the answer to a question I have asked myself for these past fifteen years.'

'Fifteen years?' Such a long time. Yet his eyes, his voice, his body, the way he moved—none were those of an old man.

'June 1795,' he said.

'What happened on that date?' She saw the flicker of pain in his eyes, there, then gone so quickly and replaced by such hard and utter ruthlessness that she felt shocked to see it.

'Ask your father the answer to that question, Lady Marianne, and see what he says.' That same half-whisper, harsher and angrier than ever.

'You are wrong about him,' she said. She did not know what lies the highwayman had been spun or why he had her father so wrong. All she knew was that she had to try, in these last few minutes they had together, to let him know the truth. 'He is the best of fathers. I know you will not believe me, but he is a good man.' She thought desperately of what she could say to convince him. 'He is a governor of the Foundling Hospital and, although he took great pains to see that it was kept secret, he contributed much of the money for its chapel to be built. He gives freely to the poor, to widows and orphans especially, yet he makes no show of his charity, and he—'

The highwayman gave a hard, harsh laugh of amusement and shook his head. 'The irony is not lost on me, Lady Marianne.'

'There is nothing of irony in what he has done.'

'Indeed? Foundlings and orphans!' In the space of a moment his eyes had darkened with the shadows that moved within them. 'He is your father. Defend him all you will, but not to my ears.'

She could feel the darkness that emanated from him, the barely suppressed anger tinged with bitterness. 'What is this hatred that drives you?'

'It is the desire for justice,' he whispered.

'More like vengeance for some imagined injustice.'

'There was nothing imagined about it.'

'What did he do to you?'

'He took from me that which was most precious.'

And she remembered the words he had spoken to her father upon the heath, before he had taken her.

'I don't understand,' she said.

'Neither do I.'

Their gazes held, locked, trapped in the moment. She could not have looked away, even had she wanted to. She stared at the tall dark highwayman with his great black coat flapping in the wind and the dark mask that hid his face, the very symbol of the villain he was. He was a man like none she had known. Strong, hard, ruthless. And yet…

The wind howled through the gravestones and the first drops of rain began to fall. Still they looked into each other's eyes, and the air was thick with a strange tension, like the unnatural calm before the storm, waiting for something she did not understand. She should have been more afraid of this man than any other. She felt that she was clinging to a great precipice, that her grip was slipping and she was beginning to slide inch by agonising inch towards the edge. And she knew what lay over that edge. She should have been grappling to regain her hold, but the edge was beckoning her closer and there was a part of her that found it dangerously alluring.

'Who are you behind that mask?' she whispered.

'Do you really want to know?' His voice was as quiet as hers as he stepped closer. She was surprised that she felt no compulsion to back away, even though her heart was pounding and every nerve in her body shivered. Her throat went dry, her mouth too. She wetted her lips and saw his gaze drop to them, before coming back to her eyes.

The tension wound tighter.

Another step forwards and they were standing so

close that, were she to inhale deeply, she would feel the graze of her chest against his. He did not touch her, yet her body tingled as if caressed by his very proximity.

'Marianne,' he whispered softly.

She looked up into his eyes and could see each golden striation within them, every dark lash that outlined them.

His face lowered towards hers and she knew that he was going to kiss her. And for one absurd moment she wanted him to do it. She wanted more than anything to feel his mouth against hers, even through the silk. And then she remembered, and stepped away.

Her breath was ragged as if she had been running and she was trembling so badly that she had to clutch her hands together so that he would not see it.

He did not come after her. He did not grab her or force his mouth upon hers. He just stood there and watched her. The wind blew and all was silent and cool aside from the thump of her heart and the scald of her cheeks. Her eyes met his once more.

A noise sounded from the other side of the mausoleum, making her start and breaking the tension between them. Part of her was relieved and another part dismayed.

Someone was making their way over the grass of the burying ground. With a tiny nod of acknowledgement to her, the highwayman turned away and went to meet whoever it was he was waiting for.

Marianne sagged back against the wall of the mausoleum. She did not understand what had just passed between her and the highwayman. But it did not matter, for the person on the other side of the tomb was bringing the document from her father. In a few moments she would be free and walking away from this.

A shot rang out, shattering the peace and silence of the place. She moved to peep round the side of the mausoleum and watched all hell break loose.

Chapter Five

'Run, governor!' the little lad yelled and began to run towards him. 'It's a trap!'

Knight saw three figures loom from behind the nearby gravestones and reacted even before he saw the first man take aim at the boy. He launched himself forwards, firing his pistol at the man as he scooped the boy up and ran for the nearest gravestone. The shot thudded into the other side of the stone as he dived behind.

'I'm sorry.' Smithy was white-faced, without a trace of his usual cocky bravado. 'They caught me. Held a pistol to my head and made me bring 'em here.'

'I understand,' Knight replied to the boy in a low voice. He knew the men would be creeping closer, knew, too, that it was him, not the boy, they were after. He reloaded his pistol and risked a brief glance round the edge. Another shot rang out and some fragments of stone crumbled to the grass on his left. 'Stay hidden,' he whispered, then dodged away through the grave-stones towards the tall obelisk stone far enough away from the lad and the mausoleum. He could only hope that Marianne had the sense to remain out of sight.

The bullets rained in force, the shots deafening in the silence of the burying ground, the stench of the powder like rotten eggs all around. The wind of a bullet whistled close to his right ear as he ducked behind the obelisk.

'Don't just stand there! Get after him!' a rough voice yelled.

Knight reloaded the pistol again, smoothly and quickly, counting the seconds as the tread of boots crept closer. The first flicker of dark shadow to his right and Knight grabbed at the villain, wrenching the man in close and compressing the vulnerable area of his neck until he passed out. The body slid noiselessly to the grass.

'Where the hell did he go?' The villain's whisper told him where they were.

The bullets ceased. There was silence, and in the waiting he heard the howl of the wind and the beat of his own heart. He ran to his left, aiming for the next gravestone, firing as he went, and heard the yelp and the slump of a body as his bullet went home. He made it behind the stone before the pistol shot cracked against it, then moved again, crouching low through the stones, working his way round towards the last of the three villains.

A bullet thudded into grass before him, tearing up the turf. One villain remained, with two pistols. Two shots had been fired. Knight didn't give the blackguard time to reload, but broke cover and ran full tilt at him, slamming hard into him, taking him down. The man struggled, but Knight's fist stilled that; then he grabbed hold of the villain's throat and hoisted him up, pinning him against the nearest gravestone.

And then he saw Marianne.

'Get back!' he yelled but, as if oblivious to the danger, she ignored him and carried on walking until she had reached his side.

'Where is the document?' she asked the man.

'Marianne, do as I say.'

She glanced up at him and he saw, before she turned back to the man, that she did not yet understand what her father had done. 'I asked you a question, sir,' she said to the man.

'I don't know what you're talking about, lady.'

She shook her head. 'But…'

'Misbourne sent you,' Knight said to the man.

'Yes.'

'With the document,' said Marianne.

'To bring me in,' corrected Knight.

'No.' The man strained to shake his head.

Knight saw Marianne look pointedly up at him. 'You see,' she said, almost triumphantly.

'To kill you,' the villain said.

She paled.

'Then you had better run back and tell him that you failed.' Knight threw the man on to the grass, allowing him to scramble to his feet and back away.

From the corner of his eye Knight saw other dark shadows slinking between the gravestones. 'There are more of them. Take shelter behind the mausoleum, Marianne.'

'So that you may keep me prisoner?' She shook her head. 'I will not do that.' She edged away from him. 'They are from my father. They have come to free me.' And then she turned to run towards them just as the closest villain took aim.

It all happened so quickly. Marianne saw the man point the pistol straight at her. 'Do not shoot! I am coming!' She saw the disregard on his face, saw the plume of blue smoke and heard the roar of the pistol, but the air was already being knocked from her lungs as something big and fast and dark threw her to the ground. A second pistol shot exploded, so close that it made her jump, but she could not see anything because the highwayman was on top of her, shielding her from the danger. In a heartbeat he had dragged her up and hauled her behind the nearest gravestone.

'Do not dare move from here,' he whispered with a ferocity no one in their right mind would ignore, then he was gone.

She stayed where he had left her, hugging her legs to her body, trying to calm the raggedness of her breathing while her mind reeled with the shock of what was happening and the knowledge that her father had not done the one simple thing that would have secured her release. He had sent men to kill the highwayman and they had almost killed her. None of it seemed real. Even though she had seen the man fire the pistol at her, there was a part of her mind that refused to believe it. It was all some horrible imagining. Yet the wind was cold in her face and she could feel the dampness from the rain seeping through the thinness of her shawl as she clutched it tight around her shoulders. She really was here, alive and unharmed—and there was only one reason for that: the highwayman.

She heard the sound of feet running and then a shout. Then the sound of fists, fighting, grunts of pain. Another pistol shot and she could smell the gunpowder in the wind and see the drift of smoke even through the rain. A man began screaming in agony and she prayed, *Please, God, don't let it be him*.

'You bast—!' someone shouted, but the words were

cut off and there came a thud of something hitting the ground hard.

Another shot. Then there was silence. A silence in which her breathing sounded too loud.

'Marianne.'

Suddenly he was there, reaching for her, helping her up, and she did not even think of drawing away.

'Are you all right?'

She nodded, not trusting herself to speak. Her gaze moved over the gravestone to the men that lay beyond. One was rolling around groaning and clutching at his lower trouser leg, which was soaked in blood. Three lay unmoving upon the ground. And another was slumped bleeding and lifeless on the steps that led down into the mausoleum. *Dead*, she thought and could not seem to move her eyes away from the grotesque sight.

'Marianne,' he said again, more softly this time.

She looked up into his eyes, at the fierceness and the urgency there. He was supposed to be the villain in all of this.

'Give me your hand.'

There was nothing she could say, no words that would come. She put her hand in his and followed him through the gravestones.

And as they left, Marianne glanced back to the ruffians that her father had sent, and the mausoleum beyond with the name of its occupant carved into the stone lintel above the door: EDMUND KNIGHT.

Knight headed towards the warehouses and timber yards, keeping to the shadows and the alleyways, alert and watchful. He kept a pistol in one hand, hiding it within the folds of his coat, and the other hand was

around Marianne's waist, both securing and supporting her. To avoid attracting attention he wrenched the
mask down from his face, letting it dangle around his
neck as if it were a neckerchief, but Marianne did not
seem to notice. Her eyes were dazed, her gaze fixed
ahead, although Knight doubted she was registering
much of her surroundings. Her face was so pale he
wondered if she was going to faint. He could not blame
her. He doubted most women, let alone one as indulged
and protected as Marianne, could have remained unaffected after being shot at and witnessing a fight so
brutal as to leave four men unconscious.

He glanced down at her dress, the dress that had
been intended for her wedding. Several of the bows
on the bodice were hanging by a thread. It was grubby
around the hem and the rain had dampened the skirt so
that it clung indecently to her legs. The fine lace shawl
wrapped around her had a rip in it and the ribbon with
which she had bound her hair was lost, leaving it long
and damp around her shoulders. Her appearance was
not so dissimilar to the women who surrounded them
in this part of town. She looked beautiful, abandoned,
wanton almost, except for her innocence and the vulnerability that she was no longer trying to hide. He held
her a little closer and knew that, whatever Misbourne
had done, his daughter did not deserve this.

Knight knew he could not risk heading home in
the daylight. There was a chance that Misbourne had
more men in the vicinity, that they were searching
for him even now. The last thing he wanted to do was
lead them to his house and his true identity. That, and
expose Marianne to more gunfire and violence. He
knew of an empty warehouse, which seemed the closest point of safety. And if Misbourne's ruffians were

on their tail they needed to get there fast. He guided her steadily towards it, unnoticed by those they passed as anything other than a man and his woman.

She had no idea where they were, other than that it was a dubious area of the city and that they were not so very far away from the church of St Luke's. The warehouse was large and almost derelict, but it provided shelter from the rain and from what they had left behind at the burying ground. The highwayman barricaded the door shut behind them and led her across the dust and rubble to lean her against a bare brick wall. She could see that the windows were small and almost as high as the roof, letting in light but showing nothing of the outside world other than the gunmetal-grey sky. Several of the panes had been broken or were missing. Pigeons nested in the exposed rafters, making soft cooing noises. One flew overhead, the flutter of its wings loud against the quiet drizzle of the rain against the roof, and sat watching them from a nearby ledge.

She did not look at him because she knew he was no longer wearing the mask. And she was afraid of what that meant…for her and for him. His hat dropped sodden to the floor and the rustle of his clothing sounded; from the corner of her eye she saw that he was taking off his greatcoat. He moved away to shake the water from it and then wrapped it around her shoulders.

She stood very still and focused on the buckskin of his breeches, the scuffed leather of his boots…anything rather than look at his face, even though it was the one place she really wanted to look. She felt suffocated by the tension. The knot in her stomach tightened. *He was unmasked.* And she knew more than anything in the world that she must not yield to the overriding temptation, swore to herself that she would not. Yet standing there alone with him in that warehouse, with his coat warm around her shoulders and the scent of sandal-wood in her nose, she could not help herself. Despite every sensible thought screaming at her to resist, she slowly raised her head and looked up into the face of the highwayman.

However Marianne had imagined him to look, the reality stole the beat from her heart and the breath from her lungs. He was a man like none she had ever seen, a vision incomparable. Such dark masculinity that made her stomach flutter and tumble and her blood race so fast she thought she might faint. She stared and could not look away, her eyes ranging over the straight manly nose, the rugged angular jawline and square chin. Over the mouth that, even hidden, had tempted her to taste it and, now exposed, made her legs feel weak and her head dizzy. Desire seemed to whisper in the warehouse all around her. Attraction pounded through her veins with such explosive force that she felt herself tremble. She met those searing eyes that were so branded upon her memory and saw the amber in them darken. Her mouth went dry. She dropped her gaze, shocked at her response.

Her heart was beating faster than a horse at full gallop. She kept her gaze low, praying he had realised nothing of her reaction, hoping he did not see the heat that was glowing in her cheeks.

Her focus fixed on the dirty hem of her gown. But the deed had already been done. She had looked upon his face. She could identify him. Both of them knew it. Her fingers gripped tight against the sides of her skirt as she waited for him to react.

And then she saw the single crimson drop land upon

the pale silk of her skirt. There was a horrible sinking sensation in her stomach, for she knew what it was even before she raised her eyes to see the blood dripping from the fingers of his left hand, and the bright red stain that soaked the sleeve of his shirt. In that terrible moment everything else fell from her head.

'You are bleeding!' Her eyes shot to his.

'The bullet skimmed my arm.'

The bullet that had been meant for her. She stared at him, understanding fully for the first time what he had done.

He moved away to sit down, leaning his back against the red dusty bricks of the wall, and with his good hand began to unfasten his neckcloth.

'Let me help you,' she said and, shrugging off the greatcoat, she knelt by his side.

His gaze met hers. Then he let his hand drop away from the half-loosened knot of his neckcloth.

She leaned closer and, pushing aside the black-silk kerchief that still hung around his neck, her fingers finished what he had started. She unfastened the knot and unwound the linen strip from around his neck. In his highwayman's guise he was not wearing the fine dress shirts she had seen in his bedchamber, but something much cheaper and thinner through which she could see a hint of the flesh of his chest and the dark smattering of hair that covered it.

He made to take the neckcloth from her and their fingers collided, but she did not release the linen.

'I must bind the wound to stop it bleeding.' His voice was low, that same half-whisper even though the mask was no longer tied around his face. 'It is no sight for you, Marianne.' The linen was taut between their hands.

'Do you think I cannot face a little blood to help you?' In the rookery he had saved her from... She could not even think the word. And not half an hour ago, in the burying ground, he had saved her life.

'Most young women in your position would not offer to help me.'

'Then you should be glad that I am not like most young women,' she replied and thought of the terrible dark secret she was hiding.

'No, you are not, Marianne.' His gaze held hers and as she looked deep into his eyes she felt something shift between them. In her hand he yielded her the linen. Then he pulled a knife from within his boot and offered it, handle first, to her. 'You need to cut away the sleeve of my shirt.'

She looked at the blade and then up into his eyes. 'With such a weapon I could do a better job than the bullet.'

'You could,' he agreed, but the knife still lay upon his palm and she knew it was more than the knife he was offering her. Trust. It was such a fragile word. Power. It was not something she had ever known.

She looked at him a moment longer, then her fingers closed around the handle. The blade was sharp and wicked, and she wielded it with great care to cut away the thin linen sleeve of his shirt. With the skin exposed she could see the wound that gaped in the flesh of his upper arm and the glisten of the blood that leaked from it.

'Lay the sleeve flat upon the ground and check that where the bullet entered none of the material is missing.'

She did not understand the reason, but did as he instructed, smoothing out the blood-soaked linen, finding the small gaping hole the bullet had made and showing it to him. To her shock he pulled his injured arm across his chest and began to poke his fingers into the wound. She could see the way he gritted his teeth against the pain; the blood flowed all the harder.

'What on earth are you doing?'

'The missing piece of shirt is within the wound. It will fester if left there.'

'Allow me.'

'Marianne,' he growled.

'Are you afraid that I will hurt you?' she goaded.

'Perhaps.'

'I do not believe you. You do not fear anything.'

'We all have fears, Marianne.'

She felt the shadow of her past fall upon her. 'And they always find us no matter how fast we run, or how well we hide,' she muttered beneath her breath. But he had heard her.

'Running from fear only makes it chase you. Hiding from it only makes it seek you. You have to face fear.'

Their gazes locked and held just for a moment. Then she took his injured arm within both her hands and examined the red pulp of the groove the bullet's path had cut through his skin. It was, as he had warned, not a pleasant sight, but she did not allow herself to balk from it. The metallic scent of blood was so heavy in the air that she could taste it at the back of her throat. She did not see the single scrap of bloodied linen at first. Indeed, it no longer looked like linen, being dark red and wet; only the edge of uneven threads made her realise what it was. She knew that it would hurt him. She glanced up at his face and saw he was watching her.

He gave her a nod of encouragement.

She reached into the wound, feeling the muscles

tense slightly, and found the end of the linen scrap. She carefully picked it out, placing it on her palm and showing it to him.

'Open it out, fit it against the hole within the sleeve.'

And when she did, they could both see that it completed the sleeve—there was no more of the material within the wound.

Using the knife, she cut the neckcloth into strips, then took a clean pad of handkerchief from the pocket of her dress, pressed it gently to the wound and bound it in place with the strips, tying off the last of them so that it would not unravel.

'Thank you,' he said.

'You are welcome.'

The silence seemed suddenly loud within the damp chill of the warehouse.

Her father had not sent the document. The knowledge hung between them, although neither of them spoke it.

'What happens now?'

'We wait until nightfall so that we can cross the streets unseen.'

'And then?'

'And then you may go home to your father.'

Her eyes scanned his, searching for lies and trickery and finding none.

'There is much time to wait, Marianne. You might as well make yourself comfortable.' He gestured to the ground by his side. He was right. She sat down on the side of his good arm, leaning her back against the wall as he did.

'The day is chilled,' he said, and when he repositioned the coat so that it covered both their legs she did not stop him. Her dress was damp with rain and when she breathed she could see the faint mist of her breath, yet she did not feel cold. Indeed, the side of her closest to him seemed to burn.

They sat in silence, their bodies so close, yet not touching.

She looked down at where their hands lay on top of his greatcoat. His, so very large, a man's hand, strong and capable, the fingers long and blunt, the knuckles grazed. Hers, so very small and pale in comparison. Both were stained with blood. His blood.

'You don't have to be afraid any more, Marianne.' He turned his right hand, the hand that was closest to her, over so that it was lying open and palm up.

And it seemed the most natural thing in the world to lay her hand upon his and feel the gentle close of his fingers.

They sat against the wall. Side by side, neither looking at the other.

They sat in silence, listening to the rain and the occasional distant sound of a bell tolling, and the howl of the wind through the roof. And the clouds moved across the sky, all the shades of grey and charcoal, racing so fast as to give her the illusion that she and the highwayman, not the clouds, were moving. And the rain drummed all the heavier before finally ceasing its attack. Even when it stopped they could still hear the run of water from the guttering. And all that time his hand was warm and strong and reassuring around hers.

'Hell, Knight! I thought he had you. I went to the burying ground, but it was empty and there was blood all over the place.' Within the kitchen of the house in Craven Street, Callerton was unwrapping the bandage from Knight's arm.

'I had to lie low until I was sure they would be gone.'

Callerton removed the dressing from Knight's arm and peered at the wound. 'The lass did a good job.'

'She did,' agreed Knight, thinking of how Marianne had helped him. Nothing about her was as he had expected. She was not over-confident, spoiled and demanding. He found her quiet dignity, her courage, the secrets in her dark eyes, intriguing. Too intriguing for a woman he had abducted. And definitely too intriguing for the woman who was the daughter of the man he had spent a lifetime hunting.

'This is going to hurt like the devil.' Callerton lifted the clean boiled rag and dipped it in the cooling boiled water.

'Do your worst,' said Knight and grimaced as Callerton began to cleanse the wound.

'Misbourne is an utter bastard. I can't believe he would risk his daughter's life for the sake of a piece of paper.'

'Believe it.' Knight's hatred of the man intensified at the thought of how he had endangered Marianne's life.

'If his men were sent in to free her, how could they make the mistake of shooting at her? You said it was point-blank range. They must have seen her.'

Knight frowned slightly as Callerton pressed harder on the wound. 'Because they weren't sent to free her. They were sent to kill me. None of the men made any attempt to retrieve Marianne. I doubt he even told them that I was holding his daughter.'

Callerton blew out a sigh and shook his head. 'So Misbourne's keeping quiet about Marianne's abduction, even to the ruffians that he's hired.' He paused and looked at Knight. 'But why try to kill you when, to his knowledge, you're the only one who knows the location of his daughter?'

'Because he thinks I know what's in the document. Whatever is written on that piece of paper, Misbourne is willing to do anything to keep its secret safe. Even if it means risking his own daughter.'

'Hell,' said Callerton. He finished cleansing the wound and started to bind it with a fresh dressing and strips of linen. 'What is in that document?'

'The explanation for what played out on Hounslow Heath fifteen years ago. And the more Misbourne tries to hide it, the more determined I am to find it.'

'And Lady Marianne?'

'We let her go,' said Knight. Her father might risk her life, but he would not.

Callerton paused in his binding. 'She's seen your face. She can identify you.'

'Only if she sees me again. She does not know my name.'

'It's risky, especially with you having to play the rake around town.'

'It's a risk I'm going to have to take.' He remembered the look on Marianne's face when she realised that her father had not sent the document to free her: shock, disbelief, confusion, hurt. Misbourne was a villain, but seeing Marianne realise it gave him nothing of gladness or victory, only a sick feeling deep in his stomach. 'I never meant for her to be endangered or hurt. I thought Misbourne would give up the document, to save her from me, at the first opportunity.' He thought of her standing before him in that burying ground, prior to the arrival of Smithy and Misbourne's ruffians. And the urge he had felt to kiss her. And his palm upon which hers had lain in the warehouse tingled, and the same desire he had felt then whispered through his body. He had to be losing his mind.

'Misbourne will think he's won.' Callerton tied off the bandage.

'He'll soon realise otherwise,' said Knight. He gritted his teeth and hardened his voice. 'The sooner she is gone from here, the better.'

Within the yellow bedchamber Marianne watched as the accomplice, still masked, poured the last of the hot water into the copper bath positioned before the fire and left. The highwayman lifted his own empty bucket and moved towards the door.

'The bath is warm to soak in and there are clothes in the wardrobe and drawers, old fashioned in style, but clean and dry. When you are ready, ring the bell and your dinner will be delivered to you. When you have eaten I will take you home to your father.'

She gave a small nod of acknowledgement. 'I have been thinking,' she began. She had done nothing else but think since the warehouse. 'The document cannot be in my father's possession. It is the only explanation.'

He said nothing, but she could see from his eyes that he thought otherwise.

'Believe me, if my father had the document he would have given it to you. I am certain of it.'

Still he said nothing. It was not as if he were arguing against her. She did not know why she felt the compulsion to explain to him. 'It is more than the fact he is my father.' She hesitated before rushing on. 'There are other reasons…very good reasons…' Of which she could make no mention. 'I know he would not have left me in such a situation if, by the production of a single document in his possession, whatever that document might detail, he could free me.'

She saw the look in his eyes and understood what it was. She faced right up to him, suddenly reckless and angry. 'Do not dare pity me!'

He did not argue, did not move, just looked at her with those eyes of his.

'You think you know my father so well. You think you have it all worked out with your plans and your machinations. But my father has not delivered you the document and there can only be two possible explanations. The first is that...' she swallowed and was proud that she did not hesitate to say the words '...is that I am not the most precious thing to him. And the second is that the document is not in his possession. Either way, you were wrong in your estimation, sir.'

There was a dark flare of fury in his eyes. The air seemed to tingle between them, making her suddenly very aware of him as a man and of all of his power. She wondered if she had gone too far, yet she could not back down.

The seconds seemed to stretch. They stared at one another across the small distance.

'Your bath is growing cold, Lady Marianne,' he said, his use of her title erecting the barrier of formality, as if nothing had happened between them in the burying ground or the warehouse. And with a small inclination of his head he left.

The hour was late by the time they travelled the first part of the way through the lamp-lit streets, in the same carriage in which he had brought her to his house. Fog drifted in patches, slowing their progress. Eventually the carriage came to a halt in an alleyway and they continued the rest of the journey on foot. There was nothing securing her wrists. He did not hold her, not her arm or her hand or her waist. He told himself that it was because she had no reason to escape, not now that he was taking her home to Misbourne. But that was not the only reason. The truth was that he liked the feel of her too much.

They did not speak, just walked side by side through the quiet streets that glistened with dampness and puddles. He did not wear the black-silk kerchief around his face, but the collar of his greatcoat was turned up and his hat pulled low on his head. Beside him, Marianne was wrapped in a long fawn cloak that brought back memories of his childhood. His mother had been taller and bigger in build than Marianne, so the bodice of the deep-blue silk beneath it had been pinned to keep it decent and the hem of the dress touched to the ground. The cloak's hood was pulled up over her head, but he knew that beneath it her hair was plaited neatly and tied with a silk ribbon that matched the dress.

They continued walking, keeping to the alleyways and mews through the occasional mist that swirled and hid them. Always in the shadows, that the few people they passed would not know either Marianne or him. Until at last he stopped at the end of the alleyway that would lead out near to Leicester Square.

He looked down at her and she looked up at him, and he was seized by the sensation that had things been different, had she not been Misbourne's daughter, had she not been the woman he had abducted, had she not been promised to another man...

But she was all of those things, and what lay between him and Misbourne was only just beginning. When it finished there would be a noose around Misbourne's neck. And he could not afford to let himself think of what that would do to the woman before him; he did not need that complication.

She was Misbourne's daughter, he told himself, and nothing more.

'We are very close to the square in which you live. All you need do is walk straight along this street until you come to your father's house. Go home to where you are safe.' His half-whispered words sounded harsh in the soft quietness of the night.

Go home to where you are safe. She shuddered at the memory his words elicited.

He saw it, but misunderstood the reason. 'You need not fear to walk alone through the darkness. You will be safe. I will be watching you until you enter through the front door.'

'I am not afraid,' she replied. *Not with you.* It was absurd and ironic, and true. 'Not of the darkness here, outside, in the open…only indoors, in chambers, when all the candles have been extinguished.' She had never spoken even this small part of it to anyone before. Indeed, she did not know why she was telling him.

'Sometimes the worst monsters are those whom we allow to play in our imagination.' He glanced away into the distance, a hard look upon his face, as if he were remembering monsters of his own.

'Not always. Sometimes the worst monsters really are those that wait in the darkness.' She bit her lip, suddenly afraid that she had revealed too much.

His eyes came back to rest on her and the look in them was one of guilt.

'I should go.' But she did not move.

'You should. I…' he hesitated as if he did not want

to speak the rest of the words '…wish you happy in your marriage to Pickering.'

She felt only dread at the prospect of the marriage. She did not want to think of Mr Pickering or anything else, not at this moment, not while she was standing here with the highwayman.

'I hope that your arm heals quickly.' She looked up at him through the moonlight and the moment seemed to stretch between them. These were the last moments they would be together. The last time she would see him.

They stared at one another and the tension that was between them, that had always been between them, seemed to tighten and strain. She could hear the sound of her breath in the quietness of the alleyway and the pound of her heart against her chest. There seemed so much unsaid. She knew she should walk away, but she couldn't.

'I…' She bit at her lip, not understanding why she did not want to go.

'Marianne.' He leaned his face ever so slightly towards her, his gaze holding hers with such intensity, as if he might kiss her. She wanted him to do it. She wanted to feel his mouth against hers, wanted him to take her in his arms. But he did neither. Instead, he touched a hand gently to her face, stroking away some strands of hair that fallen against her cheek. 'You really should go home now.'

'Yes,' she whispered. Home. And this moment and this man would be gone for ever and everything would go back to the way it had been before. To holding candles to ward off the darkness, and being guarded so carefully by her father, and being afraid of every man that looked at her. If only she could capture this moment, capture this man who was taller and darker and more dangerous than any other and who used his strength not against her, but to protect her. This man who had saved her when all those who loved her had failed. In his very danger and strength was the safety she sought.

She had forgotten what it felt like to be without fear. Just as she had forgotten what it felt like to be attracted to a man. And the attraction she felt for him dwarfed any childish fancies she might have imagined she felt for her brother's friends. She knew what she wanted to do. Time was running out. Before she could think better of it she stepped towards him, stood on her tiptoes and with bare-faced, bold audacity touched her lips to his stubbled cheek.

He did not reach for her, did not even touch her for fear that it would make her disappear into the mist that swirled around them. Yet his lips found hers and they were the sweetest, most innocent lips he had ever tasted. She stilled, startled like a deer caught upwind of a hunter. He did not move for a moment, just let their lips rest together and share their breath, allowing her to grow used to the feel of him. He inhaled her: she smelled of violets and mist and moonlight, and all that was temptation. And when she did not bolt, he kissed her. A soft kiss. A gentle kiss. A kiss that said everything he could not say in words. That he was sorry. That he had never meant to frighten her. How it might have been, had their situations been different. And when he broke away she was still standing there, the expression on her upturned face serene and blissful, her eyes closed, her lips full and parted, as if he kissed her still. Then she opened her eyes and looked at him, and he thought she was everything he had ever wanted. A woman of moonlight and mist, of innocence and mystery. Fragile, yet possessing a power she did not realise. All fine-spun glass and shimmering silver. The counterbalance to himself. And for one tiny moment of madness he was tempted to give it all up for her. And then cold hard reality crushed the foolishness of his thoughts.

'Go home, Marianne,' he said.

But she had already pulled the hood to cover her hair and shroud her face and was stepping away, beyond his reach in every respect.

They looked at one another across that small distance and then she turned and walked into the street and out of his life.

All the way down the empty street, all the way through the glow of the faint lamp-lit mist that hung in the darkness, not once did she look back at him. Not even when she reached the steps that led up to her father's house. And there was a part of him that wanted her to look. A part that wanted to know he had affected her as much as she had him.

He watched her lift the brass knocker and strike it against its plate, the clatter of it muffled by distance. Then she glanced back at him, as if she could see through the mist and the darkness to where he stood watching. And he felt a stab of primal satisfaction. The front door opened and a shaft of light flooded out into the street and she no longer looked at him, but only ahead to the butler and to Misbourne as her father pulled her inside.

Chapter Six

The house was in uproar. Marianne could not doubt that her father was pleased to see her. She had never seen him cry, but there was a sheen of tears in his eyes as he held her close, hugging her to him as if she had come back from the dead. Her mother's cheeks, normally never anything but perfectly powdered and pale, were flushed and pink. There was so much excitement and joy as her parents embraced her; her mother clucked over her and even her brother standing by the side watched with a mixture of relief and unspoken questions in his eyes. And she *was* glad to be back with those she loved. She *was* relieved. But even as she felt these things she could feel too that her family were slotting her back into the place she had left, sliding the guard closed around her, imprisoning her within that illusion of safety. She glanced at the blinds in the drawing room, already drawn low to shut out the night and the highwayman. And she smiled at her father and she hugged her mother, and she thought of the highwayman out there in the darkness and her lips burned and throbbed from his kiss.

Marianne had changed. Something had shifted in the

world. And she knew with an absolute certainty that nothing would ever be the same again. Behind her back she slipped Mr Pickering's betrothal ring from her finger and hid it within the pocket of the blue-silk dress.

It was close to lunchtime the next day when Marianne's father came into the drawing room and sat down on the sofa opposite her and her mother. She could see her brother, Francis, waiting in the background and knew, before her mother spoke, that they had come to question her about the highwayman.

'Your papa wishes to speak with you, Marianne. Be sure to do as he asks.' Then with a nod of her head Lady Misbourne slipped from the room, leaving Marianne alone with her father and brother. Francis did not move from where he leaned against the wall.

'You are well enough this morning to be out of bed, Marianne?' her father asked.

'I am very well, Papa, thank you.'

'There are some questions that I must ask you about these last few days. Questions that, although I have no wish to distress you, must be asked.'

She felt a ripple of nervousness run through her.

Her father cleared his throat and looked awkward. 'Your mama tells me that…that the villain did not…' He cleared his throat again and did not meet her eye. Marianne glanced round at Francis, but her brother's face was a mask that showed nothing. 'Did not force himself upon you,' finished her father.

'He did not,' said Marianne. 'He did nothing like that. Indeed, he treated me with kindness.'

'Kindness?' Her father's gaze riveted to hers and she saw the sudden shrewd sharpness within them and was afraid, not for herself but for the highwayman.

'He did not hurt me,' she said. 'He brought me candles to light the darkness. And when I escaped and found myself lost in St Giles Rookery he saved me from a group of ruffians who would have...' She looked away in embarrassment. 'They meant to...' And then her eyes met her father's once more. 'The highwayman saved me from them.'

She saw the look her father exchanged with her brother.

'I want to know everything about him, Marianne, where he took you, what he did. Everything.'

She swallowed and then slowly sketched a very rough outline of the past few days.

At the end of her story she saw her father close his eyes as if garnering strength or control over some strong emotion. 'At any point did you see his face, Marianne?'

A fleeting second to make a momentous decision. Her heart beat, and the seconds seemed to slow down. A pause that was so tiny, yet felt so vast. She should tell the truth, reveal a description of that so-handsome face. Especially given what he had done to her father.

'Whatever that villain may have threatened, pay no heed, Marianne, for I swear on my life that I will see the scoundrel caught.'

She knew what they did to highwaymen that they caught. The magistrates would not be lenient. Her father would see to that.

'He was masked. I saw nothing.' Marianne could not meet her father's eyes to tell the lie. Her heart tripped all the faster.

There was silence in the room and she expected them to say that they knew that she was lying. But they did not.

Her hands lay folded on her lap. She gripped them a little tighter together. 'He said he had taken me to force you to yield a particular document.' She hesitated. 'Why did you not give it to him, Papa?'

'Such a foolish question, Marianne!' Her father's face stained burgundy. 'Do you honestly think I would not have given it to him, were it that easily done?' he demanded.

'You do not have the document he seeks.' It was not a question, only an assertion of what she already knew.

'I have not the slightest notion of what he speaks. The man belongs in Bedlam. Demanding old documents of which I have not the slightest knowledge. He is both dangerous and delusional.'

'I told him you did not have it.'

Her father paled. His eyes opened wider and she saw in them a fleeting look of panic. 'He spoke to you of the document...of its nature?'

She saw her brother watching her father.

'Only that it was a document he believed you to own, that it was the reason he had taken me. He said he meant me no harm.'

'That is what villains say, Marianne.' He shook his head as if exasperated at her naïvety. 'Thank God he took fright at the strength of the men that I sent.'

'He took no fright whatsoever. And those men you sent were indiscriminate with their guns.'

'He had you with him?' Her father's face was aghast.

She nodded. 'They shot at me and he saved me, Papa, using himself as a shield that the bullet would not hit me.'

Again that exchange of looks between her father and brother.

'Marianne, are you telling me the highwayman was shot?'

'He was shot.' She glanced down at her hands, remembering that terrible moment when she realised he had been hurt.

'Are you about to suffer an attack of the vapours?' Her father was peering at her as if she were a fragile piece of porcelain that might crack at any moment. Before the highwayman she had been just that. And after the highwayman... What should have made her weaker seemed only to have had the opposite effect.

'I am quite well.' She stared at her hands, wondering what her family would say if she told them she had picked pieces of shirt out of the wound before binding it for him...or how it had been between them in the warehouse afterwards...and in the alleyway not a hundred yards from where they now sat.

And when she looked up again she could see her father was stroking his beard. 'So the villain is wounded.' His eyes were narrow and filled with such hatred that a chill ran through Marianne. He looked up at her and smiled a grim smile, then he took her hand between his and patted it. 'Have no fear, Marianne, I will see the villain caught, I swear it. He will pay for what he did and there will be an end to him. Now go and rest, my dear.'

'I am perfectly well, Papa, I assure you. I do not need to rest.'

'But you will do as I say just the same, Marianne. Your papa knows what is best for you.'

It was difficult to maintain a low profile when one was pretending to be a rake around town, but somewhat easier to stay away from the places that a respectable young lady might visit. Yet even so, Rafe found himself thinking about Marianne Winslow and subsequently keeping an ear to the ground regarding not just Misbourne, but his daughter too.

He knew that Misbourne had hired a thief-taker to find him and that he had not gone to the Order of the Wolf. He also knew that there was a considerable price on the head of the 'mysterious' highwayman. Misbourne's own newspaper carried word of it, saying that a group of London's best citizens had put the money together, but Rafe doubted there was anyone other than Misbourne himself involved. Five thousand guineas was a king's ransom—more money than some men might earn in a hundred lifetimes. Enough to tempt someone to break the underworld's code of conduct. But of Marianne there had been nothing at all, not even a whisper of a wedding to Pickering.

An image of her filled his mind: all pale and mysterious with her secrets and sensitivity that she strove to hide. He remembered the feel of her lips beneath his and the untapped passion beneath the innocence and wariness, and he felt his blood quicken, just as it did every time he thought of her. He wondered how long it would be before she was married to Pickering. Perhaps then he would have some peace from this torment.

'What do you say, Knight? Would you bed her?' Devlin asked as they made their way down the steps of their club in St James's.

Bed Marianne Winslow? He wanted her, he admitted it; wanted her with a force of lust that shocked him. He closed his eyes and pushed the thoughts away.

'Knight? You all right, old man?' asked Bullford. 'Seem a bit distracted.'

'I am distracted,' said Rafe. He gestured to the two

carts blocking the street, one of which had spilled its load of coal over half the street, and across which several children were darting, collecting up pieces of coal and running off with them.

'Not by that,' said Fallingham with a grin. 'More likely a certain little lady.'

'You are not wrong,' admitted Rafe.

'The Widow White?'

'I could not possibly comment,' said Rafe, watching the queue of carriages begin to build up in the street while they waited for the accident to be cleared.

'I was asking about Miss Fox. She's at Covent Garden Theatre tonight, playing the part of Lady Macbeth,' said Devlin. The day was bright, but cool. No sign of yesterday's rain. They walked on, leaving the mayhem unfolding behind them.

'I didn't know you like Shakespeare,' Bullford piped up.

'He doesn't. He likes well-shaped actresses with large assets,' said Fallingham. 'And I hear that she's already in negotiations with Hawick to be his mistress.'

'Not a done deal yet,' declared Devlin. 'I've got m'father's box. Are you up for a night of it?'

Everyone gave grunted answers save for Rafe.

'Knight?' Devlin prompted.

But Rafe barely heard him. He was staring at a certain stationary dark town coach with a grey-bearded and moustached man jumping down to investigate the nature of the hold up. But he was not looking at the fading bruise around the man's eye or the healing cut upon his cheek. Rather, he was looking at the young fair-haired woman still seated in the carriage.

Marianne's eyes met his. And everything else in the world faded. He could feel the steady hard beat of his heart. All that he had worked for, all that he had planned for Misbourne, could be lost in this moment. Any second now she would call out to her father and reveal the identity of the highwayman who had abducted her. Yet he could not take his eyes from hers and even across the distance of the pavement and the road that separated them he could sense the tumult of her emotion. She looked at him and he looked right back. The seconds stretched too long so that the moment seemed frozen, as if he could have walked across there and taken her for a second time.

Misbourne turned back and the movement caught his eye, breaking the intensity between him and Marianne. Misbourne's gaze slid to his and their eyes met—and it was as if Misbourne knew exactly who he was. Rafe's world became quite still; his senses sharpened and every nerve tensed. Then Misbourne turned away as if he did not know him at all and the moment was over.

'Good Lord!' said Devlin. 'Look at the mess of Misbourne's face. Coaching accident, my arse! I know the marks of a fist when I see them. The rumours are true, then.'

Fallingham and Razeby sniggered.

Rafe saw Lady Misbourne lean forwards from inside the carriage, throwing them a disapproving look.

Rafe kept on walking and did not look back, but he was poised, with every step that he took and every breath that he inhaled, for the shout of Misbourne's voice and the sound of pursuing footsteps. Every muscle in his body was tensed. Every nerve stretched tight. He felt as he had on the countless battlefields upon which he'd fought across the years. Primed and ready, sickened almost, with the wait for the fight to begin.

But the enemy did not give chase. All he heard were his own footsteps and those of his friends, and the irate voices of the passengers of the escalating coach jam. And when he glanced back, Misbourne was still hovering near the door of his coach, staring in the opposite direction at the accident, and Marianne was hidden from sight.

'Louts,' pronounced Lady Misbourne to her husband. 'Come in, sir, and close the door that we are not subject to their ill manners.' Then to her daughter, 'Avert your eyes this instant, Marianne.'

Marianne's heart was thudding so hard she wondered that her parents did not hear it. The skin on the nape of her neck tingled as if the highwayman's fingers stroked against it.

'Yes, Mama,' she replied out of habit, but she could not tear her eyes away.

He was dressed in a smart, dark, fitted tailcoat, probably one of the Weston's she had seen in his wardrobe, and dark pantaloons, just like the other men he was with. But that was where the similarity stopped. He was taller, more manly, his dark hair tied back in its queue. And so breathtakingly handsome that she could have looked at him for a lifetime and never tired of it. Even across the distance that separated them she could see the warm golden glow of his eyes and feel the intensity of his gaze. The highwayman. It seemed like everything else in the world dimmed and faded to nothing. She was aware only of him…and the strange connection between them. Her awareness of him was so intense that in that moment she smelled again the scent of him, heard again that harsh half-whisper against her ear and felt the touch of his lips upon hers.

Outside the carriage her father moved and Marianne saw the highwayman's gaze shift to him—and her father's to the highwayman's. She remembered her father's vow to bring an end to the man who had abducted her and the look of utter malice in his eyes. Her heart gave a stutter. She caught back her breath. And for a terrible moment she thought that her father had recognised him. But then he turned back to the carriage, to her and her mother, and she knew she must have been mistaken.

She did not look at the highwayman then, only at her father, lest he follow the direction of her gaze and fathom something of the truth.

Her mother scowled. 'Look at them, insolent young bucks! Out all the night long and only now, at this late hour of the morning, crawling home. It is a disgraceful way to behave.'

'Young men will be young men,' her father said with a tolerance that was at odds with everything that he was always saying about the society of the day. 'Once they are married with a nursery to raise they will soon settle down.'

Marianne blinked with surprise and saw the slight widening of her mother's eyes. Lady Misbourne gave a sniff of disapproval, pressed her lips tight shut and folded her hands together upon her lap. 'And what seems to be the hold-up on the road ahead?'

Her father explained about the accident and went back to looking at it. Marianne relaxed a little, touching a hand to the centre of her palm that *he* had held with such gentleness. She began to breathe again. And then she saw her father glance back at the small group of men, watching them for a second or two with the strangest expression upon his face.

'Papa,' she called to distract his attention. 'Perhaps we would be quicker to walk. The day is fine and—'

'Stay in the carriage, Marianne,' he snapped, cutting her off. His eyes narrowed and he cast a suspicious, almost frightened glance all around them before climbing into the carriage and shutting the door.

Rafe had reached the steps to his own house. Only Devlin remained by his side—the home of the viscount's latest conquest lay a few streets on and it seemed he was planning a visit. All the way back, Rafe had placidly followed the viscount's example, dawdling at the slow pace, smiling at the jokes, showing nothing of the turmoil within him. He had punched her father, abducted her at gunpoint, held her captive and exposed her to the seamier side of life and more danger in three days than she would have seen in a lifetime. She was Misbourne's daughter, for pity's sake. She had to have pointed him out to her father. But there had been no hue and cry, no covert shadow following him. And he knew that Marianne had not told her father.

What the hell had Marianne been doing in St James's at that time in the morning anyway?

Rafe discovered the answer to his question later that week. The gossip was all over town. Everywhere he went they were talking of it.

Rafe came home from the theatre that night and leaned against the jamb of the door, watching Callerton blackening their boots in the kitchen.

'Thought you would be back late.' Callerton glanced up. 'Told them you're tupping some woman again?'

Rafe nodded.

'You know you might actually have to bed a few or

they might start getting suspicious,' Callerton joked, but Rafe could not bring himself to laugh and Callerton stopped polishing the boots and looked at him, his expression suddenly serious.

'What's wrong? Has Misbourne come after you? Maybe the girl pointed you out to him after all.'

'She did not.' Rafe shook his head. 'Misbourne does not know me.'

'But something's wrong.'

'It's all over town that there was no accident on the way to Marianne Winslow's wedding,' Rafe said.

'They know it was the highwayman?'

Rafe shook his head. 'They think it was an excuse dreamt up by Misbourne to buy time.'

'For what?' Callerton resumed his polishing.

'It seems that Pickering has pulled out of the betrothal. They are saying that he told Misbourne on the day of the wedding and that Misbourne and Pickering came to fisticuffs over it.'

'Well, we know that's rubbish,' said Callerton. 'There was only one fist that smacked Misbourne's face and it wasn't Pickering's.'

Rafe moved into the kitchen and sat down at the table. 'Misbourne is threatening to sue for breach of promise if Pickering does not marry Marianne.'

'Again?' Callerton raised an eyebrow. 'You'd have thought he'd have learned his lesson with Arlesford the first time round.'

'It serves only to embroil Marianne in yet another marriage scandal.'

'Why do you care? There will be a damn sight more scandal by the time you've finished with her father.'

'Because had I not abducted her she would already be married to Pickering.'

'That's not the reason,' said Callerton.

Rafe met his friend's eyes.

'You're soft on the lass,' said Callerton quietly.

'Don't be ridiculous. She's Misbourne's daughter,' retorted Rafe as if that was a denial. He did not know what it was that he felt for Marianne, only that he felt it very strongly indeed.

'Aye,' said Callerton, 'she is that. And if you're set on destroying the father, you best not have a care for the daughter.' And he went back to polishing the boot.

Marianne saw him the moment that she walked into the room of the circulating library. He was standing amongst the shelves of novels, seemingly engaged within the pages of a book, but then his eyes glanced up and momentarily met hers before sliding back down to the page. Her heart skipped a beat before racing off at a gallop.

The library was quiet; only two other people were in the room and one of those was the elderly librarian seated in the corner. The other was Caroline Edingham, Lady Willaston, who immediately spotted them and headed straight for Marianne's mother, her eyes lighting up at the thought of scooping some gossip straight from the horse's mouth.

'Keep quiet over Pickering and let me deal with this, Marianne,' Lady Misbourne whispered beneath her breath.

'If you do not mind, Mama, I will have a look within the poetry room.'

'Go quickly before she is upon us. And do not return. I will come and fetch you.' Marianne made her escape, but not before she saw the false smile that her mother plastered upon her face to greet Lady Willaston. 'My dear Caroline. It has been an age.' The two women were kissing one another's cheeks as if they were the best of friends before Marianne was halfway across the room.

She was careful not to look at the highwayman, but she thought she caught the faint scent of sandalwood as she passed him and it made her heart beat all the faster.

The poetry room was empty. Marianne made her way over to the shelves of the classical poems, took the first book down from the shelf and opened it. She stood with her back to the door, her eyes scanning the open pages without seeing a single line that was written upon them. Her mind was whirring. She did not know what to think of his presence here. She was afraid he would follow her—and even more afraid that he would not. When she heard the quiet tread of a man's footsteps she did not need to look round to know it was him.

He came and stood beside her, looking at the same shelf of classical books.

She could not help herself. Her gaze flew to his, to those clear amber eyes that were fixed upon hers, and that stern handsome face.

'Why are you here?' she whispered.

'To see you.'

Her stomach gave a somersault and her heart began to thunder in earnest. 'Don't you know that there is a very large price upon your head? My father has men searching for you even as we speak.'

'I know.'

There was a small silence.

'The other day in St James's… You did not tell your father.'

'No.'

'Why not, Marianne?' he asked.

'Because there is every likelihood that they will hang you if they catch you.'

The silence hissed between them.

She felt her cheeks warm. 'How is your arm?' He wore no sling. Neither had he done so that day in St James's.

'It did not fester.'

And with those words she was back in the warehouse and the air was thick with all that had happened between them.

'I am sorry about Pickering,' he said.

'I am not. In truth, I am relieved. I never wanted to marry him. It was my father who…' She had said too much. She turned away and laid the book down open upon the table as if she meant to read it.

'My father does not have the document that you seek. I asked him,' she said, trying to change the subject.

He was standing behind her, but she heard him step closer.

Her body was in uproar, but she did not edge away. Nor did she look round.

He said nothing. He did not need to. She knew by his silence what he thought.

'You think he is lying,' she said.

Still he did not speak, and she turned on him, feeling angry and confused. 'Why won't you admit it?'

She could see the determined set of his jaw, the resolve in his eyes, and, remembering his talk of justice and vengeance, she felt suddenly afraid for her father.

'You are intent on wreaking revenge upon the wrong man.'

'I do not think so,' he said softly. 'And it is not re-venge, but justice.'

'And what is this justice you seek from him?'

'I have never lied to you, Marianne. I would see him dance upon the end of a gibbet.'

'My God, my father is right. You *are* delusional and dangerous.'

'Delusional and dangerous?' The breath of his whis-per tickled her ear.

She jumped. 'If I scream, you are undone, sir.'

'I am more than undone. My life is in your hands. You can claim the reward your father has set upon my head.'

She closed her eyes at that.

'What are you waiting for? If you really you think me delusional and dangerous, go ahead and scream.'

He did not crowd her with his body, did not touch her to coerce, yet she could sense him and the attrac-tion that hummed between them stronger than ever. The thud of her heart was so loud she wondered that it did not echo in the room around them. She should scream, but she knew that she wouldn't. Was he delu-sional? No. Was he dangerous? Very. To the men who would hurt her, to her father. But not to her. Never to her.

Slowly she raised her gaze to meet his. 'I will not let you harm him. You do know that, do you not?'

'I would expect nothing other.'

The very air seemed to vibrate between them.

'Marianne,' he whispered and stepped closer.

She knew that he was going to kiss her. She should have turned away. She should have run. Instead, she shivered with anticipation, with need, and raised her mouth to meet his.

He kissed her. And it was everything she remembered from the alleyway and more. A meeting of two mouths that were made to be together. He kissed her and it felt right. Safe and dangerous both at once, and utterly wonderful. Such gentleness, yet within it she had never been more aware of his masculinity and his strength. And she kissed him back, only a little at first, but then as her confidence grew, bolder, more fully.

Beneath her hands she could feel the hard muscle of his chest and the steady strong beat of his heart, though she did not remember placing her palms there. She felt his arms encircling her, enclosing her, yet she felt no panic at being held, only need and desire. She slid her hands up over his chest, higher, to wind around his neck, pressing herself closer until she could feel the brush of his chest against her bodice and the sensitivity of her nipples beneath her stays. The scent of him filled her nose; the feel of him overwhelmed her senses. She thought she could kiss him for all eternity and it would never be enough.

He drew back, breaking off the kiss, and she did not know why he had stopped. She felt dazed, weak, breathless. His breath was almost as ragged as hers. He eased her away so that the backs of her thighs were leaning against the table.

His eyes stared down into hers and they were dark and filled with the same torment that was fast rushing in to fill the place where all her wonder and joy had been. He stared for a moment longer and then released her.

'I should not have done that.' Still staring at her, he shook his head as if to deny what had just passed between them, then turned and walked away.

She stood where she was, her whole body tingling and aflame. Unable to think straight. Her heart still fluttering like a caged bird desperate to be free. Reeling from his kiss. Reeling from all that coursed through her body. Reeling from the thought of what she had just done. She touched trembling fingers to her lips. She had kissed him with all her heart and all her soul. Marianne Winslow, who had not thought she could tolerate the touch of a man ever again, had kissed him. A highwayman with a five-thousand-guinea price on his head, a man whose name she did not know, a man her father was paying half of London to capture. And a man who had sworn vengeance on her father.

She was still staring at the same page when her mother came into the room.

'She has gone at last, thank the lord. So many questions. Caroline Edingham could do with a few lessons in subtlety. And she's hardly one to be gossiping about anyone else. Not with the stories I've heard of her husband.' Her mother glanced at her. 'Have you made your selection?'

'I think I will take this one,' she managed to say and closed the book.

Her mother peered more closely. 'Are you quite well? You look rather flushed.'

'I am perfectly well, Mama. It is rather warm in here, do you not think?'

'Hurry along, Marianne. I told your papa we would not be long and you know how he worries about you. He will not be happy if we are late home.'

'Yes, Mama.' Marianne picked up the book and followed her mother.

* * *

Rafe Knight stood alone in his study, leaning against the mantelpiece and staring into the flicker of flames upon the hearth. Outside, across the heath, dusk was darkening the sky, yet he had not drawn the curtains or pulled down the blind. The day's newspapers lay unread upon his desk. The paperwork due with his man of business in the morning had not been touched. There was only one thing on his mind, and that was what had happened in the circulating library with Marianne.

She was Misbourne's daughter, he told himself again and again. A woman in whose veins flowed the blood of the man he despised. A woman who bore the same dark eyes as the devil. The last woman in the world he should want. Yet he did want her. He had wanted her almost from the very start. Maybe it was just physical need driving him. Maybe Callerton was right and he should be out there tupping women as frequently as he pretended. Maybe then he would be rid of the need that gnawed at him. But the thought of bedding another woman left him cold. The desire that burned in him was for Marianne Winslow alone. *Misbourne's daughter*, he thought again. Yet had it not been for her eyes, he would not have believed it. Eyes that, on first glance, looked so like Misbourne's, but when he looked deep into them there was nothing of Misbourne there. She was nothing like Misbourne. Nothing like that monster. But she *was* Misbourne's daughter and nothing he could do would ever change that.

A knock sounded at the door and Callerton came in, bringing with him the damp smell of the night. Callerton's eyes went to the bottle of brandy that sat on the table and the half-full glass beside it.

'Misbourne?' he asked.

Rafe gave no answer. He moved to the table and filled a clean glass with brandy before passing it to Callerton.

The two men sat in silence for a few minutes before Callerton said, 'It's Marianne Winslow, isn't it?'

'I had to see her.'

'Hell, why?'

He shook his head, not understanding the answer to that himself, knowing only that the compulsion gave him no peace. Nor had he revealed to Callerton what had happened in the warehouse or the alleyway. He drank down his brandy.

'She's his daughter, Rafe. And if you're going after him, then you can't dally with her.'

'I'm not dallying with her.'

'Aren't you?' Callerton demanded and topped up both their glasses. 'Are you denying that you want her?'

'I don't deny it. But that doesn't mean I'm going to act on it.'

'Christ, you could have your pick of the women in London. Why does it have to be her?'

It was the same question that Rafe had been asking himself.

'She could ruin all of this for you. One word in her father's ear, one point of her finger, and it will be you, not Misbourne, hanging from a scaffold. You have to stay away from her.' Callerton drank his brandy down in one go. 'Unless you've changed your mind over Misbourne.'

'I cannot do that,' said Rafe. 'I've dedicated my whole life to finding that bastard.'

He wanted Marianne. And he wanted her father's head on a plate. And he knew he could not have both.

Callerton was right. He needed to stay away from her.

Chapter Seven

Marianne sat in the corner of the drawing room of her father's town house that evening, the library book lying open but unread upon her lap. At the other side of the room Lady Misbourne was playing patience, the cards making a soft slapping sound as she placed them down upon the green baize of the card table. That, and the slow steady ticking of the clock upon the mantelpiece were the only sounds within the room.

Marianne was thinking of the highwayman and his kiss. She was also thinking of what he had said about the justice he meant to deliver to her father. She closed her eyes and saw again her father kneeling in the dirt on the heath with a bloodied lip and cut cheek. *Her own father.* She bit her lip and felt her cheeks burn with shame and guilt and confusion that she could be attracted to any man who had done such a thing. Now that her blood had cooled and that amber gaze was not upon her, the scent of sandalwood not in her nose, she felt a little sick at her behaviour. She had seen how the highwayman had dealt with the men in the rookery, and those in the graveyard. He would not hurt her. But he had already hurt her father, and promised much more, and nothing that she said seemed to convince him of reason.

It was true that he had saved her, in the alleyway and in the burying ground, but he was the one who had abducted her in the first place. And it wasn't as if he had not been honest from the very outset over his hatred of Misbourne. Perhaps the document was just an excuse to torture her father. Maybe it didn't even exist at all.

Or maybe her father was right and he was delusional. He was certainly dangerous to her father. She realised now too late that she had been wrong in the answer she had given within the room of the circulating library. He made her forget her fear; he made her reckless and emboldened with this madness of attraction she felt for him. A man who could have such influence over her, making her forget who she was, making her behave in ways that she had never thought possible, was definitely dangerous to her too. Betrayal. For that's what it was, she thought miserably, whatever she chose to do. She was betraying her father. But if she revealed the highwayman, it would be a different kind of betrayal. She'd be betraying the one man who had saved her.

No matter what else she imagined, the cold hard truth was he was a highwayman, a stranger, a man who was threatening her father. There was no real choice to make when she thought of it like that, not if she had any semblance of a care for her father. And once she had told her father the truth… Maybe they would not hang him. Especially if she were to speak up and tell them how he had saved her. She closed her eyes and could not bear to think of what they would do to him. She could not afford to let herself think of him at all.

Her duty was to her father. She felt sick to the pit of her stomach, but she knew what she had to do. Closing the book on her lap and setting it down on the small table by her side, she rose to her feet.

Her mother glanced up from the cards laid out before her.

'Is Papa still in his study?' Marianne asked in a carefully controlled voice.

'I believe that your brother is with him, my dear.'

'If you will excuse me, Mama.'

Lady Misbourne gave a nod and looked down once more to her cards.

Marianne made her way slowly towards her father's study. She was doing the right thing, the thing that any dutiful daughter should do, but her heart felt heavy and there was a lump in her throat that she could not swallow down.

Her slippers were silent against the marble tiles. She paused outside the study, taking a deep breath, steeling herself to the task. The door was slightly ajar, and her mother was right about Francis, for she could hear the murmur of both his and her father's voices from within. Marianne reached her hand to the doorknob and heard the words her brother was speaking.

'I told you that a bullet would not keep him from his pursuit of the document for long. He says he's coming for you and it seems to me that this highwayman is a man very much of his word.'

She froze where she was, her ears sharpening, and listened.

'Not if I find him first,' her father said in an angry tone.

'Is a document really worth your life?' Francis asked.

'Yes,' replied her father more quietly, the anger replaced by sadness. 'I would give my very life that it never existed.'

The shock of it hit Marianne hard. The blood in her veins seemed to turn to ice. She stared at the dark-mahogany panels of the door and could not believe what she was hearing. There was a cold prickle across her skin and a terrible sinking feeling in her stomach. *Betrayal*. The word whispered again in her head.

'What is in it?' Francis asked softly. 'Why will you not trust me enough to tell me?'

'It is not a question of trust.' There was the slightest pause. And when her father spoke again there was such a hard horrible quality to his voice that she barely recognised it. 'Do not ask me of it ever again. I will not be questioned. In this house, my word is law. Do you understand, boy?'

'I understand,' said Francis. 'For your sake I hope your precious document is stored somewhere safe. Because whoever that highwayman is, he's coming for *it*, as well as *you*.'

She heard the chink of an empty glass and then her father's irate voice. 'Well, do not just stand there. Ring for another bottle of brandy.'

She slipped away, hurrying to the staircase. She was halfway up when she heard the bell ring, but she did not stop, just walked briskly until she reached her bedchamber. And when she got inside she turned the key in the lock and stood with her back against the door, her hand clutched around her stomach.

Her father had the document, just as the highwayman had said. And he had not been prepared to ransom it for her. Even though he knew the dark secret that she hid from the world. Had she not heard it with her own ears, she would not have believed it. Even now, she could barely take it in. After all that had happened. After all he had promised. He had said that he loved her. He had said that he would only ever have her best interests at heart. He was her *father*. The one person she trusted over all others. And he had lied...just as the highwayman had known.

It was on the night of the new moon, two nights after he had kissed Marianne Winslow in the circulating library, that Rafe stood within the shrubbery of the garden facing Misbourne's town house. The night was clear and cold enough for him to see his breath before him, as if he breathed smoke into the night. There was no moon to relieve the stark blackness of the sky, only a scattering of small twinkling stars. He watched the house, just as he had watched these three hours past. Biding his time. Waiting for the right moment.

Every window was in darkness, each one shrouded by a blind. Rafe knew exactly what time Misbourne had gone to bed. He knew that Lady Misbourne had retired half an hour earlier and that they kept to their own rooms. Callerton, positioned in his watching place in the mews to the rear of the building, had told him that the only light still burning was that in Marianne's bedchamber at the top of the house. He knew that the candles in her room would burn long after she fell asleep. And he thought of her, despite all his best intentions not to. A woman that feared the darkness of a room, but not that of the night. A woman of mystery and secrets. A woman who he could not seem to get out of his head. He closed his eyes and turned his thoughts to a still summer's night fifteen years ago. The pain of it made him wince, but when he opened his eyes there was nothing in him but the cold hard rage of determination.

He moved his fingers to check the leather scabbard strapped beneath his coat and the hunter's knife that was in it. The pistol was ready and loaded within his pocket and against his ankle, on the inside of his boot, he could feel the cold press of the narrow metal strip that would slide beneath the window jamb. With one sleek vault he was over the metal fencing that enclosed Leicester Square's garden and moving through the shadows of the night towards Misbourne's town house.

Marianne could not sleep. So she did what she always did when she was too restless and uneasy for sleep. The maid snored softly in the truckle bed beside her own, oblivious to the flicker of the candles as Marianne stole quietly across the bedchamber. She knew exactly which floorboards to avoid. She knew just how to open and close the door without a single sound. Silent as a ghost, she made her way down the back staircase to a world below that was so close and yet so distant from her own. The kitchen.

It was a place that an earl's daughter should never inhabit. The least likely place a monster from the night would ever seek her. The only place she could be truly alone, just for the shortest of times, to think. And Marianne desperately needed to think.

She sat at the kitchen table, barely noticing the cold stone beneath her bare feet or the goosepimple of her skin beneath the cotton of her nightdress. In the days since her eavesdropping she had hardly seen her father. Hardly spoken to him. She could not look him in the eye, for fear he would see the truth in her own.

She stared at the scrubbed wooden surface before her, knowing that she could not avoid him for ever. She was going to have to face him sooner or later. And although she was angry with him, there was also sadness and a nagging need to understand.

Lifting the branch of candles, she rose to return to bed.

Her feet were silent on the stairs, the flames of the candles flickering and sending her shadow dancing against the wall. The darkness of the main hallway was broken by the slim band of light beneath the door to her father's study. All of London slept, but not Marianne and not her father. There was no Mama to interfere and fuss. And there was no Francis. She took her hand from the banister and walked across the hallway to her father's study.

The quiet knock sounded at the door and Rafe tensed, his eyes shifting to the clock that sat beside his candle on Misbourne's desk. Two o'clock. Callerton had not given the signal to warn of Linwood's return and he knew that Misbourne would not knock at his own door. There was no time to clear away the piles of papers or to even slide the drawers closed. No time to react before the door opened.

'Papa,' a familiar voice murmured. And Marianne stepped into the room.

Her gaze raised and she saw who was standing behind her father's desk and the clear evidence of what he had been about. Her eyes widened, but she did not scream.

Rafe's heart was beating too fast. She had not pointed him out to her father before. But this was different. This was an invasion of her father's castle. He waited for her to call out, or to snatch up the bell and ring it. He should have turned and climbed back out of the window. He should have run and disappeared into the darkness of the night while there was still time. But he just stood there, his gaze locked on hers.

Her eyes were black, her face as pale and beautiful as the vision that haunted his dreams. They stared at one another and those few seconds seemed to stretch to an eternity of torture and uncertainty and the attraction that was between them rippled and roared. And then she lowered her gaze, quietly closed the door behind her, and Rafe released the breath he had been holding.

She stood where she was, keeping the distance of the room between them. Her hair was long and loose and glinting silver in the candlelight. Beneath the long-sleeved shroud of a nightgown he could see the peep of her bare toes. Her gaze moved to take in the papers scattered across the desk and the drawers that hung open before meeting his own once more.

'I would ask you what you are doing here searching my father's study in the middle of the night, but I already know the answer.'

'He will not give the document to me, so I must take it.'

'Steal it, you mean.'

'No.' He shook his head and looked her directly in the eye. 'It is your father who is the thief. I seek to take back that which he stole.'

There was an uneasy expression on her face. He waited for her usual assertion that he was wrong, that Misbourne was the best of men and would not do such a thing. But she said nothing.

The silence seemed to hiss between them.

'You make no defence of him?' He raised his brows.

He saw her bite at her lip before she glanced away. And when she looked at him again she said, 'Have you found it?'

'No.' His eyes held hers as he moved from behind the desk and walked slowly towards her. He did not stop until he was standing directly before her, so close that his boots were almost touching her bare toes. So close that he could smell the scent of her, so sweet and enticing.

'What is written on that paper that, if my father did have it, he would go to such lengths to hide it, and that you will risk so much to find it?'

But he could not tell her what was written upon it, even had he wanted to. 'What has changed that you suddenly believe me?'

'Nothing has changed,' she said, but she would not meet his gaze and he knew that she was lying.

'If the document were in your possession, what, then, would you do with it?'

'The document is the evidence I need to see him hanged.'

The candles within her hand flickered wildly as if a tremor ran through her.

'Whatever my father might have done…' she bit her lip and her eyes held a haunted expression '…he does not deserve to die.'

'On the contrary, Marianne, for what your father did he should burn in hell.'

She closed her eyes at the brutality of his words and he felt the sting of his conscience.

'You would understand if it was your father,' she said.

'It *was* my father.' His voice crackled with the anger and bitterness that came whenever he thought of what

Misbourne had done. 'And my mother too,' he added, and the anger rolled away to expose the ache of grief in his soul.

'What do you mean?' She stared up at him, as if she could see the truth in his eyes.

'I should go. Your brother will be home soon.' But he made no move to leave. The air was thick with tension, with desire and attraction and everything that was forbidden between them. His gaze lowered to the nightdress that skimmed against her body, knowing that she was naked beneath it. And despite the situation and who her father was, he felt his body respond. He reached out, taking the branch of candles from her, and set it down upon the occasional table by their side. Then he took her hand and felt her cool slender fingers in his.

They stood hand in hand and he slid his thumb against the soft skin of her palm. He could see the rise and fall of her breasts beneath the embroidered bodice, see the way the cotton caught against their hardened tips. And he felt his mouth go dry and an ache within his breeches. He swallowed hard and knew there were a thousand reasons he should not be doing this, that this was madness.

'If you were not Misbourne's daughter...' But at this moment it made no difference whether she was Misbourne's daughter or not.

'What would you do?' she whispered.

'I would take you in my arms.' He slid his arms around her and felt the slight tremble go through her body. 'Like this,' he whispered against the top of her head and inhaled the scent of her hair. 'And then I would tip your face up to mine.' He touched his fingers to her chin and gently angled her head up.

'Yes,' she whispered.

'And then I would kiss you.' His mouth lowered inch by inch towards her, until their lips touched and he took her mouth with his own. He kissed her as he had dreamt of doing since the circulating library, tasting her this time, teasing her until her tongue met his, shyly at first, then more boldly. One hand rested against the swell of her hip, the other on the small of her back. He slid a hand higher to the narrowness of her waist and higher still to cup one breast, feeling her nipple pebbled beneath his palm, sliding his fingers to capture the bud through the thick cotton of her nightdress. She gasped, broke off the kiss, staring up at him with startled eyes, her breath suddenly ragged. He could feel the rise and fall of her breast beneath his hand, feel the harried thud of her heart. He stilled his fingers, but left his hand where it rested.

'I...' she whispered, and her eyes scanned his. 'We should not be doing this.'

'We should not,' he agreed. He could feel the way she trembled, standing poised as if about to flee.

Her teeth nipped at her lower lip. He kissed the hurt away with a single gentle kiss. 'I would that any other woman in the world but you were his daughter.' One last kiss and then he released her and stepped back. Then he turned and disappeared through the open window.

Marianne watched him go and did not know what to think. Her heart was racing and her lips throbbed and tingled where he had kissed. Her breasts were heavy and so sensitive that they ached for his touch. Where his hand had lain her breast seemed to burn and even just the memory of his fingers playing upon its tip made her catch her breath with the sudden sharpness of yearning that shot through her. She wanted him to touch her there, she thought with amazement. She wondered what it would be like were he to touch her without the barrier of her nightdress. Touch her, skin to skin. The imagining made her heart beat ever more wildly. Imagining was safe. And with it the darkness of past remembering seemed to fade.

She stared across at the desk with its open drawers and piles of papers emptied upon its surface. Her father's documents. His private papers. And she thought again of the document that was so important to her father that he had refused to relinquish it even for her life. The highwayman said he had not found it. She moved to the window and quietly closed the sash, the blinds and the curtains—just as her father did every night. Then she began a calm and methodical search where the highwayman had left off.

She did not know what she was looking for. But she looked through all of the papers anyway, convinced that she would know the document when she saw it. She read, looked, searched, every drawer, every cupboard and shelf. And she found many things that her father would not have wanted her to find. Things that shocked her to learn of him. A small portrait of a woman who was not her mother, a great roll of crisp white bank notes tied with a ribbon, and the most scandalous playing cards on which had been painted naked women in provocative poses. But nothing that might qualify as 'the document'.

She heard the opening of the front door and the deliberate quietness of its closing. Francis, she thought, remembering the highwayman's warning. But she did not attempt to tidy away the evidence of her search or even to extinguish her candle. She did not hear his footsteps. He opened the door with surprising speed and without knocking, stilling when he saw her, before entering and closing the door behind him as quietly as all the rest.

'I know Papa has the document, Francis.'

He made no effort to deny it.

'I need to know what it is.'

'Whatever the answer to your question, Marianne, you are mistaken if you think he will have it so casually stored with his other papers.' There was something about the expression in his eyes that made her realise.

'You have already searched for it.'

'It is not here. Nor within the safe.'

'Francis, what is this document, that a man would abduct me for it and Papa would risk my life to keep it?'

'That is what I mean to discover.' Her brother produced a piece of paper from his pocket, all wrinkled as if it had been screwed to a ball, then smoothed flat again. He opened it out and let her read the words of the highwayman's demand.

'Something happened on Hounslow Heath in 1795,' he said. 'I am going through the archives of *The London Messenger* for the whole of that year.'

'Have you found anything?'

'Not yet.'

'Will you tell me if you do?'

'You would do better to leave this to me. Our father has men searching for the villain. If they do not find him, I will.'

'You do not understand.' She shook her head. 'He could have killed Papa so very easily had he wanted to. And he could have…' she glanced away uneasily before looking at him once again '…taken advantage of me. But he did neither, even when Papa twice failed to pay the ransom and sent men to kill him. He holds Papa responsible for some heinous crime of which he does not speak.'

'Marianne, he abducted you on the way to your wedding, held a pistol to our father's head and cost you Pickering as a bridegroom. And you defend him?'

'All of that is true. Yet, even so, he is not what you think him. It is true that he is a hard man, a ruthless man. A man who does not flinch or hesitate from anything, and one in which there is undoubtedly something dark and tortured. Yet I cannot rid myself of the sense that he is, beneath it all…a man of integrity. He believes in what he is doing, that it is just and right.'

'Integrity? Marianne, have you taken leave of your senses?' Her brother peered at her in a too-knowing way. 'Do not fancy that he is some Claude Duval, a gentleman highwayman who will dance with you and quote you words of love poetry.' Her brother's gaze sharpened. 'Or perhaps that is precisely what he did and you have developed a *tendre* for the rogue?'

'Do not be foolish,' Marianne snapped, fearing her brother was coming too close to the truth. 'Given my past, I am unlikely to develop a *tendre* for any man.'

Her brother looked away, a look of discomfort in his eyes. 'Forgive me, Marianne, I should not have said that.'

'I should tidy away Papa's papers. It would not go well if he knew what I have been doing in here this night.' She thought of how the highwayman had held her in his arms, of his kiss and the feel of his hand upon her breast. And her cheeks grew warm. No, it would not go well at all, if her father knew.

'I will help you, Marianne.' And together she and Francis began to put the papers away.

'So it was not in his desk?'

'Nor anywhere obvious within his study.'

'It could be anywhere. You haven't a hope in hell of finding it.'

'I have if I rattle him enough.' Rafe looked at Callerton. 'If he thinks I'm getting close, he'll move it.'

'And how exactly are you going to convince him of such a thing?'

'A few little scares here and there. He seems to be growing more nervous by the day. I need to keep a closer eye on him.'

Definitely nervous, thought Rafe as he watched Misbourne mop his brow and glance furtively around the glasshouse in the botanic gardens later that week. Misbourne's glance lingered on him for a moment, making his heart notch a little faster with the realisation of what he was risking by being here. But then the earl's gaze moved on, scanning the crowd. Rafe had not the slightest interest in the exotic plants on display and neither, he was prepared to bet, had Misbourne. Yet the earl, his wife and Marianne were here at the event, facing down the murmur of gossip over Pickering.

Rafe's gaze shifted to Marianne standing in front of her father. By her side Lady Misbourne was engaged in conversation with a woman of the *ton*. Marianne's eyes met his across the distance. Their gazes held and the moment seemed to stretch between them. She looked away, feigning interest in some plant, nodding and listening to something her father was saying. She glanced up again, her gaze again meeting his, a small half-smile upon her face, her eyes a rich brown in the sunlight that flooded the glasshouse—shy and filled with a pleasure that mirrored what he felt filling his chest at the sight of her. Rafe knew he should look away, but he could not, even though Misbourne was standing right there and he knew he was risking too much. And then her eyes shifted to something behind him and everything in her changed.

The blood appeared to drain from her face, leaving her powder-white, her eyes widened and he could see shock, horror and abject fear in them. She stared as if the very devil had appeared before her, frozen in terror. He followed her gaze, glancing behind him at what she was seeing, but there was only the crowd that had been there before, and a neat tailored back disappearing through it.

And when he looked at Marianne again he saw what her father, standing behind her and busy in finding a fresh handkerchief within his pocket, could not, and what her mother, still engaged in conversation, did not notice. He saw her bloodless pallor and her eyes beginning to roll up in her head and he was already moving across the glasshouse towards her.

Lady Misbourne let out an exclamation as Marianne crumpled. Misbourne reacted, realising what was happening, but not fast enough. Rafe caught her before she hit the ground, scooping her up in his arms.

'Your coat, sir,' Rafe directed Misbourne, who shrugged out of his coat and spread the garment upon the ground. He laid Marianne gently down upon it. She was pale as death and limp, her long fair lashes feathering against the ivory of her cheeks. Her eyes flickered open wide, suddenly filled with the same terror he had seen in them before. And then she saw him and the terror faded. And there was in its stead such vulnerability, such raw honesty, as if she were letting him see some the private hidden depths of her soul just as she had done that day within the rookery, and in response he felt something squeeze tight within his chest. He was seized with the urge to take her in his arms and protect her from whatever had frightened her, to save her from the darkness that the world could inflict. But Misbourne was leaning over her, his face pinched with concern.

'Marianne?'

'He was here, Papa,' she whispered.

'The highwayman?' Misbourne's words were so quiet Rafe had to strain to hear them.

'Not him,' she said. 'Ro...' But it was as if she could not bring herself to say the name.

Misbourne's face seemed to sharpen and pale. Rafe thought he saw the dart of fear in those devil eyes of his before he raised them to the small crowd gathered around. He snapped at his footman, 'Have the carriage brought round at once, James. Lady Marianne is unwell.'

She tried to sit up, but Misbourne pushed her back down. 'Stay where you are, girl.'

'I am feeling better,' she said, her gaze fluttering over the surrounding crowd. 'Please, let us leave now.'

Marianne was small and slender, but Misbourne was in his sixties and run to fat. Already his face was ruddy from the exertion of crouching down. He glanced up at where Rafe still stood, his eyes meeting Rafe's directly.

'Thank you, sir. Your prompt action saved my daughter injury.'

Rafe gave a nod of acknowledgement, his expression a mask that hid the emotion beneath. 'My carriage is outside and ready, if you do not wish to wait to transport your daughter from this place.'

Lady Misbourne was flushed with embarrassment, but Marianne was scanning the faces of the crowd and he knew she was looking for the one that had frightened her.

Misbourne's gaze held his with a strange intensity. 'If it would be of no inconvenience to you, sir…'

'None at all,' replied Rafe. He did not ask Misbourne's permission, just scooped Marianne up from where she lay and carried her out to where Callerton waited with the carriage. Lady Misbourne climbed inside beside her daughter. Misbourne hesitated by the open door.

'I am in your debt, sir,' he said with a sincerity of which Rafe had not thought the man capable. Only two feet separated them. He looked the murderer directly in the eye, knowing what Misbourne had done to his parents. He felt his gall rise at the knowledge and wondered if anything of the hatred showed in his eyes. Then Misbourne climbed inside and Rafe shut the door behind him and watched while Callerton drove away.

The crowd was dissipating now that Marianne had gone. He headed home at a steady pace. It was only when he was halfway there that he realised that he had not introduced himself and neither had Misbourne asked his name.

Chapter Eight

The nightmare, which had subsided since Marianne had met the highwayman, returned that night. It started, as it always did, with Marianne blowing out the candles in her bedchamber. But this time when the villain came with his sweet scent of cigar smoke that so filled her with revulsion, she realised that they were not the only two in the darkness. The highwayman stepped out between her and the man whose name she could not bring herself to say.

'Not this time, Rotherham,' he said in her dream. 'Never again.' Then he punched the villain again and again until the limp body slithered to the floor, just like the men had fallen in the rookery and in the burying ground. She knew the villain was dead and she was glad of it. When the highwayman turned and reached his hand to her the darkness vanished and the daylight was bright. And the room in which they stood was no longer her own bedchamber, but that of the man who had saved her.

She took the hand that he offered, with its scraped and bleeding knuckles, and kissed it; then she reached up and held his face between her hands and kissed that, too, his cheeks and then his mouth, with a passion she did not know was within her. And when she awoke she was not crying out in terror as she normally did when the nightmare came. She felt safe, and in her mind was not that pale-eyed gaunt face, but a pair of amber eyes. And her thighs burned hot and her heart glowed warm.

Within the drawing room of the Earl of Misbourne's town house the next day the clock ticked too loud.

'It is not possible,' Lady Misbourne said. 'He is gone to the Continent and would not dare show his face in London again.'

'I know what I saw, Mama.'

'You must be mistaken, Marianne. It will be the fiasco with the highwayman that has stirred up dark memories of the past. Do you not recall how you were seeing him at every turn for months after we knew he had left the country?' Her mother squeezed her hand and glanced across at her father.

'Maybe you are right, Mama.' Maybe it was her carnal feelings for the highwayman that were making her remember. But she did not feel like she was remembering, she felt like she was finally beginning to forget.

'Maybe we should cancel my birthday party. I am in no spirit to celebrate.'

'I will not hear of it,' her father said. 'You need something to take your mind off all that has happened. Besides, now that Pickering is out of the picture, we need to think about arranging a new match for you. I have invited every eligible bachelor in London—including young Wilcox. That gentleman has long expressed an admiration and interest in you.'

Marianne felt a flare of panic in her stomach. She

began to count her breaths, her eyes seeking Francis's across the room.

Her brother pushed off from the wall against which he was lounging.

'Surely you jest, sir? Wilcox is a lawyer's clerk. He has neither money nor status. He is not good enough for Marianne. And after the mess with Pickering it smacks of desperation. The dust should be allowed to settle for a while before any new deals are struck.'

'You forget yourself, Francis. I know what is best for Marianne. The sooner she is married the better.' Her father spoke as if she were not even present.

'Even though the matter of the highwayman remains unresolved?' said Francis, refusing to back down.

'The highwayman is nothing in the greater scheme of things.' Her father waved a hand dismissively. 'My men will find him eventually.'

'They have found no trace of him so far. Nothing. No one is speaking, not for all the money you have offered. He is still out there. And all the while he remains free he is a threat, not just to you, but to Marianne.'

'I have two hundred men looking for him. What more can I do?'

'Bait a trap to catch him.'

'Lest you have forgotten, we have already tried that,' said her father. 'And it did not work.'

Francis betrayed not even the slightest flicker of response to his father's scorn. 'He knows our every move. He has to be watching us. Go to your safety deposit box at the bank, remove a few pages of paperwork and bring those home. They will lure him to us. And this time, we will be waiting.'

Her father looked at her brother. 'You may be on to something there.'

'No!' The word was out before Marianne could stop it.

Three faces stared at her.

'Do you not want him caught?' her father asked.

'If you catch him, then everyone will know that I was abducted. It would come out in the courtroom and not all of the court reporters work for your newspapers.' It was the only excuse she could think of. 'If it became known that I was gone from home overnight, unchaperoned and in the company of a man…' She did not need to finish it. They all knew the scandal would blight the whole family.

'You misunderstand, Marianne,' her father said. 'It is a private family matter of extreme sensitivity. It was never my intention that the matter go through the courts.'

She stared at him. 'But you said that you meant to bring an end to him.'

'And so I will, my dear,' he said as patiently as if he were explaining it to a child. 'I mean to deal with the highwayman personally.'

'Personally? I do not understand.'

'He is vermin, Marianne. And vermin must be exterminated. Once it is done you need never worry about him again.'

Her eyes widened with horror.

'Father, you distress Marianne with such details,' Francis said.

'Forgive me, my dear. My sole aim is your protection.'

Her protection. As he said the words she could not help herself thinking of the document he held more precious than her.

'Eleanor,' her father said to her mother, 'take Marianne upstairs. I am sure you ladies have many arrangements for a certain twenty-first birthday party to busy yourselves with.'

'All finished, m'lady,' the maid said and stepped back that Marianne might see in the looking glass the hairstyle she had been creating for the past hour. 'You look so different, m'lady. It suits you well.'

'She's right. You do look different,' her brother said from the doorway.

Marianne felt her cheeks warm. 'I wish that Papa had cancelled this ball. I find I have no stomach for it.'

'And let the highwayman win?' her brother queried.

'This isn't about the highwayman,' she said. But in a way it was. She had not stopped thinking about him, not stopped worrying about what her father meant to do to him, or he to her father. She was deeply anxious about the plan her father and Francis were hatching. And at the back of her mind lurked the shadow of Rotherham.

'You and Papa spoke of a plan to catch him... What do you know of it?'

'I know that it is your twenty-first birthday next week and tonight is a ball to celebrate it, Marianne, and that our father will be here in a moment to lead you down the stairs and into the ballroom to greet your guests. I know that it is your duty to look beautiful and enjoy yourself and make our mother proud and our father glad that he spent his money throwing this ball for you. Tonight of all nights you should not be thinking of that villain.'

But she was thinking of him, more so tonight than any other.

Marianne looked at the coil of hair pinned high on

her head and the loose curls cascading down from it in the classical style that was so in fashion. She did look different, she thought. But it had nothing to do with her hairstyle or the fact that almost a hundred people were waiting for her in her father's ballroom. She was not even thinking of the waxen-faced Mr Wilcox. She was thinking of a pair of amber eyes and what it would mean if her father was to succeed in capturing the man to whom they belonged.

From his place lounging against the wall by the window, Rafe watched Misbourne lead Marianne into the ballroom.

A ripple of applause broke out and Marianne blushed and looked embarrassed. The dress was white, its bodice scattered with pink pearls and fixed with a single large ribboned bow, its skirt edged in a deep scallop of pink lace. Her pale curls teased artlessly against her face, making her look like some dark-eyed Aphrodite.

'Misbourne's looking for someone to fill the shoes that Pickering recently vacated,' said Devlin. 'I'd tumble her.'

'Ever the gentleman,' muttered Rafe, unable to hide his irritation.

'And you wouldn't, given half a chance?'

'I've no mind to be caught in parson's mousetrap,' said Rafe coolly.

'None of us have,' said Fallingham. 'We're hardly suitable fodder for a débutante. Makes you wonder why Misbourne invited us.'

'We're five of the *ton*'s most eligible bachelors,' said Bullford, 'and he's looking for a husband for his daughter: that's why he invited us. He's rumoured to have spent three grand on this bash.'

'I heard Prinny's on the guest list, although quite how he managed that I don't know,' said Razeby.

'Also heard that he's lined up Frederick Wilcox as next in the betrothal line.'

Rafe had heard that too.

'Never heard of him. Who the hell is he?' asked Devlin.

'Apprentice lawyer. Works with Misbourne's man of business,' answered Rafe.

'Hardly a suitable match for the daughter of an earl,' said Bullford.

Fallingham smirked. 'Must be in a hurry to get her married off. Maybe little Lady Marianne isn't quite so pure as she looks.'

The others sniggered. Rafe knew the rake he was playing would have laughed, too, but when he looked at Fallingham he could barely smother the urge to punch his smirking mouth.

He walked away before temptation got the better of him.

'What's got into him?' he heard Fallingham asking after him, but he was out of earshot before the answer came.

Rafe kept to the background, but there was never a moment he was not aware of Marianne. He told himself that he was here because it was an excuse to make a foray into Misbourne's lair, that any extra knowledge he could glean of his enemy was of potential use. But it was not Misbourne that he watched. He knew the risk he was taking in being here, but when it came to Marianne he just could not seem to stay away.

Marianne seemed to sense him. She was dancing

with Wilcox when she saw him and he wondered if he had gone too far in coming here, to her birthday ball. Her gaze met his for those few seconds and held and he saw something flare in her eyes, but she gave no other sign that she had recognised him. And then Wilcox led her away and she did not look back until she could do so as part of the dance.

Wilcox's pate was gleaming with sweat, his hand possessive upon Marianne's at every opportunity. She seemed to withdraw, shudder almost at his touch, just as she had done with every man who danced with her. Rafe watched and knew that he should not care. But then her gaze touched his again, and he knew that he did care, more than he would have thought possible. And he knew, too, that no matter how dangerous, he could not stand here all night and watch her dance with men she did not care for. So he waited for the music to end and then made his way steadily through the crowd towards Misbourne and his family.

'Thank you, Papa, for going to so much trouble for me.' Marianne forced herself to smile at her father, knowing that he must have worked very hard to have so many of the *ton*'s best in their ballroom.

'It was no trouble, my sweet. I am glad that you are happy. You have your choice of young gentlemen as dance partners this evening.'

She bit her lip and could not help from stealing another glance towards the highwayman's group. His friends were still there, but he seemed to have disappeared. She felt her heart sink a little and something of her excitement waned. She smiled all the harder that her father would not see it.

'I have not been introduced to most of them.'

'That will not be a problem. I will ensure that the necessary introductions are made.'

'You know everyone here?' she asked.

'Of a form,' her father said.

'Even those gentlemen over by the windows, the ones who are reputed to be so very dangerous and wild and rakish?' And one of whom was more dangerous than he could imagine.

'The gossipmongers exaggerate. I see three viscounts and two wealthy gentlemen there—all young and all unmarried, each and every one of them.'

'Papa!' Marianne chided, turning away to find herself looking directly at the approach of the highwayman.

Her heart stopped. Her stomach turned a somersault. He could not actually mean to approach her before her papa, could he? But then those amber eyes met hers and she knew that was exactly what he was going to do.

'Lord Misbourne.' He gave the smallest of bows and she saw the warmth vanish from his eyes as he looked at her father.

Beside her she sensed her father stiffen.

'Lady Marianne.' Just as in the botanic gardens that day, his voice without the disguising whisper was rich and deep and delicious. Like a feather stroked from the bare skin at the nape of her neck all the way down, it made her spine tingle. Marianne felt the blush heat her cheeks. 'Would you grant me the honour of the next dance?' He had not asked her father, nor had he waited for an introduction.

'I would be pleased to partner you,' she said quickly before her father could disagree, then shot a look up at her father. 'Papa?'

Her father did not look angry or slighted, maybe because he saw only the man who had helped them at the botanic gardens. But she could not help noticing the strange expression upon his face as he held the highwayman's gaze. 'Marianne, may I introduce Mr Rafe Knight,' he said, his voice revealing nothing of his thoughts.

Rafe Knight. She had thought of him as 'the highwayman' for so long.

'Mr Knight,' she said and curtsied. Then he took her hand in his and, before her father and the best of London's *ton*, led her out on to the dance floor.

It was a Scotch reel, hardly conducive to conversation or any degree of intimacy.

'Rafe Knight,' she repeated, her eyes meeting his. She knew his name at last. And she knew, too, that the opportunity for which she prayed had just been delivered.

'Marianne Winslow,' he replied in that deep rich tone.

She couldn't help herself; she smiled and her heart felt overflowing with gladness, and then the music took them apart. When it brought them back together his hand was in hers and he was birling her around.

'I have to speak to you,' she whispered, breathless not only from the dance.

Then she was off and being birled by the next man in the line before being passed back to him. 'In private.'

The steps led them fast down the centre of the set. At the bottom, just before they peeled apart to travel back up the outside of the set on their own, she whispered, 'It is important.'

Her hand was small and cool within his. His lady

of silver and moonlight. The look in her eyes thawed the chill in his heart and her words fired his blood. He could not deny her, no matter the risk.

'Head for the ladies' withdrawing room after this dance.' Callerton would call him a fool if he knew, but then Callerton didn't need to know.

She nodded and smiled a secret smile that he knew was just for him; God help him, but he felt his heart warm and expand at the sight of it. And his thumb slid a stroke against the soft skin of her hand before he released it. They danced and he could not keep his eyes off her. They danced until finally the music stopped. Misbourne was watching him again as he returned her, watching him with something in those dark soulless eyes that made Rafe feel uneasy, as if the man knew much more than he was revealing. But he turned away from Misbourne and made his way from the ballroom to wait for Marianne.

Marianne walked slowly, her eyes scanning the bodies that crowded the hallway and staircase, looking for only one man: her highwayman—Rafe Knight.

His touch was gentle against her arm.

'The study,' she whispered and he followed her there. They slipped inside and closed the door behind them.

The desk was clear aside from a half-full glass of brandy that sat upon it and the candles in the wall sconces were alight, as if Misbourne had not long left the room. Rafe remembered the last time he had been in here: Marianne, in her nightdress, in his arms, her mouth sweet and eager beneath his, her breast and the thud of her heart beneath his hand.

'Mr Knight,' she said, and now that they were alone

she seemed shy, as if she, too, was remembering what had happened between them in this room.

'I think we know each other well enough, Marianne, that you should call me by my given name.'

'Rafe,' she said and he savoured the sound of it on her lips.

'That day in the botanic gardens…who did you see, Marianne?'

'No one,' she said hurriedly, glancing away—but not before he saw a shadow flit across her face.

He knew that she was lying. That look of terror on her face that day had haunted him ever since. He knew what he would do if he ever found the person responsible. His fingers touched her cheek in the gentlest of caresses. Her skin was so soft, so perfect, beneath his fingers.

Her eyes came to his, scanning them as if she could read the darkness that was in his soul. 'We do not have much time. My mother will notice if I take too long.'

'Your parents guard you well.' Her parents. And he was reminded again of why this was futile. There could be nothing between them save the torture of knowing what they could not have. Yet still he stayed, standing in Misbourne's study, looking at the woman who was Misbourne's daughter.

'They do,' she murmured, glancing away again with that strange uneasiness about her. But then she seemed to gather herself; when she looked at him again she was stronger and filled with an urgency of purpose. 'My father and brother are planning some means to draw you out of hiding. Whatever they might communicate to you, do not heed it; it is a trap to catch you.'

'I do not mind being caught as long as I take Misbourne with me.'

'You do not understand,' she said. 'My father has no intention of involving the courts.' She swallowed. 'He means to kill you.'

He gave a small hard laugh.

But she misunderstood his irony. 'You do not know my father, Rafe. Incredulous though it may sound, he is serious. He really does mean to kill you.'

'I do not doubt it for a minute, Marianne. I was never the one who doubted his capacity for murder.' He saw the hurt flash in her eyes before she turned away and he could have bitten out his own tongue at his carelessness.

'Marianne.' He caught her hands in his. 'Forgive me. I am wont to forget that he is your father. I did not mean to hurt you.'

She glanced up into his eyes. 'He *is* my father,' she said, 'and I am not unaware that I am betraying my family in warning you of his intent, that I seem to have done nothing other since we met. But I do not wish for him to hurt you.' She glanced down as if embarrassed by the admission. 'Nor do I wish for you to hurt him.'

Her words were soft against the silence that followed. He wished he could offer her reassurances, tell her that her father was safe. But he could not lie to her. False hope was crueller in the long term.

'I thank you for your warning…and I do understand something of your dilemma.'

'Do you?' She looked up at him.

'Of course. I am not unaffected by the situation in which we find ourselves.' She had no idea of the way she affected him, or what it did to him knowing that he could not stop until he watched her father dance upon the gibbet.

He saw the blush touch pink to her cheeks and

thought what a cruel game fate was playing with them both.

His thumbs slid against her small slender fingers and in return he felt them close around his.

'Did you come tonight that you might continue your search?' He could see that she was holding her breath.

'No, Marianne. I came to see you.' He pulled her closer. The air sparked between them, the tension was so tight that he felt his blood rush hot with it.

'It is dangerous for you to be here.'

'Very dangerous,' he agreed, lowering his mouth to hers.

He kissed her as he had been dreaming of kissing her all of these nights past. He kissed her until she was breathless and weak-legged. Her arms wound around his neck, her fingers threading through his hair, freeing it from its queue. He sensed the untapped passion in her that contrasted so starkly with her innocence and shyness. He could feel it in her kiss, feel it in the tremble of her slim body pressed to his.

Rafe forgot all about Misbourne. He forgot about the document and the quest that had spurred him through the last fifteen years. There was only Marianne Winslow and the depth of feeling and passion that was exploding between them.

His hands were on her breasts just as she had imagined every night as she lay in her bed. But this was real. He was touching her and his touch was gentle, not greedy or grabbing or hurtful. Her body was flush against his, fitting as if they had been made as two halves of the same mould. She let herself relax against him, revelling in his strength and his sheer size, and in the hardness of his muscles.

The scent of him and the faint undertone of sandalwood made her feel heady and safe and excited all at the same time, drunk as if on the bubbles of champagne that her brother had let her sip from his glass when she was sixteen. Her mouth was filled with the taste of him, her tongue meeting his in a dance that she did not want to stop. He caressed her, every part of him against every part of her. Tongue to tongue. Lips to lips. His hands on her breast and her hip. His heart against hers, and as he kissed her, as he touched her, she felt the barricades she had erected around herself begin to crumble.

Even through all the layers of her clothing she could feel the stroke of his hand against her nipples. His fingertips traced against the very tops of her breasts that only just showed over the neckline of her dress. She caught her breath at the sensation and felt her blood rush all the wilder and her nipples tighten unbearably as if they ached for his touch. She did not remember the darkness of the past. She did not remember her fears. She thought only of Rafe Knight, of the magic he was stoking within her body and how much she wanted this intimacy with him.

His breath caressed the crook of her neck and she angled her head, allowing his lips to tease where his breath had been. He touched his lips to the small tender hollow at the base of her throat, then kissed all the way along her collarbone, tasting her, making her thread her fingers through the length of his dark hair and hold on to him. And when he reached the small puff sleeve of her dress he eased it off her shoulder that he might kiss the skin beneath.

The sensation made her gasp so loud that he drew back a little and looked into her face. She did not release him, just kept her hands where they cradled on either side of his head, her thumbs stroking tiny caresses. His eyes looked almost as dark as her own, and there was a look in them that she knew was desire. She knew it, yet she was not afraid. For she felt the same hunger, the same need in herself.

'Marianne,' came his highwayman's whisper as he placed a kiss in the middle of her *décolletage*. 'Marianne,' again as his lips slid lower.

'Rafe,' she replied and arched against him, desperate to feel him all the more.

Within his arms he bowed her gently, as if she were a willow, as his mouth closed over the top of her breast, as his fingers edged her bodice infinitesimally lower. A moan escaped and she did not know it was her own mouth that made the sound. She clutched his head tighter to her breasts, holding him as if she would never let him go. She was so lost in the moment that she heard nothing save the beat of her own heart and of his.

She did not understand at first when Rafe stiffened and glanced swiftly round at the door. Her mind was dulled with passion. And then, when she looked again, her father was standing in the doorway, grey-faced with worry, eyes wide with shock. Her mother, standing behind him, gave a little shriek.

Her father pulled her mother inside the study and closed the door behind them both. 'Good God, woman, cease your hysterics unless you have a mind to broadcast this affair to every last one of our guests.'

Rafe had released Marianne and positioned himself to shield her from her parents' view, but he could not hide the truth. Awareness of precisely of what she had been doing hit her like a deluge of cold water. She could not believe it. Even as she clutched an arm around herself, her father's gaze swept over her and

Marianne felt that Rafe's every touch, every kiss was branded upon her for her father to see. Her cheeks scalded hot with shame. And then her father's gaze moved to Rafe and she saw it harden.

'Papa...' she started, but her father ignored her.

'I think we have something to discuss, Mr Knight,' he said.

'Indeed we do, sir.' She saw Rafe give a nod, but his eyes were anything but submissive.

'Take her upstairs,' her father hissed at her mother. 'And try to make her look as if she has not just been seduced.'

'Papa, it was not like that.'

'Do as I say, Marianne,' he snapped, his eyes so dark and clouded with anger that she feared what would unfold between him and Rafe.

'Papa, it was my fault. Mr Knight was—'

'Marianne,' Rafe said and only then did he shift the lethality of his gaze from her father. His eyes met hers and they were dark and meaningful, conveying a message that she should do as he asked. 'Go with your mother. Everything shall be well.'

Yet still she hesitated to leave the two men alone.

'Marianne,' Rafe said more softly and she realised that she had to trust him. She gave a nod and, with one last lingering look that spoke all that she could not say, she turned to her mother.

Chapter Nine

Misbourne waited until the door closed behind Marianne and her mother before he spoke. 'You have ruined my daughter, Mr Knight.'

'I am aware of the situation,' Rafe said. He knew that there was no way back for Marianne after this. Only one ending to this evening could save her.

The door burst open and Linwood appeared, a feral look in those black eyes of his. 'You abominable rake! By hell, I will call you out, sir, for what you've done to my sister.'

'Get out,' said Misbourne coldly. 'I am dealing with the matter.'

'You cannot seriously mean to—'

'I said get out.'

Linwood glowered at his father, then turned and walked away, closing the door behind him.

'Ignore him,' said Misbourne.

'Surely you mean to call me out too?' Rafe asked, part of him hoping that the bastard would, even though he knew it would never come to that. For no matter how much he hated Misbourne, he could not stand back and watch Marianne's reputation crumble to dust before all of London. The writing was on the wall; it had been ever since Misbourne had opened the study door.

'Do I need to?' asked Misbourne.

'Only if you have an objection to my marrying your daughter.'

'I shall organise the wedding for Wednesday,' said Misbourne. 'I think you will understand the need for a speedy and discreet affair.' He lifted the glass decanter from the occasional table and poured brandy into two glasses, one of which he passed to Rafe. Rafe ignored the proffered glass, his eyes holding Misbourne's.

'We should return to the ballroom.'

'You are right,' Misbourne conceded. 'We must keep up appearances.'

'But I cannot marry him!' Marianne exclaimed after her father finished his announcement to the family in the breakfast room the next morning.

'You seemed to like him well enough in my study last night.'

Marianne felt the heat glow in her cheeks. 'It was just a kiss. He did nothing more.' She was lying; it had been so much more than a kiss. It had been something that made her forget herself, the past, her fears. In those moments she had felt alive and vibrant and unafraid, a thousand miles removed from everything that was Marianne Winslow.

'Just a kiss, Marianne?' Her mother raised an eyebrow. 'Your father and I both saw exactly what was going on.'

'Merely being alone with Rafe Knight in my study was enough to compromise your reputation,' said her father more calmly. 'Knight is no green boy. He knew the risk he was taking.'

A risk far greater than her father understood.

'Honour decrees that he offer for you.'

'But you don't understand.' She glanced round at her family, at her mother's pursed lips and her brother's dark gaze, and the stubborn set of her father's jaw. Rafe was the highwayman her father had set half of London to kill. Her father was the man against whom Rafe had sworn a dark vengeance. The two men she loved, each sworn to destroy the other. And no matter what she felt for Rafe, no matter how much the idea of becoming his wife might entice her, she knew that it was far too dangerous.

'I understand very well.' But he didn't. He had no idea.

'It was my fault. I asked him to meet me in the study.'

'Good Lord!' she heard her mother mutter beneath her breath. She did not look at Francis, just kept her eyes on her father, on the angry disapproval in his eyes and the curling of his lip. She knew they were all disappointed in her.

'And why would you do that, Marianne?'

'Because I wanted to...' *Warn him of your plan.* She closed her eyes and swallowed down the guilt and warring emotions. 'Because I wanted him to kiss me,' she finished, and felt her face flame all the hotter.

'And he obliged.'

'Yes.' She glanced down. 'So you see, it was my fault.'

'He is hardly the innocent in this.'

'And neither am I,' said Marianne quietly.

The words hung in the room, all clumsy and uncomfortable.

'It makes no difference,' her father said, but the look in his eyes had softened.

'But, Papa—'

'No buts,' her father said. 'You will marry him on your birthday.'

'Wednesday!' she said. 'So soon?'

'Wednesday,' her father said. 'And that will be an end to it.' The strength and angry stubbornness was back in his eyes. No argument was going to sway him.

She turned to walk away without asking to be excused.

'Marianne!' her mother exclaimed, but Marianne ignored her and kept walking.

Her father's words made her hesitate halfway across the drawing room. 'Until you become Knight's wife you do not leave this house, Marianne. Knight is procuring the special licence. The ceremony shall take place in this very room so there is no need for travel. After the last attempt at a wedding day I'm not taking any chances. I want you kept safe from the highwayman.'

Marianne felt like laughing and crying both at once. If only her father knew that he had just betrothed his daughter to that same highwayman. She did not look back, just walked right out of the room.

'Treat her gently,' Misbourne said to his wife, then waited until the door closed behind her before turning to Linwood. 'Ensure that all windows and doors are kept locked. No one enters the house without being vetted by me, you or your mother. And I mean no one, not even the lowliest of tradesmen.

'He may not be the bridegroom I would have chosen…' Misbourne stared off into the distance and thought of the past '…nor this the means of their betrothal, but he will marry her and that is good enough.'

'He's a damnable rake, taken to running with Devlin and his crew of late. He seduced Marianne, despite what she says. She is young and her head filled with foolish notions of romance. She fancies herself in love with the rogue and seeks to protect him by taking the blame on herself. You never should have invited him and his cronies. I don't care what he did at the botanic gardens.'

'You are too hard on him. We all make mistakes when we are young.'

'It is unlike you to be so solicitous. Few people knew of their being in the study alone. We could hush this up. Knight does nothing save drink and game and womanise. Are you so desperate to see her married off that you would have her wed such a man?'

'I cannot deny that I will be happy to see her wed.' Misbourne felt the stain upon his soul grow heavy and dark as the shadows seemed to whisper in his ear, reminding him of what he had done, what he could never forget. 'I long for the day that she is settled...and safe.' And then he realised that he had revealed too much and that his son was watching him too carefully. He pulled himself together, closed his ears to the voices that whispered to him. 'So she will marry him, and there will be no more gossip. Now, I wish to hear no more about it.' When the door closed behind his son, a dark frown creased his face, and the darkness of the past rolled in to turn the dust-flecked sunlight of the breakfast room to cold grey shadow, and Misbourne longed for Wednesday.

'What the hell do you mean you are marrying Marianne Winslow on Wednesday?' Callerton stared at him aghast. 'Have you forgotten who she is?'

'You do not need to remind me of her relationship to Misbourne; it is ever in my mind. But I have compromised her and I will not leave her to face the shame of it alone.'

'I told you to stay away from her. You could have any woman in London and you have to go dallying after Misbourne's daughter. Hell's teeth, Rafe!'

'I do not want any other woman. I want her!' Rafe raked a hand through his hair.

'Enough to marry her?'

'Were Misbourne not the complicating factor, yes.'

'But Misbourne is in this as much as she. Are you are prepared to call Misbourne father for the sake of having her? For that is what it comes down to, Rafe.'

Rafe's hand flexed so hard that the brandy glass within it cracked. 'What else can I do? Walk away and leave her ruined?'

'Yes, if that is what it takes.' Callerton's face was pale. 'I would not see any woman's reputation hurt, but no good can come of this.'

'You know I cannot do that.'

'Your blood cries out for vengeance, Rafe. Do you think it to be so easily silenced to save his daughter's honour?'

'What is between Misbourne and I can never be silenced. It plays out to the end.'

'You will not stop until there is a noose around his neck.'

Rafe looked at him, the confirmation in his eyes.

'And yet you still mean to marry his daughter?'

'Marrying Marianne will not prevent me from bringing her father to justice.'

'Think of what that will do to her. If Misbourne

hangs for murder, his family will be destroyed. You will be a part of that family, Rafe.'

'I will never be a part of Misbourne's family. Marianne will take my name. She will be my wife. I will take care of her.'

'Do you think she will forgive you for destroying her father?'

'If I do not fulfil my oath, then I will not forgive myself. It is a matter of honour both to marry Marianne and to see her father executed. And I will do both.'

Callerton shook his head. 'You are making a mistake in marrying the girl, Rafe. There can be only trouble down this route. You can choose to save her honour or your own, but you cannot have both.'

'Mr Knight,' Marianne said politely and made her curtsy. And when she peeped up through her lashes, that steady amber gaze was on hers and she blushed at the sudden heady rush of anticipation and longing.

'Lady Marianne,' he replied and the sound of his voice seemed to stroke a caress all the way down her spine. He was dressed impeccably in a tailcoat of dark-blue, buff-coloured breeches and riding boots. In one hand was his hat, riding gloves and crop, and in the other a bouquet of flowers.

'For you.' He passed her the bouquet, not large and showy as Mr Wilcox's had been, but small and plain and made entirely of white rosebuds.

'Thank you, Mr Knight. They are beautiful.' Marianne inhaled their perfume.

'They reminded me of you.'

She felt herself blush and lowered her eyes. 'White roses are my favourite flower,' she murmured.

'How lovely, Mr Knight,' said her mother with a

false smile, whisking the bouquet into the hands of the footman to find a suitable vase.

'Indeed, Lady Misbourne,' he said, but his gaze did not move from Marianne's and the look in them was passionate and possessive and everything that was contrary to the pale innocence of the flowers.

The silence in the room was heavy and awkward. Her mother lifted her tambour and worked upon her embroidery. Marianne swallowed. There was so much she wanted to say to Rafe, none of which could be spoken in front of her mother.

'The weather is uncommonly fine for the time of year,' she said, trying to fill the silence.

His eyes looked golden in the sunlight that flooded the drawing room. His face, so handsome and serious that she longed to press her lips to his and tell him that she loved him. To tell him that she understood all that he had done for her and all that he was prepared to do to save her once again, even though she could not let him.

In the silence the knock at the front door was so sudden and loud that Marianne jumped. Then the butler appeared, whispering soft words in her mother's ear and her mother frowned. 'I shall come at once.'

She looked at her daughter, then at Rafe. 'Excuse me while I step out of the room for a few moments.' She left the drawing-room door wide open in her wake. Marianne glanced towards it and lowered her voice.

'I am grateful for your desire to save my honour, but I cannot let you do this, Rafe.' She looked up into his eyes. 'You cannot possibly marry me.'

'Marianne, we do not need to have this conversation.'

'Yes, we do. It is too dangerous. If my father were to discover who you are…'

'We will deal with that if it happens.'

'He has sworn to kill you!'

'I know what your father does to those who cross him.' There was an underlying bitterness to his tone that made her shiver.

'And you have sworn vengeance upon him.'

'Not vengeance,' he said, correcting her as he had done before. 'Justice.'

'Justice that involves you wishing him dead.'

'I cannot deny it.'

Her blood ran cold at how adamant he was about it. 'He is my father, Rafe. And I love him, even with his imperfections. I cannot bear that you should wish to hurt him…'

His expression remained hard.

'…or he, you.'

His hand closed around hers, his thumb stroking the centre of her palm.

'I will not marry you, Rafe. I cannot. Surely you see that?'

'I see that if you do not marry me you are ruined.'

'I will survive a little social embarrassment.' She glanced away. 'I have survived much worse.' And her mind flickered back to touch on a shadow from the past that was fading more with every day that passed.

'After Arlesford and Pickering you will not survive this.'

'I will not marry you,' she said again, even though he was the only man in the world she would willingly marry.

She saw something flicker in his eyes.

'What is between us, Marianne, cannot so easily be

extinguished. It will burn whether we marry or not, whether we will it or not.'

'You are mistaken,' she said, even though she knew he was not. Her heart was already lost and nothing she could do would reclaim it.

'Am I?' he asked, stepping closer.

She swallowed, feeling her heart begin to thump and that same fluttering in her stomach that she felt whenever he was close.

He raised her hand to his lips and kissed where his thumb had traced.

'Marry me, Marianne,' he said in the highwayman's harsh whisper. And when his arms came around her, she went into them willingly. When his mouth touched hers, she kissed him with all the love that was in her heart.

'Your mother has left you unchaperoned?' Her father's voice shattered the moment.

She jumped and felt a panic over whether he had heard Rafe's whisper and recognised it as the highwayman's. 'There was a caller at the front door; she went to deal with it.' She stood slightly in front of Rafe.

Her father's eyes slid to meet Rafe's.

She tensed, ready to protect her highwayman. But when her father spoke she knew he had heard nothing after all.

'Mr Knight.' He gave a small bow of the head.

'Lord Misbourne.' Rafe's bow was so slight as to be insulting and Marianne heard the anger and dislike that edged his words. They were like two dogs facing one another, hackles raised. She could sense the energy in Rafe, a barely contained snarl, ready to pounce and rip out her father's throat. Her father was less aggressive, but watchful and uneasy just the same.

'I will call for Marianne to take her for a drive in Hyde Park tomorrow afternoon.' He should be asking her father's permission, not telling him what he intended. She held her breath, waiting for her father to respond to the insult and remembering his decree that she was not to leave the house.

'I do not think so,' her father said carefully and there was nothing of the angry voice he would have used had anyone else uttered such a slight. 'Marianne has much to prepare for the wedding ceremony. We would not want her to over-exert herself.'

'Indeed not. But she is in good health and a carriage trip in the park is hardly likely to over-exert her. Do you doubt my ability to protect her?'

'Never that.' Her father smiled as if Rafe had just cracked some secret joke. 'Like myself, Mr Knight, you are not a man to be lightly crossed. I think you will make my daughter a very good protector.'

Like myself. The words seemed to hang in the air between them, offered by her father like an olive branch and unwittingly the very comparison that would inflame Rafe.

'Come Wednesday, Mr Knight, Marianne will be your wife and her care passes to you. Until then, she is under my protection.'

She felt Rafe stiffen.

'I do not need a protector,' she said. 'I am perfectly able to protect myself.' But both men ignored her. 'And as for a trip in the park, Mr Knight, it would be very pleasant, but I am afraid I am busy all of tomorrow afternoon.'

'Perhaps we should have a drink in my study, Mr Knight, and discuss the wedding plans.' Her father smiled, but it was strained and there was something in his eyes that she did not recognise.

Her hand hung loosely at her side. She moved it surreptitiously so that the edge of her little finger touched ever so lightly against Rafe's hand. Her gaze slid to his, imploring him to be civil, telling him with her eyes what she could not tell him with her words.

'Another time, Misbourne,' Rafe said. 'I am already engaged to attend a meeting. I bid you good day.' The rejection was tempered by a bow of his head, a concession she knew was only for her sake. 'Lady Marianne.' He pulled her to him and kissed her mouth, his lips searing against hers. It was an action to claim her as his before her father—an action both of defiance and possession. Her father watched with dark eyes and to Marianne's surprise said not one word of disapproval. 'Until Wednesday,' Rafe said as he released her and disappeared through the door.

Her father looked at her and said nothing.

'If you will excuse me, Papa.'

He gave a nod. 'Of course, my dear,' he said as if nothing untoward had happened.

Misbourne watched his daughter leave. Three more days and she would be married. 'Every cloud has a silver lining.' He smiled grimly to himself. No matter who Rafe Knight was, no matter what he did, Misbourne could only be glad of the turn of events. 'Wednesday—only three more days,' he whispered, but he knew he would not sleep until Knight's ring was upon Marianne's finger and she was safe as his wife.

Without Rafe's presence Marianne's fears over the marriage seemed to take hold once more, to magnify out of all proportion. Her appetite waned so that she did little more than pick at her food. At night she lay restless, tossing and turning on her bed, unable to sleep for the turmoil of thoughts tumbling in her head. Preparations of valerian did not help. Counting her breaths did not help. Nothing that she did in the longest hours of the night made any difference. And when she did sleep, out of sheer exhaustion, there was nothing of rest, only of the worst imaginings.

She was in the country, standing beneath a leaden sky, while the wind howled like a banshee and blew a chill cold enough to freeze the stoutest of hearts. Before her was a lonely hill at the top of which grew a solitary tree, tall, its branches gnarled and twisted as a demon from a hellish tale. The light was so grey and dismal she could not see clearly. She stared up the hill, at the tree and saw the movement of a shadow against it. Something about the sight gripped her heart with terror.

She began to run, desperate to prevent what was about to happen, clambering up the steepness of the hill. But the grass was wet and slippery beneath her feet and the wind was like a great hand forcing her back, stinging her face, roaring in her ears. She fought for all she was worth, but by the time she reached the summit, the night had come and she could no longer see. In the silence she heard the creak of a rope swinging heavy in the wind. *Rafe!* she cried in the dream. *Papa!* But in reply came only the crashing of thunder that rolled across the sky and the fork of white lightning that, in the transient moment of its flicker, lit the man's limp body swinging from the noose strung from the tree. And no matter how hard she tried, she could not see whether it was Rafe or her father. But it did not matter, because she was too late, and when she woke her maid was peering down anxiously into her face and Marianne's cheeks were wet with tears.

The horror of the dream would not leave her, but grew only worse so that as the days crept by, hour by agonising hour, she could not dispel the sense of impending doom. She imagined persuading Rafe that she would not marry him a hundred times, even practised what she would say to him. She both longed and dreaded to see him. But Rafe did not visit again. Not on the first day, or the second or even the third. And all the while there were dressmakers and florists and menus, everything that went with the preparations for a normal wedding, except for the announcement of the betrothal in her father's newspaper. There was no mention of that.

Her mother fussed incessantly, and her father and Francis were always in the background, always guarding and watching. Marianne was not left alone even for a minute. And every night the door to her bedchamber was locked from the outside.

By Tuesday night Marianne could think of nothing other than Rafe and what the morning would bring: her twenty-first birthday and her marriage.

She heard her father go to bed a little after one o'clock. Her body was tired, but her mind was racing; she pushed back the covers and rose from the bed, moving to the window. She edged the curtains open and looked out into the night. The lamps were still burning and overhead the bright light of the moon was hidden behind the charcoal clouds of the night. She looked out over the houses and the dark foliage of the gardens opposite that stirred in the breeze. And as she watched she thought she saw the dark figure of a man standing there amidst the shrubbery. Rafe. And despite everything her heart lifted and something of the worry diminished.

She pressed her palm to the window as if to touch him. But the figure made no similar gesture, only stood there watching. She stared all the harder and, as she did so, the clouds parted to reveal the moon. In the ethereal silver light she saw not Rafe, but Rotherham.

She jumped back, wrenching her hand from the window, her heart thudding so hard that she could scarcely breathe, her legs trembling violently. She took a deep breath, trying to calm the nausea that was roiling in her stomach. Then she stepped to the window once more, determined to see if it really was Rotherham. But the clouds had covered the moon once more and the figure had vanished, absorbed by the blackness of the night. *Had it been real, or simply her imagination?* She stood there a while and watched, but there was no movement and no sign that anyone had been there.

'My lady?' the maid whispered from the truckle bed behind her.

'Go back to sleep, Polly. I am all right.'

But she wasn't all right. She wasn't all right at all.

Chapter Ten

Wednesday came both too quickly and not quickly enough. Rafe declined the seat that Misbourne offered and stood at the front of the drawing room of the town house in Leicester Square. The room had been dressed with both white and pink flowers, and huge bows and swags of ribbons. The heavy perfumed scent of lilies tickled his nose. Although the day was overcast and the wind held the chill of autumn, the fire had not been lit and he was glad of it. The chairs had been set out in rows and the guests, who were only around ten in number, sat within them, the quiet hum of their chatter filling the room, speculation glinting in their eyes at a surprise wedding organised so close to the bride's betrothal to another, that had allowed no apparent time for a new courtship. It could not have escaped their attention that there had been no mention of a wedding at Marianne's birthday ball only a few days earlier.

Callerton glanced round at them again, easing his cravat a little looser as if it pressed too tight around his neck. Rafe could see the unease in his friend's eyes; so at home on a battlefield, but clearly uncomfortable in the drawing room of a high-society town house.

They watched a footman enter the room and whisper in Misbourne's ear. The earl slipped away.

'Look on the bright side,' Callerton whispered to Rafe as they turned to face the front. 'You'll be able to search to your heart's content. You'll find out where he's hiding it eventually.'

'That's not why I'm doing this.'

'I know.' Callerton touched his fingers to the pocket watch of his white-worked waistcoat. 'If I've forgotten the ring, do you still have to marry her?' He risked a smile.

Despite everything—the severity of the situation, what he was about to do—Rafe returned the smile.

Then the string quartet in the corner began to play and the guests rose to their feet and Rafe knew without looking round that Marianne had entered the room. Callerton had turned to watch her, but Rafe resisted the temptation. He knew what he was about to do. Marrying the daughter of the man he had spent a lifetime hating had not been part of the plan. But he was honour-bound to marry her and he would not let her face ruin at the hands of the *ton* simply because he hadn't been able to resist her. And if he was honest, there was a damn sight more to it than that.

She was inside his head, inside his heart. She flowed in his blood and was in the very air that he breathed. He could not get enough of her. He cared about her. And he wanted her as he had never wanted a woman in all of his life, for all that she had Misbourne's blood flowing in her veins, wanted her with a passion that seemed to simmer and nag and plague him night and day. There was the faint smell of violets and the rustle of silk. And inside, his heart leapt even at the same moment that the resentment began coursing through him, the utter distaste that he was about to ally himself to Misbourne.

He remained facing forwards, refusing to turn while he reined in the disgust and hatred he felt for the man, knowing that at this moment, more than any other, he must mask his true feelings. And when he turned his head to the side at last, Misbourne had retreated to the first row of seats, leaving Marianne standing there alone.

The sight of her made Rafe's heart miss a beat. Every time he looked at her it was as if he was seeing her for the first time—yet simultaneously as if he had always known her. That feeling of familiarity and tenderness as if she were already his, and always had been. And protectiveness. His woman, he thought, with a fierceness.

Gone were the bows and swags and heavy layers of lace. The dress was a plain ivory silk, devoid of all decoration, yet cut to fit Marianne's slim figure perfectly. The neckline was square and low enough to expose the smooth perfect skin of her *décolletage*. Even her neck was bare, devoid of so much as a ribbon— a fact that reminded him of the outsized ugly pearls that Pickering had bought her. And he realised with a stab of shame that Marianne had probably expected him to bring a necklace as his gift to her. But Rafe had brought no gift, either for the wedding or for her birthday. His gaze swept up to her hair, simply styled and caught up in a chignon from which several curling silver-blonde tendrils escaped to tease against her neck. The simplicity suited Marianne. He had always thought her a beautiful woman, but today Rafe could not take his eyes from her.

Her gaze fluttered up to meet his and he saw the

uncertainty in her dark eyes. And without thinking he took her hand in his, and gave it a small reassuring squeeze. Her fingers felt cool beneath his, and he could feel the slight tremor that ran through them. He wanted to tell her that she had nothing to be afraid of, that all would be well, but then the priest opened his Book of Common Prayer and began to speak the words that would bind them together.

Marianne had seen the hard line of Rafe's jaw and the way he could not bear to look round at her. She knew that he was only doing this out of a sense of honour, that she was the last woman on earth he would have chosen to marry. And her heart ached because she loved him; she knew that whatever he felt for her, it was not love. How could it be when, every time he looked at her, he was reminded of the man he despised?

And then his fingers closed around hers. And the warmth of his skin seemed to spread throughout her, thawing the ice and the fear and dread that flowed in her veins. It was such a gentle gesture, small and surreptitious in nature, but the strength of the man seemed to seep into her from that one point of contact, calming her nerves and all of her fears, buoying her, rekindling that tiny spark of hope that in some way, against all the odds, all might be well between them.

Marianne felt that what was happening was unreal, as if it were part of some dream. The priest's words droned on and all Marianne could think of was that this could not really be happening. She was marrying the man who had abducted her *en route* to her wedding with Pickering. The man who had sworn to destroy her father, a man who was darker, stronger, more dangerous than any man she had known.

'I, Marianne Elizabeth Winslow, take thee, Rafe Knight, to be my lawfully wedded husband,' said the priest for the second time, peering at her with exasperation. And Marianne wondered if she could do it, if she could close the door of no return and bind him to her. She glanced around.

All the guests were staring with bated breath, almost gleeful at the prospect of her ruining yet another betrothal. Her mother's mouth was tight, her eyes signalling frenziedly that Marianne must say the words. Her brother was looking at her with his usual closed expression. She could see the sheen of the sweat upon her father's forehead, see the way he gripped his hands tightly together and the pallor beneath the grizzled grey of his beard, and, worst of all, the anger and fear that vied in his eyes. And finally her gaze moved to Rafe, to those clear warm amber eyes that seemed to reach through everything and touch her very soul, just as they had done that first day on Hounslow Heath.

His face was as if chiselled by the hand of a master sculptor from the marble of the gods—that strong manly nose, those perfect sculpted lips, the hard line of his jaw clean-shaven and strong. She remembered how he had saved her from being attacked in St Giles Rookery, how he had taken a bullet for her in the burying ground. And how he had not ridiculed her fear of the dark, but brought candles. He was the only man in the world she wanted to marry. The man that she loved. She did not think of anything else. All her fears were forgotten, all her worries were gone. She looked into his eyes and she said the words straight from her heart.

'I, Marianne Elizabeth Winslow, take thee…'

And when she had finished all that had to be said, Rafe slipped a gold wedding band on to the third finger of her left hand and the priest pronounced them man and wife.

'Let no man tear asunder what God has blessed and put together.'

Rafe lowered his face to hers and he kissed her, not some formal polite touching of lips, but a kiss in which all of the passion that was between them fired and blazed with a fury, so that she felt herself almost consumed by the fierceness of it. And when he drew back, the guests and even her mother were staring as if they could not believe it. Her brother's eyes were narrowed, dark as thunder, and her father looked… relieved.

The wedding breakfast was held within her father's dining room. They ate fine steak and drank the best of champagnes. And in the centre of the table was the elaborate sugar palace that had been sculpted for her wedding to Pickering and beside it a cake that had been iced for her birthday. Her father was the soul of the celebration. He laughed and joked, and, contrary to his usual demeanour, was the very best of hosts. And Marianne felt the squeeze of her conscience that he did not know the truth of the situation.

She glanced up to find Rafe's eyes on her, as if he could see every thought that was in her head, and beneath the table she felt him take her hand and rub his fingers against hers. He smiled, a smile that was all for her, and her heart glowed with the happiness that only he could light. She smiled back—and it was enough to get her through the rest of the breakfast, the conversations with the wedding guests and the string quartet renditions that her father had arranged for the celebrations.

* * *

By the time all was done and the hour had come for her to leave with Rafe, Marianne was aware of a new nervousness. Especially when her mother held her close, kissed her cheek and whispered a reminder that Marianne did not want to hear. Her father only looked into her face, and he nodded, as if everything had come right. Then he took her hand and kissed it, before giving it to Rafe.

'She is your wife now,' he said, and there was a catch of emotion in his voice. 'Look after her.'

She felt the slight underlying tension in Rafe directed at her father, but as his fingers closed around hers, he showed nothing of it.

He said not a word, only led her out to the waiting carriage and settled her inside before taking the opposite seat.

All of the wedding guests had assembled in the street to cheer them on their way. Her mother and father stood on the steps to the town house, smiling and proud. Behind them, leaning against the frame of the opened front door, stood her brother, his eyes dark and angry, his expression sullen. When she turned away, she heard the shadow of the past whisper in her ear.

Ahead lay the night, and a fresh breath of fear breathed upon Marianne.

Rafe could sense Marianne's nervousness and knew it must be difficult for her to return as his wife to a house where once she had been his captive. The clock ticked loudly in the silence of his drawing room.

'An eventful day for your birthday,' he said.

'Yes.'

The silence stretched between them.

'The day has been long, Marianne,' he said. 'We should retire for the night.' He wanted to make her his wife in truth, to make love to her.

She did not meet his gaze, just kept her eyes trained on the tea cup before her.

'I have not finished my tea,' she said and took another sip from the delicate bone-china cup. She had been so long in the drinking of it that any tea remaining in the cup must be stone cold by now.

'Then bring it with you.'

She glanced up at him, a shocked expression on her face.

'This is your home now, Marianne. There are no servants save for Callerton. We do not stand on ceremony. You are mistress here and may do as you please.'

A small shy smile fluttered briefly to her mouth, then it was gone again and she was gripping so tightly to the cup's handle that her knuckles shone white.

'Come,' he said, holding out his hand to her.

She set the cup down upon its saucer with very careful precision, keeping her eyes steadfast upon it. He saw the deep breath she took before rising to her feet with the air of a woman going to her execution. Her gaze moved to his hand and she hesitated before reaching out and placing her fingers within it. The room was warm, a fire blazing in the hearth to drive away the autumnal chill, yet her skin felt like ice to the touch. And still she would not look at him. He pulled her gently into his arms; her whole body was rigid, tense, chilled.

'Marianne,' he said gently.

She swallowed and stood stock still. He could feel her nervousness as if it were a living breathing thing in the room between them. He touched the point of her chin and tipped her head up so that she could no longer hide her face from him. In her eyes, before she masked it, he thought he saw the ghost of fear.

'There is no need to be nervous. We will do nothing that you do not wish,' he assured her gently. 'I promise you.'

She looked at him then and reached up to stroke her hand to his cheek, cradling it with such tenderness. 'You are a good man, Rafe Knight.' Her touch was light and loving and tender.

'I am many things, Marianne, but good is not one of them.' There was a five-thousand-guinea price on his head. He had abducted her at gunpoint and sworn to destroy her father. They both knew the truth of what he was.

'Whatever you say, you have been good to me.'

She moved her hand and the new gold wedding band glinted in the firelight. He captured her fingers and touched them to his lips, kissing the ring he had placed there earlier, and felt a possessiveness surge through him. She was his wife, he thought, his woman. And he kissed the skin of her slender fingers. Trailed his kisses over the back of her hand and round to the tender white skin on the inside of her wrist where he flicked his tongue to taste her.

He heard the small breathy gasp she released and felt her body soften its resistance as she leaned into him, splaying her other hand flat against the lapel of the same black tailcoat in which he had married her.

'Marianne,' he whispered and took her mouth with his, kissing her gently, wooing her with his lips, tempting her with his tongue. She was so sweet and innocent, opening to him, her nervousness melting away as the passion that had always been within her kindled and ignited. He felt the blossoming of her need as keenly as he felt his own. He scooped her up into his arms and carried her upstairs to his bedchamber.

The house was in complete silence. Callerton had left them in privacy for their wedding night.

He kicked the door shut behind him and set her down on the Turkey rug without releasing her from the circle of his arms. The room was warm. A fire still burned on the hearth, the coals glowing orange and red. She glanced over at the bed and again he felt that stiffening of her body.

'Rafe...' she whispered and there was such dread in her eyes that it shocked him. 'I...' She bit at her lip.

'There is nothing to be afraid of, Marianne. What happens between us will be pleasurable for us both. And I meant what I said: you need do nothing you do not want.'

She only smiled at him in grateful relief. But when he touched his hand to the buttons of her dress she shrank back.

'Marianne?'

She backed away further, increasing the distance between them. 'I...cannot...' Her eyes were wide and sparkling with tears as they flicked between him and the bed.

He stared at the panic escalating in her.

'Marianne.' He spoke the word as softly as he would to a skittish mare; stood stock still, keeping his hands low and open, as if he would soothe her, calm her. 'We do not have to do this tonight. If you wish to wait...'

'Yes,' she said as a drowning woman might clutch at a lifesaving hand. 'But we are supposed to...'

'No one need know, Marianne. Only you and I.' His gaze held hers.

She bit at her lip. 'You would not force me?'

'Of course not. I would never force you.'

'Even if it is your right as my husband?'

'It is never a man's right to force a woman, Marianne. No matter what you may have been told.'

She dropped her gaze.

'I shall not bed you, Marianne, until you ask me—maybe not even until you beg me. I give you my word.'

Her gaze came back to meet his. And the raw emotions in her eyes—relief and gratitude and love—reached right through his chest to touch his heart. He held out a hand to her. She hesitated only a moment and then placed her own in his. He closed his fingers around hers and felt the tension in her relax. She slipped her arms around him and buried her face in his chest, pressing her lips to his breast bone through the cotton of his shirt.

'Thank you,' she whispered.

He dropped a kiss to the top of her hair, then released her. 'I will leave you to change into your nightclothes. A man and woman might share a bed to sleep and nothing more. When I return, that is what we will do.'

They looked at one another and he could see the guilt in her eyes.

'I am sorry, Rafe.'

'You have nothing to be sorry for, Marianne.'

She closed her eyes as if she could not bear to hear the words.

He kissed her forehead and walked away, wondering just why the hell his wife was so afraid of the marriage bed. But he knew this was a matter of delicacy and could not be rushed. He needed to be patient and teach her gently of how it could be between them.

* * *

Marianne did not look. She kept her eyes fixed firmly on the wall while Rafe stripped off his clothing, her body tensing with the prospect of him climbing in next to her. But when she finally felt the bed dip and her heart thunder so hard that she thought it would leap from her chest, he did nothing more than kiss her eyebrow and bid her goodnight. They lay side by side, not touching. And yet they did not need to touch, for she could feel his warmth thawing her fear steadily with every hour that slipped by. She listened to the sound of his breathing. And when he slept she rolled on to her side and studied his profile in the candlelight.

In sleep he looked younger and the severity was gone. He was so handsome: those dark brows sitting low over his eyes, the strong masculine nose, the full firm lips and the line of his jaw. He was so strong, so irascible. He had no fear and could stand undaunted by the world. Yet his words from the warehouse whispered through her head. *We all have our fears, Marianne.* She could not imagine that he had ever felt afraid or powerless or small. Nothing frightened him. He was the one from whom others fled.

There was definitely darkness in him, and danger. And yet she had never known a man of such integrity. A man who did what he believed was right without a damn for the rules. A good man. The man that she loved. She did not understand why, when all of these things were true, she could not give herself to him. She feared that it might always be this way—she feared that Rotherham had ruined her for ever.

She woke in a dapple of autumn sunlight. For a moment she thought she was in her own bed in Leicester

Square, but then she remembered: her wedding and her new home in Craven Street. In her line of view she could see that the curtains framing the window were a deep dark blue, not pale-pink chintz. And the faint scent of sandalwood in the air made her shiver in a response over which she had no control. She was tired from too many hours spent awake, but the fear that had gripped her so intensely last night had gone this morning.

She heard the sound of toothbrushing from across the room and shifted her eyes, but nothing else, to the sound. Rafe was standing with his back to her at the wash cabinet. He was not wearing the breeches he had worn all night, only a towel tied around him so that from the waist up he was naked. Marianne felt her mouth go dry.

She knew that she should avert her eyes, but she found she could not tear them from him. Wearing his clothes he looked tall and strong and athletic, but without them he was…magnificent. Like one of the marbles in a book of the classics. She could see every line of muscle that rippled beneath the skin of his back and shoulders and upper arms as he moved. He was a pale-golden colour and damp with water droplets that glittered in the sunlight. His hair was dark with water and slick against his scalp and over the nape of his neck. She felt the breath catch in her throat and her nipples grow taut and more sensitive as she looked at him. Yet still she could not look away. Her eyes traced the breadth of his shoulders and the way his body narrowed at his waist and hips and she wondered what it would be like to trace her fingers down the length of his spine. Her heart began to beat faster.

He spat the toothpowder into the basin and rinsed his mouth with water from the glass. When he turned round it was too late to shift her gaze and pretend she was still sleeping.

'Good morning, Mrs Knight,' he said in his velvet voice.

His eyes were the colour of clear orange-blossom honey in the sunlight. The shadow of beard stubble had been scraped from his face and when he smiled at her, her heart skipped a beat and she felt pure unadulterated desire flash through her body.

'Good morning.' Her words sounded strangely husky. She didn't dare glance down to the towel wrapped around him like the kilt of a Scottish highlander, or stare at the sprinkle of dark hair across his naked chest. The blush burned on her cheeks.

'I have almost finished. Then I will bring you warm water and cook you breakfast.' He turned away and pulled on clean drawers beneath the towel while he spoke.

'Ham and eggs. And coffee. Or would you prefer hot chocolate?' The towel dropped away and she could see a hint of the firmness of his buttocks through the linen of his drawers before he pulled up a pair of dark pantaloons to cover them.

'Coffee would be very nice, thank you.' It came out high enough to be almost a squeak and the heat in her face intensified.

Rafe reached for a clean ironed shirt and turned to her once more before pulling it on over his head. She caught a glimpse of a flat abdomen ribbed with muscle and a line of dark hair that led into his breeches before the fine white cotton slid down to cover it and she felt the slither of desire low in her belly.

Oh, my! It was all she could do not to speak the words aloud.

'Callerton will not return until this afternoon. He wanted to give us some privacy.' He smiled again, but she felt guilty, knowing what Callerton thought they would have been doing last night. What they should have been doing. What she wanted to do...but could not.

He sat down in the easy chair by the fireplace. 'We need to hire some servants. I thought you might wish to take charge of that...as you are now mistress here.' And when he stood up he was wearing stockings and shoes.

'I...' She was not sure she knew how to do such a thing. At home her family allowed her to do nothing.

'Or Callerton could do it, if you prefer.' He fixed the collar of his shirt.

'I will do it.' She wanted to do something for him. If she could not fulfil her wifely duties in the bedroom, she would at least undertake them everywhere else.

He looked into the peering glass as he tied his cravat in place.

'How do you wish me to run the house?'

His eyes met hers in the glass. 'However you see fit.'

She watched in continued fascination as he donned his waistcoat and tailcoat, and when he came to stand by the bed again he was fully dressed. 'If you wish to discuss anything of it, Marianne, then we will discuss it.'

And she had the feeling that it was not only the housekeeping of which he was speaking.

She nodded.

He turned and went to fetch her water.

* * *

They breakfasted together in the dining room. Unlike when she had been here as his captive, she ate all that was on her plate, but there was a new awkwardness between them that had not been present before.

He took her with him on his morning ride over the Wenlock Barn fields, saddling up one of his horses for her. The hour was still early, the fields quiet save for a few other horsemen. They walked their horses for a while, breathing in the nip of morning air, fresh and invigorating and filled with the scent of autumn—dampness and brambles and dew-laden grass. The sky was white-grey, but the light bright. The russet leaves of the surrounding trees whispered even though there was no breeze. The quietness of a day just awakening. The calm that had been his respite on all of the days in the past months, the chance to breathe between playing the parts of the rake he was not and the highwayman he had forced himself to be. He glanced across at Marianne. She filled her lungs with the air and put her face up to the sky. He could see the pleasure in her eyes.

'It is wonderful,' she sighed.

'Do you see that great oak tree over there by the barn?' He gestured to the distance.

She nodded.

'I'll wager you a kiss that you cannot reach it before me.'

'We cannot race! What would everyone say?' But her eyes sparkled and her face shone with excitement.

'Do you care so very badly what everyone says?'

Marianne considered it for a moment. 'No, I suppose I do not.' She gave a laugh, as if the realisation astonished her, and then she spurred her horse and took off for the oak tree.

He laughed, too, to see such gladness, then galloped after her.

She was a good horsewoman and it was a race in earnest to the end. Afterwards they walked their horses to cool them and chattered and laughed some more. Only as more horsemen began to appear on the grounds did they leave and head home.

At the stables they dismounted and saw to their horses, removing saddles and tack and brushing them down. For a woman who had never done such things she learned quickly and with a relish that surprised him. Her fingers were quick and deft with the buckles and she was strong for her size. She dealt with all the low parts. He dealt with all the high parts. They were the perfect team.

'You are looking very happy for a woman who did not win the race,' he said, looking at the roses in her cheeks and the sparkle in her eyes and the windswept curls that had escaped from her pins to dangle enticingly around her face.

'I am feeling very happy.'

He laughed at that. 'I admit that you would have won were I not riding the stronger horse and were you not riding side-saddle.'

She smiled even more at that. 'Do you really think so?'

'I know so,' he said. And then they were looking intently at one another and sensual awareness rippled between them. All was quiet. They could hear the murmur of distant carriages and the cries of delivery men and hawkers, and, in the stable stalls, the soft whicker of a horse.

He reached over and lifted a stray curl from her cheek, tucking it behind her ear.

'And now I suppose you wish to claim your kiss,' she said quietly.

'I was under the impression that you liked my kisses.'

'I do.'

Her eyes held his.

He made no move.

'But someone might see us,' she said and knew she was just making excuses.

'There is no one to see us, Marianne. As I told you yesterday, Callerton will not return until much later and you know there are no other servants.'

The tension stretched tighter between them.

'Rafe,' she whispered, stepping closer and reaching her face up to his. When their lips touched, he took her in his arms and kissed her, fully, properly, as he had wanted to kiss her last night. He made love to her with his mouth, teasing her, nibbling her, tonguing her, until she was clinging to him, until she was kissing him hard, with passion, with want and desire.

'Rafe,' she said again, gently nipping his lower lip with her teeth.

He pulled the pins from her hat, removing it and setting it aside, before starting on her hair. Plucking the pins from it, mussing it, threading his fingers through the long silken waves, wrapping it around his fist, angling her head to kiss her neck and lick at the tender spot where her blood pulsed as strong and fast and hard as his. He sucked her, tasted her, grazed her. And the passion that flared between them was not gentle, but raged hot and urgent and dark with desire. She arched against him and he felt the press of her body, the tease of her thighs. He was hard for her, his shaft straining as if it would burst through his breeches.

He slid his hand down to cover her breast and it seemed he could feel the hard nub of its peak even through the thickness of her deep-red riding habit, through the layers of her underwear that separated their skin.

She moaned as his fingers closed over her breast, massaging her there—and it was a sound of relief and of growing need. Her hands slipped beneath his coat, moving over his stomach, against his chest, over his throat, his jaw, pulling the ribbon from his queue.

He released her hair, stroked his hand down to find her other breast, teasing its bud through the layers of her clothes before sliding both hands to her hips. She groaned her dismay when he left her breasts, pressing herself closer to him as if she wanted him to touch her there again. But his hand stroked over her buttocks before lifting her up and perching her on the edge of the wooden tack table.

Her legs opened naturally and he stood within them feeling the graze of her riding boots against the outer edges of his calves. He kissed her harder, finding her breasts once more, closing his hands over them, flicking his thumbs against their peaks until her breathing was hard and her eyes were a dark-midnight black. He nudged her legs wider and pressed himself to her.

She gave a small breathy gasp and stilled before pulling back from his kiss.

'Marianne,' he said, never shifting his gaze from hers, his voice a whisper and husky with need. 'I gave you my word. I will not break it.'

'But…' She glanced down to where their bodies touched.

'We are fully clothed,' he said. 'And it will stay that way.'

Her eyes met his once more.

'Trust me,' he whispered.

She stared into his eyes as if peering into his very soul. 'Yes,' she said.

And he lowered his mouth to hers and began to kiss her all over again, kissing her until he felt the tension ease from her body, kissing her until she was pulling him to her and his hands were on her breasts, teasing and playing. Then he wrapped his arms around her and bowed her, arching her back to mouth at her breasts as he had done on the night of her birthday ball.

He longed to unfasten the thick high-necked riding habit, to peel it from her body. He knew how soft her skin was, had tasted a flavour of what her breasts would be like to suckle.

'Yes,' she whispered again, clutching his head tighter to her.

He slid a hand to her hip, then lower, stroking against the wool of her skirt, caressing her thigh, feeling the heat grow in it, sliding his fingers round to stroke the inner edge while his teeth scraped through her bodice to excite her nipples. And when his hand finally touched her core, finding it, feeling it, through all of the layers of clothes, she jerked and gasped, and he raised his eyes to look into hers, watching her as his fingers set up a rhythm between her thighs. Watching her until her breathing became louder and more ragged, until he felt her slight movement against his hand. Then his mouth closed over her breast and he bit her very gently: first one nipple, then the other. She let her head drop back, moaning aloud, glorious gasps and groans of utter pleasure, as she found her orgasm. And it did not matter that he was hard and straining like a green boy. He took her in his arms and he kissed her mouth and her eyelids and the tip of her nose. And he held her close until the frenzied thump of her heart calmed.

And when the daze had gone from her eyes she looked at him and whispered, 'I don't understand what just happened. What was it?'

'It was the beginning, Marianne,' he said and took her hand in his to lead her from the stables and into the house. And that night when they went to bed he held her in his arms, just held her.

Chapter Eleven

Callerton sought him out the next day. Rafe left Marianne writing letters at the little desk in the drawing room while he spoke with his friend.

'Misbourne was out on the town celebrating last night,' Callerton said. 'Bought everyone in White's a glass of champagne and announced to all of London that his daughter was married to Mr Rafe Knight.'

Rafe said nothing. He was related by law to Misbourne. And he was married to Marianne Winslow. It was both his nightmare and his fantasy.

'What happens now in the Misbourne stakes?' asked Callerton, a deliberate blank look in his eyes.

'I do not know. We have to let things settle for a while.'

He thought of Marianne and what it would do to her to learn what her father had done. To see him dragged through the courts; to watch her family fall apart; to watch her father's execution—and know that it was her husband that had brought them to it. He winced at the thought.

Callerton said nothing, but the look in his eyes was too knowing.

'I cannot turn back from this,' Rafe said. 'I owe it to my father. To my mother too. They deserve justice. What would it make me if I were to turn back now? After all these years. After all that it has taken to get this far. That it was acceptable for Misbourne to kill them?' *Or that he loved his wife?*

Callerton poured them both a brandy and they drank it in silence.

Marianne watched her husband undress and slip beneath the sheets beside her. It was the third night she would sleep next to him in his bed. She felt the brush of his fingers against hers as they lay side by side. She turned her head on the pillow and looked at him in the candlelight. At the man she so loved. At the man who was risking his life to be her husband—the man who held such hatred in his heart for her father.

He smiled and gave her hand a squeeze. Despite everything, she felt something inside her blossom.

'Does the light disturb you?' she asked, knowing that many people found it difficult to sleep in the candlelight. And the candles had burned all through the past two nights.

He shook his head.

There was a small comfortable silence before he asked, 'Have you always been afraid of the dark?'

'No.' He didn't ask the natural next question, but she answered it anyway. 'Only for the past few years. And I suppose it is not so much the darkness of which I am afraid, but more what it hides. In corners and cupboards. Under beds and…behind curtains.'

'Monsters,' he said as if he understood.

'Of the worst kind.' She felt a chill prickle through her at the mere thought.

'Like highwaymen,' he said softly, with the strangest look in his eyes.

She shook her head. 'There are worse things than highwaymen.'

'Are there?' he asked. His focus shifted to the distance as if he were thinking, or remembering, before switching back to her. 'Will you tell me what frightens you, Marianne?'

'You would not understand,' she said. 'You are so strong, so invincible. How can you understand fear when you have known none? Or understand what is like to feel utterly powerless, when you are so powerful? To be dangled at the mercy of another? To feel terror? You know none of these things.'

'I understand more than you realise, Marianne. I have known all that you name.'

She could not imagine it. He seemed utterly fearless. 'Yet you are not afraid now.'

He shook his head. 'I faced my fear. I embraced it.'

'What was it that you feared?' she whispered, knowing it must have been something truly terrible.

He paused for so long that she thought he was not going to tell her, then he said, 'Highwaymen.'

'I do not understand.'

'I feared highwaymen. The fear paralysed me. Terrorised me.'

She understood how that felt.

'But you became a highwayman yourself.'

'Yes.'

'You robbed and you stole.'

'From six men only, Marianne. To conquer fear you must face it.'

She nodded.

'May I blow out the flame of one candle? There is still light enough from the remaining two.'

'No,' she replied.

He did not argue or try to persuade her. He just squeezed her hand in reassurance.

'Blow them all out,' she said, her heart beating very fast, the fear sliding through her blood just at the thought.

'You don't have to do it all at once,' he said.

'I know,' she replied. 'But I want to.'

He did as she asked. It seemed the darkness was sudden and complete. She shuddered with the terror of it, and struggled to harness the fear running out of control. Her eyes were wide and staring, but all she saw was the inky blackness. Then Rafe pulled her to him and held her, and she felt the beat of his heart against hers and the strength of his arms encircling her. His breath was steady and calm. She did not count her breaths, only matched them to his. After a while the panic subsided and she grew calm, noticing for the first time that the blackness was no longer black. The curtains were not drawn and faint silver moonlight spilled into their bedchamber. She turned her head to look at it.

'What do you see in the darkness now?' he asked.

'I see moonlight and starlight.' She returned her face to his. 'And I see you.' And she touched her lips to his.

A ball at the town house of Lord and Lady Chilcotte. It would be their first public occasion as a married couple. Marianne smoothed down the silk skirt of her silver-gauzed white evening dress and tried to calm her nerves. There was bound to be gossip. Over the speed of their marriage following the abandoned wedding to Mr Pickering, over the seeming lack of a courtship. She just hoped that no one had heard the truth of what happened at her birthday ball. A knock sounded on the door of the bedchamber they shared. And then Rafe was standing there.

'I am ready,' she said.

'Not quite,' he replied and as he approached her she could see that he was holding a black-velvet box. He handed it to her.

'It is my wedding and birthday gift to you. I am sorry that it is late.'

She opened the box and there inside was a fine string of diamonds that sparkled in the candlelight, with a large single dark sapphire at the centre. It was the most exquisite necklace she had ever seen, beautiful enough to take her breath away.

'Starlight and moonlight…and darkness,' he said, taking the necklace from where it lay in the box and holding the sapphire up to the candlelight so she could see that the stone, which had appeared black, now glowed a deep rich blue. Their eyes met and she remembered lying safe and snug in his arms all through the night.

'Rafe…' she whispered. 'Thank you. It is beautiful.'

'Like you,' he said. 'I should have given it to you on the day of our wedding and your birthday.' He took the necklace from where it lay in the box and draped it around her neck. She felt the cold of the diamonds and the warmth of his fingers where they touched the nape of her neck to secure the catch of the necklace, and her skin tingled and a shiver rippled right through her body. His fingers seemed to stroke and tease and the sensation shimmered all the way down her spine. Her nipples prickled. Her stomach sucked in tight. Her breath caught in her throat at the heady intoxicating sensations tingling through her. She could not move, just stood there transfixed by the depth of desire that the lightest brush of his fingers created.

She looked at herself in the peering glass and did not recognise the dark-eyed woman that looked back at her. Her cheeks were flushed pink. Her lips looked full and ached to be kissed. And her eyes glittered dark with such undisguised passion that even Marianne recognised it. She looked so different from the timid, nervous girl that was Marianne Winslow. The woman reflected in the mirror was beautiful, just as he had said, and confident and unafraid, just as she had always longed to be. And the tall, dark, handsome man standing behind her was looking at her with desire.

She lifted her hand to adjust the necklace, but Rafe was there first. She felt the heaviness of the stone shift to lie just above the cleavage of her bust. His fingers adjusted the sapphire so that it lay perfectly central, but the feel of his touch so close to her breasts, however transient, made her nipples tighten for him. In the peering glass it looked almost as if he were touching her there, and God help her but she wanted him to. Wanted it so much that it shocked her. But Rafe did not shift his fingers from the sapphire or his eyes from their joint reflection in the glass.

Yes, she wanted to say. *Please*, she wanted to beg. She had to bite her lip to prevent herself. His eyes had darkened to an intense smoulder. She willed him to touch her, willed it with all her might, never taking her eyes from his.

His fingers slid infinitesimally lower.

Her breath was as ragged as if she had been running. He must have felt the frenzied rise and fall of her chest beneath his fingers, but she did not care.

He moved lower still so that he was touching the tops of her breasts pressed full against the low neckline of the dress.

Her throat was dry with anticipation. She swallowed and wetted her lips. She wanted to groan. She wanted to reach her hand round to his and clasp his fingers tight to her breast, wanted them to slide beneath her bodice.

He traced a delicate teasing pattern over the upper globe of her breast, toying with her as he felt the hard fast thump of her heart and the need that quivered right through her body, yet his every move was light and sensuous and slow.

Yes, she wanted to scream.

He traced all the way across her other breast and back before dipping his finger into her cleavage. The sensation was so exquisite that she could not prevent the little breathy sigh escaping her. She watched his eyes darken at the sound. His hand slid over her dress to cover the whole of her breast. She gasped again and could not help herself from arching against him, driving herself all the harder into his hand. He moved his other hand so that both were cupping her breasts as he pulled her back flush against his chest and she could feel his warmth against the length of her. She watched their reflection in the peering glass—watched his hands moving over her breasts with a possession that felt so right. Her breasts were so sensitive that, where his fingers stroked and massaged, it was as if his touch passed through the layers of her clothing to brand her naked skin—just as it had done in the stables. And she remembered what he had done with his mouth, with his teeth…with his hand, and her breath shook with anticipation.

His eyes looked as black and glittering as her own. He was as racked with this strange tension as she, a tension that hummed so loud the whole room seemed to vibrate with it. She should have been embarrassed to watch herself behaving so wantonly, but she felt nothing of that emotion, only impatient desire. His touch was a taste of heaven, and her breasts ached for release from the tight strictures of her corset. She arched again, driving herself into his hands, wanting to feel him all the more. And in response the fingers of one hand rubbed gently against the hard nub of her nipple while the other unfastened the upper buttons of her dress. She felt nothing of fear, only of relief that he was doing what she so desperately wanted. And impatience and a thrilling urgency.

The bodice gaped, but did not fall. She watched and could not look away, holding her breath with anticipation. A flash of white skin that strained for release from its imprisonment within the corset.

'Please, Rafe…' she gasped, unable to prevent it.

'Do you want me to stop?' the man in the peering glass asked, his voice thick with desire and need.

'No,' she said and her whisper was husky and breathless. 'Don't stop.'

His eyes never left hers in their reflection, watching her as he inched her bodice lower with agonising slowness. Teasing her with such sweet torture until at last her corset was revealed in full. Against the top of it the pale swell of her breasts was taut and longing for his touch. But he did not touch her. His left hand rested lightly against her stomach.

She reached her arms up so that her pale-pink nip-

ples peeped over the edge of her bodice, needing them
to be free, and higher still until they erupted over the
edge of the corset and its underlying shift. She stared
at the woman in the glass—a different woman from
the one Marianne had always believed herself to be.

'Tell me what you want me to do,' he murmured,
his voice deep and gravelly beside her ear, his breath
tickling the skin of her neck. She angled her head to
allow him greater access and where his breath had
scalded he traced a small trail of kisses. 'I am under
your control.'

She was trembling with need for him.

'Tell me, Marianne,' he repeated between kisses.
'Say the words.'

Her head felt dizzy with the force of the desire
surging through her body. Her breath was ragged and
strained, her breasts almost fully exposed, and all the
while the sapphire burned like a blue fire against the
pallor of her skin.

'I want you to touch me,' she whispered.

In the peering glass Rafe's gaze was dark and intense, simmering with something she did not understand. He moved his right hand so that it hovered over
her right breast, so close that the skin tingled and
seemed to burn, so close that it looked as if his hand
was already clutching her breast in the glass.

She held her breath and trembled with the strain of
the wanting and waiting. And still his eyes held hers,
unyielding, unrelenting, binding her to him in this
madness that held them both. She swallowed. 'Touch
me, Rafe.'

His hand edged closer so that she could feel the
very tip of her nipple brush against his palm. 'Here?'

'Yes,' she said.

And at last he closed the space and at last her naked breast was within his hand. She sighed her relief, feeling the ecstasy of his touch, feeling the magic of his fingers weaving a sensual pattern against her sensitised globe, feeling them pluck and tease the tight bud.

And when his other hand captured her left breast and played the same teasing pattern upon it she felt she was melting against him in a rich heady sensation of pleasure and need. This man who was her husband, this man whom she loved.

'Rafe,' she whispered, watching in the glass as her hands closed over his, pulling him to her, wanting him never to stop. She was trembling with the force of the need throbbing through her. She moaned and her legs began to crumple.

His arm fastened around her waist, holding her upright as he turned her in his arms. The passion in his eyes when he looked at her razed all else in its path.

'Marianne,' he said, his breath as ragged as hers. And then their lips found each other, and what exploded between them was so much more than a kiss. It was filled with need and heat and passion, while at the same time exposing something vulnerable and intimate that only two lovers could share. And then he pulled back to look into her face.

She felt dazed, unable to think straight, like there was no one else in the world but them, no world at all beyond this room. She wanted the moment to last for ever. 'Why have you stopped?'

He smiled and touched his thumb to her lips. 'So that we might finish the rest of it later.'

'Later?' She blinked, unable to think about anything

other than wanting his lips on her breasts and his hand between her legs.

'I will be yours to command,' he whispered against her neck. And then he helped her dress again and, wrapping the deep-blue cloak around her, he took her hand in his and led her down to the waiting carriage.

At the entrance to Lady Chilcotte's dining room, lit by the light of a thousand candles within the two massive crystal-tiered chandeliers, Marianne felt the sudden stiffening of Rafe by her side. She followed the line of his gaze and saw her father across the room, standing by the French windows. Despite the open windows the room was overly warm and airless. The whole of the *ton* seemed to be present and she knew that they were watching both Rafe and herself. She heard the whispers and saw the stares and speculation, reminding her of why she had not wished to come here tonight. Her grip upon Rafe's arm tightened ever so slightly. He must have felt it, for he slid a surreptitious thumb over her hand and his eyes met hers.

'I had Callerton start the rumour it was a love match,' he murmured for her ears only.

A love match. She looked up into the amber eyes of the man who did everything to defend her from the world. A man from whom even the toughest of criminals ran, a man who was much more fierce and powerful than anyone in this room could guess. Yet with her he had been only gentle. For Marianne this really was a love match. She wanted to tell him, but knew she could not. There were so many reasons why. What they had together, this strange connection, the overwhelming attraction—none of it could last. And were he to discover the truth…

'Thank you,' she whispered, her voice thick with emotion.

His hand closed over hers, so warm and reassuring, and she felt his strength filling her.

They shared a smile and she felt safe and confident and happy.

And then together they stepped into the Lady Chilcotte's dining room to face the whole of London's *ton*.

Rafe watched Marianne speaking to Lady Fothergill across the room as Devlin pressed a glass of champagne into his hand. He wanted the evening to be over. He wanted to be alone with Marianne. He wanted to pleasure her a thousand times over, to touch her, to taste her as she lay naked beneath him. He wanted to hear her cry out his name as she came again and again, all through the night. He wanted to slide into her body, to love her, to ride together and spill his seed as she climaxed. He wanted to consummate his marriage. But he knew he must not rush this. In his own single-minded selfish pursuit of Misbourne he had not considered how frightened Marianne must have been when he abducted her. He had taken away her power, her control, her freedom, subjected her to his will through his own greater might. Now he would give her all of that and more. If and when they consummated their marriage was her decision. And for every night, every hour, every minute of his torture, he had only himself to blame.

'Congratulations, old boy—or should I say commiserations? You have been well and truly caught in parson's mousetrap. Now I know why you were asking those questions over Misbourne's banking details.' Devlin tapped a finger on the side of his nose. 'Strictly hush-hush, of course.' Devlin swigged half of his champagne down in one gulp. 'Thought you would have waited for the answer before taking the plunge from bachelorhood.'

'The matter was too pressing to wait.' Rafe did not move his gaze from Marianne. The diamond chips sparkled around her neck. His eyes dropped lower to the sapphire that glinted dark against the smooth pale curve of her breasts.

'Judging by the way you are looking at her, I think I can imagine just how pressing.' Devlin smirked.

Rafe did not smile. Devlin had no idea of his feelings for Marianne, or of just how desperate his body was with the need for her. He turned his mind to other matters, shifting his gaze to meet Devlin's, and took a sip of champagne from the glass in his hand. 'So, were you able to access Misbourne's details?'

'No problem,' said Devlin. 'When one's father owns the bank, no one asks too many questions. Kept it quiet from the old man, of course.'

'Of course.' Rafe gave a small cold smile.

'You struck gold, quite literally, with Marianne Winslow, you sly dog,' said Devlin. 'Misbourne's loaded and no mistake. He has a substantial quantity of bullion. And his safety deposit box was full of jewellery, mainly diamonds and rubies, one of the stones the size of an egg. Plenty of investments. A broad spread of stocks and shares, ownership documents for coal mines in the north and tobacco plantations in the West Indies. He also has a whole pile of bonds worth over a hundred grand, and the deeds for several properties around the country.'

'Any gaming debts? Any vowels or secret letters?' Rafe asked nonchalantly and took a sip of his champagne.

'Nothing like that, you'll be glad to know,' said Devlin.

Rafe smiled at just how wrong Devlin was with that remark.

'Didn't think you cared much for Misbourne—or Linwood, for that matter.'

'I don't,' replied Rafe coolly.

Devlin raised an eyebrow. 'You're a cold-hearted bastard when you want something, Knight.'

Rafe smiled.

'Don't underestimate old Misbourne. He used to run with m'father when he was young.' Devlin threw him a significant look. 'I've heard some wild stories—of women and gaming tables. Doesn't gamble any more, but still likes the women. Got a temper on him like the devil himself. Not a man you should cross…especially over his daughter. So have a care and be discreet if you mean to dally.'

'I have no intention of dallying,' said Rafe. His eyes shifted to Marianne again. She seemed to sense his gaze and glanced round to meet it, holding his eyes for a few seconds across the floor and then looking away with a telling blush.

Devlin looked from Rafe to Marianne and back again. 'Good God, it's true what they're saying.' Rafe could feel the weight of Devlin's shocked stare on him. 'I thought it was about the money, but it isn't, is it? You *do* want her.'

'Oh, I want her, all right,' said Rafe, and set his barely touched champagne on the tray of a passing footman. 'Thank you, Devlin.' He made his way across the room towards his wife.

At supper Marianne had only picked at her lobster and pushed the creamed potatoes around her plate. The butterflies fluttering in her stomach had quelled her appetite. And when they did settle she just had to glance in Rafe's direction for them to start all over again. She had fielded Lady Routledge's questions over the speed and secrecy of her courtship with Rafe, kept up a steady and polite conversation with Mr Dobson seated on her right, and felt her cheeks warm and a secret pride in her heart at the many looks levelled between her and her husband. She glanced over at him and saw that he was making his way towards her and the spirals of excitement low in her belly danced and burned at the sight of him. And she thought of what would happen later between them, when they returned home.

Chapter Twelve

She was sitting on the edge of the easy chair by the fireplace, still wearing her white-and-silver ball gown when he entered their bedchamber. He walked to where she sat and placed the branch of candles on the mantelpiece.

She rose to her feet, her eyes scanning his face. And he could see the desire in them and the slight nervousness as she wetted her lips. He reached to her and touched the silver-blonde tendrils that dangled against her cheek.

'Is it later?' he asked.

'Yes,' she whispered.

'What do you want me to do, Marianne?'

'Kiss me,' she said.

So he stepped closer and, sliding his palm to cup her cheek, he looked into her eyes and kissed her, as gently as he had kissed her that very first time.

Her whole body seemed to give a sigh of relief. She came into his arms.

He slid the pins from her hair and kissed her until her lips were swollen and pink and moist. He kissed her until her eyes were black with passion and her breath was uneven and fast. He slid a caress over her shoulders, down the length of her spine, over her hips, against her stomach, but not once did he touch her breasts.

Her arms were wrapped around him, her hands splayed against his back, the pressure light at first, then harder as the desire began to pulse stronger through her body. He felt the glide of her hands over his hips, then up the front of his coat before they slid beneath the lapels. She hesitated for a moment, her hands resting lightly against his waistcoat.

'I am yours, Marianne,' he whispered against her ear, then grazed his teeth against the soft lobe before taking it into his mouth and flicking his tongue against it.

Her fingers slid within his waistcoat, palms against him, and her hands crept against his chest.

He touched her breasts then, feeling for her nipples through the layers of her clothing as she felt for his through the fine linen of his shirt, mirroring every press of her thumb, every slide of her fingers until she understood what he was doing.

She squeezed harder at his chest.

His hands closed more firmly around her breasts.

She scraped her nails against his nipples.

He licked along the delicate line of her jaw as his nails flicked against the silk of her bodice.

She opened his coat and pushed the lapels back as if she would wrench the coat from his shoulders.

'Take it off,' she whispered.

He released her long enough to do as she said, dropping the coat to the floor and never taking his eyes from her.

She watched him and he could see the pink flush

of excitement and desire in her cheeks, the sparkle in her black eyes and the rapid rise and fall of her breasts bound tight by the white-and-silver bodice.

'And your waistcoat too.'

He shrugged it off and saw her swallow. She bit at her lip, looked at him with both daring and hesitation. He kissed her again, a full rich kiss on her mouth. She hesitated no more, but pressed her mouth to his chest, kissing first one nipple, then the other, licking him through the thin linen of his shirt, scraping her teeth there. And when she was done she raised her mouth to his and kissed him. She broke the kiss to look into his face, searching his eyes for a moment before she stepped a little out of his arms and turned around, presenting him with her back. With one hand she swept up the curtain of silvery waves, holding them high, baring the nape of her neck, exposing the line of buttons that ran down the back of her dress.

He moved closer, let his breath stir the wisps of fine hair around the nape of her neck and saw the tiny shiver that rippled through her in response. Then he let his mouth follow his breath, touching his tongue to that tender skin. He felt her inhalation, watched as she dipped her head, allowing him great access to the sensitive spot. He teased his tongue there, kissed it.

'When you touch me there I can feel it right through me, all the way down to the soles of my feet,' she whispered.

He bit her lightly and she moaned in pleasure.

He kissed her neck, while his fingers traced slowly down the line of her spine until he found the first small silk button of her dress. Her head lolled to the side and he bit her again and slowly, one button at a time, began to unfasten the bodice of her dress. It gaped wide long before he reached the final button. He kissed her ear and then helped ease the dress down. She slid her arms free from the small puff sleeves, and in a soft rush of silk the dress landed around her ankles. She wore only one petticoat—plain white cotton. He stroked it from her until it lay on top of the silver-and-white silk.

Breathing in the scent of her, he pulled the tape of her corset loose from its securing bow. As his fingers began to unlace it his mouth traced kisses along one shoulder to the edge of her shift, then the other, kissing the soft white skin until the corset fell away to land on the floor with a thud.

He stilled his lips where they were, feeling her breath, feeling the rush of her blood. She stood very still, then she slowly turned and looked at him.

The white shift was plain and loose, covering her all the way down to mid-shin. But through its fineness he could see a hint of the flesh and shadow of her body.

He took her in his arms, kissing her mouth, their tongues entwining, dancing, mating. And while his lips made love to hers, he placed one hand flat against the small of her back, arching her body towards him, tightening the shift against her breast as he slid his hand over it.

She moaned against his mouth as his hand found first one breast, then the other, feeling them fully freed from the confines of her corset for the first time. He trailed the kisses over her chin, down the centre line of her neck by the side of the sapphire-and-diamond necklace, over her *décolletage*, to the edge of the shift. His mouth paused there while his eyes sought hers.

'Yes,' she said. 'Oh, yes.'

He moved against her breast, kissing all round the small mound, teeth scraping lightly through the linen, teasing round the nipple without touching it. She arched more, thrusting her breast to his mouth, her fingers winding in his hair, clutching him tighter. He touched his tongue to her nipple, feeling it bud hard against him. He licked it once and felt her heart leap beneath it. And then he closed his mouth over it, tasting it, suckling it, flicking his tongue again and again against the tip until he could see it pink and straining through the wet translucent linen.

Marianne could not think. She could only feel. And what she felt was Rafe and her need for him, and the wonder he was bestowing on her body. Her thighs were burning, the secret place between her legs slick and wet and filled with a strange dull ache.

He brought her upright again, one hand resting lightly against the small of her back, the other on her hip. His eyes were a rich dark mahogany in the candlelight; she stared into their depths, and touched her hand to his jawline, trailing her fingers along its edge, rubbing against the roughness of the faint shadow of beard stubble that had grown there since the morning. She felt the bob of Adam's apple as she touched it and could not help herself placing a kiss there, caressing it with the tip of her tongue before drawing back. Then her fingers touched the end of his cravat, touched the knot that was tied there and she remembered the warehouse: removing his neckcloth and cutting the sleeve from his shirt and all that had passed between them then and since.

I am yours, Marianne. The knowledge seeped through her like the soft streaming smoke of a candle extinguished in the darkness. She breathed it in, allowed it to permeate.

Her fingers struggled with the collar of his shirt;

he came to her assistance and the buttons opened. The lawn of his shirt was fine, soft, white. Through it she could see the darkness of the hair that grew across his chest. She laid her hand lightly against it, feeling the soft spring of hair and the hardness of the muscle beneath. And her eyes moved to his left arm, to the sleeve beneath which she knew the bullet had sloughed. Her gaze moved back to his.

'Take off your shirt,' she whispered.

He pulled it free of his breeches, peeled it off over his head and stood there before her. The candlelight flickered across the hard lines and muscle of his chest, his stomach, his shoulders and arms. She looked at the nakedness of his skin, at the size of him, at how very different his body was to hers, at the strength, the power, the potential. His arms were loose by his side, allowing her to do whatever she would.

I am yours.

Between the elbow and the shoulder of his left arm was a patch of pink puckered skin. When she looked at it her heart swelled to fill her chest and she felt the prickle of tears in her eyes. She leaned forwards and touched it with her lips, light as a feather, letting them rest there against the newly healed scar.

'I am yours, too, Rafe,' she said softly as she kissed the scar. Her hands slid slowly against the muscle of his chest, feeling the roughness of the hair and the warmth of his skin, feeling the beat of his heart.

And then she stood back. *She was his.* She stepped out of her shoes. Unfastened the tape of first one stocking to slide it from her foot, then the other. Her gaze met his and held it. She pulled the end of the bow in the ribbon that threaded through the neckline of her shift. The ribbon unfastened. She pulled the shift over her head, letting it fall to the floor, and stood there naked before him.

'Marianne,' he whispered, the same whisper of a highwayman a lifetime ago. His gaze moved over her. She could see the bulge in the front of his breeches, the way it strained against the material. She knew what he could do. But she trusted him.

He slipped off his shoes and stockings and came to stand immediately before her. She glanced down at their bare feet, at his and at hers, and stepped closer so that the tips of their toes were touching. And then she looked up at him.

'Kiss me,' she said.

He kissed her mouth until she was breathless, kissed her breasts until she was panting. And when he laid her on the bed she pulled him down with her so that their mouths shared and tasted and breathed as one, so that his lips were hot and hard, teasing and stroking against her nipples until she was gasping and pulling his hair, until her thighs gaped open to him.

'Take me,' she said, needing him, wanting him. Her body tensed with the knowledge of what lay ahead, the sharp penetrating pain, the invasion, yet even knowing it, she needed him; she wanted him and whatever it encompassed.

'Not yet,' he said, then she felt the touch of his hand on her, the slide of his fingers against her moisture. He stroked her, his mouth kissing hers, keeping time. She opened her eyes and looked up into his. He stilled, his hand resting against her woman's place as if he would shield it, protect it from all intrusion. And his gaze on hers was dark and smouldering with passion and desire.

'Take me,' she said again.

But he shook his head and he kissed her again, a deep rich, thrusting kiss that matched what was in his eyes. Then he began to stroke again between her legs, massaging that same part of her that he had touched in the stables. A magical steady rhythm that made her gasp with the pleasure that was building, that made her blood rush and her heart thud harder and faster, and her body strain and chase something she did not understand. She opened her legs wider, exposing her vulnerability to him. But his fingers worked that same rhythm that was so tuned to everything her body strove for, teased until her hips bucked up off the bed and she was gasping aloud for need of him and everything exploded in shards of light and colour and a pleasure so immense that it took over all of her mind and body and soul. She could do nothing other than tumble headlong into the surge of it, to give herself up to the roaring of it all around her, sweeping her up, taking her out of the bedchamber, taking her out of her herself to another place she did not know, overwhelming her with its ecstasy. Gasping for breath, clutching at Rafe, pulling him to her, kissing him as the furore ebbed, and the crashing waves gentled until, like a receding tide, they washed over her, rhythmically, leaving only the echo of the pleasure pulsing through her.

He blew out the candles and lay down by her side. He stroked the long mess of her hair from her face and he kissed her, then he settled her in his arms and pulled the covers over them. And they lay together in the darkness and she wondered at how much he had given her and taken nothing himself, wondered at how much she loved him, until at last, safe in his arms, she slept.

* * *

Rafe sat at his desk the next night, his cravat hanging loose around his neck, his collar unfastened, his waistcoat abandoned. The tumbler of brandy had barely been touched. He ignored the glass and continued to stare at the rows of neatly penned numbers in the books that lay on the dark polished wood before him. It did not make any sense, yet Bradley was right: the evidence was there in the figures before him. Had he not instructed the man to audit all of his affairs as part of the process of amending his will in favour of Marianne, the anomaly would never have been discovered.

Marianne. He thought of his wife in bed upstairs and wondered if she would be awake. And the memory of the passion between them the previous night stoked the desire in his blood. She was all that he wanted, all that he needed. She was the light in a lifetime of darkness, the cooling touch to the fire of his anger, the balm to his pain. But always in the background, even though he did not let himself confront it, lurked the shadow of Misbourne and the burden of duty. And Rafe knew he could not hide from it for ever.

A quiet knock sounded at the door and he knew it was her even before she entered.

Her feet were bare, her pale hair hanging long and unbound, soft as silk, and he wanted to wrap his hands in it, bury his face in it. Her nightdress was expensive, embroidered in white work, high-necked and loose, hiding what he knew lay beneath. She had a shawl wrapped around her shoulders, long and silken, the silver-threaded fringes swaying and glinting in the light of the candles from the branch she held in her hand.

He rose to his feet, coming out from behind the

desk. 'The hour is late,' he said. 'I thought you would be sleeping.'

She set the candles down on his desk and looked at him. 'I could not sleep. Not with you out on the streets of London alone at night.'

'You were worried about me,' he said quietly. The thought was so sweet that it made him smile.

'You have a five-thousand-guinea price on your head and my father and brother are sworn to kill you. Of course I was worried.'

He reached to her and, taking her hand, touched his lips to her knuckles. 'But you got my note saying I would be late?' He did not release her hand, just kept it within his own.

She nodded. 'Did you resolve matters with your man of business?'

'Not entirely.'

She glanced over at the ledgers lying open on the desk. 'Was there a problem?'

'It appears there is a discrepancy with the monies in my bank accounts.'

'You mean there is money missing?'

'Quite the opposite,' he said and the worry was back with him again. 'I was the recipient of an inheritance held in trust until I reached my majority. The initial sum was small, but I thought my income through the years came from its successful investment. Now I have discovered the investments were so poorly made that, had someone not been making regular payments into my accounts, I would have very little.'

'How strange,' she said. 'Wouldn't it be possible to check with the bank and find the identity of your mysterious benefactor?'

'Under normal circumstances, yes. But whoever is

behind this has taken great pains to hide their identity. My lawyer has tried every avenue available, but no name is forthcoming.'

'Perhaps it is some relative of yours who wishes to remain anonymous.'

'I have no relatives, Marianne. I am alone in the world.' And he thought of the man who had made it that way.

'Not any longer.' She smiled shyly.

His eyes traced her face, seeing nothing of Misbourne there before meeting her gaze. It was true she had the same dark eyes as her father, but whereas Misbourne's were soulless as the devil's, Marianne's were gentle and filled with passion. 'Not any longer,' he repeated. 'Now that I have you, Marianne.'

They looked at one another. And in the silence he heard the slow steady tick of the clock and the settling of the glowing embers from the hearth.

'Come to bed, Rafe,' she said and he felt the slight squeeze of her fingers around his.

He lifted the branch of candles from his desk and followed her up to their bedchamber.

And so the nights and the days passed. Marianne employed servants who worked with precision, seeing to his every need, and slowly the house began to change from a place where he slept and ate to a home once more. The floors were swept; the furnishings cleaned and tidied. Soon there was the clean sweet smell in the air of beeswax and lavender wood polish, and cut flowers in the vases, and her own sweet scent of violets. The paintwork on the door and windows was pristine. The brass of the door knocker was polished until it gleamed. The house began to take on a new life, a vibrancy that reminded him of his youth, before his parents had died. Callerton officially became his steward. Every day he watched Marianne's confidence grow and he did not think of Misbourne. And every night he loved her more.

'Not this room, or the adjoining bedchamber. Both are to remain untouched,' said Marianne.

The two maids, clutching their basket of dusters and cloths and polish, bobbed a curtsy each and hurried away.

Marianne stood in the silence of the yellow bedchamber alone and looked around.

The daylight shone in from the landing, exposing what she had only seen by candlelight or the daylight that had stolen through the cracks of the shutters. Since the last time she had been in this room the surfaces had been shrouded with holland covers. Her hand caught at the cream-linen sheet covering the dressing table and let it slither to the floor. The ivory-and-tortoiseshell hairbrush sat in three parts on the exposed mahogany surface of the dressing table, just as she had laid them after gathering them up from the floor. Rafe's mother's brush. She touched her fingers to it and was filled with a feeling of such fierce tenderness, that it took her breath away, and a sadness upon which she did not want to dwell. She could not hide for ever; *they* could not hide for ever. Her father stood between them, an unspoken barricade they could not cross.

She did not know what made her glance round at the doorway, for he made not one noise. But when she did, she saw that Rafe was leaning against the door frame watching her.

'I know it cannot be easy for you, Marianne. The

last time you were in this room, things were very different between us.'

'Very,' she said.

'It was…wrong of me to take you from your father, regardless that I would never have hurt you. I'm sorry that I frightened you.'

'Are you sorry that you took me?'

He looked at her. There was a pause before he answered. 'I have never lied to you, Marianne. I will not start now. So the answer is no. I am not sorry.'

'Even though my father refused to yield you the document?'

'That has nothing to do with it.'

She glanced round at him. 'It has everything to do with it!' she said, shocking herself with the anger in her voice.

'It was the reason I took you, Marianne. It is not the reason I am not sorry.' He paused. 'Nor the reason I made you my wife.'

'We both know why you made me your wife. To save me from ruin.' She wished so hard that it could have been for another reason, the same reason that she felt in every beat of her heart and every breath that filled her lungs.

'You know what is between us. You must know how I feel about you.'

Desire. Attraction. Not love. How could it ever be love considering what lay between Rafe and her father? Yet at his words she felt her heart somersault in her chest, felt it thump harder and a dizziness bubble through her blood.

'Must I?' she said, holding his gaze, willing him to say the words. The silence hummed loud and awkward. She turned away, glancing around the yellow bedchamber. 'It was your mother's room,' she said.

'Yes.'

'The shutters are still nailed closed.'

He said nothing.

'And those in the adjoining bedchamber too. Your father's?'

He nodded.

There was a pause, a quiet in which she could hear the sound of her own heart and, she fancied, his heart too.

'What happened to your parents, Rafe?'

The silence hissed in the room. At first she thought he would not answer, but then he said, 'They were killed—murdered in a robbery.'

'I am sorry for your loss.' She ached with compassion for him.

'The shutters were closed that night. I swore that they would remain so until the man responsible for their deaths was brought to justice.' His voice was calm, controlled, devoid of emotion.

'Justice,' she whispered. *Not vengeance.* An icy finger stole down her spine at the word. And she remembered his strange remark about his parents in her father's study on a night that seemed so long ago.

'Justice,' he said.

'When did they die?' She felt suddenly deeply uneasy.

'1795,' he replied.

'The mausoleum in the burying ground,' she said and saw again in her mind's eye the lettering chiselled into its stone lintel—EDMUND KNIGHT, 1795—only now realising its significance.

'That of my parents.'

There was a cold feeling in her chest, a deep seeping dread. '1795, Hounslow Heath. The document that was taken in exchange for your daughter.' She spoke the words of his ransom demand.

'I am surprised that he showed you.'

'He did not. It was my brother.' Her heart was pounding hard now and there was a sick feeling in her stomach. 'What happened to your parents is at the root of what is between you and my father, is it not?'

He said nothing, but she saw the flicker of tension in the muscle of his jaw and the slight darkening in his eyes.

'He is my father. You are my husband. Surely I have a right to know?'

'You have every right, Marianne. But he *is* your father. Do you think I have no care for you?'

The words were bittersweet, for she understood now why he did not want to tell her, why he had not told her at the start: because he knew she loved her father. 'You do not wish to hurt me.'

'No.'

But she had to know. And she was sure, no matter how much she loved him, that he was wrong about her father. 'My brother is searching through *The London Messenger* archive for all of that year, seeking anything to do with Hounslow Heath. What will he find, Rafe?'

'He will find that my parents were robbed and shot dead by a highwayman upon Hounslow Heath.'

'A highwayman,' she said. 'In the same place that you held up my father.'

His eyes never shifted from hers.

'The same place you took me from him.' And she remembered the words he had answered when she asked him what her father had ever done to him. 'When you said that my father took from you that which was most precious, you were not talking of the document, were you?'

'No,' he said softly.

'Are you saying that my father was the highwayman?' She could not keep the incredulity from her voice.

He gave a laugh that held nothing of happiness. 'As if Misbourne would dirty his hands.' He shook his head. 'No, Marianne. But your father was behind it. He was the one who paid for it to be done.'

'That is ridiculous! Why on earth would he do such a thing?' The thud of her heart was loud in the silence. His gaze was steady, everything about him so quiet and focused and controlled.

'He wanted the document, and he wanted my father dead. My mother just had the misfortune to be with him at the time.'

'You cannot know that.'

'Oh, but I can, Marianne.'

'How?'

He could see that she didn't believe him, that she still believed in her father over him. And part of him was glad of it and part of him railed against it. He didn't want to tell her, but he needed to. Needed to tell someone after all these years and she was the one, the only one.

'I was there that night,' he said and felt a strange kind of relief in saying the words aloud.

'You witnessed your parents' murder?' He could hear the horror in her voice.

He gave a nod.

'Your fear of highwaymen…' Realisation dawned on her face.

He glanced away to the shadows that edged the room, his face grim. 'I watched what he did to them and there was nothing I could do.'

'Fifteen years ago. You must have been a child at the time.'

'Ten years old. Old enough to understand.' He shook his head again and darkness of the past closed in upon him so that he could see again the nightmare playing out before his eyes. 'He took my mother's jewellery, my father's watch, his purse of money. I thought he would ride away and leave us safe. But he did not.'

He knew that she had come to stand before him, but he did not look up. 'He demanded the document from my father's pocket. But my father would not yield it.'

'Just as mine would not,' she whispered.

'Indeed,' he said. 'I heard him lie and say that he carried nothing. Even with the muzzle of the highwayman's pistol touched to his forehead.' It seemed he was back upon Hounslow Heath, watching the horror unfold before him, and his body felt that same overwhelming fear, that same rage, that same impotence. He could hear again his mother's screams, see the highwayman shoot her, feel the crack of the highwayman's fist against his face. 'When he was dead, the highwayman took the document from his pocket. There was blood on his fingers when he opened it out and showed it to me—my father's blood. I have never forgotten what he said: "These few words, whatever they say, are worth a grand and your pa's life."' He glanced at her with a small tight smile that belied all he was feeling. 'And he rode away and left me there.' He felt the grief raw and ragged as he had done on that day on the moor fifteen years ago and turned away so that she would not see his weakness.

She caught one of his hands, holding it between both of hers.

'I have made it my life's work to find that highwayman…and the man who set a bounty of a thousand pounds on my parents' lives. I traced every link in the chain, all five of them, Marianne, until I found him.' His gaze met hers. *Misbourne.* Her father's name whispered silently between them.

'My father would never sanction murder. Someone has misled you. Whoever gave his name lied.'

But Rafe knew what he had done to the men he had found. 'No, Marianne,' he said gently. 'No one lied… of that I can be certain.'

He saw the small shiver that ran over her. 'There must be some mistake.'

'There is no mistake.' Yet no matter what he said, no matter how much he told her, the denial was still there in her eyes.

'I know my father, Rafe, and he is far from perfect, but to kill an innocent man and woman…?' She shook her head. 'I cannot believe it of him. There is no way back from such a crime.'

'There is not,' he said quietly.

He saw the sudden comprehension in her eyes and the fear that followed in its wake. Justice and all that it implied loomed black as death over both of them. 'He is innocent, Rafe. He has to be.'

He felt his heart ache, for her pain and for his own. She came to him, wrapping her arms around him. Pressing her face to his chest, breathing him, holding him, her eyes shut tight. And they stood like that, entwined, with only the soft sound of their breath and the beat of their hearts, in defiance of the past, in spite of the future, and all it could bring. They stood there until she turned her face up to his…until she took his hand in hers and led him from the room.

Chapter Thirteen

Marianne led him to their own bedchamber, to their own bed. The daylight was only now beginning to fade, the sky darkening as the night breathed black upon it. She sat him down on the edge of the bed and stood between his legs. There were no words she could offer that would comfort him. Denial would not salve the pain and grief that drove him. Such a strong fearless man, yet he had feared as much as she. He had suffered. He suffered still. She felt his pain worse than any of her own. She stroked his hair, caressed his cheek, placed her lips upon his and kissed him with everything that she felt in her heart, as if by so doing she could draw his hurt into herself and carry it for him. She kissed him once more, then drew back and looked into his face.

'Let me comfort you as you comfort me. Let me pleasure you as you pleasure me. Let me make us forget, even if it is just for this moment, just for this night.'

'Marianne, I…' She saw the turmoil of emotion in his eyes.

'You need me…' she said, 'and I need you.' And she began to loosen his cravat. Together they peeled off their clothes until he stood there clad only in his black breeches. She looked at him, this big, strong, dauntless man. Invincible. A man like no other. Yet when she looked into his eyes she knew that she had spoken the truth: he needed her every bit as much as she needed him. She reached her fingers to rest lightly against the top of his breeches.

His eyes held hers.

'I want to see you,' she said.

He unbuttoned the fall. Drew them from his hips, easing them down his legs until he could step clear of them. Marianne had never seen the front of a man's underwear before; the white linen covered where his breeches had and reached almost to his knees.

'All of you,' she insisted quietly.

He unfastened the drawers, let them drop to his ankles, and stepped out of them.

She looked at him, at the whole magnificent nakedness of him, her gaze tracing down over his chest, over the hard ribbed stomach and abdomen, following the line of hair that led lower. Down the long muscular lengths of his legs, right down to his toes, then back to the part that made him a man. Masculinity and strength and power. He looked more than she had expected, overwhelmingly so. And beside him she could not fail to be aware of how much slighter she was compared to him, of how much weaker, how vulnerable... and how feminine. Yet when she looked at his body she felt something happening deep down low in her belly, felt a heat stirring through her blood. There was nothing of fear.

She was standing so close that she could smell the scent of his skin and see the pulse that beat at the side of his neck. She looked up into his eyes and saw only the man that she loved. Her hands slid up his chest, to his shoulders. She reached her mouth to his and kissed him. A soft, sweet kiss. Tasting him. Dipping into his mouth, teasing his tongue. Kissing him while his hands swept a glorious caress against the nakedness of her back. They kissed and then they lay down on the bed together. When he took her breasts in his hands, when his fingers worked their magic upon her nipples, she kissed him harder, more passionately before drawing back with a slight shake of her head.

'Not yet,' she said, just the way he had said to her. She wanted to share the wonder he had given her, wanted to make him forget the pain. This was not about her, only about the man who was her husband. 'May I touch you?'

He nodded and let his hands lie loose by his sides, giving her permission to do what she would.

She knelt over him, her knees straddling one of his thighs, and plucked the pins from her hair, uncoiling its length until it hung free over her shoulders the way she knew he liked it. She ran her fingers down its waves the way he always did, skimming her nipples, her belly, her hip, and saw his eyes darken as he watched. Then she reached out and touched the tips of her fingers lightly against his lips, letting him kiss them, letting him flick his tongue against them, but sliding them beyond his reach when he would have taken them into his mouth. Her fingers trailed over his stubble-roughened chin, before moving down his neck, his Adam's apple bobbing as she caressed it. Her fingers journeyed on, lingering over the small springy hairs on his chest, pressing down on the hard muscle beneath it. His chest was so different to hers—hard, muscular, flat. She laid her palms over it, felt the beat of his heart. She teased against his nipples, plucking them, rolling the tiny buds between her fingers. Everything she enjoyed, everything that made her blood rush and her heart race, everything that made her breathless. All of it, she would do to him, *for* him.

She lowered her mouth to his nipples and licked, working her tongue over the flat dark skin, and beneath her lips she felt his heart beat harder. She drew back so that she could look down into that most beloved face as he lay there. The man she loved. Slowly she traced her hand lower, feeling his stomach suck in, feeling his rapid inhalation of air. Her fingers caressed each hard band of muscle that lined his abdomen then she paused, feeling the warm steady beat of her heart, knowing how much he had done for her, how much she wanted him. Her hand slid closer to the centre.

'Marianne!' She heard his whispered warning. She hesitated, her gaze meeting his. His eyes looked black in the dusky light. He was breathing harder now, the pulse in his neck visibly throbbing, and she was surprised by how much she could affect him. She looked at him and then down to that part of him that was close to his belly. That part she had so feared. And then she slowly stroked her fingers against it.

He gasped and she felt the slight jerk of him beneath her fingers. But he did not move his hands, nor did he try to stop her.

Contrary to all that she had expected, his skin was silky smooth there—the only place on the entirety of his body that was so. But even beneath the silkiness she could feel the rigidity, the hardness, the strength. She slid her fingers down the length of him from the very tip all the way down to the root. He groaned, a low guttural sound of need that mirrored those she made when he touched her, mirroring what she felt for him.

She wrapped her hand around the girth of him.

'Marianne,' he gasped and beneath her hand he grew even harder and longer. *Such power wielded by the lightest touch*, she thought. She squeezed him gently and felt the way his whole body stretched and tensed, the muscles of his thigh rippling beneath her.

'A man's weapon,' she said softly, knowing how she had feared it.

'And his weakness,' said Rafe. Her eyes met his. Yet his hands remained by his sides, trusting her. 'You hold the power, Marianne.'

'Yes,' she said. Then she bent and placed a single kiss on the silky skin at the very tip of him.

He groaned and jerked again.

She rubbed her fingers along his length, trying to emulate the way he touched her. And then she stilled and wrapped her fingers around him again, showing that she had no intention of letting him go.

'Show me how,' she said.

His hand moved to cover hers and he showed her.

She watched him while her hand moved on him, watched him with eyes that were dark and burning with desire and felt all that was within herself rise to meet it. Watched him while he shifted his thigh to touch her womanhood, making her gasp and catch her breath—but she did not still her hand.

'Marianne.' It was a plea, a cry from the soul.

'Rafe,' she whispered, needing his body, needing his heart, and she laid her body over his even while her hand still slid upon him.

'Marianne,' he gasped and his arm came around her, freeing her hand from him and rolling her on to her side, so that their bodies were flush together. And he stared into her eyes as he pulsed against her belly and she felt his warm wetness between their skin.

'Marianne,' he said again, then took her mouth with his and kissed her as if his soul touched hers.

His fingers moved between her legs, slid to one single place and it was enough; she arched against him and felt her heart merge with his in utter ecstasy and joy. And when it eventually rolled away and left her in his arms he rose and she heard him pouring water into the basin. She watched him wring out the cloth. He washed her, gently, with tenderness, as if she were the most precious thing to him in the world, and then he washed himself. They lay down together in the darkness. And he held her as if he would never let her go.

She stood by the bedchamber window and watched the dawn break over the rooftops. From the bed behind her came the sound of Rafe's breathing, soft and even as he slept. As she stood there in the coolness of the new morning there was something on her mind, something of which she could not stop thinking and which made her clutch her shawl more tightly around her shoulders. Her father had the document Rafe sought. She had heard the admission from his own lips. And if he had the document, the question was how it had come into his possession. The unease whispered all around her. He would not murder. He would not kill an innocent man.

And then she thought of his promise to find the highwayman and how he would deal with him and shivered despite the warm wool of her shawl. She heard a slight noise and glanced round to find Rafe watching her.

'Marianne.' His voice was low and husky from sleep, his eyes warm and sensual. Her husband. Her love. She felt like she were standing in a sunbeam with him, but the clouds edged around the sky and soon the shadows would close in upon them. Time was running out on the small haven of happiness, like grains of sand running through a timer.

'I must visit my family today, Rafe.'

'I understand.'

'Do you?' she asked and turned fully to face him, her gaze scanning his.

He nodded.

She wanted to capture this moment in time and preserve it. She wanted to still the clocks and remain here for ever, but she knew she must face the world.

He peeled back the edge of the bedcovers. 'Come back to bed, Marianne. The hour is early enough yet.'

She smiled, but there was a lump of sadness in her throat. She went to the warmth and protection of his arms.

'I have missed you,' her father said and kissed her cheek. He looked well, more than well; he looked like a man from whom the weight of the world had been lifted. 'But it is good that you are married.' He smiled and chucked her beneath the chin as if she were still his little girl. And when she looked up into his eyes, eyes that were so like her own, she thought of what had happened on Hounslow Heath on a night fifteen years ago.

'How do you find married life?' her mother asked.

'I am very happy,' she said.

Her mother leaned closer and lowered her voice slightly. 'You did as I said?'

Marianne felt her face flush warm. 'Mama, that is hardly a topic fit for the drawing room,' she said with a calmness that belied her embarrassment and anger.

Her mother looked unabashed. 'We have been anxious about you.'

'You have no need to be,' said Marianne.

'Then I am relieved,' said her mother and peered more closely at her. 'You look different,' she said. 'Almost...' she angled her head to the side and considered her daughter '...radiant.'

Her father gave a nod of satisfaction. 'Where are your footmen, Marianne? It is not safe these days for a woman to travel with a maid alone. A husband should take care of such things. It is his duty to protect his wife.'

'I am in the process of taking on new staff. The carriage is waiting outside.' She had forgotten how much her family worried over every small thing, their paranoia feeding an atmosphere of fear, coddling her to the point of suffocation.

'You should have a care, Marianne,' her father said. 'Especially when the highwayman is not yet apprehended.'

She felt her cup rattle in its saucer and quickly took a gulp of tea to disguise her response. 'There is such a great price on his head that I am sure he will not dare to show his face in London or the surrounding villages or towns again. We need think no more about him.'

Her father shook his head and gave a grim smile. 'My enquiries are ongoing even as we speak, my dear.'

'Are you close to catching him?' She sipped at her tea as if his answer was not so very important.

'Let us just say I am making progress. But never

fear, Marianne, I shall find him even if it takes me a lifetime.'

'I wish you would not, Papa. Please, do not seek him.'

He peered at her and she could see that she had shocked him. And in the background, where he stood silent and listening, she saw her brother's face sharpen.

She set the cup and saucer down upon the table. 'He is a dangerous man. I do not want you to get hurt.' *And I do not want you to hurt him.*

'My dearest girl, you need have no fear on my account. I have made my preparations to deal with him, most thoroughly.'

She closed her eyes at the menace in his voice.

'You have paled, Marianne. I should not have reminded you of the villain,' he said. 'If you will excuse me, my dearest, I have an appointment I must keep elsewhere. But I am glad that you are married to Knight. He will keep you safe.'

She could have laughed out loud with the irony of it were it not so very terrible. She wondered what he would do if ever he discovered that her husband and the highwayman were one and the same.

And when he had gone her mother chattered over inconsequential fripperies. Marianne was worrying so much over her father's words that it was a struggle to pretend an interest and she was relieved when it came time to leave. But when she would have done so her brother, Francis, drew her into her father's study, with such a dark intense expression upon his face that her stomach knotted and she felt the prickle of foreboding over her scalp.

Once inside he closed the door behind them.

'Does Knight treat you well?'

'He is good to me,' she said. But he would not be good to their father.

'You are certain?'

'Of course. Why do you ask?'

'Because there is something about him…' He glanced away into the distance. 'I do not like him.' His gaze returned to hers. 'And I do not trust him.'

She felt the stir of both anger and fear. 'Have a care how you speak of my husband, Francis.'

'After the way he seduced you at your ball I don't think I need have any care over him.'

'He is my husband.'

'Even so, you barely know the man, Marianne.'

'If that is what you brought me in here to say, you will excuse me.'

'Not so hasty, little sister.' She felt his hand upon her arm. 'There is something that you might want to see.'

Her heart gave a stutter. 'You have found the document?'

'Not yet.' He shook his head. 'Father will discuss little of the highwayman matter with me, so I took the liberty of looking into it myself. Remember the first ransom note that he sent?'

She nodded. The words were engraved upon her heart.

'1795. Hounslow Heath. The document that was taken in exchange for your daughter,' said Francis as if reading them again. He took a piece of paper from his pocket and when he unfolded it she could see that it was a page that had been cut from a newspaper—a newspaper that was yellow with age. He passed it to her. At the top of the page in tiny letters she saw the page was from *The London Messenger*, and the date was June 22nd, 1795.

'1795,' she said and when her eyes dropped lower on the page she saw the article entitled 'Robbery and Murder upon Hounslow Heath'. She swallowed down the nausea.

'Read it,' her brother said.

The names leapt out at her before she even began to read. She read, in silence, a small part of what Rafe had already told her.

'Edmund Knight,' he said slowly. 'And his wife, Catherine.'

'A tragedy,' she said.

'Do you know who they are?'

She nodded, but did not meet his eye, just kept her gaze fixed on the sheet of newsprint before her.

'Rafe Knight's parents,' he said.

The silence hissed between them.

'What is your point, Francis?'

'1795. Hounslow Heath. A highwayman. A strange coincidence, don't you think?'

'What are you suggesting?' She looked at him then. Her heart was thumping so fast, so hard, that it threatened to leap from her throat. 'You think that the man who killed Rafe's parents is the same one who abducted me?' But she knew that was not what he was thinking.

'No. But the two crimes are connected in some way.'

'There must have been hundreds of happenings upon Hounslow Heath in that year.'

'There were not,' said Francis. His gaze held hers and the look in his eyes made her shiver.

'Then maybe the reference is to some event not reported in the newspapers.' She hoped he could not see her nervousness.

He shook his head. 'It is the strangest thing,' he said,

'but when I started asking questions about the murder of Rafe Knight's parents I discovered that no one is willing to answer them.'

'Then maybe you should stop asking questions about something that is long since dead and buried.' The blood was pounding in her head and she felt a fear worse than any she had known, for this fear was not for herself, but for the man she loved. She did not trust herself to raise her eyes to her brother's. She gripped the newspaper page tighter so that he would not see the tremor that ran through her fingers.

'Don't you want us to catch the highwayman, Marianne?'

No! she wanted to shout. 'I want to put the past behind me and move on with my life.'

'Even if he's still out there?'

'There are worse men than him out there, Francis,' she said quietly. She hated to see the pity that flashed in her brother's eyes and wished she had not spoken.

'Not in England,' he reassured her.

She prayed he was right, and when she went to leave this time her brother did not stop her.

Rafe was in his study, discussing matters with Callerton, when Marianne returned from her father's house. Her face was pale and he could see the worry in her eyes. She had not even removed her pelisse, bonnet or gloves when she came to him. He sent Callerton away before coming to stand before her.

'Francis has found it. He knows, Rafe!'

He felt his heart miss a beat. 'The document?' he asked quietly.

She shook her head with impatience. 'The article from *The London Messenger* archives for 1795. He knows of the murder of your parents.' She untied her bonnet and set it down on his desk.

'It is no great secret, Marianne.'

She peeled off her gloves and thrust them down beside the bonnet. 'No, but it is the only incident reported for Hounslow Heath for 1795.'

The silence hissed between them. He knew what she was saying.

Her eyes held his and he saw the fear in them.

'He has already been asking questions about your parents…about you.'

He had not cared if they caught him before, not as long as he took Misbourne down with him, but things were different now.

'Do not underestimate my brother, Rafe. He seeks to protect me and that makes him tenacious, and determined, ruthless even. He will not let the matter rest, not until he has found all there is to know of you… and the highwayman. We have to go away before he discovers the truth.'

'We can't run from this, Marianne.'

'Why won't you understand?'

'I do understand,' he said softly and drew her into his arms.

She stared up into his face. 'My father will destroy you,' she said. 'And you will destroy him.'

'You know that he has the document, don't you?'

She nodded and he saw tears sheen her eyes.

'And you know what that means, Marianne.'

'I know, but I cannot believe it of him, Rafe.' She shook her head. 'All of this for a sheet of paper. What is written on it that it is worth so many lives? You saw it that night.'

'Only the smallest part of it.' Only the three vowels written large and clear.

She placed her hands on either side of his face and stared up into his eyes. 'He is my father, Rafe, and I love him.' She paused and a single tear overflowed to trickle down her cheek. 'And I love *you*. More than anything.'

'I know.' It seemed he could see right into her very soul. 'I love you, too, Marianne.'

She squeezed her eyes shut at his whispered words, but the tears escaped to flow none the less.

'What are we going to do, Rafe?'

'We are going to face what will come.'

'I cannot,' she sobbed.

'I know that you can, Marianne,' he said.

'If I lose you, Rafe…' The words choked and finished.

He held her in his arms and he could not tell her that everything would be all right, for they both knew the truth: it would be his neck or Misbourne's in the noose and, either way, it would break Marianne's heart.

Chapter Fourteen

They lay in bed together that night. The wind rattled at the window panes and the sky outside was a sheer sheet of black. There was no moonlight, no starlight. Only the glow of the fire's red embers broke the darkness of the room. But there was no need for light. They lay naked and entwined, breast to breast, heart to heart. So close that she could feel his eyelashes against hers, so close that they shared the same breath. Every hour was precious. Every minute. Too precious to waste on the past or on worries of the future. All they had was now.

'Make love to me, Rafe,' she whispered against his lips. 'I am asking you.' Then, remembering the words he had spoken so long ago, 'I am begging you.'

'As I would kneel at your feet and beg you, Marianne.' And then he kissed her and it made all his other kisses fade to oblivion. In his kiss was everything that had been between them and all that love could ever encompass. He kissed her lips and then he kissed her breasts, tenderly, with all of his love, so that it felt like he was worshipping her with his mouth. His breath seared her skin, branding her, making her his, as if she could ever be another's. Tasting her, touching her, taking them both on a journey that could only have one end.

Their hearts beat in unison. She could feel the rush of his blood as surely as she felt her own, feel the convergence of their desire to a blaze of unimaginable intensity. He kissed her until there was no thought in her mind save for him, kissed her until her body was begging for his. She needed this union with him, wanted it with all her heart, all her soul. To share their bodies. To lose herself in him. For ever. Against her belly she could feel the press of the long thick length of him and between her thighs the dull throbbing ache was almost unbearable. She slid herself against him, needing to feel him between her legs.

'Marianne,' he breathed her name.

'Rafe.' There was nothing else in the world. No fear. No hurt. Only her love for him and his love for her.

He rolled her on to her back, taking his weight on his elbows as their bodies clung together. Her thighs gaped wide, opening herself to him, and she could feel him touching her, letting her taste the place to which he would take them both. A promise. A vow.

'Yes,' she whispered. She wanted to love him in every way she could. She needed him, him and only him, as desperately as if her life depended on it.

His lips brushed hers, their breaths mingling, warm and intimate, and then he slid inside her. It was the most wonderful feeling in the world, being filled with him, as if their bodies had been made to fit together. A sense of coming home. A sense that everything had been made right. She sighed with relief, with delight, the sensation of it making her dizzy. She kissed his mouth and only then felt him begin to move within her.

Thrusting, in long strokes, a rhythm that cemented the love that was between them. Deeper and faster until she was clutching him to her so hard that her fingers dug into his back, into his buttocks. Until she was moving with him, pulling him in even deeper, even harder. Until their breaths panted loud and their skin was slick and sliding with sweat. Faster and faster in a whirlwind that tumbled and turned and drove and urged. Until she arched against him and cried out his name and heard him cry hers, as everything seemed to explode in an ecstasy that stole her breath and stopped her heart, and shattered her body, her very being, into a thousand pieces scattered across the heavens, like stars in the darkness of the night sky. She clung to him, revelling in the heavy weight of his body upon hers, feeling his love all around her, within her, filling her heart and her body and her soul as, together, they floated back down to earth.

They lay there, and he kissed her, a single kiss both tender and possessive, then rolled his weight from her.

She heard him climb from the bed, watched the dark shape of him move across to the fireplace. She saw the tiny flare on the candle he lit from the red embers on the hearth. And the two small flames flicker in the darkness as he used the first candle to light the others. She could see his nakedness as he returned across the room and set the branch of candles down on the bedside cabinet. He did not climb into the bed, but sat on its edge, looking round at her, his eyes very dark, his face shadowed in the flicker of the candlelight.

There was silence, a pure silence, raw and unbroken. And she felt her heart tighten because she only now remembered, and she knew what he was going to say.

* * *

Rafe looked into the eyes of the woman he loved.

'You were not a maid.' The candles flickered in the draught, making shadows dance upon the walls, upon her face.

'No.' Her voice was quiet. She did not try to deny it, made no pretence.

'Why did you not tell me?'

'The right moment never came, and then I…forgot.'

'Forgot?' He raised an eyebrow and looked at her.

'You made me forget,' she said.

'Does your father know?'

She nodded. He closed his eyes, tried to close his ears to the horrible little voice that whispered possibilities of which he could not bear to think.

'The night of your birthday ball, when your father caught us in his study… Was it all a ploy he devised to catch you a husband?'

'No! Never think that!' He saw the shock that flared in her eyes, and the distress that followed in its wake, and he knew that she was telling the truth. And besides, it was too late, because he loved her.

They looked at each other across the small distance.

'Tell me what happened, Marianne,' he said gently.

Her eyes scanned his face as if she were committing him to memory, then she glanced down and began to speak. 'It was the night of my eighteenth birthday. My father wanted it to be a quiet family celebration so we did not even leave the house that day. I retired as usual. My maid helped me change into my nightclothes and put me to bed, and then she left. It was a mild night and the fire had almost died upon the hearth and…' She hesitated, and took a deep breath as if willing herself to continue. He reached his hand across the covers to take hers. She felt cold to his touch. He folded his fingers around hers to warm them.

'The curtains were drawn,' she said. 'I blew the candle out and it was so dark.' He felt the slight tightening of her fingers. 'He came from behind the curtains. He said he would kill me if I cried out or struggled and I was so shocked, so very afraid, that I made no sound, not until he was gone. I could not see him in the darkness, not until he left and the streetlight shone on his face as he climbed out of the window.'

Rafe felt her pain as raw as if it were his own. His heart was thudding hard in his chest and he was aware of the metallic taste of blood in his mouth. And more than anything of the quiet deadly certainty that he hid from his face and his voice. He placed his other hand over hers, enfolding her one small hand with both of his, protecting it, warming it.

'Monsters in the darkness,' he said quietly.

'Yes.'

He paused. 'Who is he, Marianne?'

'He is gone. Fled to the Continent before my father and brother could find him. They would kill him were he ever to return.'

They would not, for Rafe would get to him first. 'His name, Marianne.'

'The Duke of Rotherham.'

There was a small silence before she said, 'I tried to block him from my mind. I tried not to let myself think of him or what he had done. And then I met you...'

And he had made her father grovel hurt in the dirt while she watched. And he had abducted her at gunpoint and held her prisoner. He only now realised the truth of what he had done.

'I never would have abducted you had I known.'

She looked up at him then and her expression was one of devastation. 'Now you are sorry for it.' And she began to weep.

He moved across the bed, pulling her into his arms, trying to make her understand. 'I can never be sorry for taking you, Marianne. Had I not, you would always just have been Misbourne's daughter. How would I have come to love you? How would I have made you my wife?'

'You made me truly forget what Rotherham had done.'

'I am glad of it,' he whispered.

'My mother told me there was a way that you might never know. To pretend the pain and scratch my skin with a pin so that the blood would mark the bedsheets. But I could not deceive you like that.'

'I know you would not. I love you, Marianne. You are mine. And I am yours. Nothing can ever change that.' He kissed her and took her in his arms and made love to her again, gently, with all that was in his heart, to show her the truth of it, to show her that nothing else mattered.

In the week that followed they lived and loved minute by minute, hour by hour, one day at a time. There was nothing of fear, nothing of darkness, only a love so strong that it seemed to etch itself upon time itself. Marianne knew they could not live like this for ever, that sooner or later, reality must intrude upon the world they had constructed for themselves. And it did.

The note was delivered by hand on Tuesday afternoon. She recognized the neat slope of her mother's handwriting and cracked open the red wax seal of the Earl of Misbourne.

Leicester Square, London,
November 1810
My dearest Marianne
Your father and I would be delighted if you and
your husband would come to tea at three o'clock
tomorrow afternoon. We look forward to seeing
you both.
Ever your loving mother

She passed the note to Rafe, who read it without
a word.

'Will you come?' She knew what she was asking of
him—to take afternoon tea with the man he believed
responsible for the murder of his parents. She hoped
with all her heart that he was wrong and prayed for
the miracle that would prove it both to her and to Rafe.
And deep within her was the small glimmer of hope
that, somehow, the breach between her husband and
her father could be healed.

He nodded.

Her heart gave a little squeeze. She reached her face
up to his and kissed him on the mouth. 'Thank you,'
she whispered.

At three o'clock the next day her father's butler led
them into the drawing room. She knew the minute the
door closed that she had made a mistake in coming
here. There was no sign of her mother. There was no
tea tray. Only her father and on the table, where the tea
cups should have been, a crumple of deep-blue silk and
Mr Pickering's betrothal ring. She felt her heart miss
a beat and her stomach sink down to meet her toes.

'Where is Mama? What is going on?' She played the
game, feigning an indignation and innocence, anything

that would protect Rafe. And even while she played it she prayed and prayed that she was wrong.

'Sit down,' said her father in a voice she barely recognised.

'No.' She manoeuvred herself to stand in front of her husband, as if she could shield him from them. 'We are leaving.'

She tried to back away towards the doorway, but Rafe was solid and unmoving as a rock. Behind them she heard the closing of the door and the key turn in the lock; when she looked Francis was standing there, barring their exit.

'Do you recognise this dress, Marianne?' Her father lifted it from where it lay on the table. And when she said nothing, 'You should do, it is the one the highwayman sent you home in.'

She felt Rafe move, coming to stand slightly in front of her. She swallowed and felt her blood chill. She did not look at him, just kept her eyes on the dress that was gripped so tight within her father's hand that his knuckles shone white.

Her father began to speak. 'Your brother was most interested in this dress. It appears that one can discover so much from a dressmaker's label. The dress was made in March 1795 by Madame Voise of New Bond Street, a dressmaker with a very select clientele.'

She waited, and the sense of dread she had felt on entering the room expanded and grew to fill the entirety of her chest. But she showed nothing of it, determined to yield not one thing that might implicate Rafe.

'Madame Voise died some years ago. Her nephew runs the business now, under the name of Sutton. But he still had his aunt's old records.'

The tension in the room was so tight she thought she could not bear it.

'No one would have anticipated such a thing after all these years,' he said.

She said nothing. She did not dare look at Rafe, but she could sense the strain emanating from his body.

Please, God, she prayed. *Please.*

'The dress is made from Parisian silk,' he said.

Say it if you know, she wanted to shout.

'The material cost one pound, sixteen shillings and thruppence a yard.'

Every word was a torture of waiting, for she had a very good idea of where this was leading.

'And do you know the lady for whom it was made?' He smiled, but it was not a smile of happiness, nor even one of victory.

She held her breath and felt the tremble go through her as the seconds stretched.

'Mrs Catherine Knight.' He paused. 'Your husband's mother.'

In the silence there was only the fast frenzied thud of her heart.

'Rafe Knight is the highwayman who held us up on Hounslow Heath. Rafe Knight is the man who abducted you.'

'What nonsense—' she began, but her father cut her off.

'But then you already know that, don't you, Marianne?'

'This is madness! Rafe has done nothing!'

But her father and brother just looked at her.

'Do you think I would not know if my own husband was the highwayman? Do you think—?' But

Rafe stayed her with the gentle pressure of his hand on her arm.

'They know, Marianne.' His eyes were very dark and his face the sternest she had ever seen it. There was about him such a certainty, such an aura of danger and power, that she feared the terribleness of what was about to be unleashed within this room.

She shook her head as if doing so would deny that he had said the words. 'No,' she whispered, and looked up into his eyes. 'No.' And stroked her fingers against where his hand rested upon her arm.

'Your brother was right,' her father said. 'You love him.'

'Of course I love him,' she said, loud and angry, and faced her father with defiance. 'I love him,' she said again. 'And I will not let you hurt him.'

Her father ignored her and kept his attention focused on Rafe while he spoke to her brother. 'Take your sister upstairs.'

Francis took a step towards her.

'No!' she shouted. 'I am not going anywhere.'

'My wife stays with me,' said Rafe, his voice low and uncompromising.

'Very well,' her father said, but his mouth tightened. 'Are you going to tell me what manner of game you are playing, Mr Knight?'

'There is no game, Misbourne. You know what I want.'

'I am sure I have not the slightest notion. I played along with the highwayman's demands for the sake of my daughter's safety.'

'June 17th, 1795,' said Rafe. 'Hounslow Heath. You may have forgotten that night, Misbourne, but I have not.'

'I am not unaware of the tragedy of your parents' demise, Knight, but I fail to see how their unhappy fate has anything to do with me.' It made sense what her father was saying. He would have been so very plausible, had she not already overheard the betrayal from his own lips.

'I was there that night, Misbourne,' said Rafe in the highwayman's deadly quiet whisper. 'Did not your henchman tell you?' He stepped forwards and his eyes had nothing of gold in them, nothing of lightness, only the promise of death. 'I watched what he did to them. I saw what he took from them.'

Every last vestige of colour washed from her father's face. 'If you believe that I had anything to do with your parents' murder, you are mistak—'

'Five men,' said Rafe. 'Tommy Jones—brother of Billy Jones, the villain who dressed up as a highwayman and did the deed—who you ensured was hanged so that he might never reveal the truth. James Harris—Billy's handler, the one with whom your man made the arrangement. Frederick Linton—your man with whom the liaisons were made. Alan Brown—the corrupt Bow Street Runner who led the investigation—and George Martin Fairclough—the magistrate who was in Linton's pocket.'

Her father swallowed hard. His eyes seemed to bulge as he realised the significance of the names. 'They were the ones you robbed? The ones you...'

'Yes,' said Rafe darkly. 'You paid them well for their silence—they kept it for fifteen years. But they talked to me.' He smiled without humour. 'How they talked.' And those words spoken so quietly sent a chill through the room.

Her father tried to laugh it off as an absurdity, but

the sound was hollow and unconvincing, and across his face was unadulterated fear and a guilt that endorsed Rafe's accusation better than had he held up his hands and admitted it. 'You have got this all wrong, Knight.'

The two men stared at one another.

'Give me the document, Misbourne.'

Her father shook his head.

Rafe slipped the pistol from his pocket and pointed it straight at her father's heart. 'I will not ask you again.'

She saw her brother edging closer to Rafe, positioning himself ready to act.

'Go ahead and pull the trigger, Knight,' her father said.

Marianne saw the slight tightening of Rafe's fingers on the pistol. 'No!' She stared at her husband, at the hardness and the hatred in the focus that held her father. She did not take her eyes from Rafe's face as she moved to stand between him and her father.

Rafe's eyes moved to hers. 'Stand aside, Marianne.'

But she shook her head. 'You know that I cannot let you do this.'

They stared at one another and she knew what she was asking of him. She saw the pain and the anger and the grief and all that he had spent a lifetime working towards. But she could not let him pull the trigger. She stood there, her eyes fixed on his, willing him to understand. Slowly he lowered the pistol.

From the corner of her eye she caught the movement of her brother charging at Rafe. 'No, Francis!' she cried, but it was too late; Francis launched himself at her husband, knocking the pistol from his hand and the two men were down on the floor landing such savage blows on one another that the blood reached to splatter against the hem of her skirt. Crimson against ivory. So stark and so awful. She stood stock still and stared at it in shock for a moment, while the furore erupted around her. Her brother's blood. Her husband's blood. She bent down and lifted the pistol from where it had landed at her feet, then she pointed it at the sofa behind her and fired.

The noise was deafening. The plume of smoke was acrid and stung her eyes. And when it cleared, both men were on their feet, staring at her with alarm and concern.

'Enough,' she said. 'No more.' She dropped the spent pistol to the floor with an almighty thud. Her ears were still ringing with the echo of the pistol shot. She looked first at her brother, a searing glance that made him look away in shame. And then she looked at her father. She looked him straight in the eyes.

'After what you have done to Rafe, do you not think an explanation is the very least he deserves?' she said quietly.

He stared at her as if he had not thought she knew the awfulness of his crime. As if he only now realised the truth—that she knew what he had done. For a moment there was such a terrible tortured expression in his eyes. It was a pain like none she had ever seen, as if his very soul was writhing in agony. He closed his eyes as if he could not bear for her to see it.

'I am sorry, Marianne,' he said in a voice that was barely above a whisper. 'I am so very sorry, my darling girl. You are right, of course.' There was nothing of fight in him, nothing of his energy and strength. 'I never meant for the Knights to be killed. It was to be a highway robbery only. The fool was supposed to rob them, nothing more.' And then he waved Francis away and looked at Rafe. 'I have spent a lifetime regretting the loss of their life, what I did to you…' He shook his head. 'I am sorry, truly I am.'

'The document.' Rafe's voice was harsh.

'The damnable document.' Misbourne gave a laugh, except it came out like a sob. 'Your father and I were both members of a particular club…some might call it a secret society. He was taking the document to the Master of the Order. There would have been an investigation. It would have all come out. I could not let that happen.'

'So you killed him that you would not be black-balled from your club?' Rafe said with incredulity.

But her father shook his head. 'I would take the shame on myself a thousand times over, if only it had been that simple.'

'Then what?'

'I could not risk that the document might find its way back to its owner.'

Rafe sneered and shook his head. 'So the document was not even yours to steal?'

'It was not,' said her father. 'But I had to have it,' he added quietly. 'I would have done almost anything in the world to possess it.' He raised his eyes suddenly to Rafe's. 'But it made no difference. I had unleashed a monster and I could not call it back.'

'Where is the document now?'

Her father's eyes flitted to hers before returning to Rafe's. 'I will give it to you. And you may do what you want with me. Only send Marianne upstairs, to sit with her mother, first. I beg you, Knight.'

'I have been treated as a child for too much of my life,' she said. 'I want to know what this document is that cost Rafe's parents their lives and my father his honour.'

'Marianne has every right to see exactly what you refused to bargain for her safe return. She stays.'

Her father seemed to shrink before her eyes. With every breath in the silence he aged a lifetime. His eyes sunk. His cheeks grew gaunt. Her proud strong father looked old, defeated, grey. His gaze moved to hers, and there was in his eyes such a terrible sadness and regret that it broke her heart. He looked at her, drinking in her face as if it were the last time he might look upon her, the seconds stretching too long before he looked at Rafe once more. He said not one word, just turned and walked over to the small boxed bookcase by the fireplace and withdrew a blue leather-bound book that looked like every other in his collection. He hesitated only for a moment, holding the book in his hands as if he had held it a thousand times before, then opening it and turning the pages to find the one he sought. He creased the spine open and she realised that the document had been bound into the book like a proper page. Then he passed the wide-opened book to Rafe, who had moved to stand before the fireplace.

Marianne watched Rafe's eyes scan the page. She waited for him to reveal the document's secrets, but there was only a deafening silence. Her heart beat once, twice, three times. She saw Rafe's eyes widen, saw the way his gaze shot to her father's and the look that was in them—utter incredulity and condemnation and comprehension all rolled into one. The silence was deafening. A piece of coal cracked and hissed upon the fire. And still Marianne waited and her stomach was clenched tight and for all the heat in the room and the sweat that prickled beneath her arms her fingers were chilled to the bone.

'Why the hell have you kept this all these years?'

She could hear the horror in Rafe's whisper and it frightened her more than anything else had done.

'So that I could never forget what I did. So that I would always remember that it was my fault,' said her father, and he seemed a shadow of the man he had been. 'It is my penance, my punishment.'

'Rafe?' she said and began to walk towards her husband. She had a horrible feeling about what was written on that page. A dread like none she had ever known. She feared to discover its terrible dark secret, yet she was drawn to it like a moth to a flame.

She saw the flicker of something in Rafe's eyes. In one rapid move he ripped the page from the book, balled it and threw it into the fire. 'No!' she gasped in disbelief, racing towards it as if to save it from the flames, but Rafe stopped her, capturing her in his arms so that she could only watch the page darken and crinkle and shrink to nothingness within the roar of flames.

'You *do* love her,' whispered her father in his old man's voice as he stared at Rafe.

'The only reason you are still alive is because I love her.'

'What have you done?' she cried and stared up into Rafe's face.

'What your father should have done long ago,' he said.

'Are you mad? After all these years of seeking… after all that you have gone through… Why would you do such a thing?' She shook her head, unable to believe it. 'What was written upon that page?'

The question that Rafe had spent fifteen years asking. The thing he had thought the most important in the world. He understood now how wrong he had been.

He understood now that the most important thing in the world was that Marianne never discovered the answer to that question.

'You must think me the very devil,' said Misbourne.

Rafe did not disagree.

'But you understand, do you not, why I had to move heaven and earth to retrieve it? Why I could not yield it? He needed the paper in his possession to redeem it. I thought that if he did not have it I could stop him.'

Rafe felt sick to the pit of his stomach. Yet he gave a nod. He understood too well.

'What the hell is going on?' Linwood asked.

'Take your sister upstairs to her mother. Then come down and I will tell you,' Misbourne said. 'I owe Knight the truth. And whatever he decides to do, you should know the reason for it.'

Linwood gave a nod.

'You cannot seriously think to send me to another room as if I am of no consequence in any of this. I am not a child.' Marianne looked from her father to her brother and back again. 'I have been as much a part of this as any of you,' she continued.

Rafe saw Misbourne wince as her words struck home. Marianne did not know that she had been at the very centre of the whole thing.

'I shall stay with my husband,' she said and looked to Rafe for support.

'You should see how your mother is, Marianne,' he said quietly.

She looked at him as if he had just slapped her. He knew that she must think he was letting her down, but rather that a thousand times over than she learned the truth.

'Rafe?' She stared at him with shock and hurt in her eyes.

'I'm sorry, Marianne.' God only knew what he would do to protect her. 'Please trust me in this one thing. Believe me, it is for the best.'

'The best?' she said. And she gave him a look of utter strength and anger and disappointment. 'I have spent a lifetime doing what other people deem best for me. I thought you were different, Rafe.'

'Marianne, you do not understand…' But there was nothing he could say to make her see, without telling her the truth.

'You are right, I do not understand at all,' she said, then she turned and strode away, slamming the door behind her.

'Thank you,' said Misbourne.

'Don't thank me,' snarled Rafe, 'I didn't do it for you. I did it for Marianne.'

'I know,' said Misbourne. 'And that is why I thank you.'

'Is someone going to tell me what is going on?' asked Linwood.

Rafe's eyes slid to Misbourne.

The earl slumped down into the chair and in a quiet monotone he began to talk.

Marianne did not make her way up the stairs to her mother's little parlour. She felt angry and hurt beyond belief over Rafe's attitude. Everything had changed in the moment he read the document. What secret did it hold that he would rather ally himself with the man who was behind the murder of his parents than reveal it to her? He said he loved her, but what had just happened in the drawing room did not feel like love. It felt like betrayal, by both her husband and her father. And what did anything written on a piece of paper mean in comparison to that?

She could not go and sip tea and chat about the latest fashions with her mother, closing her mind to all that was around her, pretending that nothing had happened. She could never be that cosseted, fearful, stifled woman again. Marianne slipped out of the front door, closing it noiselessly behind her.

Callerton had not yet returned with the coach to collect them. She could not very well go back inside and start ringing bells and summoning servants to ready her father's carriage to take her home. Although she was uneasy about the idea of walking alone through the streets of London, she would damn well do it. Better that than the alternative. And then she saw the hackney carriage at the end of the street and her dilemma was solved. She glanced back at the window of the drawing room and was relieved to see that no one was standing there. She squared her shoulders, held her chin up and, with a determined grip on her reticule, headed towards the hackney carriage.

'You bastard!' Linwood landed the blow against his father's chin and Misbourne did not turn away, let alone raise an arm to defend himself. 'How could you do such a thing?'

Misbourne said nothing, just stared at the carpet with deadened eyes as the blood trickled down his chin and his lip began to swell.

The flames had died away within the fireplace. The coal was devoured and in its place was a mass of glowing embers. Rafe did not know how long it had taken for Misbourne to explain every last detail, but he had done it and the silence that followed had been deafening. He could not blame Linwood. Only the thought of what it would do to Marianne stayed his own fists... and pistol.

'It was you, wasn't it?' he said. 'Paying the money into my account. Trying to appease your conscience.'

'I had taken your parents from you. Paying for your education, ensuring that you would never want for money—these were the only things I could do. I stood in the shadows and watched you grow from a boy to a man, easing your way when I could, safeguarding you when it was necessary.'

Rafe felt sick.

'I was right,' said Linwood. 'You would have married her to anyone.'

Misbourne nodded. 'Anyone to save her from him.'

'It is why he fought so hard to secure first Arlesford, then Pickering—why he had me wed her so quickly,' said Rafe. 'It had to be by her twenty-first birthday.'

'He would have come for her otherwise,' Misbourne said, 'and no matter what protection I built around her he would have found a way to breach it.'

Rafe balled his fingers into a fist at the thought.

The door slammed closed and the hackney carriage drew away. It stopped again a few minutes later; the coachman was speaking to someone, declining a fare. And then they were off again, making their way steadily through the streets.

Marianne thought about Rafe. And in her mind all she could see was the look in his eyes when he had sent her away, a look she did not understand and yet seemed to reach into the very core of her and touch where no other could. A look that had such a grim irascibility about it that she knew he would not falter. Whatever he had read upon that page, he was never going to tell her. He was shutting her out. Treating her as her father had done all of these years. Overruling her, without discussion or explanation. Always knowing what was best for her. Marianne knew she could not just sit back and let that happen. She knew she had to fight for what was between them. And just as she thought it, the sun peeped from behind the clouds, lifting away the heavy dull greyness and shadow that hung over the day. She glanced out of the window at the patch of blue sky above and the beautiful shimmer of the sunlight upon the water below and felt the finger of unease down her spine. She moved closer to the window, looked out properly, focusing on the route the carriage was taking and saw they were on London Bridge, crossing the Thames…heading in the opposite direction to St Luke's and Rafe's town house. The panic was sudden, like a fist slamming into her stomach, making her catch her breath, making her feel sick. She banged a hand on the door and called out to the driver in a loud clear voice.

'Stop this carriage at once.'

But the carriage did not stop.

She told herself that the driver was just a villain chancing to fleece her for a higher fare by taking her on a longer route. She prayed to God that that was the case. But in her heart she knew, even though she did not want to believe it. She felt the panic roil, felt her limbs stiffen with terrible fear so that she could not move, could not make a sound. And then she heard the whisper of Rafe's words. *Running from fear only makes it chase you. Hiding from it only makes it seek you. You have to face fear.*

She stopped struggling inside herself and stilled the turmoil of her thoughts. With traffic as it was in London it was only a matter of time before the coach had to stop. But the carriage did not slow. Instead its speed increased until it was rattling dangerously fast over the pot holes and ruts of the poorly kept road. Marianne gripped tight to the securing strap and knew there was no chance of jumping from the speeding vehicle.

She shouted as loud as she could, thudded her free hand against the glass of the window, anything to attract attention. But the carriage driver was taking her through a place where there were no houses or shops, only large warehouses and derelict-looking manufactories. There was no one to see, no one to hear. She stopped shouting and saved her energy for the fight ahead.

The carriage eventually came to a halt outside a seedy tavern. There were men on the narrow street, unshaven, unkempt, with bloodshot eyes and blackened teeth, sitting on steps and old broken wooden crates, drinking from dark and dirty bottles. And women, too, women who lounged in doorways with their petticoats showing and grimy skin beneath, who looked at her with malice and amusement in their eyes. There would be no help here. It reminded her of the rookery in St Giles from which Rafe had saved her. But he would not save her now. He thought she was upstairs in her father's house, drinking tea with her mother. She had only herself to rely on. She sat very still, watching, waiting for what was going to happen.

The door opened and it was not the carriage driver that stood there, but a tall thin gentleman, as old as her father. A gentleman with a black lacquered walking cane, who had just climbed down from his seat beside the coachman. He was impeccably dressed, as out of place in this seedy place as she was herself. He climbed inside, sat down opposite her and made himself comfortable. And she knew even before he looked round to face her who he was. There had been no imagining in the botanical gardens, or that night in her bedchamber. She looked across the hackney carriage into the cold pale eyes of the Duke of Rotherham.

'What do you mean, Lady Marianne is not there?' Misbourne demanded of the footman.

But Lady Misbourne was hurrying down the staircase at that very moment, running up to her husband, breathless and uncaring of social graces. 'I thought she was down here with you! She did not come upstairs.'

Rafe saw the whites around Misbourne's eyes grow larger. The fear that crept across the man's face was transparent. He sent his wife and servants away. 'Oh, my God, he has come for her!' he whispered as if to himself. 'It cannot be...' He stared at Rafe. 'I thought she would be safe once she was wed. He is such a stickler for precision. Everything to the letter. Everything just as was agreed. I thought once she was married he could not...' He clutched his hands to his face and could not continue.

Rafe looked at Misbourne and the man quailed beneath the look in his eyes. 'You should have warned me that he was coming back for her, that I could have guarded her against him,' he said in a deathly quiet voice. 'Had you shown me the document...'

'Had he shown you the document you would have killed him for the bastard he is and what would that have done to Marianne? Besides, we are jumping the gun,' said Linwood. 'She was angry and upset with us all.'

But most of all with Rafe. He knew it was the truth. From Marianne's point of view he had let her down when she had needed him most.

'She has probably returned to Knight's house,' continued Linwood, but Rafe could see the fear in Linwood's eyes. And he felt a ripple of the same fear.

He strode to the front door and opened it. His carriage sat waiting directly outside in the street, with Callerton standing by the horses. Callerton moved to open the carriage door when he saw Rafe, slipping the step down into place. By that one small action Rafe knew that Marianne was not within the carriage, that Callerton was expecting her to emerge from the house on his arm. The dread pierced right through him, sharp and cold as the blade of his sword. And he knew in that moment that Misbourne was right. The fact that the document was destroyed and that Marianne was his wife changed nothing. Misbourne had made a pact with the devil, and the final day of reckoning had arrived. Misbourne had indeed unleashed a monster. And the monster had come for Marianne.

Chapter Fifteen

'**R**otherham,' Rafe whispered and the intensity of the word cut through the room like the lash of a whip.

'How could he have slipped back into the country? I have eyes and ears at every port,' said Misbourne.

'Men that can be so easily bought are always open to a deeper pocket,' said Rafe.

'He has her and there is nothing we can do.' Misbourne crumpled to his knees, his face ashen, a stricken look in his eyes.

'On your feet, Misbourne,' Rafe snapped and dragged him up with nothing of compassion. 'Where is his town house?'

'It no longer exists. It was burned to the ground the week after he fled to the Continent.' It was Linwood who answered, and there was something in his voice that meant Rafe did not have to ask who lay behind the property's destruction.

'She is already wed to Knight.' Misbourne seemed to be talking to himself. 'He cannot marry her. But he means to have her regardless. I had not thought he would deviate from what was agreed.'

Rafe thought of the words written upon the second

half of the page he had torn from the book. *I give to you my daughter, Marianne, once she has reached her twenty-first year, to be your wife.* Rotherham was a man who wanted precisely what he had been promised. And if that were the case then Rafe thought he understood what the villain was doing.

'He could have her anywhere,' said Misbourne and covered his face with his hands. 'We haven't a hope in hell of finding them.'

'We do not need to find them,' said Rafe.

'What do you mean?' Misbourne let his hands fall away and stared at Rafe.

'I think we will hear from Rotherham before the afternoon is out.'

'Good afternoon, Marianne,' Rotherham said in the soft voice that had so haunted her nightmares. 'We meet again, just as I said we would.'

'How did you…?'

'I have been watching you, my dear. How very fortuitous that you escaped your "guard" to travel all alone and by hackney coach…when the coachmen are so easily and quickly persuaded. All the money in my purse and the promise of even more when we reach home.' He leaned forwards and dropped his voice slightly, as if he were telling her a secret. 'Although he might be in for something of a surprise when we get there.'

'You villain!'

'Come now, my dear, that is no way to speak to me when I have come all this way to rectify a little misunderstanding.'

'Misunderstanding? It was hardly that, sir.'

'I wish only to make my apology and put matters right.'

'I do not want your apology! Take it and return whence you came.'

The cool pale gaze flickered over her face, appraising her. 'How much you have changed, Marianne, in three short years. You are not afraid of me.'

'You are the one who should be afraid,' she said. 'You should be very afraid.'

He smiled in a condescending way as if she were a simpleton who did not understand the words she was saying. 'And why exactly should I be so fearful? Hmm?' He wetted his narrow lips.

'Because if you do not release me, there is a man who shall not rest until he has hunted you down.'

'Really.' He seemed amused, more than anything else.

'And when he catches you...'

'If he were to catch me...' Rotherham sat forwards in his seat as if riveted by her words. 'What would he do, Marianne?'

Marianne thought of Rafe in the rookery and what he had done to the men who had stood in his way. She thought of the burying ground and the bullets and the blood. And most of all she thought of the way a city of thieves and villains had parted to let him pass.

'You think you are dangerous,' she said and shook her head. 'But you have not met my husband.'

'Rafe Knight,' said Rotherham and something of the smile vanished from his face.

She laughed to see it and felt Rotherham's eyes shift to hers, and in them for the first time was a flicker of anger. 'How hoydenish you have become, my dear. You should learn to mind your manners.'

'I do not think so, your Grace,' she said. 'My husband likes them just the way they are.'

He paused, then said very carefully, 'Then Rafe Knight is an unfortunate fool. Just like his father before him.'

The wind dropped from her sails. 'His father? What do you mean?'

'Poking his nose into affairs that were none of his concern, taking documents that were not his to take. It was Knight who stole the original document from me, you know. Once it was in my possession again, I had a copy made. A precise replica, so good that Misbourne could not even tell it apart from the one he had written with his own hand when he went to such lengths to retrieve it. I take it your husband has told you the story of how his parents met their death?'

She gave a single stiff nod.

'Billy Jones, the highwayman that night, worked for me, of course. I always remembered him with a degree of affection as a reliable sort of man, until Rafe Knight started asking questions and I realised that Jones had not been so very reliable after all.'

She stared at him, unable to believe what she was hearing. 'It was you who ordered the murder of Rafe's parents!'

'Indeed, my dear. But it would have been so much harder to silence Edmund Knight had your father not arranged the robbery.'

'And why was it necessary to silence Rafe's father?'

'Knight was taking the matter that very night to those who would have made what was agreed within that piece of paper impossible. And I had to have you, my dear.'

Everything in the world seemed to pause in that moment. She thought she must have misheard him, but when she looked at his face she knew that she had not.

'The piece of paper…' she began, but her lips felt too stiff to form the words.

'Did your father not show you?' He arched his thin grey brows. 'You know he should not have let you marry Knight, and so slyly done. No betrothal, no courtship, not even a hint of gossip. I had no idea. I thought I was coming back to the matter of Pickering. I hope you have recovered from your little coaching accident.' He smiled, but the look in his eyes was one of anger. 'I really am most disappointed in Misbourne.' From the inside pocket of his waistcoat he produced a sheet of paper folded like a letter except it bore no name or direction, and no seal. 'A gentleman's gaming debt is a matter of honour, after all, and your father has more than proven he has none of that attribute.' His eyes dropped to the paper in his hand.

Marianne's gaze followed.

'Do you know what this is?'

She could hazard a very good guess.

'It is the original document written in your father's very own hand.' He offered it to her.

She stared at the folded paper, but made no move to take it. She knew that within that document lay the explanation for all that had happened.

'Do you not wish to read it? Do you not wish to know what your father gambled on a turn of the cards? What he staked when he was in his cups?'

She had a horrible, horrible feeling. Inside, she was trembling, but when she reached out and took the document from him her hands were still and calm. The paper betrayed not so much as a quiver as she opened it out and read it. It consisted of two separate IOUs written by her father to Rotherham in 1795. In the first he had given her maidenhead—to be claimed when she turned eighteen. In the second he had given her hand in marriage, if Rotherham so wished it, redeemable when she turned twenty-one.

She stared at the sprawl of her father's handwriting, and in that moment everything ceased to be. Whatever she had imagined had been written in the document, whatever she might have expected, the truth was a zenith away. Nothing could have prepared her for it. Those few seconds seemed to last an eternity. Her mind was thick and slow-witted, unable to comprehend, unwilling to accept the magnitude of what he had done. She could feel the beat of her heart and hear the sound of her breath within the silence of the carriage. Her eyes blinked. From outside came the sound of a man's whistle, followed by a woman's coarse laughter. A seagull cried. Her father, whom she thought had loved her. Her father, who had always tried to protect her. All of her beliefs shattered and cracked apart. She could not weep a single tear. She could not utter even one word. She just sat there, frozen in the likeness of the woman she had been.

'I thought you would understand, my dear,' Rotherham said, taking the document from where it lay in her hands and folding it neatly once more into his pocket. Then he gave a single thud upon the roof with the head of his walking cane and the carriage moved off, swaying and dipping over the uneven surface of the narrow road.

The curtains were drawn within the study of Rafe's town house. Four men stood around the desk: Rafe, Callerton, Linwood and Misbourne. Four men with cold determined eyes. A letter lay discarded on the desk between them.

London, November 1810

My dear Mr Knight

The lady that you seek is within my care. I hold her for one reason and one reason only. That is, to bring about an end to that which was agreed between the lady's father and myself fifteen years ago.

I am grown old, and my health feeble of late, and with each day that passes the burden of guilt over my part in it weighs heavier upon my soul. I wish to return abroad unhindered, to live out the rest of what days I may have in solitude and penitence for my sins. You are husband to the lady at the centre of this tangled web and thus I make my proposal to you, and you alone. I will release her only in exchange for the document that her father still holds, that I might destroy the last evidence of our wickedness…and my guilt.

I seek to avoid capture only that the noble name of Rotherham is not blighted. Therefore there can be no question of involvement of the law, or otherwise. Come alone to Hounslow Heath at four this afternoon with the document, if you wish to proceed as I have suggested. If not, I will be forced to revise my plans for the lady and myself.

Your remorseful servant

Rotherham

The letter had been addressed to Rafe and marked private, yet every man in the room knew the words that Rotherham had written upon it. They had spent the last hours readying themselves.

Misbourne checked the ink was dry, then folded the

freshly written piece of paper and passed it to Rafe. 'You will find it faithful to the page you burned in every word and every stroke of the pen. Their very image is engraved upon my memory, for there has not been a day in the last fifteen years that I did not force myself to look at them.' He paused and then said, 'Thank you for doing this for my daughter.'

Rafe looked into Misbourne's eyes, the eyes of the man he had spent a lifetime hunting and hating, the man whom he would never forgive for what he had done to his parents and to Marianne, and he gave a nod of acknowledgement.

'It has been an honour to know you, Knight.' Misbourne's voice was quiet within the room; respect burned in his eyes. 'For all that you have done for my daughter. For all that you would do for her this night. I thank you, sir.' Misbourne held out his hand to Rafe.

Rafe looked at Misbourne's hand and only the ticking of the clock punctuated the silence. Sometimes a man had to make sacrifices for the woman he loved. Even if it meant sacrificing all that he believed in. Even if it meant sacrificing his own life.

For Marianne, only for Marianne, he thought. He met Misbourne's gaze and took his father-in-law's hand within his own. And it was done.

The men moved to leave for Hounslow Heath.

The late afternoon air grew damp as the sun began to set, casting Hounslow Heath in an orange-tinged hue and silhouetting the hackney carriage to a black-blocked shape that was as dark and sinister as Rotherham himself by her side. Her shawl was lost within the carriage, and the cold seeped through the thin muslin sleeves of her gown, right through her skin to chill her very bones. The rope that Rotherham had used to bind her wrists behind her back was immovable. No matter how hard she strained against it, or stretched her fingers to reach the knots, it gave no sign of yielding. The coach driver had long since been dispensed with, leaving them to travel here alone.

Rotherham checked his pocket watch again. 'Five minutes before four o'clock. Not much longer now, my dear. And then all of this…fiasco…will be over and you shall be with your husband.'

She wanted to believe him. She prayed that he was telling the truth. But she could not trust him. Not for one second, not for all that calm measured look upon his face, or the soft reassuring lilt of his voice. And even if he was telling the truth, there was the small matter of the document her father had held, the document upon which all of this centred, the document that was now ash within the ashes tray of a fireplace. But Rafe would think of a way round that problem, she did not doubt it for a second.

The globe of the sun began to sink down beneath the horizon, firing the sky a vivid pink. The heath was silent in its waiting; not a bird called, not a bat fluttered. Even the distant streets of Hounslow that bordered it were hushed as if holding their breath. Four faint chimes of a church bell sounded, and as she watched the sun slip lower and the glorious glow of light begin to fade, a solitary horseman appeared on the horizon, riding straight out of the sun so that it seemed he had been born of the sun itself; a dark-caped figure galloping fast towards them, with such purpose, with such lack of fear. And as he came closer she saw the old-fashioned tricorn hat that she knew so well, and the dark silk kerchief across his face…and the pistol held high in one hand. And she felt her heart lift. Rafe had come for her.

Rotherham grabbed at her arm, pulling her before him as a shield for any bullets that Rafe might fire and producing a pistol of his own to hold against her head. 'Very amusing,' said Rotherham and his eyes flicked over Rafe's highwayman attire as her husband brought the horse to a halt fifty yards away. 'And somewhat appropriate.'

Rafe slipped down from the beast's back.

'Please divest yourself of the weapon. Over there.' Rotherham indicated a spot some distance away, where the gun could not be readily reached.

Rafe hesitated, as Marianne knew that he would over such an order.

'I am aware of the fragility of trust, Mr Knight, but I am afraid I cannot dispense with my own pistol until I know you are unarmed. I would not wish my finger to grow tired where it is positioned upon the trigger... not when Lady Marianne is in such proximity.'

Rafe threw the pistol to the place Rotherham had gestured.

'And the rest of them, if you would be so kind, sir.' Rotherham's voice was smooth, his hand held across her *décolletage* cold and calm. She could smell the sweet scent of tobacco that came from his coat and the familiar heavy scent of his cologne.

Rafe took two pistols from his pocket and threw them to land by the first. He stood facing Rotherham, unarmed and unafraid if the defiant tilt of his head beneath his low-slung hat was anything to judge by. Marianne felt her stomach grip in fear, and not for herself. Her focus was fixed firmly on Rafe and the danger that he was in. The touch of muzzle was light against her hair, yet she could feel the prickle of her scalp beneath and a gladness in her heart, for all the while Rotherham aimed his pistol at her he could not shoot Rafe. She watched her husband intently, while every nerve in her body was poised and alert, ready for that first hint of movement in Rotherham's hand.

Rafe held his hands up to show there was nothing in them, then, with slow clear movements so that Rotherham could see exactly what he was doing, he produced the document from within his greatcoat.

'Open it. Lay it down on the ground before me. But do not make the mistake of coming too close.'

Rotherham cannot be trusted, the little voice whispered in her head. And every nerve in her body strained to free herself from her ropes that she might save Rafe. Rotherham must have felt her surreptitious movement, for his arm tightened ever so slightly around her.

'Patience, my dear,' he whispered in her ear.

Rafe walked closer; she held her breath, waiting for him to produce another pistol from some unknown hiding place and shoot Rotherham. Or for him to move fast, landing a blow that would send Rotherham reeling. But the man from whom the worst of villains had scurried, the man who could best seven men with his fists alone, did only as Rotherham instructed. She realised in that moment that he would do nothing to endanger her life.

The IOU looked very convincing where it lay upon the grass. *A copy of a copy*, she thought, and prayed that Rotherham would not realise.

Please, God, she prayed for her husband's safety. *Please*. She prayed that somehow this mess would all work out for the best.

'Thank you, Mr Knight.' Rotherham gave a sigh as if in relief.

Rafe said not one word, just faced him with a steady determined patience.

This was the moment. Rotherham thought he had the document. He had Marianne and a loaded pistol, and Rafe unarmed before him. Every muscle in her body tightened. The breath stayed lodged in her throat. Her heart gave a stutter.

'It is over,' Rotherham said, 'at last.' She waited for him to squeeze the trigger, for the roar of the pistol as it fired its bullet. But whether it would be into her head, or Rafe's chest, she did not know. She felt the slight movement in Rotherham's arm and she closed her eyes and prayed his aim would find her.

But there was no explosion, no plume of gunpowder. Rotherham's grip slackened and dropped away. She opened her eyes and for a moment she just stood there, unable to believe it. And then Rotherham gave her a little nudge forwards.

'Take her,' he said in a soft voice in which the regret was unmistakable.

Marianne ran the small distance to her husband.

Rafe swung her behind him, shielding her from Rotherham. He gave a grim nod at Rotherham and then turned to her, urging her forward towards his horse, always keeping himself between her and the duke.

They walked away and Rotherham let them go, just as he had said he would. They were almost free. Five paces and they would be on Rafe's horse. And for the first time since Rafe had placed the document down she allowed herself to hope. Maybe Rotherham was telling the truth, maybe both she and Rafe could escape this nightmare alive.

Four paces. Maybe Rotherham did mean to go back to the Continent and never return.

Three paces. Maybe it really was going to be all right.

She wanted to look round at Rafe, to look into his eyes. Two more paces and she could do it. Two paces and they would be upon the horse's back. Two paces and they would be safe.

The shot rang out, ripping through the quietness of the heath.

'No!' She turned to see Rafe collapsing down on to his knees, his gloved hand clutched to his chest. 'No!' But he was already face down upon the grass and in her line of vision, through the haze of drifting white-blue smoke, was Rotherham, standing where she had left him, the pistol still smoking in his hand.

She chafed at the ropes that bound her until her wrists bled, but it made no difference, she could not free herself to help her husband. She dropped to kneel by his side.

'Rafe!' Her voice was guttural and ragged. 'Rafe!' she cried, but his body lay still and unmoving.

'What have you done?' she yelled at Rotherham.

'I have made you a widow, my dear,' he said in a voice devoid of all emotion, 'a widow who is set to re-marry with indecent haste.' He dropped the pistol and produced another from his pocket. 'But let us take no chances.'

Marianne had not thought it was possible to feel such pain, such rage, such madness.

'No!' she shouted. 'You are the vilest of creatures to have walked this earth!'

'That is no way to speak to your future husband, Marianne,' he said and began to walk towards her.

The tears were streaming down her face. She wanted to launch herself at him. She wanted to kill him. Rotherham smiled at her. She stared and could not look away. She stared and thought that what had just happened had driven her mad, in truth, for behind Rotherham a man was crawling closer on his belly. And as she watched the man rose up to his feet and the man was tall and dark and powerful. He was a man who wore no hat or dark silk kerchief around his face, yet had seemingly risen from the dead—the man was her husband.

She did not know if his image was the product of her own imagining or the soul of her husband come back to save her from beyond the grave.

She saw him aim his pistol and heard him call Rotherham's name in his own strong harsh voice.

'He has a pistol!' she yelled in warning.

Rotherham turned and fired at the man who looked like Rafe. But he was not fast enough. Rafe's bullet landed in Rotherham's thigh, sending the duke sprawling on the grass.

'Rafe?' She was on her feet, running towards the spectre before it could vanish.

'Marianne.' He reached her, cutting the ropes from her wrists, hugging her briefly against him, his body warm and hard and strong.

She glanced back at the fallen body of the highwayman in confusion, but Rafe grabbed her hand and ran to the man.

She watched while he rolled the man over so that he lay on his back. And the man gave a grunt and opened his eyes.

'Did you get him?' The words were muffled behind his mask.

'Rest easy,' said Rafe and freed the hat from the man's head and the mask from his face that he might breathe easier, and checked the wound to the man's shoulder. At first she did not recognise him, for the beard had been shaved from his chin and the moustache from his lip. And then the man's eyes met hers.

'Papa,' she whispered.

'My daughter,' he said and his voice was thick with emotion. 'Whatever you think of me, it is deserved. But know that I love you and that I have spent a lifetime ruing those vowels so wickedly and thoughtlessly and drunkenly written.'

She clutched his hand in hers, feeling the wet blood that smeared upon it.

'I love you, too, Papa.'

He wept at that, silent tears rolling down his cheeks.

Rafe pulled her aside, speaking quiet words for her ears only. 'We have to get him home. There is a doctor waiting ready.'

'Was there no other way?'

'None that would not endanger your life all the more. And none of us would risk that. He wanted to do this for you, Marianne. I could not deny him the chance to regain some measure of honour.'

She nodded.

'Help me get him into the carriage.' Together they moved her father into the hackney, supporting him as best they could and laying him across the seats. Then Rafe tied her father's horse on a lead to the carriage.

Rafe walked over to Rotherham and grabbed him, flipping the man to lie flat on his back. He took a fresh pistol from his pocket and pressed the barrel against Rotherham's temple.

Rotherham paled even more and gave a whimper.

'No.' Marianne came to stand by Rafe's side, touching her hand to the tight tense muscle in the curve of his arm. 'Do not do this, Rafe.'

'For what he has done to you he deserves to die.'

'If you kill him, they will hunt you down and hang you.'

'It is a price I would willingly pay.'

'But I would not.'

She felt the tremble that ran through Rafe's arm.

'He is nothing to me. And you are everything.' It was true, she thought. Rotherham no longer held any power over her. She was not afraid of him. 'And besides,' she said in a quiet voice, 'you once told me that you were not a murderer.'

He closed his eyes at that and she knew that he understood the truth of it—that if he killed Rotherham in that moment he would be no better than the villain himself.

'Do not give him the power to change the man you are.'

Rafe lowered the pistol, but he did not shift his eyes from Rotherham. 'The document,' he growled.

Rotherham scrabbled in his pocket and passed him the copy.

'He has the original too,' she said. 'He has had it all along.'

'Then the one in your father's possession…?'

'A copy Rotherham had made. Billy Jones was Rotherham's man. He killed your father under Rotherham's instruction.'

She saw the darkening in Rafe's eyes and wished she had not blurted the truth here and now, when the pistol was still in Rafe's hand and Rotherham lying helpless before him.

'Rafe,' she said softly. And he looked round at her. Their gazes met and held. All that was in her heart reached out to him. He touched his fingers gently to her cheek. Then he took the original document, the one her father had written all those years ago, and stuffed it into his pocket. Taking Marianne's hand in his, he turned and led her away towards the carriage.

'You cannot mean to leave me here?' said Rotherham.

'I shall not kill you, Rotherham. But neither shall I help you.' Rafe's voice was quiet and controlled.

'This place is not safe. And my leg…'

'Nowhere in England is safe for you, Rotherham.' Rafe's voice was grim and dark and filled with promise. 'In the eventuality that you escape this heath you would do well to remember that.'

'Damn you, Knight!'

But Rafe had already turned and was helping Marianne into the carriage. She sat beside her father, whose face was white and strained from Rotherham's bullet lodged in his shoulder, and held his hand in hers. And as the darkness of the night began to close in, Rafe drove them home.

'Now that Mama and Francis are not present to hear, tell me honestly…' Marianne paused briefly '…will he survive the wound?'

'There is likely to be some impairment in his left arm, but aside from that, and assuming that he takes no fever, then your father should make a good recovery.'

She nodded and closed her eyes; when she opened them again they were blurry with tears.

'I should not have let him do it,' Rafe said, misunderstanding why she was weeping. 'I should have—'

But she did not let him go on. 'I thought it was you,' she whispered and the tears flowed harder. 'I thought Rotherham had killed you.'

'Marianne.' Her name was like a sigh on his lips. He took her into his arms, trying to hold her against him, but she did not yield, just stared up into his face, determined to tell him.

'I thought it was you, and I could not bear it.'

'I'm sorry, Marianne. If there had been another way...' He traced the outline of her face with his eyes. 'But I did what I had to, to save you. And I will always do that. Because I love you.'

His words were a whisper, the same whisper a high-wayman had used on a heath what seemed an eternity ago. And they meant more to Marianne than anything else in the world. She stared into his eyes.

She reached up and touched her fingers to his lips and there was no more need for words, only the need of a woman for her man. After all that they had been through, after all the day had brought. They undressed each other, one garment at a time. And then he carried her to their bed, and he made love to her, and the union of their bodies, the physical manifestation of a love that had been born in spite of vengeance and hatred and wickedness, began to heal their hurts.

It was two weeks after that fateful day upon Hounslow Heath. The house was very different from the one that the highwayman had first brought her to. There was a full staff of servants. The shutters had been opened in the yellow and master bedchambers and the rooms were filled with late autumn sunshine as she and Rafe carefully packed away his parents' possessions.

'You must choose the paints and wallpapers, and

materials, Marianne. I would fill this house with light and laughter…and children.'

She smiled and gave a nod. 'Most definitely.'

'I will hold you to that, my love,' he said.

'Please see that you do.' She leaned across and kissed him on the mouth, and everything in the world was right.

* * * * *